Awake

A ROSE WORLD TALE

H. C. FITZPATRICK

AWAKE

Sleeping Beauty isn't asleep... but her household is.

Despite Aurora's bold attempt to escape and stop the painful sleeping curse, it descends on her household. One step beyond the threshold and it takes hold. Her betrothed was supposed to kiss her and break it but sends his army to destroy her instead.

Donning a new identity as Rory, she sets out to break the curse, but the soldiers close in. A dragon shifter and his magical friends help her avoid capture and navigate a dangerous forest filled with magic beings and humans persecuting them.

Their path takes them closer to Rory's betrothed, but also towards danger. Because the man she's supposed to kiss, is torturing and killing the magic folk in her kingdom. She must win them over to claim her place on the throne.

But the curse is expanding, and if she doesn't stop it, no one will survive.

Contents

To the readers who were given a future
by someone else,
and who decided to make your own way instead.
You are my heroes.

To my mom.
You were one of my first readers.
Thanks for telling me this book belonged in the forest.
I miss you more than I can say.

1

Aurora was out of time. The clock struck the first chime of midnight, deafening against the eerie silence of the chateau. The curse was upon them, and Princess Aurora's betrothed had not come to break it, as he vowed. Not that she'd expected it, not anymore. Her hands clenched when she thought about his betrayal. But she didn't dwell on it. Now wasn't the time. She would save her household.

Princess Aurora took a deep breath as she stood at the window, at the edge of her tower, looking down at the ground below. She'd already hung the rope she'd made from the turret outcrop, and it waved in the slight breeze below. She stuffed her cloak in her travel bag and passed it over her shoulders, over the stable boy's clothes she'd stolen. Muriel hadn't noticed her nephew's clothes missing. She sent him away to avoid the curse. If Aurora survived, she would choose another name. Hers was cursed.

As the second chime sounded, she tied the loose rope which hung through the rafter around her waist and grabbed the swaying one with her right hand. She turned back to look at her room one last time, the place they had confined her for the past sixteen years. Thick, colourful tapestries softened the stone walls, telling stories of the land of Elsass. Ornately decorated, with everything she could ask for, it was a beautiful prison. Her heart pounded in her chest, not for the exertion or fear, but for excitement. She hadn't been outside these walls in years.

The third chime sounded as she leaned back out of the window, and held her body upright as she braced her leather-clad feet on top of the sill. She checked the rope above her head, but thick as it was, there was no fraying. She took pride in her handiwork, then looked down. Bile filled her throat as she stared down at the five stories. The rope swayed in the breeze. She gripped the rope tightly; her knuckles white. She couldn't move.

The fourth chime sounded. If she didn't get down soon, she never would. She didn't want the curse to put her to sleep while she was hovering in midair. It might kill her. Though perhaps that way her household would be free. She wanted her household to live. But Aurora didn't want to let go of life to the curse. She wanted to *live, too.*

The fifth chime sounded while she inhaled deeply through her nose and out through her mouth. It helped enough where she slid her feet out to the chateau wall sides. She loosened her grip and started the descent. It was slower than she'd hoped.

The sixth chime sounded above her head, but she'd barely made it two steps. She steadied her breathing. As long as she didn't fall asleep, slow progress was better than too fast. She kept going. With the rope around her waist, she loosened her grip slightly, then gasped as she slid down two stories at once. *Too fast!* She gripped the rope tightly with both hands, wincing as it burned her hand despite its fine finish.

She stopped as the chime sounded again. *Was that seven? Or eight?* She looked down. Three stories to go. Holding on tightly to the rope with her left, she pulled her sleeve down on her right hand and tested its grip. It was smoother, but still had some tooth to it. She did the same with her left hand. The next chime sounded as she wrapped her covered hands around the rope. This time, prepared for it, she slid down smoothly.

By the next chime, this one she assumed was number ten, she was above the second-storey window. She kept descending.

She heard another chime. *Eleven?* It was hard to tell.

As she drew level with the second-story window, she realized it was open. She pushed herself to the latch side of it. She lowered herself down until the sill was below her arms, then reached over and peered in.

The chime sounded, and she flinched as she stared into the candlelit room. A woman sat at the foot of a bed; shoulders slumped forward. In the woman's hand was a goblet, and she gripped it tightly. Aurora breathed a sigh of relief. Her plan worked. She broke the curse. Her household was safe.

Another chime sounded, and she nearly lost her grip in surprise. The woman arched her back and screamed in pain, joined by many more voices throughout the chateau. Aurora's eyes widened as the woman fell back on the bed, facing the window.

"Muriel?" Aurora gasped and nearly let go of the rope to cover her own mouth.

"Aurora?" Muriel's eyes widened as she saw Aurora's face outside the window, lit up by the candlelight. Her mouth dropped open, first in surprise, but then turned into a grimace. More cries rang out through the castle.

"No!" Aurora cried out. "Not like this!" Gripping the rope with her left hand, she reached her right hand into the window threshold and gasped. As her fingers crossed the window frame inside, the tips started to tingle. A strange numbness worked its way up her arm the further it passed through the threshold. She gasped, touched the window, but couldn't feel it. Her fingers couldn't hold a shape. The tingles in her arm grew stronger, like pins and needles. They jabbed her, forced her to give up on Muriel, and pull her arm back out of the opening. A burning sensation rushed down her arm, almost as painful as the tingles, until both feelings finally subsided. She tested her hand around the rope: it felt solid underneath, her fingers once again strong.

In the room, Muriel lay on the bed, her body frozen in place in sleep. The agony that had just crossed her face disappeared, and all her muscles relaxed.

"It didn't work," she whispered to herself. "If it wasn't my home anymore, it should have worked. They shouldn't be asleep." Tears streamed down her face as she stared at Muriel.

They're all asleep because of me!

Aurora wiped her sleeve over her face to dry her eyes, but as she did, she lost her footing, and free-spun down towards the ground. She reached out to catch the rope, but her hand couldn't grip it and it yanked hard on her arm. She cried out as she lurched to a stop. A burning sensation rushed through her shoulder as the rope pulled her arm out of her body, then pushed back in. She struggled to wrap the rope around her hand, but her arm was weak. She spun again, bounced her shoulder against the wall and cried out in pain. The sound echoed in the forest beyond.

She faced the ground while hanging above it, blood rushing to her face. It took three attempts to right herself. Her arm was weak but regained function. Once upright, she sat on the ropes, tangled below her and around her legs. She looked around for a way to get down. She couldn't call for help. The curse had claimed her entire household.

Tears welled again, but she blinked them away.

Now is not the time.

She pulled at the tangled mess of ropes and corrected her balance, but remained tangled. Her bag and knife fell to the ground below. As she sat there, her toes felt a distinct numbness, the tingles climbing her legs.

The curse!

She took a breath and stared at the rope. As a spinner, she knew knots. Her movements to untangle the rope were methodical as she tested each one to see if it would give. The tingling turned into prickling, and she started to sweat. But when it stopped at her hips, where the rope wound itself around her legs, she breathed out.

I'm awake!

She stopped struggling, and the prickling sensation got worse. She then took a deep breath and focused on the ropes around her hips and thighs, loosening them. The tingling stopped as the feeling returned.

The clouds parted, and the moonlight lit up her tower.

Her body shuddered out a breath of relief.

I am awake!

2

Aurora spent most of the night slowly working through the knots which held her legs trapped within the rope. Just before dawn, they gave way, and she found herself face down on the earth. She exhaled from the impact and shivered until her body remembered to breathe.

She flipped over and glared at the small rock she landed on, rubbed her stomach, and closed her eyes for a moment. She stood up slowly, her shoulder complaining, her stomach sore. All things considered; she was okay.

She was *awake!*

She couldn't say the same for her household or her home. Muriel's face flittered through her mind, deep in the throes of agony. Rory collapsed to her knees, hugged her stomach as she shook her head to rid herself of the image. But it stayed. Her eyes burned as tears fell down her cheeks.

She tried to escape, so her home wasn't asleep, but she couldn't stop it.

It was her fault.

She fell back to a seated position, hugged her bag close to her chest, and let the tears fall. She thought about the last year leading up to this point. Maybe if she'd gotten out sooner, gotten help sooner, she could have saved them. Saved Muriel.

Last year, on the eve of her eighteenth birthday, Aurora received a letter from her father. It was his last words before his passing. A lengthy tome, it described the reason for her stay in the tower, and everything he'd done to try to fix it.

At her one-hundred-day naming ceremony, she'd been cursed by the Seeress. She'd known the detail from the household staff who wouldn't let her outside. But it was the curse's wording he'd described in detail that she hadn't known.

5

As Aurora's eighteenth year rings its end at midnight,
so the curse begins.
Asleep, the household, one and all.
Where she calls home, there she'll lie,
to sleep until kissed by the King of Kehl,
whose love must overcome hate,
to unify their lands.
Without an heir, their lands will fall to waste,
and war will never cease.

When Aurora was two, her mother died in childbirth, along with a brother who would have been heir to Elsass. Her father tried to remarry, to produce another heir, but the women competing to be queen felt uncomfortable with Aurora's presence. They begged him to send her away, and by the time she was three, he agreed.

But he never produced another child who could be an heir in her place.

As Aurora neared her sixteenth birthday, her father decided to take matters into his own hand. Her marriage was arranged with the King of Kehl. Since his son, his heir was named in the curse itself, Kehl's future King was the only one willing to accept her. The only stipulation was that Kehl could never keep the kingdom without an heir. Her father's promise to do everything in his power to break the curse and unify the kingdoms sealed the deal.

But the King of Kehl was assassinated shortly after.

His son, instead of coming for her himself and breaking the curse, chose to marry Aurora by proxy one year later as she turned seventeen. The young king sent a letter to tell her of this news, claiming he was at war and had no chance to come for her yet.

When Muriel heard this, she disappeared for a moment, then came back. "I've had a letter dispatched. I'll get some answers." She patted Aurora's hand for comfort. "He'll come for you."

She received a letter from the young King of Kehl a few weeks later, with promises that he would soon come to collect her. The proxy was simply a convenience because there were problems with the refugees in his kingdom. He didn't mention the kiss or broken curse, but it was implied in the letter as he reassured her he would be there soon. She also received a letter from her father, saying he was withdrawing support from the King of Kehl's battles until he came to collect her.

By the time she turned eighteen, the King hadn't come. But Rory's father's final letter came, and with it, a single intricately carved wooden ring.

Muriel saw the ring and nodded. "This is your wedding ring. I've been told it will keep you safe. Protect you." It was too large for her, so Aurora made a small rope to carry it around her neck. She'd spun for years and made a single small group of strands strong enough to carry the heavy weight of the oversized wood ring.

Hope was a strange thing. Muriel had enough for both of them, constantly reassuring her. But Aurora understood what Muriel wasn't saying. The King of Kehl had no intention of rescuing Aurora from her curse. He had access to Elsass now and didn't need her. He would control both kingdoms. She didn't consider herself married, not when it was by proxy. He would remain her betrothed in her mind, one without honour.

So she made rope. Strong, thick rope. At first it was just something to do, a way to pass the time. Then, as she thought through the curse, a plan formed. Unfortunately, it took much longer to make the rope than she thought. She'd barely made it out in time.

If only she'd started sooner, made her way to the young King of Kehl, gotten him to kiss her and break the curse. Or at the very least, dismissed her household. But leaving home should have meant no curse without one.

A rustling overhead drew her attention to the present, and Aurora looked up to a small group of grey jays fluttering towards her window. She smiled as they fluttered around her windowsill, looking for the crumbs she usually left for them. They kept trying to land, but immediately leaped off the sill. A series of annoyed chirps flitted through the air. She whistled softly to them as she did every morning. The male's attention turned to her below, and he flew down to investigate, landing beside her.

Aurora opened her bag, pulled out the small loaf of bread and pulled off a few large crumbs, laying them before the male. He chirped once, and three females landed beside him. They tilted their heads sideways, then each took a crumb.

"You're lucky I'm out and that you have any crumbs at all." Rory sighed, then pulled a few more crumbs for them. "I'm lucky I'm out. But I couldn't save them." Rory wiped another tear away.

"So," she said to the grey jays. "Any ideas on how I get to Kehl to kiss a man who wants nothing to do with me?"

The male grey jay tilted his head sideways and peered at her. He looked at the others, let out a chirp, and bounced away down the path along the side of her chateau. A low rose bush started growing around the chateau's perimeter, about a foot thick. Aurora wondered if Muriel had them planted. They chirped at her again, before they continued to hop away. She shoved a piece of bread in her mouth before wrapping the loaf up and placing it in her bag. She stood and followed them as they hopped and flew for short amounts of time, landing just ahead of her.

They ventured down the path for a while, stepping over new rose bushes, and headed into the nearby forest until they landed at a signpost. One arm pointed to her chateau, one pointed to the main castle stronghold of her kingdom, another to Riquewihr, and finally one to Kehl.

She smiled at the grey jays. "Thank you," she said. She pulled out her loaf, dropped some small pieces for them, then put everything away. She hiked her bag over her shoulder and headed down the trail to Kehl.

Aurora walked for a few hours down the path to Kehl before exhaustion overcame her close to lunch. She looked around for a quiet place to rest and stepped off the path to a small crop of trees, which stood near a boulder. She could see the road from her view. Once she checked to make sure nothing else made its home there, she sat down and pulled the bread and cured meats she packed. The small meal did not satisfy her, but saved the rest for later.

Aurora wrapped her cloak tighter, shivering from the slight dampness in the trees, but more so from fatigue. She took her maid's fire starter sticks, hoping to make a fire later that night. No one taught her, but she watched Muriel do it. Although she didn't want to start one now. She would also have to hunt if she wanted meat. For now, the forest was in full bloom with the later summer berries, and she'd foraged as she walked.

I am unprepared, she thought. *I've barely covered any part of the main roads, and at this rate, I won't get to Kehl for at least a month.* Aurora yawned and stretched before wrapping her cloak around her. *But at least I'll get there. And I'll break the curse.*

Aurora woke up with a start, thinking the curse had found her. She searched around her, looking at everything. Her bag and cloak remained undisturbed, so she carefully searched around her little hiding place. Nothing moved on the roads, but her neck was sore from sleeping on her right hand. Aurora felt sharp pains moving up her arm as she flexed her wrist, no doubt from falling asleep and holding her head. She sighed. It was probably the sharp pain and numbness that woke her.

She thought she heard a cry which sounded like Muriel. Aurora rubbed her eyes and looked around again in the silence. *I'm just remembering my dream.* She crawled out from her hiding spot, venturing back to the road. She looked into the sky, caught her bearings, and started along the path. It was only a couple of hours after noon, so Aurora could get plenty of walking in.

She paused on the way when she spotted blackberries in a bush beside the path. She gathered several clusters, eating a few as she picked them and saving the rest for later. As she bent over to pick the last handful, she heard a cry again.

Aurora looked around but saw nothing. She fixed her pack, then stepped back to the edge of the path. That's when she heard the cry again, only it sounded more like a whine. Aurora pulled out her knife, holding it out for an attack, looking around again. The cry, or whine, ricocheted around her forward off the path, into a grassy knoll.

Aurora crept closer to the meadow as the forest went silent.

She stepped forward again when a loud wail caught her attention. She looked down into the grass to find a fawn lying down, leaning to one side. Aurora stared at the fawn, its leg caught in an iron trap.

"Oh!" she breathed out softly. She held her knife out as the fawn flinched. *This could feed me for a while.* But she shook her head. She couldn't hurt the fawn. And anyway, it would be a waste. She couldn't cure or eat the meat in time. The scavengers and predators would find it, then come find her.

For a moment, she stared into the fawn's eyes, her knife held at the ready.

Aurora put the knife away and studied at the trap. It was solid black iron, with sharp jagged teeth which should have broken the fawn's leg, had it not been for the small rock wedged beside the hoof. Though the gap was big enough to hold the fawn's leg, it was irritated and bloody from trying to escape. There was no way its hoof could fit through.

She slowly crouched down to eye level with the young deer.

"I'm going to help you get out," she whispered. "But you can't panic, or kick me in the face, or I might drop it, and it will do you more damage than good."

The fawn stared at her and nodded. Aurora blinked. Then nodded to the fawn.

"I'm going to gently pry this trap open and pull your hoof out."

She reached down as the fawn flinched when her hands approached.

"Easy," she breathed. Aurora pushed her fingers through the trap and pulled, but it wouldn't budge. She tried again, unsuccessfully, cursing under her breath. She looked up at the fawn. "So, what else should I try?"

The fawn turned its head sideways, making sure it could see her with one eye, and scan around for predators with the other. It whined softly.

Aurora looked around to her right and found a few more rocks. She picked up the one slightly bigger than the rock wedged into the iron trap. When she found the small end, she pushed it beside the one already stuck. She wiggled it back and forth, widening the trap until the smaller one fell through. It still wasn't big enough for the hoof. She looked up at the fawn, who stared at her calmly.

"Well, that's a start," she whispered, as the fawn held its hoof away from the iron teeth of the trap.

Aurora grabbed another stone, but it was smaller than the last. She found another one and wedged it in. Then found another and did the same. She tilted her head at the trapped hoof, then looked up at the fawn. It watched her, its chest breathing heavily.

"I think I can get your hoof through, but I need to touch it to make sure it goes the right way." She waited for a moment while the fawn snorted and calmed down.

Aurora took a deep breath before she reached through the trap, touching the hoof just beyond the irritated leg. The fawn flinched but otherwise stayed calm. "Good job," she crooned. "I'm going to touch you again." She brushed her fingers along the hoof to maneuver it. "I'm going to twist it a little to get it through. Can you try not to kick me if I hurt you?" She asked, but didn't expect an answer.

Her gut clenched at the idea that the fawn would kick the stone and her own hand might get trapped or severed. She took another deep breath and wrapped her fingers around the animal, guiding it through the trap. She just made it through when something hit her from behind and knocked her over with a snap.

She waited for the pain, but then turned over and saw the trap beside her. The fawn was gone; the trap was empty, and Aurora breathed in a sigh of relief.

A shadow passed overhead as she looked into the eyes of a large stag. He snorted in her face until she scrambled back, grabbing her things at the same time. She backed her way to the path, holding her satchel to her chest. The stag advanced on her, his antlers large, sharp, and aimed at her.

"I just wanted to help," she said, holding her hand out. It was a mistake, because she'd grabbed her knife and pointed the blade at the stag. It snorted at her and kept advancing. She gulped and put the blade away. "See? I just wanted to help."

The stag lunged at her, at the same moment she tripped backwards. The air whooshed out of her lungs, as the stag leaned his head over her, before everything went black.

"She's human!" A man bellowed. Aurora tried to groan, but nothing came out.

"But she saved me!" A child's voice argued. "She saved me when you couldn't! I won't let you hurt her!"

Several voices murmured, some louder than others.

"She saved him," a woman's voice said. "We cannot take a life when she saved one."

"She wouldn't have saved him if she'd known what he was." He grumbled.

"You don't know that." The woman's voice said. "They're not all monsters."

"Fine, we'll leave her here." He acknowledged.

"No, we can't!" The child pleaded. "She's hurt. She needs help."

"That doesn't have to come from us." He grumbled.

"Then let's find someone who can help." The woman said.

More grumbles, but a decision must have been made. She tried to ask what it was, but nothing came out. Aurora felt herself floating through space.

She woke in the moonlight. She found her bag, but she wasn't on the grassy knoll. Had she dreamed it? Her hands were sore and scraped, and she felt behind her head. A large bump formed and was tender to the touch. A small shimmer floated in her vision, and a shadow seemed to pass overhead, so she stopped trying to touch the bump. She rolled her neck and sat up, felt something solid right behind her. She must be in the meadow. Except it wasn't a large boulder, it was straight and ridged. Blackberry clusters were beside her. It wasn't a dream. In the moonlight, she looked around and found a large wood gate, and large stone walls with an emblem she instantly recognized.

The wooden gate outside of her Elsass Chateau.

3

Riel held back from aerial acrobatics, and instead soared on leather wings. Flying in his dragon form was as close to freedom as he could get. He dived, then used his wings to break and spin back up the air, using the air currents to take him higher. Then repeated the action until a shock of pain took over his body. The pain was nothing new, just a reminder to focus and use his night vision to scan the ground below for refugees. The King of Kehl called them spies, but the refugees were escaping Kehl's king.

Movement in the distance drew his attention. He focused his gaze on the fields, then swooped above for a closer inspection. Two hooded figures stood still on either side of a mass of creatures moving, huddled in the chilly night air. A series of concerned bleats reassured the dragon of the group's nature, shepherds with a flock, making sure the sheep didn't fall prey to anyone like him.

He debated grabbing one for a snack. The midnight colouring of his dragon shape would hide him until it was too late, but reports of the refugees nearby stopped him. Taking a sheep meant the herd would bleat, and draw the attention of the shepherds and the predators seeking a snack from either the flock or the refugees. This trip was merely reconnaissance.

Out of habit, he swooped towards the chateau in the forest beyond the fields, but tonight it was dark. The small fortification held nothing of beauty. He stopped by to perch on the tower whenever he was in the area and felt at peace when he was nearby. It had been a few weeks since his last visit, but whenever he was in the area, he tried to see what was happening.

Tonight, the chimneys weren't lit, and no one moved. On previous visits, a single candlelight burned from the tallest tower. But tonight, everything was dark. What struck him as the oddest was the silence. No animals cooed, no movement, nothing. He looked around, then flew down. His soft wings were silent in the still, stale air. A strange rosebush grew at the base of the building.

As he touched his hind feet on the tower roof, a strange power ran through his leg. It jolted him like the lightning dragons of his kin. As the sensation travelled through him, it seized his legs and shocked his wings. He pushed himself off the tower, falling until the excruciating pain stopped, and caught himself before hitting the ground.

He landed, his enormous head at eye level with the window a few stories above the ground. Peering in, he saw a woman lying awkwardly on the bed. He let out a soft growl, but the woman didn't stir. He nosed in the window, but felt the strange sharp tingling and jerked away, crushing the new rose bushes beneath his enormous claws.

The bushes latched onto his feet. More than a foot tall, it meant they'd grown rapidly for the last few months. He leapt back into the air, stretched his wings, and flew over to the stables. Vines tore apart, while thorns stuck into his feet. Still, no one moved, no horses whinnied. They were usually the first to recognize the predator in him.

He flew higher, back towards his friends to tell them the news.

On his way, the small herd of sheep and their shepherds drew his attention. He took a slight detour, circling above them for a moment, studying them, wondering if they knew when the curse had started. He couldn't very well land and ask, not in the dark and not without terrifying the small animals and shepherds. Except, now that he thought of it, the two shepherds were smaller than a human. The smaller one had a strange, hobbling walk. *Were they refugees too?* They were well off the path, and he had seen none of the magic folk migrating with a herd. As many of them hunted their food or foraged, a herd of sheep was an easy target. If they were refugees, the King would order their execution, and Riel would have to stop it, despite the pain.

As he left the herd and flew towards his friends, he spotted smoke in the distance, near the boundaries between Elsass and Kehl. He changed direction, flying towards the smoke. It came from a clearing just on the other side of the boundary stones.

Judging by the leather armour, and the small purple circle embossed in the right shoulder of the men below, it was his brother's men, the only ones who acknowledged his existence. He circled for a moment as he watched the smoke. Every few minutes, the smoke made three separate billows; a sign there was a message for him.

Riel let out a huff, then sent a crosswind to the fire, flapping his wings until the smoke blew sideways. The men on watch started at the smoke in their eyes, before looking up at him, his gigantic shadow barely visible in the night sky. One man pointed to the boundary stones and the small clearing around it, as he flew off towards it, while the man ran to get his superior.

He landed in the clearing, then scuttled into the woods to hide from plain sight. It took some time for the guardsman to meet him. He looked around, before carefully approaching the boundary stones. He waited.

"I know you're there," he said. "I can't see you, but I feel your eyes on me. Show your face, Riel. I have a message from your brother."

Riel recognized Laniel, leader of his brother's men, and stuck his large angular head out of the forest. To his credit, the man didn't jump, but his hand gripped the sword at his side.

"It's going to be like that, is it?" Laniel asked.

Riel snorted a puff of smoke at him in answer, his lips curling upward at the sight. He didn't trust the man, so he stayed in his dragon form.

"Fine. Your brother asks you to enact the second phase." Laniel stood at attention and waited for a reply.

Riel squinted at the man, then waited, blowing puffs of smoke in the soldier's face. Laniel didn't move until he coughed, the smoke overtaking the air in his lungs.

"You know what he means?"

Riel huffed, then nodded. Laniel sighed, relaxing until Riel leapt into the air and grabbed the soldier in his right claws. A muffled yell came from Laniel, who then fell silent as they rose high in the air. Riel held the man with his arms wedged between his claws and pointed to the castle with his other hand. In the distance, the chateau was nearly invisible against the moonlight. The man squinted, then looked back at Riel.

"I don't see anything!"

Riel grunted, then raised an eyebrow.

Laniel squinted again, then his eyes widened. "Then it's true?"

Riel dove back to the small clearing, swooping down at the last moment to drop Laniel on the ground. The soldier rolled like a stone as Riel flew off into the night. Laniel's curses faded as he soared away.

Riel chuckled to himself until he remembered what they commanded him to do as part of the second phase. His gut churned, the sharp current of command echoed in his body, and he raced back towards his friends.

The curse had started, and Kehl's King was not wasting time in his plan to take over Elsass. Riel would not have much time to help the refugees now that war was upon them.

4

AURORA DISENTANGLED HER CLOAK and stretched, taking a few deep breaths. She gathered her sack of supplies, her vision blurred as she tested the lump behind her head. It was still tender, but smaller than the night before.

She shielded her eyes as the sun came pouring through the trees on her left, and a chill ran over her. During the night, she'd had nightmares of being watched interspersed with her dreams of Muriel, blaming her for the curse. She looked up at nothing but the blue sky of dawn, and the moon setting to the west. The lingering feeling wouldn't go away. It settled deep in her bones and mixed with a shadow in her dreams, flying overhead.

A few grey jays landed beside her. They tilted their heads sideways as Aurora smiled.

"Bet you didn't expect me back here so soon." Aurora chuckled, then pulled out a few crumbs for them. "At least I know which way to go this time." As she spoke, she wondered if that was the best course. Should she go to Kehl and confront the king?

She faced the chateau. *Home.* The single word echoed in her mind. It drew her in, its magnetic pull echoed a deep-seated longing, despite the weariness from her dream. It was the only place she'd known and felt comfortable. She belonged to her people, and they were cursed because of her. Sure, the curse had taken over, but she was clearly ill-prepared to the world outside her doors. Her stomach tightened as she placed her hand over her belly. *Was that why the Seeress cursed her to sleep? Because she couldn't survive out here? Because she couldn't rule?*

Aurora shook away the thoughts and walked around the chateau. There was no use standing around. She had to do something. Get back in, move on with her plan, *something*.

A small cry came from around the corner. Rose bushes surrounded the chateau's base, a tall thorny barrier that snagged at her clothing if she got too close. They were new since she'd left and flourished in the last few days. She wandered around the side, but the cry faded as she walked. Turning back, she continued slowly; the crying getting louder, until it faded again. She found where the sound was loudest, then peered into the bush.

"Hello?" Aurora called softly.

A painful cry answered. She lowered herself to her knees and peered in. In the middle of the bush, a tiny figure with wings no taller than the length of her palm stared back at her, thorns crisscrossed and hooked on to its clothes. It looked like an insect, but stood on two legs, and stretched its arms and four wings. Three of them were fine, but its upper right wing was bent at a strange angle. Rory stuck her arm in and cringed as the thorns scraped her through her woollen clothes. She slowly extracted her arm.

"Hello little one, are you okay?" Aurora asked softly.

The crying stopped and a flutter of wings answered her, though the thorns still held the creature in place. For a moment, the fawn's face and otherworldly eyes flashed before her, and her head throbbed. She hesitated, but the tiny creature kept crying, and it pulled on Aurora's heart.

"Hmm, how are we going to get you out?" Aurora asked. She pushed and pulled at the thorns, but they wouldn't budge. Looking at them again, it was as if the thorns grew around the creature, holding it in place. She straightened and stepped back. As she did, she gasped when she saw the gap she left in the bush, as if it grew around her too.

Aurora pulled out her knife, knelt near the gap, but not fully inside of it. She watched as the rose bush grew and expanded around her. Her heart thundered. She stepped back again, while the rosebush stilled. The creature did not. It cried. She could hear its struggle to follow her voice. Aurora winced, shushed it until it once again grew calm.

"What are you doing?" She whispered to herself.

The rose bush pulsed in the light, flashing the underside of its leaves at her before settling down. Rory stepped back, her jaw open, eyes wide.

"Do you... understand me?"

Another flash of the leaves.

"May I... touch you?"

Nearest her hands, the leaves pulled away to reveal a thick stem with thorns, along with a tight rose bud nestled inside. She knelt down and put her knife away. Her hand approached the vine slowly, gently, as she did with the frightened creature. Her fingertips brushed the vine, running along the tip of the thorn. The thorns aimed at Aurora's hand as she approached the rosebud, so she stopped. The bush pushed towards her.

"You are beautiful." She whispered reverently.

The thorns aimed away from her hand, pulled back.

"Do you need the creature?"

The thorn bush retreated further from her, revealing the creature and the partially severed vine at the base of the bush.

"Was it cutting you?"

The thorns crisscrossed in between Aurora and the small creature, tightening around it.

"No, please! It's just a child." Aurora looked at the tiny thing, a faerie, she believed. "I think it's learned its lesson. Right?" She looked at the faerie. It stopped crying.

The rosebush relaxed its hold on the faerie and created an opening for it to come through. Of course, the faerie rested on the vine, wary of her.

"Hey," she called out to it. "I promise I won't hurt you." The little thing approached her, creeping along slowly.

The rosebush opened further until Aurora felt something whack her upside the head. Her vision blurred as she stumbled backward onto her hands and knees. She held the aching spot at the base of her skull and looked at the blurry face of a short cloaked man with pointed ears, a round nose, and a scruffy black beard. Was he a troll?

"Who are you, and what are you doing here?" The troll glared at her, menace in his eyes. He held out a knife as he limped forward.

Aurora held her hands up in peace and blinked her eyes into focus. "There's a faerie inside. The thorns caught it, and I was trying to help."

The troll narrowed his eyes at her, brandished his knife, and tried to shove her aside.

The rosebush hissed and surrounded her, aiming its thorns at the troll. It pulsed repeatedly at him.

"Please, stop!" Aurora called out.

The troll's eyes widened as the bush grew, leaning over his short frame. He held out the knife, prepared to attack. Aurora felt the faerie flutter down to her cheek as the rose bush enveloped them. Her breathing grew shallow, and the faerie cried out as daylight disappeared with the thickening leaves and flowers facing them. Aurora put one hand on the ground, the other near a bud. Her vision blurred as her heartbeat raced. The air felt too thin. "Please," she whispered. The flowers tilted before they pulled back. The bush gave her and the faerie space, leaving one vine under her fingers.

"Please troll, sir, stop!" Aurora called, stroking the plant's stem. "He doesn't understand. He's just trying to protect the faerie." She looked back through the plant to see the troll surrounded by the thorns. "Drop the knife. It just wants to live."

"What're you talking about?" He roared, gripping the knife, wincing as some vines wrapped themselves around his wrist.

"Drop the knife! Leave the plant alone!" She cried. "Please!"

The troll dropped both the knife and his staff before the rosebush paused. It loosened its vines around his wrist.

"Monsieur troll?" she asked.

"What just happened?" He asked roughly.

"Are you okay?" The rosebush opened between them, and Aurora pushed through, checking the troll for injuries. He yanked his hand away, glaring at her and the faerie.

"I'm fine," he growled, reaching back to smack her. The rosebush hissed again, and he stopped, slowly lowering his hand. "I'm fine," he grumbled softly. "Thank you." The rosebush settled. "What are you?" He asked, staring at Aurora's hand on a vine tendril that reached out to her. "Where did you come from?"

"It's been here for a while, but it's growing quickly." Aurora shrugged, avoiding answering him by choosing the plant. "It was defending itself against the faerie, thinking it was cutting it. Then it was defending me against you."

The troll nodded but didn't take his eyes off where her hand touched the bush. "Will it let us go?"

"Will you?" She asked the bush. "Please?"

It shuddered against her fingers, flashed its leaves, then pulsed before opening toward the sky.

"Thank you," she answered. The three of them stood and walked out into the clearing beyond. It closed itself behind them once again.

The troll scowled at her for a moment, then yelled at the faerie. "What's wrong with you? What were you thinking?"

The faerie leapt off Aurora's shoulder and spun around in circles. In a flash, it turned into a small girl with overly large lavender eyes, only standing as tall as Aurora's stomach.

"I wanted a flower. I should have known it wouldn't want to give me one."

Suddenly, the troll took his staff and swung it up and down, bonking the child's head.

"Hey, don't do that to her!" Aurora yelled. The rosebush behind her shivered.

"You shut your mouth," he pointed the staff at Aurora, who held up her hands in surrender. Pointing a gnarled finger at the child, he said, "how many times do I have to remind you?"

"I know," the faerie rubbed her head. "Stay away from the castle and the roses. It's cursed."

"Child, of all of us, you should know better than to try that with them." The troll looked back at Aurora. "You! Why aren't you asleep with the rest of them?"

"My mother was the lady's handmaid, and she needed me to do some of the harder things because her hands didn't work so well." Aurora's lie about being Muriel's daughter rolled her stomach, but she didn't want the troll or faerie to worry about themselves. "They sent me to earn my keep with my skills."

"What skills?" The troll's eyes narrowed.

Aurora held up the rope around her tunic. "Spinning. I made this."

"You made that?" The troll looked it over, pulled an end towards him and rubbed the fine texture with his fingers.

"Yes, out of the wool they brought in." And a good thing she made it, or she'd still be up in the castle, asleep, because the king wasn't coming.

The troll's angry squint was the only warning he gave before he yanked on the rope. Aurora fell forward on her knees while he swung the staff up at her chin. Aurora blocked the end with her arms, but the impact hurt. The rosebush hissed behind her, and several vines reached forward.

"Ow!" Aurora rubbed her arms. She felt nauseous. She looked at the faerie and wondered if the girl felt a lump on her head. The faerie smiled back. Aurora held her hands at her sides, palms back to placate the rosebush, and the vines stopped moving.

"The curse has fallen now." The troll stated. "Why didn't it hurt you? Don't lie to me now." He waved his staff at her.

"I'm not part of the household." Aurora answered. It was her curse, in her home, but she wasn't part of the household. She was its ruler. At least, she assumed that's why she wasn't asleep outside the walls. It was the only explanation she could come up with. As she rubbed the new bruise, she thought of the people affected by the unnatural sleep. She'd walked away from the only family she'd known, hoped that by no longer calling the chateau home, she could save them, but it hadn't worked. They were still her household, asleep in her home. Aurora blinked back tears. They didn't deserve it. She ran her fingers over the wooden ring hanging on her neck.

"What's that?" The faerie asked, leaning in to see the ring.

Aurora clutched it tight to her chest, her knuckles white, her palms sore from the descent. "A gift for my birthday." She looked away to hide the lie. Her stomach rolled again at the reminder of her betrothed's betrayal.

"My name's Luiselle," the faerie said. "That's Reinhold."

"You don't just give her your name! It's not the faerie way of things." The troll grumbled. "No wonder your lot is fading away."

Luiselle tilted up her chin. "She offered me help. It's the right thing to do!"

The troll swung his staff, but Aurora stepped forward and smiled at the two. "My name's A-, um, Rory. It's a pleasure to meet you."

The troll rolled his eyes, and they became an eery white as a silence stretched over them. Finally, they returned to their natural colour. "I can offer you work." Reinhold finally spoke.

"What kind of work?" Rory asked.

"Hard work nearby. Tending the sheep. You won't find shelter in the open fields. There'll be no home for you to rest your head."

Rory smiled. No home meant no danger of creating a household that would endanger the two beside her. No more sleeping inside a room with only a window for fresh air and birds for company. It meant the entire world at her feet, trees, and forests, open sky, and grassland. It was a world she could touch rather than look at from a distance. It meant she could survive. Rory smiled. "Will you let me card and spin some of the wool?"

A twinkle appeared in the old troll's eyes. "Yah, of course." Then he poked Rory and Luiselle both on the shoulders with his staff. "Just remember who's in charge."

Luiselle clapped her hands. "This is going to be so much fun!" She grabbed Rory's hand as Reinhold turned to walk away from the chateau. But Rory turned back to the roses.

"May I visit you again?" She touched a nearby leaf with one finger.

The rosebush extended a bloom at the end of the vine, opening to Rory's fingers. She rubbed the stem, and it detached from the vine, wrapping itself around her index finger. She looked back at the bush.

"Thank you," she whispered, then placed the rose in her hair. It held on to a lock above her ear.

"Let's be off," Reinhold grumbled.

Rory looked back once, waved, then followed the troll and the faerie back to their herd. The rose bush waved back.

5

REINHOLD STUDIED RORY AS she checked over the second last sheep for wool rot. In the last few months, the young woman excelled at shepherding. She never shied away from any task he gave her, no matter how menial and disgusting. Her palms, once soft and callus-free, were now those of a shepherd. They bore dirt, broken nails, bite marks and splinters from her staff. She motioned the sheep to go, then massaged her knuckles and stretched them out before starting on the last ewe.

Rory never complained.

She never asked for anything.

Reinhold frowned. For months now, he'd been waiting for Rory to extract her promise from Luiselle. She'd saved a faerie from the rosebush. She'd saved him, too. By law, they owed her a promise equal to her intervention.

And by Draconis, he was going to eliminate the debt.

Reinhold looked up into the forest beyond where Rory knelt, and watched the shadows move closer, golden eyes studying her too. They blinked at him twice, and he nodded. Then they disappeared.

He still didn't understand what happened at the chateau. He knew of the rosebush's origins, and it should not have attacked Luiselle. But Rory? He didn't trust her. As a human, she had no inherent magic that he could determine, just an eager nature to please and help. No one was that kind without reason, or without it beaten out of them. And she'd escaped the curse. Her home was the chateau; he could tell from the way she gazed at it; brow furrowed. She'd wander off to the chateau every chance she got. In the midnight hours, he sensed her inner turmoil,

24

anger as she clenched her hands into her fists. She rubbed her chest, as if her lungs hurt. But she never shared her burden.

She was restless but channelled it into her spinning.

The sheep trusted her, and she spun some fine wool. Her rope was strong and of good quality. It made them a decent profit in trade. Luiselle loved her. She fluttered around Rory when she wasn't on shepherd duty, slept in Rory's pockets during her daytime naps, and sat on her shoulder while shepherding. She often curled up in her lap as a child, listening to Rory tell her stories.

Rory had some good ideas. When Reinhold mentioned Kehl's refugees, she suggested culling an extra sheep now and then, drying out the meat and leaving it at the nearby signpost. Her kindness, at odds with his own views, had their merits. Rather than fight the refugees who would attack their sheep as a source of food, she saved her own food, offered it up freely. And it worked. His herd thrived, and he had to cull more sheep to keep it manageable. This made it easier to keep feeding the refugees.

So he kept her around.

For now.

The voice had also whispered in his mind to watch out for her, so he started training her, too. He instructed Luiselle to play games with her. How far could they throw their staffs? Could they hit a tree or land within a few hands of the sheep? A moving target? Rory's accuracy improved, and more often than not, she hit her target.

Reinhold searched the forest for the golden eyes, but saw nothing. His fingers tightened around his staff; his knuckles turning white. Bile churned his stomach, but he ignored the feeling.

Reinhold eyed the rose in her hair, a gift from the rosebush. It sat above her ear, today in full bloom. Other days, it remained tight as a bud when the wind and rain picked up. At first, it hissed at him every time he was near. The cursed rose would warn her he was ready to teach her a lesson. Nothing dangerous. He would knock her off her feet or startle her into defending herself. Rory started to sooth it, and tell it to ignore him, that he meant no harm. And the rose listened!

Rory did not know how to defend herself against a real predator, someone whose baser needs or desires couldn't be met with kindness.

So Reinhold enlisted help from some refugees, the hunters, who protected the weaker members. The hunters found out they were testing a human girl, and their grins became feral. He made it clear they weren't to hurt her. He'd sacrifice the sheep. But he'd given them a token for payment, some rope Rory made.

Now he waited. He licked his lips and swallowed to ease his dry throat.

Dusk turned the greens and browns of the grazing area and the forest beyond into a mix of shadowed greys. The full moon was rising, but the forest hid its glow. Reinhold watched as three sets of golden eyes appeared in the shadows. They moved forward, grey wolves that padded silently, hiding behind rocks and trees as they stalked her.

The rose tightened into a bud as Rory looked into the forest. The sheep she was working on bleated, sensing danger even with the wolves down wind. Rory calmed the sheep with steady hand movements, and the sheep stood closer to her. Rory squinted her eyes, looking around her, her gaze focused on one shadow.

The first wolf, a wiry grey beast, bigger than the rest, stepped into the grassy opening. He would draw her attention.

Reinhold watched the other wolves circle around her, one on each side, targeting the sheep. Reinhold let out a breath as the plan unfurled.

"Rory!"

Everyone stopped moving as Luiselle's voice came over the grassy knoll.

"Lu?" Rory asked, never taking her eyes off the wolf. "Lu, stay back!"

"Why?" Luiselle asked as she skipped into view. The wolves on either side of Rory stalked towards the sheep, one silent step at a time.

Do not hurt her, Reinhold willed.

"Stop moving, Lu!" Rory's harsh whisper echoed in the silence.

Luiselle came up right to the sheep. Then looked around. When she saw the large grey wolf, Luiselle rolled her eyes. Rory didn't see her do it. The wolf snarled, its ears straight up, as Luiselle frowned, then grasped Rory's hand. Rory shook it off and stood between the wolf and Luiselle. The wolf snarled again, while the other two bared their teeth at Rory.

Rory closed her eyes for a moment, breathed slowly. The wolves closed in.

"Do you know where Reinhold is?" Rory asked Luiselle.

"No," she said. "I came to ask you."

"There's three at least," Rory said. "They've surrounded us."

Rory looked between the sheep and Luiselle, then focused on the gigantic wolf as it lunged at her. The wolf on her left attacked the sheep while the one on her right stalked Luiselle.

Rory hit the enormous wolf in the neck with the butt end of her staff, then swung around and hit the one after Luiselle in the ribs. She herded them so a large bolder protected her back, but now she faced three growling wolves.

The large one bared its teeth, and all three had their ears up. She held her own, swung her staff and hit the right side of its head. They stalked her, staying back for the faerie's sake.

"Run Lu!"

"But they won't-" Luiselle's protest stopped as Rory grabbed the girl by her waist and threw her over the boulder.

"Hide!"

The wolves growled in unison; eyes focused on Rory. All the hairs on Reinhold's body stood up on end as the largest wolf lunged at her. She swung against them, but it left her vulnerable to the others. One grabbed her cloak, another her arm. The enormous wolf stood over her as the others held her down.

Reinhold stepped forward before he realized what he'd done.

The wolf snapped at Rory's head as she shifted it to the side.

Do not hurt her!

Reinhold stepped forward again, and the enormous wolf looked at him. It narrowed its eyes, then barked at the others. The one holding her cloak grabbed the sheep and ran off, the other let her arm go and followed. The large lone wolf growled at Rory; his teeth bared.

Reinhold scrambled towards Rory; his short legs struggled to make up the distance.

"Hey!" He yelled and threw his staff at the wolf.

The wolf huffed, growled again at Rory before running away. The staff landed at Rory's feet and embedded itself into the earth.

"Reinhold!" Rory got up and grabbed her staff. She looked back to where she'd thrown Luiselle, then after the sheep. She looked at Reinhold. "You stay with Luiselle. I'll go after the sheep."

"No Rory," he said, out of breath. "Leave the sheep. It's theirs now."

"But-"

He whacked her on the shoulder with his staff. "Leave the sheep. And next time, pay more attention to your surroundings. Luiselle could have gotten hurt."

Rory rubbed her shoulder, looking at where the wolves had disappeared. Then down at her feet. When she looked up at him, grim defeat in her eyes, he narrowed his gaze. She rubbed her arm where the wolf had held her.

He ignored the twist in his stomach and focused on Rory. "Let's go check on the flock. I had to leave them because of you."

Rory nodded as they walked back to the sheep. Luiselle hugged her and fussed over her. Rory hugged her tight, comforting the little girl, and ignored the pain in her arm. She glanced over at the chateau, closed her eyes, and clenched her hands.

Luiselle knelt down beside her and rubbed her arm, little purple sparks lighting up the night. Once Luiselle healed Rory's arm, and lit a fire, she nestled in to sleep beside her as Rory rubbed her back in comfort.

From upon a rock, Reinhold watched the flock and studied Rory as she stared at the fire. As he looked back at her, she stared up at him.

"Sorry about the sheep," she said, then turned her gaze back to the fire. "And thank you for coming to help. I'll train harder so it won't happen again."

She lay down to rest while he stared into the night sky, his hands clenched around the staff. The test was a success. He swallowed the bile rising from his stomach.

Sort of.

6

R ORY LEANED ON HER staff, staring at the rosebush flourishing around the chateau. She visited the rosebush daily, and the plant made space for her to sit among its thorns. But it never stopped growing. A month after Rory's escape, the rosebush reached the moat. A few tendrils climbed the walls. Rory counted the stones, and the tallest vine was now only two stones below Muriel's window.

The vines would soon cover her home in the beautiful thorny bush.

Rory was relieved the plant would protect her household. But at night she dreamed she was stuck in the chateau, awake but unable to move. The rosebush wrapped itself around her until she could no longer see. The rose in her hair woke her from the nightmare when it rubbed her temple with its stem. It comforted her, as if it understood her dreams.

She shivered from the reminder of the nightmare and rubbed her chest, feeling the ring that lay there as she checked the sun's position in the sky. Rory's visit was almost an hour now; it was time to head back. She picked up her things and started off.

Rory loved Luiselle and respected Reinhold. Luiselle never had a family, only the troll, so Rory treated her the way she imagined a big sister would. While Reinhold used his staff to discipline and direct them, he tempered his use to gain attention or for correction, not for pain. He was shorter than Rory. Even Luiselle, almost seven, was as tall as him in her human form. After watching the troll come to her defence against the wolves, Rory trusted him even more.

They were Rory's... friends.

She didn't dare think of them beyond that. Not with the curse so close.

At the forest entry, Rory stopped and looked back. The tendrils reached Muriel's window, but instead of going inside, they wrapped around the stone sill, up to the frame before growing sideways. Rory's chest stopped aching as she breathed out, the raspy sound echoing in the silent morning.

She entered the forest and walked towards the herd. She knew the path well, but as she approached the markers, she thought about her curse. Rory was awake, but if she decided somewhere new was her home, it would trigger the curse to shift. It couldn't be just anywhere. Rory had to mean it, claim it. She tried calling a nearby cave her home, but she wasn't inside it, so it hadn't worked. Muriel and her household still slept. She loved being with Luiselle and Reinhold because they had no home and slept outside under the stars and used only modest shelters at other times.

Rory stared at the sign, pointing to Kehl.

She knew what she had to do. Rory didn't want to trigger the curse and hurt her new friends. If she wanted to save Muriel and her household, she would have to leave for Kehl. She rubbed her chest, the ache tighter now.

The rose tugged Rory's hair over her right ear, distracting her. She glanced over to the right, seeing Luiselle skip towards them, a slight tilt to the right side of her mouth.

"Hi Rory. Hi flower." Luiselle greeted them. The rose bloomed in a wave, then tucked itself back into a bud by her ear.

"What made you smile?" Rory asked.

"Reinhold asked me for a favour."

Rory smiled back. "And what did you ask him for in return?"

"The next batch of wool, for you."

"For me?" Rory squinted at her friend. Her fingers wiggled around her staff in anticipation, but she tried to hide her joy. "And what are you asking me in exchange for the wool?"

"Not much," Luiselle said as she tugged Rory's hand down to hold. "Just a new belt to wrap around my cloak." She held up the tattered coil wrapped around her slight frame.

"But what I make won't shift and changes sizes."

"Oh, silly!" Luiselle rolled her eyes. "That part's mine to do."

"What size do I make it to start?"

"Full size." Luiselle looked at the base of the path marker. "Is that the food you left this morning?"

"No." Rory pulled out the pack of food she intended to leave today. "They didn't eat yesterday's food, and it's still there. Do I wrap them both up in case someone's still there?"

"Reinhold said the refugees are still moving through Elsass lands." Luiselle shrugged. "Maybe they didn't stop last night."

Rory rearranged the food, so it all sat in the same package. She saw something reflected in the sunlight. It looked like a piece of metal wedged into the rock.

"What is that?" Rory ran her fingers over it, the sharp, jagged edge pricking her. She shook her finger and pressed it into her palm to stop the bleeding.

Luiselle leaned over and examined it, then backed away several steps. "Iron!" She yanked Rory away. "It's harmful to us."

Rory got closer again.

"Careful Rory!" Luiselle said.

"I know, Lu. I want to see it." Rory ran her fingers along the bottom of the metal, feeling the sharpness of the edge. "This is the tip of a sword."

As Rory stood up again, she shivered. She felt the rose push her scalp to the left as Luiselle rubbed her left shoulder. The touch got lighter and lighter until Rory didn't feel it.

"Maybe they were being hunted," Rory said. "Luiselle, hide in my cloak hood."

"Already there." Luiselle's tiny voice said from behind her left ear.

Rory crouched into a ready position, leaning to the left of the stone marker to check out the forest beyond. She searched the trees. The small hairs on her arms rose. Ever since the wolves, she'd trained harder with her staff and with the troll, but she was never a match for him.

"What's out there?" Asked Luiselle.

Rory scanned the trees. Her gut pointed her to a set of trees opposite the stone and the path to the chateau. The rose tapped her head in that direction too.

There.

A set of flat dark brown eyes stared at them from the trees. One closed in a slow blink, then the other. Rory held her breath, staring at the eyes. She gripped her staff in her hands, waiting for it to move.

"What is it?" Luiselle whispered.

"I don't know," Rory whispered back.

The eyes blinked again, and a growling noise came from its direction. A cross between a gargle and a snarl, Rory's body tightened while Luiselle whimpered.

A large, clawed bird's foot stepped out of the tree, along with a massive head, complete with a sharp curved beak the size of Rory's head. A second foot followed, along with the creature's body, full of fur rather than feathers. It beat wings with skin so thin Rory could see the outline of the trees beyond. A scaled serpent's tail lashed behind it.

"A cockatrice!" Luiselle said.

The creature strode forward. Its growling intensified; the forest, silent behind it. The cockatrice moved to the right, and Rory stepped in the opposite direction. In response, it spread its massive wing, blocking the way back to Reinhold and the sheep. It closed the space between them. Rory moved back, keeping the stone marker in between them.

"It's herding us! What do we do?" Rory asked. The rose tugged her hair to the right. She moved in the direction until the cockatrice tilted its head sideways. She paused before the cockatrice lunged its beak at them. Rory jumped out of the way, raised her staff and hit it underneath the beak's joint before stepping back.

The cockatrice let out a screech, making both the rose and Luiselle press into Rory's head. Luiselle pulled Rory's cloak hood down over her eyes. Rory dropped the staff to pull the hood back, only to see sheer black leather-like material. The cockatrice wing came crashing into her head. Rory rolled out of the way of impact, then stood. Its tail coiled around her fee and yanked her legs from underneath her. Her back hit the ground hard, the air rushing from her lungs.

"Get up, Rory!" Luiselle shouted in her ear.

Rory used her staff to stab at the tail, which loosened enough for her to get one leg free. She stabbed at the tail again, but the rose tapped her. Rory saw the beak approach and moved her head away from its snap. The hooked tip scraped the dirt near Luiselle. Rory rolled over, but the cockatrice's tail still had her foot. It pulled her back until she found her body between its large bird feet as she grasped her staff. The beak snapped at her face again, but she held it back with her staff. The large, leathery wings dimmed the sunlight. She kicked at the tail with her free foot and held the beak back.

"A little help, Lu?" she called out, but Luiselle didn't answer. "Lu?"

Suddenly, a flash of light shot out and the wings pulled back. With a squeal, the cockatrice's tail loosened around Rory, so she pushed herself out from between the predator's legs.

"Hah!" yelled Luiselle, spiralling above the cockatrice's head. It snapped at her form before Rory saw the small fairy fall.

The cockatrice lunged at Luiselle. Rory thrust her staff on the side of its head in a devastating blow. It stumbled sideways as she reached out to catch her friend, gently tucking her into her pocket. She scrambled away, but the creature shook its head and came at them again. Its eyes focused on Rory, it charged. Rory stepped back, her staff held high. She swung at the cockatrice, but it caught the staff in its beak, and threw her to the side. Rory landed on her arm, crying out as pain shot from her elbow into her shoulder.

The cockatrice growled again and lunged at her when a brown hooded figure tackled it to the ground. It pinned the cockatrice's wings down. The figure poured an orange powder into its hand and blew the substance into the cockatrice's face. The creature went limp.

Rory watched as the hooded figure turned towards her. It brushed a lock of red hair behind a pointed ear. The figure opened the cockatrice's beak, squeezed a dark liquid out of its mouth before slitting its throat. Rory felt the rose caress her ear, at ease with the hooded figure's presence.

The figure turned to Rory and nodded at her arm.

"Is it broken?" A woman's voice asked.

Rory shook her head.

"Good," she responded before she disappeared into the forest, away from both the chateau and the flock.

"Was that...?" Rory started.

"Yep." Luiselle said, then clapped. "Wait till we tell Reinhold about the elf!"

7

"WHAT DO YOU MEAN, an elf saved you?" Reinhold asked Luiselle.

"You should have seen it!" Luiselle paced around the fire, making grand gestures as she described the scene. "After Rory landed on top of her arm, the elf swooped in from the trees, knocking the cockatrice down! She pinned its wings down, took the venom from its beak and..." Luiselle paused in front of Reinhold, then made a cutting motion with her hand across her neck.

Reinhold's staff bopped Luiselle on the head before she could continue. "Not what she did, you silly girl. What was the elf like?"

Luiselle rubbed her head. "Oh. She had long red hair, pointy ears, a brown cloak."

Reinhold scowled at her. "That's it?"

Luiselle shrugged and sat down on Rory's lap.

Reinhold looked up at Rory, who stifled a chuckle at his exasperation. "She had a soft voice," Rory told him. "She asked me if I broke my arm. When I said no, she left."

Reinhold squinted at her. "Is your arm broken?"

Rory flexed it out in front of him. "No, just bruised."

"Good." Reinhold ran his fingers through his bearded chin. "Odd for the elves to be out here. Odder that she cared enough about your arm."

"What do you mean?" Rory asked.

Luiselle tilted her head up to Rory. "Elves, like faeries, are from the area in the mountains northeast of Kehl. They don't venture down to this area without reason, and they *never* take an interest in outsiders."

"Why not?" Rory asked them both.

"For generations, kings in the areas surrounding the elves' territory valued them for their healing abilities." Reinhold said. "A few years ago, the previous King of Kehl was upset about something with his sons. They weren't able to fix it."

"And faerie and elf alike were hunted ever since." Luiselle broke in.

"They now offer their services to only the magic folk who come their way." Reinhold said.

"But not human." Rory brushed the rose above her ear. Reinhold narrowed his eyes as Luiselle shook her head. "So that she sounded concerned for me is... odd."

"Yah." Reinhold stood up abruptly. "It's time to move the sheep to a new pasture." He started packing up his things. "We'll leave in two days."

"Leave?" Rory asked.

"Too bad," Luiselle said. "This was good pasture. The sheep ate well here."

"What do you mean, leave?" Rory asked.

Reinhold gave Luiselle a stern look, then hobbled away.

"What did he mean, leave?" Rory asked her friend.

"It's just Reinhold. He moves the sheep around." She shrugged. "You'll come with us. And it will be fine."

Rory looked in the chateau's direction. "But what if I don't want to leave?" Luiselle's hand rubbed Rory's left shoulder, and the rose caressed her ear.

"Sometimes we have to do things we don't want to do," Luiselle said softly. "But I trust him. He will keep us safe." With that, Luiselle marched over to stop a few of the sheep from wandering away. Rory wondered what Reinhold was keeping Luiselle safe from. Especially so far from her home and kind.

Rory stared at the chateau as Reinhold came back to the fire.

"Get some rest." He grumbled. "We'll have some long days starting tomorrow."

"Reinhold?" Rory asked. "It's not safe to stay anymore, is it?"

He narrowed his eyes at her, gripping his staff tightly. "No, it isn't."

"For me, or for Luiselle?" Rory asked, rubbing her arm.

Reinhold studied her for a long moment. "For either of you. You're too naïve to stay with the refugees coming and the predators hunting. But Luiselle..." he glanced over to where she stood. "Luiselle was in poor condition when I met her. The King of Kehl imprisoned a lot of her kind and tortured them."

"Her wing?"

Reinhold nodded.

Rory's gut turned. She forced herself not to ask if it was the current King. "Why?"

Reinhold glared. "She never said." But from Reinhold's challenging gaze, he knew.

"Where will we go?"

"Southwest. We'll follow the refugees, but make our own path with the sheep." He pulled out a small brass bowl from behind him, offering it to her. "For your arm."

Rory took the bowl and sniffed it. The concoction smelled foul but was warm to the touch. "Thank you." She pulled her cloak and tunic out of the way and rubbed the concoction on her arm. When she was done, she handed the bowl back. Her arm heated, and her muscles relaxed.

Reinhold left to tend the sheep, while Rory focused on the chateau. She felt the pull of her home to her core, a distinct tug in her heart which made her want to run back to it. But she couldn't go back now. The roses had surrounded the chateau. They wouldn't let her in. And none of her attempts to break the curse worked.

She rubbed the ring under her tunic and sighed.

Reinhold and Luiselle would travel away from Kehl. If she went with them, she wouldn't be able to break the curse and save her household. Muriel's anguished face came to mind again, and Rory hugged her knees.

She had to leave Reinhold and Luiselle, and her chest ached.

Rory packed up her things, setting some of her best rope aside for her friends before she left. She mentally went through what she needed, rehearsed what to say to Reinhold.

"What are you doing?" Luiselle asked, startling her. Rory suddenly felt the rose caress her ear.

Rory shook her head, then turned to face her friend, smiling despite her stomach's turmoil. Her chest tightened as Luiselle took Rory's hand in hers.

"I'm so glad you're coming with us." Luiselle said simply. Her enormous smile lit up her face. "I love having you with us."

Rory swallowed, but stayed silent.

The next day, Luiselle's faerie form fluttered through the rosebush as Rory said farewell to the plant. The single rosebud clung to her finger as she held it out to the larger plant.

"Don't you want to stay?" She asked the flower. Its stem tightened on her knuckle. "Don't you want to bring it back?" She asked the bush. A vine reached out; thorns tucked down. It caressed her cheek with its leaves before pushing her outstretched hand back to her hair. The offered rose took up its residence above her ear, wiggling itself firmly in place around her lock.

"But..." Rory felt tears fall from her eyes. A single vine wiped them off her cheeks.

Another vine came out with Luiselle on a leaf, as she hugged another tight bloom bud.

"I think it understands," her little voice said. She looked at the rose in Rory's hair. "This way, it will always be with you." Luiselle gave the bud a little kiss before flying up to Rory's shoulder.

Rory caressed the plant one more time. She looked up at the chateau tower to her window. The ever-growing plant obscured the view from this angle. Missing Muriel, Rory felt herself leaning in, wanting to go into the tower. The rosebush reached out with two vines, pushed her away from the tower, and closed off all access. It fingered the thin rope around her neck holding her wooden ring, then turned her around and pushed her away.

As they left, Rory waved at the plant, but it closed in on itself, a mass of thorns pointing out.

That evening, the three of them checked the sheep for the journey, trimming the errant wool. Rory checked the lead rope, mended the wear and tear, while Luiselle grabbed herbs and berries from the nearby trees. Reinhold filled their skins from the nearby stream.

Rory took the first night watch to stay up and think. The full moon shined brightly, creating a shadow of the chateau in the distance. Muriel and her household would stay asleep if she joined her friends to journey to new pastures. It broke her heart to leave the ones who loved her since she was a child. She wanted to go with Luiselle, but how could she start a new life when her household was asleep?

The whisper of a shadow fell over her. Rory looked toward the sky, seeking the moon and the stars. Draconis, the dragon star, shined brightly to the north, and Reinhold and Luiselle would keep it behind them on their journey south towards Vaud. Legend had it all the stars obeyed Draconis. To wish upon it was perilous, because the dragon star never granted wishes in the expected way. But tonight, Rory wished her household free of the curse, and how she would one day see Reinhold and Luiselle again. The star winked in response, disappearing entirely before shining again, which sent a shiver through her entire body. The hair on her arms stood, but she was always worried at night. Draconis continued to shine as it always did, and Rory decided her imagination played a trick on her. At night in the chateau she often left a candle burning because she felt like something watched her. She laughed to herself about the thought when she remembered how far she scaled down the wall.

Luiselle sat up and checked the dragon's constellation's location in the sky.

"Go to sleep Rory," she said, touching Rory's shoulder.

Rory tried to stay awake with her friend, to spend as much time as she could with the little girl. But soon her dreams overtook her as she stood in the Chateau, looking for her household. They were nowhere to be found. The tingling returned to her body, and Muriel screamed from somewhere in the chateau.

"Muriel!" Rory cried out.

"Rory!" came her distant cry.

Rory ran to find Muriel, searched every door, but never found her as she cried in agony.

"Muriel!" Rory stumbled as the chateau descended into darkness.

"Rory!" Muriel's voice sounded far away, but the screaming continued, louder than before.

"Muriel!" Her voice broke.

"Rory!" a deep male voice called, with a hard shake to her body. Her nightmare shattered, and she sat upright, staring at the chateau. A cloud floated over the moon. She gulped deep breaths of air, trying to clear her mind of the echoes of the scream. Her body tensed at the grating sound. The cloud moved upward instead of sideways, but Rory couldn't focus because the screaming continued. She looked over at Luiselle and Reinhold, both awake, staring at her.

No, not at her, but at the side of her head.

The *rose* was screaming.

8

T HE ROSES WERE *SCREAMING!* At first he thought it was the chateau's residents, but the fire hadn't breached the rosebush. Yet.

Riel twisted his angular head away. But he couldn't escape the screeching sound. It came from the writhing bush that enclosed the chateau. The cries echoed through him and wouldn't stop. His body shook from nose to tail as the sound joined the choir of tortured cries he'd tried to forget for the last five years.

His brother's soldiers brandished torches, setting dry kindling on fire underneath different parts of the bush. But fire-laden vines whipped out at them, tripped them up, knocked them down, and dragged them into their thorny trenches.

He flew away from the firelight to hide his enormous form from the soldiers. Their painful cries mingled with the rosebush's. The vines gripped the walls of the chateau, trying to climb out of the flame's reach. Unfortunately, it just gave the fire a path to climb. He soared above the tower and watched as one soldier broke through the flaming plants. He made it to the chateau gate, torch blazing. A vine reached out to grab his torch-bearing arm, but the soldier cut it off with the sword in his other hand. The soldier threw dried kindling down at the gate's base and set it on fire, too.

This isn't part of the plan! They were supposed to get inside!

Riel dropped closer to the gate, an old thick wood, which struggled to light. Riel breathed in relief until flames inched closer to the door.

The soldier celebrated by lifting the torch above his head. One vine grabbed the torch from him, while another one wrapped around his torso with elongated thorns. The soldier cried out, his face a mask of anguish, as the rose set his clothes on fire.

Riel looked from the tortured soldier to the others pillaging around him. Fires started around the castle, lit by bow and arrow, or from the vines trying to climb away from the flames. The burning plant trapped dying soldiers, their throats now too charred to cry out.

This was a reconnaissance mission!

The soldiers were supposed to confirm the curse's reach and see if they could breach the chateau. Instead, they were destroying it, murdering the people inside. There wasn't supposed to be anything living outside of it, either. He clenched his front claws together, nails scraping the scales on his palm. His brother changed the plan, as he often did, and innocents were about to perish. Not that his brother cared.

Riel tried to land on the castle until he felt the curse's power flow through his body. He flew upward, turned around, and then soared in. He exhaled into the sky before coming close to the castle and inhaling the smoke and fire from the charred plants and doors. The smell of burned rose petals mixed with human flesh made his stomach spasm. He ignored the feeling, took the smoke and fire deep into his lungs and let its energy flow through him. He exhaled hot, charred breath into the night sky. Ashes exploded from him and floated to the ground. He looped around and continued to disperse the fire. Riel inhaled again, when small sparks of purple lightning hit him in the face.

"Leave them alone!" A tiny voice said near his ear.

He turned sideways, striking a tiny insect with his head as it fell away from his face. He faced the burning bush and inhaled the fire when he heard a growling shout.

"Luiselle!" yelled a man.

He was about to exhale again when a stick blocked his nostrils. No, not a stick, a straight staff. He choked out the built-up heat, and coughed onto the rosebush, withering what the soldiers left of the poor plant.

"Leave it alone!" said a girl, holding another staff like a lance. *Stupid git!* he thought. He shook the stick out of his nose, but not before a second one nearly poked him in the eye. It bounced off his armoured head and fell as the girl ran through the flaming and wilted bush to pick it up.

He stopped flying for a split second, then looked again.

The bush parted *itself* for *her*.

He exhaled the heat into the sky before inhaling the flames again from the rosebush. As he did, purple sparks hit him in the face. A tiny insect fluttered around this head but wouldn't hold still long enough for him to identify it. More sparks flew toward his face until a fine mesh net snatched the insect out of the air. The net dragged the annoying thing down off to the side. Riel looked down below at his friend Kuri, grateful for her interference. Then he inhaled the flames again.

"Lu!" said the girl.

The man below - a *troll* - launched himself onto Riel's tail, but he flung the troll off to the side, in the opposite direction of Kuri. He fell outside the burning plants.

"Reinhold!" yelled the girl. She stood up among the dying rosebush, her hood fallen from her shoulder to reveal dark hair, tears streaming down her face. Not a girl, a woman. She looked at the chateau, raced towards the troll, and cradled his head before setting it down again gently. The woman glanced at the chateau, then in Kuri's direction. She stopped to caress the charred remains of the rosebush before focusing on him again.

"Leave them alone!" She picked a fallen soldier's sword and ran at him. She tripped and fell over charred vines. The rosebush no longer moved out of her way. When she stood up again, he noticed the red stain at her temple. His heartbeat thundered in his ears. He cursed to himself for hurting another innocent person, then swooped down and picked her up in his front claws. He held her tight, but she kicked at his claws.

The woman gasped and gripped her sword. While one clawed hand held her, the other immobilized her, holding her arms to her sides.

"Let me go!" She yelled.

Riel glowered at her until she fell silent. He exhaled heat into the sky, and inhaled the dying flames, making them embers with one final breath before releasing it again.

She watched him, her mouth open, her brown eyes wide. She looked down at the carnage below, tears gathered in her eyes. Only then did he hear the silence. The screams and flames stopped. He soared for a moment and checked for embers when she spoke again.

"Please, can we check on the people inside?"

Riel lifted an eyebrow before he swooped down and flapped his wings to hold himself above the lowest window. Any lower and the curse would hurt his body. He released one of her arms and she tried to open the window, then yanked her arm back as if in pain. His lower foot approach the castle, and the shock shot through him.

She looked at him with tears in her eyes. "Will you put me down?"

He descended until he saw movement in the shadows. A lot of movement. *Trouble.* In the opposite direction, a flicker of light caught his eye. He rose into the night, followed his friend's signal, taking the woman with him.

9

As Rory watched the chateau disappear behind her, the knots in her stomach grew larger. The dragon carried her deep into the night, away from the flames, the roses, and her home. Her household remained alive, for now. The curse's sharp sting shocked her and the dragon when she saw Muriel through the window, asleep.

Alive!

Rory tried to rub her chest, but couldn't move. The rosebush was ash, and the small bud that screamed her awake, lay still above her ear. Silent. She couldn't comfort the only remaining friend she had left. It broke her heart, but it kept gripping her hair. Tiny pulses pulled at her scalp. The bud was okay, for now.

She looked up to the dragon who held her beneath him, but saw only its dark, armoured underbelly. It didn't hurt her, and honoured her requests, so she wasn't terrified. But it was a dragon. She didn't know what his purpose was. When she and Luiselle first saw it flying over the burning remnants of the roses, they raged, trying to stop the dragon from destroying it. Which was foolish for so many reasons. It turned out the dragon was trying to *stop* the fire.

Reinhold tried to hold them back, to warn them. They didn't listen and now Luiselle was gone, and Reinhold had a broken leg. She'd checked on him before the dragon grabbed her.

"Find Luiselle and save her!" He'd grabbed her cloak and yanked her ring into his hand.

"I will!" Rory answered, no doubt she'd go after her little friend.

"When you find her, take her home, to the Rätsel caves so she can fulfill the role she was born into." Reinhold grabbed her hand, squeezing the ring between their hands. "Swear it!"

"What role?" Rory asked.

"Swear it!" Reinhold said. Sweat poured down his face, agony stretching his mouth.

"I swear!" Rory answered. The ring heated, scorching her hand, its warmth going straight to her heart. Then it flashed cool but left no mark.

Reinhold released the ring and shoved her away. "Go! The dragon is key!"

"But..."

"Go!"

So Rory went. When she looked back, Reinhold was gone. He simply... disappeared. Though Rory was with the dragon, she wished she hadn't left Reinhold behind. The troll was gone, the one who took them both in, and her chest hurt. Despite her love of her friends, she'd planned to leave him and Luiselle behind to go to Kehl. Now she had no choice. She'd made an oath and would honor it. But she would still break the curse and help Muriel. After she helped Luiselle get to the Rätsel caves.

Now the wind circled around her head. Looking around, she realized the dragon soared higher, using the air current to glide upward like a kite. They were stationary but always in motion to capture the wind.

It lifted her to eye level, with her back towards the chateau. From the north, an undulating shadow stalked towards the chateau, larger than anything she'd ever seen before. She heard the faint cry of sheep in the distance, their pleas shattering her already broken heart. The mass overtook the sheep, her hard work protecting them all for nothing. Tears burned her cheeks, cascading wildly as the wind pushed them towards her ears.

"What is that?" She whispered.

The dragon scrutinized her for a moment before returning its attention to the shadow.

In the distance, flashes of silver glistened in the moonlight and penetrated the shadow. It circled the chateau and was full of silver spikes. Sections approached the chateau, while the rest stayed behind. Her home, Muriel and the servants were vulnerable, and she had no way of protecting them. She wished to return, but felt a burning sensation travel up her arm, a reminder of her oath to Reinhold. A small part of the mass broke off, heading north where it came from, other fragments towards the east, west, and south. *Towards them.* Rory understood.

"It's an army?" She asked the dragon.

It nodded once, as they turned, flying to the north.

"Wait! My friend! I need to-"

The air left her lungs as they dropped from the sky, gliding over the dense forest. The dragon pulled her close to its body, keeping her safe from the treetops as he scanned the forest from side to side. His nostrils flared, sniffing for something. They pivoted to the right. There it landed, still holding her close, sheltering her within its wings.

Rory wondered why they stopped here and peaked around the wings and front legs until she saw a firelight coming from the forest. Rory gripped the hilt of the sword, still trapped in her hand, ready to draw if necessary. She'd never used one, but wouldn't let that stop her.

That's when she saw the green arm of an ogre carrying a torch.

10

CLAUDE GLOWERED AT THE moon as it lit up his kingdom in an ethereal glow.

"Can't sleep?" Ilse asked, standing in the doorway. She kept her blonde hair cut short like a man, which kept the soldiers from grabbing it when she trained them. They saw Ilse's elegant attire and thought her weak. Fools. "What are you staring at?"

"It's a full moon."

"Thinking of her again?" She responded from beside him. She kept her distance, hands to herself, but he never heard her move. No one did.

"There's no one else but you, Ilse." Claude answered.

Though that wasn't quite true. Once upon a time, Claude composed odes to the lady of the night sky. He ascribed to the fickle lady, the beauty of a woman with amethyst eyes whose skin glowed in the dark when she was content. Swore by Draconis, his love was true, as true as the dragon's love of the moon's maiden. Tonight, though, he didn't compose sonnets, her loss a mere echo in his life. He shook off the dream that woke him. What others would consider a nightmare fuelled his passion once again.

Claude had plans. They didn't include the lady of the moon or the woman with unnatural amethyst eyes. He would never play a sentimental fool again. It was the reason Ilse stood by his side. She made an excellent partner, pragmatic above emotion. Loyal to him.

"I see the plan is progressing." She gestured with an open palm to the glimmer of red light shining in the distance.

Claude nodded. The mission was going as intended. Elsass's chateau and its inhabitants would soon be engulfed in flames. His men hunted the refugees, and the Elsass kingdom was in his grasp.

The sky reddened in the distance, making Claude smile. The dragon was more useful than Claude imagined. More than even the Seeress predicted. He caught his reflection sneering and relaxed his face. Thoughts of the Seeress brought back memories of her rejection of his love. She paid for that rejection. He smiled to himself. She paid, but not enough. Claude frowned. Again, he caught his reflection, his hand running through his blond hair. He took a deep breath and made his face neutral. A leader gave nothing away in his expression.

"What's wrong?" Ilse asked, squeezing his hand. He permitted her touch because he knew her hands were useful for his defense.

"Someone is working against me." He ran his fingers through his short hair.

"It's just a matter of time before we find her." She said, turning her lip up. It was as much emotion as Ilse would show unless you found yourself on the wrong end of her sword. Then her eyes lit up from within. "You'll have your revenge." She squeezed his fingers and left him staring at the moon.

The red glow died down in the distance as he smiled. When he had her at his mercy, he would eliminate her and the dragon both. Then, his revenge would be complete. Nothing would stand in his way, not even the war the Seeress predicted.

11

R ORY PEERED AT THE ogre from behind the dragon's wings. Brown leather armour clothed the green skin of a muscled warrior, who carried a broadsword in one hand, and the torch in the other. They strapped a bow and quiver to its back over an axe. It had dark green hair shaved on the sides and brushed longer over the top from the right side to the left.

"Took you long enough."

The low feminine voice surprised Rory, and she let out a small gasp, then flinched as it focused on her.

"What you got there?" The female ogre asked the dragon.

Wings unfurled, unveiling Rory. She shrank back, but the dragon pushed her forward in the ogress' path. She tried to step away, but the dragon stretched beside her, front legs out with its angular head down, and tail pointed to the sky. It nosed Rory forward, and she noticed a scar bisecting its left eyebrow. It watched her stare and blew a puff of smoke into her face. Rory coughed as she spun around, suddenly face to face with the ogress. Or face to chest. The ogress towered over Rory by a span and a half. A large, green hand with long, dark green fingernails gripped Rory's entire jaw. It tilted her face as gold eyes squinted at her. The ogress sniffed before glancing at the dragon.

"You picked up a human?" She asked, the left side of her mouth raised in a sneer.

The dragon huffed, blowing smoke in their faces again.

Rory gripped the hilt of her sword, but the ogress lifted her by the jaw, so she was barely standing on the tips of her toes. Lights flashed at the corners of Rory's

49

vision as she grew dizzy from the position. She swung the sword, but the ogress dropped her suddenly to the side before she could lift it a foot off the ground.

"Why on earth would you bring a human here, let alone this weak little thing?" she asked, crossing her hand over her chest.

"She had blood on the side of her head."

Rory jumped at the man's deep voice, coming from where the dragon stood. The ogress arched an eyebrow at him. Rory looked around for the dragon, but didn't see it anywhere. She faced the man again, noticing he too had a scar bisecting his left eyebrow. Fully clothed, he wore leather armour similar to the ogress, a cloak, and linen clothes underneath.

"So you kidnapped her?"

"I thought Kuri could look her over."

The ogress rolled her eyes, then grabbed Rory's chin again in her calloused hands. She tilted Rory's head from side to side, then glowered at the man.

"You idiot. It's not blood, it's a flower." The ogress let go of Rory's jaw and sighed. She picked up Rory's hands in hers, flipped them over to see her palms, then grunted. "She's got calluses, so at least she's done work."

"I had to bring her, Nega."

"Whatever for?" The ogress crossed her arms over her chest. Her stance made Rory think of the guards who attacked the chateau. She wanted to weep, but not in front of Nega.

"The army is on its way," he said, his hands clenched. "They're headed in every direction."

Nega flinched, barely, but Rory saw it. "So why bring her here with you?" Nega faced Rory. "Do you even have any skills?"

Rory opened her mouth to say something, but the man spoke instead. "I will not leave her at their *mercy*." He spat out the last word, and bared his teeth, then took a breath and relaxed. "And she was with the faerie. I think they're friends."

The ogress looked at Rory again, one eyebrow up. "A human, friends with a faerie?"

"And a troll." The man said.

The two stared at each other before they both turned towards her. The ogress reached around Rory, yanking the small bag she carried off her back.

"Hey!" Rory said, as the ogress dumped the contents onto the ground.

"She doesn't even have a weapon."

"I have a sword," Rory argued.

"That you don't know how to use," the ogress answered, looking through her things. "You have rope, at least. What is this?" She pulled out the two spiked brushes and the fleece, then dropped them on the forest floor. "How would you fight someone with this?" She held out the spinner and touched her finger to the tip. "This couldn't hurt anyone, except maybe to give them a splinter."

Rory yanked it out of the ogress' hands.

"It's for carding wool." Rory grabbed her pack and shoved the contents back in. "I card it, then I spin it, then I make rope."

"This rope?" Nega asked, grasping the end that cinched Rory's waist.

Rory rolled her eyes. "Yes, *that* rope."

"You made *this rope*?" Nega asked again.

"Why are you surprised?" Rory clenched her hands. "I shepherd sheep. They have fleece that make wool, and I can make rope. It's not a stretch."

The man behind them chuckled.

Nega watched Rory, tilting her head again, and narrowing those golden eyes. "This is nice rope." She said.

"Thank you." Rory answered her.

"That's probably the only compliment you're going to get," the man said, smirking.

"Idiot." Nega retorted. She faced Rory again. "So why were you making rope with a faerie and a troll?"

Rory breathed deeply, looking directly into the ogress' golden eyes. She wouldn't lie, but she didn't know them. They didn't need to know her history. "They took me in when I lost my family, taught me how to shepherd to earn my keep. Three shepherds are better than two." She shrugged. "I made them rope. Sold it in trade too."

"If you're a shepherdess, where's your staff and why are you holding a sword?"

The man behind them snorted. Nega stared at him, then back at Rory.

"I, uh, threw the staff at him." Rory pointed to him as she tiptoed back from the scowling ogress.

"You threw it at him?" Nega trod forward.

"Threw it like a spear. Good aim too." The man laughed. "Got it right up in my nose."

"You attacked him?" The ogress growled. She bared sharp, jagged teeth.

"I thought he was attacking the roses!" Rory argued, stepping back again. The ogress strode forward. "They were on fire, and he was, you know, a *dragon*!"

"Flowers?" Nega halted and glanced at the man, her face scrunched up, trying to understand. "You were attacking flowers?" She punched the man in the shoulder. Taller and more muscular than him in human form, she knocked him sideways before he regained his balance. "What is wrong with you?"

"Hey!" He said, rubbing his arm. "The *soldiers* set fire to the flowers, and they had grown around the entire chateau. They were trying to light the building on fire. I was extinguishing the blaze."

"The roses were screaming and there was fire and a dragon," Rory argued. "What would you think?"

"The king will hate that you intervened." The ogress pointed her sword in his direction then turned toward Rory. Rory's mouth went dry at her scowl. "I don't know what's more idiotic. Saving a plant or attacking a dragon when you can't even lift a sword. I mean, throwing a piece of *wood* at something that breathes fire? Do you have a death wish?"

Rory's chest ached at the insult, and she dropped her sword at her feet. "No, just a desire to help my friends." The ring on her chest pulsed beneath her tunic. "Speaking of friends, do you know where the faerie is? I need to find her."

The man glanced at Nega, who scowled further. She shook her head. He nodded. Rory considered them both, confused by their silent conversation.

"She's with another friend," the man answered.

"Safe?" Rory asked. At his nod, she let out a breath.

"There's a village nearby," Nega said. "We'll leave you there."

"What? No!" Rory said, grabbing the ogress' arm. Everyone froze. Rory's heart pounded in time with the pulsing ring. The man arched an eyebrow and Nega clenched her sword tighter in her hand. Rory let go immediately. "Please, I made a promise to look out for her. She's very young, only seven, and helped me out. I'm here because of her, and I made an oath."

The ogress studied the man again, then back at Rory.

"Fine." Nega answered, lifting a torch ahead of her. "Stay close. We won't wait for you."

The man patted Nega on the back before she punched him in return.

"I don't know what's worse," Nega mumbled. "Working against the king with you or bringing this puny thing with us."

Rory exhaled in relief as the ring stopped pulsing. Her heartbeat slowed until she heard Nega grumble under her breath, "I'm going to regret this."

12

T HE CROW LANDED ON the old crone's entry way, puffed out his feathers, and leaned heavily on one leg. He hopped into her home, but she wasn't there, so he hopped back outside. He found her in her garden, on weathered knees, hunched over and tending to her yarrow and a few other plants.

She hummed to herself. A purple glow flowed out of her hands, plumping the flowers and their leaves twice their size. Her staff, sturdy with a curve at the top, and carved in runes, lay beside her, placed so the protection runes faced up. As he approached, they glowed beside her, drawing her attention off the plants. He was relieved. He couldn't caw at her with what he carried. The crone's humming ceased, and so did the growth of the plants.

The woman rubbed the rune with her thumb, then used her staff to help herself up to her feet. Her body straightened, and she brushed her deep black robes, lined with streaks of purple, out of her step. She didn't need the staff, but affected its use to hide herself from attention.

The crow spread his wings out before her, while tilting his head down low, a kind of awkward bow with his damaged foot.

The old woman grinned, recognizing him, but her grin only reached the left side. Her white hair was the only thing that gave any indication of her age. The crow never knew if her grin meant she thought up some sort of joke or punishment. Her porcelain, wrinkle-free skin contrasted the deep violet of her eyes. Their intensity made most look away from her in fear of her sight.

"You're back." She looked around him. "Alone?" Her eyes narrowed at him.

The crow rose from his bow and hopped backwards as she stepped forward.

"Oh, come on up," she said, offering him the curve in her staff as a perch.

He flew, relieved that he wouldn't have to hop on his damaged leg any further. He wiggled for a moment, making sure his feet didn't rub any of the runes. The last time he did, they hit him with magic so strong she'd had to revive him.

The crone brought them into her home, where she traced the runes in her doorway before entering inside. There she leaned the staff against a wall, and the crow flew to the perch beside the fireplace where a hearty stew bubbled away.

She sat down in the chair by the fire, focused on the stew, and gave it a stir. "Well? What news?"

The crow pumped his wings to get her attention.

She turned violet eyes on him until she noticed something in his beak. She held out her hand as he gently placed the small piece of charred wood into her palm.

The crone looked it over, holding it up in the firelight.

"A thorn?" she asked him. "From the roses?"

He bobbed his head.

"And where's the girl?"

The crow looked down and cawed.

"What do you mean, she's gone?"

Immobilized by the look in her eyes, he didn't see her hand until she gripped him, squeezing his wings to his body. He didn't flinch, but felt every feather crush. He couldn't breathe as her magic wound itself around him.

"You failed me?" She ground her teeth, violet eyes storming as she stared into his small black ones.

She released her grip, tore her gaze from his, and looked down at the thorn in her other hand. Blood seeped into her palm, connecting the life and fate lines into a bloody mess. The burned thorn sat embedded in her heart line. She stared at the bloody stains; her eyes glazed over. When she focused on the crow again, she grinned at him.

"I see." She released him back to his perch. After washing her hands, she walked back to the stew and sat down.

He stretched out his wings, fluffing the feathers until they realigned.

"Well, my friend," she said, pouring herself a bowl of stew. "You haven't failed me completely, but this changes things." She faced him, eating in silence. "Rest up. You'll need your strength. I have plans for you."

The crow tucked his wings in and sighed. He was getting too old for this.

13

A ROUND DAWN, NEGA STOPPED their group in the forest. Nega and Riel communicated silently, with only hand gestures. The pair halted, then Nega shoved Rory behind a tree while they separated. She'd learned his name earlier, after he asked the ogress to stop calling him Idiot. They hadn't bothered to ask hers.

"Stay here," Nega said, showing her overly large incisors.

Rory nodded and crouched down low at the base of the tree. Pulling off her bag, she opened it for her canteen and got her food ready. She looked up to find a family of grey jays staring at her, twittering. She smiled at them, broke off some crumbs from her bread crust and placed them on the branch of the tree.

The birds tilted their heads at her, then descended on the crumbs, eating them silently. In a flurry, they flew off. Rory heard the crunch of leaves and studied the trees. She slung her bag over her shoulder and gripped the hilt of the sword she still carried.

The noises grew closer. She tucked herself against the tree, blade held forward, facing the sound.

The flat side of a blade pressed against her neck just as Riel reappeared in front of her. Rory froze. Riel halted too, then smiled at her.

"Nega, leave the poor girl alone."

The blade swung away as Nega appeared to Rory's right. Rory looked up at her. Nega's lips snarled, disgusted with Rory's skills. Nega put her blade away in her back holster.

"Come on," Nega said. She gestured to the side with a nod of her head. "Stay alert!"

Rory followed her, Riel coming up behind her. Rory gripped the sword tighter, furious the ogress caught her off guard. She could take care of two dozen sheep alone, fending them off from predators, but she couldn't hear an ogress?

"Get out of your head." Nega said.

Rory stumbled, surprised, and frowned. "What do you mean?" She wanted to yell in frustration, but knew it wouldn't help her case with Nega.

"You're in your head, too busy thinking, not paying enough attention to what's going on around you." Rory stepped on a twig, the snap loud in the forest's quiet. "Like that. You're not being careful where you're walking. Not using your senses." They came upon a stream, and Nega crossed her arms over her armoured chest. "I shouldn't have caught you off guard. What were you doing, anyway?"

Heat creeped from Rory's cheeks down into her neck. "Um... Giving crumbs to some grey jays."

Nega's eyes widened as she stepped forward, clenched her fists in front of her, as if restraining herself from punching Rory. "Feeding the birds?" She whispered. The seething sound made Rory shudder more than the ogress's growl. Nega turned to Riel. "She was feeding the birds!" Nega clenched open hands over her head in an angry grab at the sky, then looked back at Rory. "What in Draconis' name is wrong with you, child?"

"I-"

"You can't fight. You're wasting whatever food you have on the woodland creatures, and you've got no head on your shoulders. What use are you?" Nega walked away. She whipped her axe out and sent it flying into a nearby tree, where it struck so hard she had trouble getting it out.

Rory felt her blush deepen with shame; tears stinging her eyes. Luiselle popped into her mind, and she remembered her promise to Reinhold. But if the ogress was right, how would she ever succeed? She wiped the tears away.

"You should fill your canteen," Riel said. Rory looked at him under her eyelashes. "Just make sure you don't let Nega sneak up on you again." He paused and watched her movements. "What's your name?"

"Rory," she answered, stepping closer to the river. She looked in the clear water, filled her canteen to take a drink, then refilled her canteen again. Setting it in her pack for later, she ate some cured lamb. She spotted a broadleaf maple, some yarrow, and a branch decent enough to make a staff. Once she made a bowl out of leaves, she mixed pollen of the yarrow inside. She set it down in front of her, then carefully unhooked her rose from her hair. The rose gripped her finger tightly, its bloom closed in a tight bud covered in soot.

"Come on," she whispered to the rose. "Take a drink."

The rose trembled.

"Please? I don't want to lose you too." Memories of Reinhold, his oath, and Luiselle snatched out of the sky, made Rory's hands tremble. Fresh tears stung her eyes. She swallowed, forced back the memories, and focused on the rose. "Please?"

The rose loosened its grip on her finger, and tenderly reached its stem into the leaf bowl. Rory grabbed onto her staff and took comfort with it in her hand as she watched the bud step into the bowl. It sank into the water, and she gasped, ready to fish it out when the bud bloomed, opening wide on the water surface, stretching as if after a long nap.

"There you are, my friend." Rory smiled at the plant.

Suddenly, it closed in on itself, and Rory spun around.

Crack!

Rory held her staff in two hands, blocking the strike of Nega's arm, the hilt of the sword aimed at Rory's head. Nega's gold eyes widened slightly, and Rory kicked out at Nega's knees. The ogress jumped out of the way but didn't resume her attack. Nega's smile curled up on one side.

"Well, Riel," she said as he stood to Rory's right. "She may prove useful after all."

Rory set down her staff and checked on the rose, but kept her mind on the ogress. The rose bloomed again, so Rory offered it her finger. It grabbed on, and she placed it back in her hair.

"Thanks," she whispered.

The rose tugged back.

Riel lit a fire, roasting some sort of a small animal by the time Rory joined them. She sat across from the ogress, putting distance between them. Riel, who sat to Nega's right, stood and stretched. He blew softly on the fire until the flames brightened, then sat down again. They spoke softly, eating as they did. Their low tones and unfamiliar language kept her from understanding them. She assumed it was the ogre's language.

Rory ate a small amount of the meat, then pulled out her drop spindle and the roping she'd already carded. She spun the small stash of wool and allowed the repetitive motions to bring her comfort in a strange place. Her heart ached as she longed for the calls of the nearby sheep, only to have the birds twitter in their place. She missed Luiselle, snuggled up to her as she spun. Rory realized she never made Luiselle's belt. She decided that's what she'd make now. A few finches landed near her and watched her motions with avid interest.

"Sorry, no crumbs for you now," Rory said to them.

Two little finches hopped towards her, then laid something on her cloak. Rory looked away from her spinning for a moment, and spotted small clusters of gooseberries. She stopped spinning and looked at the birds.

"For me?" she asked, then looked over at Nega and Riel. They were still in deep conversation. A third finch laid out a small cluster for her, too. "Many thanks." Rory ate the berries as the finches flew off.

Rory resumed her spinning until she realized the silence surrounded her. She looked up to find Nega and Riel staring at her. Rory stared back, the spindle coming to a stop.

"A troll taught you to spin like that?" Nega asked, her eyebrow arched.

Rory laughed out loud, picturing Reinhold's thick, stubby fingers trying to do the delicate and even work. She shook her head. "He was a troll, not an imp."

Nega glared at Rory. "So, who taught you? It's not a skill a shepherd would know."

Riel leaned forward, his elbows on his knees, his fingers pressed together in front of his mouth.

"I have only been with them for a few months." Rory answered.

"And before that?" Nega clenched her jaw.

Rory gulped. "Before that, I lived in the chateau of Elsass. A servant named Muriel taught me." Rory didn't hide her eyes. She left out a few things, but it was the truth. She fought tears as she thought about Muriel, still asleep in the castle. Hopefully, still alive despite the advancing army.

Nega and Riel glanced at each other, then back at Rory. She didn't know what their looks meant, only that they agreed about something concerning her.

"Muriel was the one you wanted me to check on in the chateau?" Riel asked, his voice gentle but his face neutral.

Rory nodded. "Until I met Lu and Reinhold, she was my only family."

"So why aren't you still there?" Nega narrowed her gaze.

Asleep. Nega didn't have to say the word, but Rory understood. She decided on the truth, or as much of it as she could under their scrutiny. "I got out before-"

Nega held up her hand, halted Rory's explanation, and closed her eyes. Riel looked at Nega, then kicked sand over the remnants of their fire. He inhaled the flames and smoke before exhaling the heat into the air. It drifted towards Rory, and she held her cloak over her mouth to stop from coughing. She sat motionless until Nega opened her eyes.

Nega angled her head to the left, putting her fingers to her lips for Rory's benefit. Rory opened her bag, slipped the spindle and unfinished roping back in, then closed it softly and slung it on her back. She grabbed her staff and handed over her sword to Riel. Nega nodded her approval.

Crack!

The sound came from the North. Finches flew overhead, circling around the three of them before heading south. Rory pointed her staff toward the birds and arched her eyebrows at Nega.

Nega nodded. The three of them followed the birds, Nega in the lead, Riel behind, and Rory in the middle. Rory paid close attention to where Nega stepped. She gingerly picked out the ogress's large strides on the forest floor with her shorter legs. Rory tried to step on the mosses and bare earth, rather than the branches and sticks. Nega checked back every so often to make sure they still followed her. Rory assumed that meant she was doing fairly well. After a while, it became easier to pick out her steps, tiptoeing through the forest.

Rory looked back to see Riel close behind her, so she kept following Nega. The forest grew increasingly silent. The birds and woodland creatures hid from the invisible predators who stalked their group. Rory tightened her grip on the staff in her hands, looked around, and nearly bumped into Nega. The ogress snarled at her. Riel came up behind them just as a growl broke the silence. It was close behind them.

What are they? Rory mouthed to Nega. They both looked at Riel. Nega pushed Rory to the side, then pulled her bow. She strung and notched it with an arrow from her quiver with an efficiency that impressed Rory. Nega took aim at something in the canopy, tracking its movements. Nega's fingers twitched as her arrow took flight.

Rory held her breath as she waited. Then they heard a pained cry followed by a loud thud.

Suddenly motion surged through the trees, towards them. Leaves moved and branches snapped, followed by a guttural cry. One word from Nega sent shivers down her spine.

"Run!"

14

T HE THREE OF THEM jumped into action. Rory followed Riel as Nega sent a flurry of arrows into various parts of the tree canopy and ground. Rory heard several cries before Nega joined them. The ogress overtook them and lead them through the dense forest.

Rory struggled to keep up, stumbling forward. Rory caught herself with her hands on the soft ground below and got back up. But the others didn't wait. She cried out as she stumbled again, her knee slammed down on a tree root.

Rory saw Riel glance back. Nega, noticing him hesitate, grabbed his arm, and dragged him away. Rory got to her feet, ignored the pain in her knee, and watched them disappear into the forest shadows.

She froze as she took in her surroundings. The light filtered through the trees, creating a series of moving shadows. She grabbed her staff and hobbled forward. Tears stung her eyes as the pain shot through her kneecap and up the tendons in her thigh.

She limped on her tiptoes in the direction Riel and Nega had departed. The pain lessened as she used her leg. Rory sighed as she realized her knee wasn't broken, but bruised.

A rustle in the trees behind her made her pick up her pace. She stepped as Nega had shown her, but her heartbeat thundered in her ears and drowned out any other noise. A shadow moved on her right, so she veered left. The cracks of branches to her left had her moving back, but the shadow still ran alongside her.

They surrounded her, picking off the weak link in their group, just as the predators did with her sheep.

She was no sheep.

Rory raced forward. She noticed a clearing up ahead and ran as hard as she could towards it, ignoring the pain in her knee. In the open, she could see the predators she was up against, figure out how to fight them. Her heart thundered in her ears as branches behind and beside her broke. Each sound was closer than the last.

Just before she reached the clearing, something sharp pierced her cloak, just missing her torso. She dodged the spear that stuck out of the ground on her right. Rory leapt over the bush in front of her, just as the branches behind her broke.

Bracing herself to land with a roll on the ground, she gave a startled cry as her body didn't land, but continued to fall. She had a brief glimpse at the brush above her, before tumbling over again in a midair roll. She caught sight of the ground below, split by icy blue water.

Rotating toward the forest, she glimpsed the predators who were chasing her. They had misshaped faces on their chests, and arms raised above square shoulders in anger at losing their prey. She stared too long at their headless bodies. Her body unrolled itself as she crashed belly first into the river below.

The sudden shock of the frigid water made her gasp, but her stomach spasms made her unable to breathe. It kept her from inhaling the icy water. She sank for a moment until the shock stopped and she kicked her legs, swinging her arms to the surface. The current eddied, and it pulled her under, bumping her arms and legs against the river's rocks.

Her feet met the ground underneath, as she pushed herself through the current, back to the surface. She spied a branch above, and tried to grab it, but couldn't reach it with her icy fingers. Her head dipped under the water, the wool cloak dragging her down. She pushed again.

Another tree branch hung in her way, so she grabbed it. Her fingers held, but the branch broke, and she spun around backwards, bobbing in and out of the water. Rory's body struggled against the current, which dragged her down. Her body jerked back and pulled forward, but her cloak was stuck on a rock or branch. The water cascaded over her head and pushed her down with relentless pressure.

She fought with all her strength and reached out her arms for something, anything, when her fingers brushed something smooth. Her hands slid along the surface to find something to hold. She pulled herself forward but remained stuck until her cloak released, and the water dragged her down stream. The thing she held onto gripped her back. It lifted Rory out of the water enough to see she held onto a green arm hovering in the air.

"Hold on!" Nega said. The dragon carried her and together they pulled Rory out of the river. Rory's strength collapsed while black clouds formed in her vision's periphery. She looked at the forest below for a moment, and her fingers lost their grip.

"Don't let go, Rory!" Nega reached forward with her other arm to grasp Rory's forearms in her larger hands. Rory forced herself to hold on. She dangled with the weight of her torn wet cloak attached to her body, pulling her back down to the frigid water below. She forced herself to stare up at Nega, whose golden eyes glared back.

"You *will* hold on!" Nega ordered, her white teeth shining in contrast to the strain of holding a soaked and heavy Rory. Rory nodded. She and Nega dangled in the air for what seemed like hours when the dragon veered to the side. Rory's body swayed as she struggled to hold on with the directional change. Nega's grip tightened, but Rory felt only pressure on her arms. The dragon landed, so Rory's feet touched the ground. Nega rotated Rory in her grip until she laid down on her back. Rory rolled onto her side and coughed up the water, still stuck in her lungs. Nega leaned beside Rory and pulled her wet hair out of the way. The dragon's large angular head watched them both.

Rory coughed again, then groaned, "I thought you left."

Nega glanced at Riel. Then everything went black.

15

Riel and Nega sat together across the fire from Rory, still asleep after surviving her plunge into the river. In his dragon form, Riel had blown heat over her until her clothes dried. Her lips were no longer an unnatural shade of blue. Now she rested as comfortably as she could on the forest floor. Nega stared at the food they set aside from their hunt earlier, then turned back to Riel.

"So what now, fearless leader?" Nega asked while she poked at the fire. "We've gone in the wrong direction and were chased by Blemmyes. The King sent an army to destroy the Elsass Chateau. You're nowhere close to removing your oath. And you picked up that... thing." She gestured at Rory's sleeping form with the poker.

"You're an excellent motivator," Riel said. He watched Nega's grin grow before she shook it off. Nega punched him in the shoulder, but Riel managed not to fall over from the impact.

"I didn't join your ridiculous crusade to motivate you."

"I know."

Rory moaned in her sleep, so they waited to see if she'd wake up. They sat in silence for a few moments until she stopped moving, and they heard her soft snores.

"You should have left her behind." Nega jabbed at the fire.

Riel stared at the flames. They pulled at the dragon, comforting him no matter his circumstances. He inhaled the smoke, letting it swirl in his lungs before releasing it into the air again. The fire dropped to a comfortable warmth.

"Why did you go back?" Nega looked at him.

Riel sighed. "I can't explain it."

"Try."

Riel looked at Nega with one eyebrow up, her face hard like olivine. She stabbed the fire until it flared up.

"I'm drawn to her." His voice was quiet in the night. He breathed in the flames, quieting the fire.

Nega stayed silent, waiting for him to go on, but he had nothing. She punched him hard on the shoulder.

Riel fell over. "Ow!" He rubbed his arm and sat back down. Rory stirred again, but soon she snored.

"Are you serious?" Nega whispered. "That's it? You're just... drawn to her?" Her other eyebrow went up as her fists clenched.

Riel held up his hands in surrender. "I know it's not the best reason, but yes. I'm drawn to her. She's... intriguing."

Nega's lip curled into a snarl, revealing one sharp canine tooth. "Is that code for pretty?"

Riel smiled. "Noticed that too, did you?"

"My heart already belongs to someone else." Nega stabbed at a log in the fire and broke it in two.

"Yes, I know." Riel said, punching her in the arm. "And yes, pretty. But also brave."

Nega growled. "You mean stupid."

He shrugged. "She tried to defend the rosebush from a dragon."

"I didn't realize the way to your heart was through a stick up your nose."

"Ha!" Riel smiled, then went pensive again. "You know that's not it. At the castle, I had to take her with me." He shrugged. "I don't know. I'm drawn to her. I couldn't let her drown."

Nega poked at the fire. "I don't like it. It feels strange." She looked over at Rory, who continued snoring, before facing Riel. "Does it feel like what happens around your brother?" Nega asked in a whisper.

Riel thought for a moment. He compared his compulsion to help his brother with his desire to save Rory. One he had to do even when he disagreed. Rory required protecting to make sure she survived. "No."

Nega stared at him for a long moment while he held her golden gaze.

"Fine." Nega looked back at the fire stabbing the wood, making millions of sparks fly for a few minutes. "Are we going to Kuri now?"

"Yes, I think that's best. She'll have answers."

"By flight?"

Riel hesitated. It would be faster, but it was harder to hide as a dragon. "I need to think about it."

"Because of your diversion to get *her*, we're at least three days away from Kuri. And now we have someone else to worry about." Nega poked the fire again. "You can check on the chateau again."

Riel shook his head. "I don't need to." He wanted to, but the king's army would wait for him there.

Nega stared at him. "Are you certain?" He shrugged in response. The fire flashed under her prodding. "She's not even useful. Can't even hold up a sword to defend herself."

"So teach me." Rory's soft voice drifted over the fire.

Nega and Riel looked over at her when she sat up, cheeks rosy with warmth, and her brown hair a tangled mess in all directions. Nega scowled at her. "Been awake long?"

Rory examined the tear in her cloak. "Long enough to know you think I'm useless." She sat upright for a moment, checking her hair above her ear, and rubbed the side of her head. Red flashed out from the side.

She's injured, he thought. Riel's body tensed until he saw the rose bloom under her touch. He exhaled a long breath.

Rory relaxed again and smiled, then frowned at Nega. "I know a little about self-defence, and I could protect the sheep with my staff. But I know nothing about sword fighting." Rory pulled out a thread from her pack and pinched the tear.

"That means I should teach you?" Riel didn't think he'd ever seen Nega look so disgusted by anything. Being an ogress; that was saying something.

"Of course not." Rory said. "But if anything else attacks us, I would like to hold my ground. At the very least, I don't want to get in your way."

Riel hid his grin as Nega grunted, looking away.

"You said it yourself. I'm useless," Rory retorted as she stitched. "I made an oath to protect my friend, and I won't be able to unless I learn from a master like yourself."

Nega glared at her, her golden eyes glowing in the firelight. "Suck up," she said under her breath as she handed Rory the extra food they salvaged. Rory looked at her curiously. Nega just pointed at the food. "You'll need your strength if you're going to be useful. Eat up, get some rest. I'll go take watch."

As she stalked away, Riel saw the ogress's lips curl at the corners and he smiled to himself. Rory had no idea what Nega planned.

16

RORY SHOULD HAVE GUESSED Nega would be brutal when she asked to be trained in sword fighting. Two days in, they weren't even using blades yet, and Rory's arm muscles burned from striking and taking blow after blow, defending against the muscular master. Rory took more blows from the ogress than she delivered. Her sides ached from all the twists, and her hands cramped.

Rory wiped her brow again, while Nega stood relaxed in a soldier's stance. Rory now understood that was Nega's natural posture. Riel stood calmly next to the fire, cooking pheasant or some other bird they found in the ground cover.

"Again." Nega said.

Rory took a breath to ready herself. Before she could lift her wooden blade, Nega attacked her, forcing her back until she tripped and found herself with a wooden blade at her throat. Again.

"I wasn't ready."

"You think your enemies are going to *wait* until you're ready to fight?" Nega shook her head, her lips contorted in a sneer. She walked back to her original position and took the same stance. "Again."

This time, Rory jumped up and stepped forward to attack. She realized Nega defended her left knee the most, stretching it out between sets. So she stepped, swung her sword, then kicked at the knee, only to be blocked by the ogress, and knocked down again on her back. Nega's blade aimed at Rory's throat and brushed her skin with its tip.

"Get out of your head. You're thinking too hard, and you're giving away your strategy."

Rory groaned and slammed her hand on the ground. The rose rubbed her earlobe, and she shook her head, closing her eyes.

"I'm not getting it, am I?" she breathed out as Nega stepped aside to let her up.

"That's enough for now. Go fill up your skins." She pointed her blade to the nearby stream. Rory sighed. She couldn't decide if Nega's break was pity or strategy. Rory got up and collected her water skin from near the fire. Riel glanced up at her and she stopped.

"Do you want me to fill up yours, too?"

Riel nodded and held out two. She took the skins, including Nega's, and walked down to the stream's edge, her face warm with frustration. *Why couldn't she learn to fight?* She could defend the sheep. It wasn't so different, was it? When Rory arrived at the stream, she kicked the dirt a few times, then threw small stones into the water.

She took a deep breath, dumped whatever was left of the skins, and submerged them under the flowing water. Her fingers grew icy holding the skins under, but she didn't mind. It eased the burning from gripping the wooden swords, allowing her to straighten her fingers.

"I don't know how she does it," Rory mumbled to the rose.

After filling up the skins, Rory continued to massage her fingers under the water. The hairs on her neck and arms stood up. She felt more than heard the silence. She pulled her hands out of the water. Rory reached for the sword as she looked around her, then cursed as she found the wooden blade instead of a real one. Her fingers protested her grip on the sword again, but she ignored the burning pain. The rose sat motionless at her head. As Rory searched the forest, she sensed the threat came from her right, downwind of her.

Rory spun around to face that direction and waited. Either whatever watched her would attack, or it would move on. She scanned the area, down in the grass, then to the canopy above. Her breath caught as she looked into the trees.

On the lower branches, a full head above Rory, a lynx stood motionless, poised to pounce.

Its golden eyes stared at her, sizing her up. A smaller female, Rory knew it could kill her easily if it got hold of her. Rory rolled her hood over to protect her neck. She tightened the ties, then grabbed hold of the sword just in time for the lynx's attack.

Its long legs and enormous feet propelled it forward, its front claws extended out to grab her body and hold on. She dodged to the side and swung the wooden sword, using it as she would her staff to knock the paws and shoulders of the lynx off its course. The lynx rotated mid deflection, shifting its body so it could pounce again. Rory shifted her staff, readying for the lynx.

The lynx pounced again, but Rory deflected it with her sword. Rory's footing slid on the mossy forest floor as she landed sideways, bracing herself with her sword hand. The lynx took advantage of her stumble, attacked again, yet Rory shoved herself to the side. She hurtled her sword into the lynx's hind quarters. It spun around and attacked, but Rory found her footing and swung the wooden blade directly on the lynx's fragile ears. The cat took longer to recover, and Rory prepared herself to strike again. The lynx paused in a stalk position before it attacked. Slower this time, she struck its ear again with her wood sword, but it splintered into several pieces.

She shook the broken wood, but it was useless. The lynx recovered from the blows to her head. It stalked Rory, who backed up to the trees. She held her hands up in front of her, waiting for the attack, until the lynx hissed at her. Rory tilted her head, and the lynx stepped forward, but then hissed again, arching its back. It lowered his head, hissing again. Its hairs stood up, making itself larger, until it then backed away.

Rory stared after the wild cat, confused, until a puff of smoke came from behind her, and she understood why the lynx cowered in fear. A larger predator was behind her.

She turned to face the dragon, seeking the familiar scar on its angular eyebrow. Nega stood beside Riel's head, leaning against it with arms crossed. "You hurt?"

"No. Thank you."

Rory went back for the water skins, then drank from hers before filling it up again. She brought them over to where Nega still stood, but the dragon had disappeared.

Nega accepted her waterskin and looked Rory over.

"What? No advice this time?" Rory asked.

Nega punched her in the arm, and Rory caught herself from stumbling to the side. "Only one." Rory looked up at Nega, who sneered at her. "Next time, take a proper weapon with you."

Rory snorted. "Yes, that would have been the obvious thing to do."

Nega smiled, baring her teeth. It didn't make her any less intimidating. "It's a good day when you're still alive after facing a predator like that. Where did you learn to fight the lynx?"

"Predators are always after the sheep," Rory answered, thinking of the wolves that attacked her. "If you don't learn to avoid them, beat them off with your staff, or kill them outright, there's no point in being a shepherd."

Nega nodded. "I can say the same for war. It's a matter of knowing which battle to fight, when, and how much to hurt the enemy." Rory looked up at Nega, whose eyebrows pressed together in thought. "The way you handled the wild ones makes me think there's hope for you yet," she acknowledged, as they walked back to their camp. "You just have to treat me like one of your predators."

Rory tried not to celebrate Nega's small praise, but the rose bloomed outright in her ear.

17

"Y ou're getting better today," Nega told Rory's hunched form the next morning. "Less clumsy and predictable."

Rory bent forward, hands on her knees. She looked up, tried to say thanks, but gulped deep breaths instead.

"We're two days away from Kuri and your friend," the ogress added.

Rory straightened and stretched to expand her lungs, then faced Nega. "How do you know?" The words didn't come out like a raspy squeak, and Rory breathed a sigh of relief.

Nega stepped to the side and waved her forward to a tree next to the small clearing. She pointed to a series of markings made on the tree's roots.

"They look like scratches," Rory examined. Her brow furrowed as she squinted, trying to decipher their meaning.

"Imagine them with a mirror here," Nega said. She held her hand flat, aligning it to the bottom of all the scratches on the tree branch.

Rory squinted and imagined the marks with a mirror beside them. The scratches were crude, but she recognized poorly shaped numbers.

"It's a date?" Rory asked. Nega nodded. "What's this last mark?" Rory questioned, pointing to the angular lines at the bottom. Nega traced it, then its mirror image. "An arrow? They went that way yesterday?" Rory asked, pointing in the arrow's direction.

Nega smiled at her. "You're a fast learner. Though I'd never meet a shepherd who knew how to read." They started the walk back to the campfire.

Rory blushed. "They roped me into shepherding. I didn't mean to, but it made sense, especially after meeting Luiselle and Reinhold."

Riel stoked the flames as they arrived back at the campfire. He kept the flames warm, but inhaled the smoke to prevent it from being seen further away.

"What do you mean, they roped you into it?" Nega asked.

Rory thought back to meeting Luiselle and Reinhold. "I found them after I left home and had nowhere to go," Rory answered. She looked straight ahead but tried not to hide herself from Nega's stare. "I found Luiselle caught in the rosebush and helped her out. When they realized I have beneficial skills, they allowed me to join them."

"Because you can spin and card wool?"

"Pretty much. They gave me wool. It gave them income from my skills, and they had a third for shifts."

Nega nodded and contemplated the fire. Riel offered them a small meal of some dead animal, while Rory pulled out the berries and mushrooms she'd collected on their walk.

After their meal, they rested during the warmest part of the day. Rory pulled out her drop spindle and worked her wool. There wasn't much left after her spill down the river. The others took a brief nap, getting a quick rest before it would be Rory's turn. They laid down on the dirt, heads on their packs, hoods over their eyes.

Rory's mind wandered as she spun and thought back to her third night outside the castle, her first night with Luiselle and Reinhold, and her poor sleep outdoors. She still woke up in the night, afraid the tingling sleep would overcome her. It took weeks for her sleep to regulate. She never slept a full night, but at least it was consistent. Nightmares of Muriel, roses, fires, the sharp tingling and vibrations of the curse woke her in a panic. She knew it was her guilt when her stomach felt sick. Rory was out, but her household was asleep. She could feel the vibrations now, the phantom sensations crawling up her body as she trembled with fear.

Rory closed her eyes and counted as she breathed. Reinhold taught her how to focus with her senses on the things surrounding her. It helped with her nerves. The breeze on her face. The smell of the damp earth. Birds chirping. Light filtering through the trees. The taste of berry juice, still on her tongue. Her fingers pressed against the forest floor. Those things she knew with her senses brought stillness and peace.

Today it didn't help. She went through her list again, but when she pressed her fingers against the forest floor, the vibrations intensified. The tingles didn't come, but she felt tremors.

Rory got onto her knees, both hands and feet pressed against the ground. She felt the vibrations everywhere her body pressed down. She lowered her head, tilting it sideways, and pressed her cheek to the ground.

It rumbled beneath her ear, a steady, relentless tremor with no rhythm. The hairs on her neck and arms stood up. She counted several beats, and after twenty, realized that the tremors were getting louder, more violent with every breath she took.

Rory crawled over to Nega first, shaking her.

"This had better be worth waking me." Nega's growl made the hair on Rory's arm stand up.

"Shh!" Rory hissed, and Nega sat upright, scanning the area.

"What's the threat?" Nega whispered, looking into the forest.

Rory grabbed Nega's hand and pressed it into the earth. "Can you feel it?" She whispered. Nega tried to pull her hand back, but Rory held it in place with both of hers. Rory waited for a few seconds, searching Nega's face until the ogress's eyes widen. "What is it?"

"Horses and people. Lots of them. Wake him up." Nega pointed to Riel, then donned her cloak, pack, and grabbed her weapons, holding them at the ready.

Rory shook Riel's shoulder, and he opened his eyes, green with vertical slits for a moment, until they focused on her and returned to their normal green human pupil. "What is it?" he whispered.

Rory pointed to the earth and pressed his hand into it. Once he realized what was happening, he jumped up, inhaled the fire to snuff it out, then donned his gear as well. Rory shoved everything in her pack and got ready. She kicked dirt onto the fire, and leaves on the ground to remove traces of their presence. She turned around to find Nega offering her a sword. Rory looked at the ogress and tilted her head.

"Don't want you to be surprised again." Nega winked, then tilted her head to show the direction they should travel. Rory followed behind her with Riel trailing, heading up a hill in the woods. Nega stopped and checked her surroundings, then dropped to her knees and crawled through the underbrush. Rory looked behind her, then surveyed the trees before dropping and following Nega. She made her way through the path Nega travelled and heard branches break behind her as Riel did the same.

Crawling on her belly twice more, Rory came up to where Nega lay. She crawled to the left side of the ogress at the edge of a cliff. It overlooked the forest below, with a clearing at the centre. There stood hundreds of soldiers, dressed in black, some mounted with horses, while most of them marched on foot.

"Who are they?" Rory asked.

Riel crawled to Rory's left and cursed to himself.

"Those are *your*s." Nega growled.

"Mine?" Rory glanced down at the soldiers below. Their armour glinted in the sun from all the metal made into the shell. But she knew her soldiers. They made Elsass armour of thick hide, with only metal fasteners.

"Humans," Nega spat.

Rory watched the soldiers. Several held banners of red with gold zigzagging across them. "Those aren't my people's colours, or banners." The banners displayed the gold in a shape, not just a zigzag. "Are those dragons on the banner?"

Riel cursed again.

"What are they doing here?" Rory asked.

"I don't know," answered Riel, his teeth clenched.

"What do you mean, you don't know?" Nega asked, smacking at Riel's shoulder over Rory.

Riel grunted at the blow. Rory ignored their silent communication and focused on the soldiers in the field below. They were all heading in one direction, horse mounted riders directing the men with the banners, who led the men towards...

"Wait, Nega, are they headed to where Luiselle and your friend are?"

Nega gripped her sword and looked in the direction the men were heading. She cursed, then looked back at Rory. "Their army is too big. We won't be able to get around them. Riel, we could..." her voice cracked as she glanced at the soldiers below.

"If we fly, they'll see me. At night, the campfires will light the sky. There won't be anywhere to hide." Riel ground his teeth together and growled.

Rory put her hand on his forearm, making him pause and look at her. "Will your friend know how to handle them?"

Nega growled this time. "Kuri is skilled, but not against an army."

"It's not just an army." Riel said, pulling his arm away. "Look down there."

Rory's gaze followed his pointed fingers, the nails elongating in front of her for a moment, until Riel shook his fingers, then clenched his fist again. "The red tent?"

He nodded. "That's the *Beül Richter's* tent."

"What's the Beyool Reekter?" Rory struggled to wrap her tongue around the foreign words.

"Their butcher. He hunts the magic folk," Nega sneered. "He's after the refugees from the kingdom of Kehl."

"The King of Kehl sent his soldiers here to butcher my... our people?" Rory's voice rose in pitch, drawing Nega and Riel's attention. She swallowed again before continuing. "Isn't it considered war to send the soldiers into Elsass land?"

"A year ago it would have been." Riel answered. "The kingdoms have united with the marriage of the King of Kehl to the Princess Aurora."

"But... the princess is asleep and cursed." Rory looked from Riel to Nega. "The whole chateau is asleep under the curse." She thought about how to word it without giving herself away. "Didn't he have to marry her to break it?" She knew the answer, but wanted to hear it from them.

"The princess was married to Kehl's king by proxy the year before she turned nineteen." Nega answered.

"And that's... legal?" Rory asked. In her mind, he was still her betrothed. She still didn't understand how it was legal, but had her wedding ring as proof. She rubbed her chest, where the ring lay underneath her clothes.

Riel cleared his throat, and Rory focused on him. "Yes, it's binding. Under the marriage agreement, the King of Kehl is the steward of Elsass until the Princess has escaped her curse."

"Isn't he supposed to break it?" She asked.

"Yes, he was," Riel snarled. Rory watched his nails grow into claws, but then they receded. "He needs to kiss her, though. But now he can't."

You mean he won't, Rory thought. As she looked at the soldiers below, Rory remembered what Muriel said about the curse and her wedding ring. Her husband, a man she'd never met, had sent an army into her territory under the pretext of their union. These soldiers hunted the refugees like Luiselle and the elf she'd seen, even Riel and Nega. She noticed the armour the soldiers bore and recognized it from those who attacked her chateau.

The king attempted to assassinate her and kill her household. She looked at Nega and Riel again, realizing they saved her home and the people she loved. They saved her. Rory's gut cramped, wondering if she should tell them who she was. They were allies. Maybe, one day, friends. Then she looked at Riel's clenched hands, and Nega's contained snarl. Her husband was a monster, they would understand. Maybe even help her get him to kiss her and break her curse. The ring sent a sharp current through her body. Then again, the way Nega snarled the word *human,* she might not help Rory take Luiselle to the Rätsel caves. They might be angry once they discovered she lied and decide to eliminate her. With her out of the way, they could take over her kingdom and fight against Kehl.

Rory cleared her throat. "So, the refugees escaped Kehl to Elsass with their lives, only to be hunted here, too."

"Precisely," answered Nega, her fists clenched. "Some of them left with just the clothes on their backs and their children in their arms to escape the torture and death the *Beül* inflicted on them. Just like when I was a child."

Elsass should have been a safe place for the residents to escape torture. She wanted to ask Nega what happened to her, but the ogress didn't trust her. It was enough to know humans had hurt her. Rory clenched her fists. The rosebud caressed her ear. "Where will they go now?"

"South through the mountains," Nega answered. "At least until they're stopped by the Cave Kala. The Elsass kingdom borders their lands."

Rory thought about the stories of the merciless cave dwellers who came out to slaughter anyone who approached their territory. "So... they'll be trapped?" Rory's fingers covered her mouth. "Luiselle and your friend, and all the other refugees, will be cornered between the Kala and the soldiers of the *Beül* of Kehl?" The ring heated on her chest as she rubbed it absently.

Riel shifted beside Rory. "There's a chance that our friends stayed on this side of the soldiers." He sat up and studied Nega. "Which way do you think Kuri would go?"

Nega stared over the soldiers, down into the valley. "I think she would have followed the stream. She likes to hide up high. It's easier to hide her tracks, and the tree canopies are taller in that direction." Nega pointed across Rory, past Riel, but his gaze focused somewhere else. "She also would have guided the refugees away from them, too."

"Then we should go after them." Rory faced Nega again. "You said they were only a day ahead of us. Maybe less with all the soldiers here?" Nega nodded, her face hard with determination. Riel's gaze remained focused on something in the distance. Rory touched his shoulder to get his attention. He faced her, his eyes a slit of green, unfocused until he saw her. "We should go after them now."

Riel nodded, looked back out, then back at Nega. "Let's go get them." Nega backed her body up, and they followed her out of the underbrush, heading to Kuri and Luiselle.

18

N EGA MARCHED THROUGH THE forest with so much purpose, Rory worried the soldiers would hear them. As she looked around for them, she stumbled several times, but each time, Riel or Nega helped her up.

They only stopped to get a drink of water or pick some berries. Every once in a while, Nega looked up, spotted something in the canopy Rory couldn't identify, then looked down at the base of a tree. Sure enough, the markings were there. Rory guessed the latest markings were only about twelve hours old.

Rory's legs burned and her feet blistered. Still, Nega pushed them forward. The few times she felt ready to complain, one look at Nega's face reminded Rory of why they were rushing. The ring on her chest warmed. Luiselle and Kuri were at risk from the *Beül*. Riel and Nega moved too fast for her to complain, anyway. They didn't light a fire at night and slept little. Rory found some berries and mushrooms, and they ate lightly. She also found a couple of plants whose leaves would ease her blisters. She made a paste for them before she slept and dried out her socks, then cleaned her feet before they headed out the next morning. Riel would often check the trail behind them, lagging before joining them again, covering their tracks.

By midday, Rory's body hurt everywhere, and her mind drifted to Luiselle. Was she safe with Kuri? Rory, Riel, and Nega barely spoke, a kind of urgent agreement on their journey in order to maintain energy. She didn't train, but watched carefully where Nega stepped, followed her and made sure she didn't fall behind. She thought of the soldiers. How close were they?

To keep her calm, she let her mind drift to her own situation. She was married to the King of Kehl, who had legally invaded her land. She absently rubbed the ring tucked under her shirt, the physical reminder that she was bound to both him by marriage, and Luiselle by a vow. How could one small object bind her future so tightly? Rory's oaths trapped her between two hard places, both forced on her. But unlike being trapped in the castle, waiting for a king who wouldn't save her, she would have helped Luiselle. Worry for her friend pushed her forward.

The rose yanked her hair, and she watched Nega and Riel scowl at the base of a tree.

"What's wrong?" Rory asked.

"There's no mark," Nega said. She grunted. "The signs are all here, but there's no mark."

"Any signs of others?" Riel's eyes shifted into their dragon shape as he examined the area. His brow creased with every movement.

Nega shook her head, looking around. "Nothing. There's just... nothing."

The rose tugged on Rory's head again. She rubbed her finger against the bud to soothe it, but looked around anyway. It had warned her before, and she wouldn't ignore it.

"I don't understand it!" Nega punched the tree. "Kuri would have left a sign. She would have told us." Riel closed his eyes and breathed deeply through his nose.

The rose tugged again.

"Did we go the wrong way? Did she leave a false trail for the soldiers to follow?" Riel asked.

The rose tugged harder. Rory ran her fingers over the bud again and looked around.

"No," Nega answered. "I'm sure of it."

"Do you think they have her?" Riel asked quietly. Rory's heart stopped.

"No," Nega said. "No signs of a struggle."

The rose tugged hard enough to pull out hair. "Ow! Stop that!" Rory hissed, and Riel and Nega looked at Rory. Nega's eyes flashed and her nostrils flared.

"What is it?" Riel put his arm on Nega's shoulder, but she shrugged it off, clenching her fists.

"The rose is tugging on my hair." She lifted her fingers up to the rose. "I'm sorry. I can't understand what you're trying to tell me." The rose stem grasped her fingers, and the bud pointed into the trees over Nega's shoulder. They looked in that direction. Nothing. "I don't understand," Rory whispered. The rose tugged her, so she stepped that way. It kept tugging, so she tiptoed forward, still looking for anything out of place.

Riel and Nega followed behind Rory as she searched the forest. "It's pointing up?" Nega whispered from behind her. Sure enough, when Rory looked at the rose, it was pointing up.

The three looked up and glimpsed motion in the trees. "What is it?" Rory asked, squinting. They waited, and several starlings appeared on a branch just out of reach.

"It's just birds," Nega growled. Rory ran her fingers through her hair, but the rose pulsed into a point at them.

"You want me to talk to them?" Rory asked. The rose bloomed slightly, then became a bud again, and pointed back at Rory. She lifted it back to her hair as it took its normal place. Rory pulled her bag forward, removed the last grains she had. She laid them out on a nearby rock, then stepped back. The male bird descended, picked up a seed, then swallowed it. He chirped, and the others descended.

Rory knelt down to their level. "Have you seen my friend? She's a young faerie." Rory asked them.

"We're talking to birds now?" Nega asked Riel, who shrugged. Nega glared at Rory, her nostrils flaring again.

The birds finished the crumbs, then in a flurry of fluttering wings, disappeared into the canopy. Rory sighed.

"Well, that was useless!" Nega complained. She swung her fist, and Rory stepped out of the way.

"I-"

Riel held his hands up and said, "Wait." His eyes closed, hiding their dragon shape. "Listen."

Rory closed her eyes but heard nothing until... *there.* She saw a small starling coming back. The bird landed on the same stone, something small in her mouth.

"Is that a bug?" Nega's nose wrinkled in disgust.

Rory smiled as the bird flew away. With a *pop!* Luiselle sat before them in her child form. "Hi Rory! Hi flower!" She said, launching herself into Rory's arms.

Rory hugged Luiselle tightly, tears pooling in her eyes as she held the girl. "You're okay?" Rory checked Luiselle's face, her chin, her arms, and legs, while the faerie giggled. Rory's chest muscles relaxed, the heat in the ring lessened its intensity, and she hugged Luiselle tight to her again.

"I'm good. Kuri took good care of me." Nega and Riel stepped forward at Kuri's name, and Luiselle's eyes widened. "Rory," she whispered, "there's an *ogre* behind you!"

Rory smiled at the girl. "Yes, and they're looking for Kuri. They're friends, and we've been looking for you for a while now."

"But Rory," Luiselle clutched her tightly, "ogres eat *children!*"

"Oh, by Draconis!" Nega threw her hands in the air, then punched Riel. "Your mother is very proud of that stupid rumour."

Riel grinned and winked at Rory. "My mother, part ogress, thanked that ridiculous chef for creating that story. No one invited her to baby naming ceremonies after that." He knelt down next to Rory and Luiselle. "My friend Nega here does not eat children. And she would gladly hurt anyone who tried."

"Promise?" Luiselle asked him, peering out from under Rory's hood.

"I promise." He smiled at Rory, then looked back at Luiselle. "Now, where is Kuri?"

"She's resting in the cave there," Luiselle pointed. "I promised her I would wait with the birds while she tended to her ankle."

"She's injured?" Nega growled. Luiselle jumped into Rory's cloak.

"Relax, you brute! You're scaring the child." A woman's voice came from behind them. They all turned. "I'm fine. It was just a sprain from running."

Rory stared at the same red-headed elf who had slain the cockatrice.

19

R IEL WATCHED NEGA EMBRACE Kuri before leaning her tall frame down to the elf's smaller one. She pressed her forehead to Kuri's and breathed in the peace of being back in her presence. He looked away. Witnessing any tenderness from Nega would earn him her wrath when they sparred later. He would tease her anyway, egg her on later, but at least they were together. He breathed out a sigh, warm moist air instead of the inferno he'd been holding in.

Rory and Luiselle were different. She was not old enough to be the faerie's mother, but Luiselle snuggled up with her. Rory wrapped her cloak around the two of them. He knew some women to be tender to their offspring, but never different species like the human woman and the faerie child. His own mother, rumours of eating children aside, treated him more like Nega did: less affection, and more like a soldier. His mother was only half ogress, but that was their way with their young, especially for the younger siblings. Dragons were no different, and his father, only half dragon, treated him as a soldier too. Luiselle rested, and Rory cradled the child against her, her serene face at odds with her discomfort at being a chair with nothing to lean against. A memory of his human grandmother doing the same with him overlaid the pair, then was gone. He rubbed his chest, a slight ache over his ribs.

Rory looked up at him, concern in her eyes. Luiselle was asleep in her arms. "Is it safe to rest here?" She whispered.

He looked away from the younger pair, back to his friends. Nega and Kuri whispered something to each other, then they broke apart and looked at Rory and Luiselle. Nega searched the forest for a moment, then looked back at Kuri, who nodded her ascent.

Darkness settled over their group.

"We should be fine here for a night." Nega pulled Kuri to the stone and made her sit, then lifted Kuri's foot and examined it.

Riel hid his smile behind his hand at the warrior ogress, trying to take care of the healer.

"For the last time, I'm fine." Kuri rolled her eyes but didn't fight the large hands that held her feet. "I've already spread the ointment, and I will be ready to go by sunrise." Kuri then looked at the others. "So you're Rory. Luiselle has spoken of you *at length*."

Rory's face lit up with her smile. "She likes to chat," Rory whispered. "It's nice to meet you, Kuri. And I owe you my thanks for stepping in with both the cockatrice and for taking care of Lu."

"Cockatrice?" Nega's brow furrowed. Her knuckles grew white, trying not to crush Kuri's ankle in her hands. "When did you run into a cockatrice?" Kuri rolled her eyes again at Riel as he smiled. Kuri told him but not Nega because she knew the ogress would worry. "I'm your *bodyguard!* Why on earth didn't you tell me?"

"Not anymore, Nega. We've been through this." Kuri patted Nega's hand. "And I killed it. So relax."

"Relax? You put yourself... I wasn't... you... ugh!" Nega set Kuri's ankle down, then threw her hands in the air and stomped off into the forest.

"Is she okay?" Rory asked, her gaze following Nega's direction. She brushed Luiselle's hair with her fingers.

Kuri scowled at Rory, and Riel bit his tongue at the elf healer's rare display of jealousy. Rory's concern for the ogress was who she was. But Kuri didn't know that. He thought about correcting her, but changed his mind. Kuri deserved a little tension for making Nega worry these last few days. "Nega has been teaching Rory how to fight with a sword. She's getting very good at it. Must be all that proximity to Nega." He stoked the fire with his breath to avoid showing Kuri his grin. "That or Nega's softer on her."

When he looked back, Kuri's eyes flashed, but she forced a smile at Rory. "You're learning from a true master."

Rory glanced at him. Her eyebrows pressed together as she frowned, then faced Kuri. "I am grateful for her teaching. She's being generous in sharing her skills." She answered.

Kuri scowled. "I'll bet she is," she mumbled.

Riel chuckled to himself, then stood. "I'll go after Nega for you," he offered Kuri. But Kuri ignored him, watching Rory stroke Luiselle's hair. They didn't see him walk into the forest in the opposite direction of Nega.

As soon as he found a clearing, he shifted into his dragon form. His clothes shifted with him. It was part of shifter training to hide from the humans. No one wanted to surprise them with nudity. Carrying clothes around in your mouth as an animal was degrading. It also meant he could only smell his clothes, nothing else. So shifters adapted.

Riel flew into the night sky and took the long way around the massive army to the signal he saw from their perch the day before. He circled outside the army for an hour, counting, studying the soldier's assignments and ranks based on their arrangement. He took a chance in doing so, but he needed to know. It was a large army, sent to decimate the remaining refugees and enlist local Elsass townspeople in the King of Kehl's cause. In showing up with the army, the King was persuasive. But with so many soldiers here, Kehl's north-eastern borders remained vulnerable. The King was a fool to separate the humans and other species within his borders. They would be stronger together.

As he flew, he caught sight of the shimmering light hidden by campfire smoke. Spotting a clearing outside the army, he batted his wings, sending the smoke in its direction, then landed there. He scuttled into the forest, wedging himself between two trees. A few minutes later, an armour-clad soldier came into the clearing. Riel tilted his head. The armour was unusual for a Kehl soldier, with far more metal than normal. The helmet came off, and he saw a young wolf shifter, a teenager based on his size. They both stilled, listening for a moment. Riel shifted, then stepped to the edge of the forest clearing, staying in the shadows.

"The water is wide." Riel whispered.

"But I can cross over." The soldier stated, signalling they were alone.

"What news?" Riel asked.

"The king is chasing the refugees through the territory." The wolf shifter answered.

"Nothing new." Riel ran his fingers through his hair.

"But this time he's looking for a specific refugee. A young faerie girl, one with a broken wing."

Riel's chest tightened as his breath stilled, picturing Rory cradling the child. *I made an oath,* she'd said. What part did they play in this war? Could he use this to his advantage with the King? He swallowed before answering. "Why that one? Why now?"

"No one knows. But the *Beül* gave out specific instructions not to harm her."

"I wonder why he wants her alive." Riel thought of the pair again, how they fought him at the Elsass Chateau. "What of the princess of Elsass?"

"Her chateau still stands." The wolf paused and held himself still. Riel heard and sensed nothing. The young man looked around, then relaxed back into his stance. "No one can penetrate it. The rosebush has regrown into a dense set of vines. Fire can't burn them, and if anyone gets within feet of the chateau walls, they crumble to the ground, asleep. The curse expands, as the Seeress swore it would."

"So she remains safe?"

"For now. The orders are to keep trying to destroy it."

Riel wondered if there was a way to get to the princess with the expanding curse. If not, the King's choice not to kiss her would make them all suffer. "Anything else?"

"Louvret has pulled the pack to the North."

"To avoid persecution?"

"To prepare for-"

Fallen leaves rustled in the clearing behind them, and the young wolf put his helmet back on, hand on his sword. Riel stepped into the shadows and scaled a tree to see who was coming. He didn't want to risk a shift and draw more attention to himself.

Another soldier came into view, and Riel struggled to hear their words. They spoke for a few moments before Riel released a breath as his friend relaxed. Then the new soldier ran his sword through the shifter's gut. Riel covered his gasp with his hand.

Why didn't he shift?

He crumpled to the ground. The other soldier looked around before heading back. Riel stifled his growl. He climbed down the tree and checked his surroundings before heading into the clearing to check on his friend. The wolf teenager lay immobile. Riel sighed, leaned forward, and closed the boy's surprised eyes. He brushed the visor of the helmet, flinching at the burning sensation.

Iron. The pup *couldn't* shift. He wondered why Louvret sent this youngster into Kehl's military, but Louvret was a strategist. The teenager had lined the interior with sheep's wool to lessen the iron's impact.

"Many thanks," Riel whispered, breathing hot air into the night. "Rest now, warrior wolf. I'll see you on the other side." His stomach rolled at the young wolf's horrible death.

Leaves crunched from the direction the other soldier disappeared. Riel grabbed Louvret's sword and ran into the shadow of the trees where he'd first hid. He peered around the side in time to see six soldiers step into the clearing with their swords drawn. They each had a blood red 'X' on their chest, visible under the just waning moon.

The *Beül's* team.

"Fan out." One soldier, a double 'X' on his chest, commanded the others. *The Captain,* thought Riel. He stepped forward and looked at the dead shifter, kneeled beside him. "He's missing his sword."

"He said the dragon ran him through." A soldier replied as they stepped out wider. "Too bad. I heard he was an excellent soldier on the field. Good instincts."

Riel clenched his hands around the sword. The soldier spotted him. And he never would have hurt the shifter. Which meant they didn't realize the boy was one. Only the one who made his armour did. Unless they all wore iron armour now.

The soldiers stepped forward again. Riel studied the armour details and confirmed the metal was iron. Which would hurt the refugees if they fought back.

"The dragon didn't need the sword to kill him." The captain said.

Riel looked around, evaluating his options. He was too big to shift in the forest. He could, but he would break the trees and branches in the canopies overhead. Which would draw attention to him faster than he could escape.

"He's a traitor to Kehl and needs to be eliminated." The second soldier answered him.

Riel snorted his anger at the soldier's response. They didn't know all he did for his King and country. If they did, they would have backed off.

"Did you feel that?" The third soldier asked. The others looked at him. "A wave of warm air. It came from that way." He pointed his sword in Riel's direction as the others stepped forward.

"Careful," the captain whispered. "The dragon is strong."

Riel covered his mouth to stop the heat as he exhaled in anger. He looked around again. His choices were limited. In the clearing ahead, he could run, shift and fly off, but the soldiers fanned out in front of him, standing between the trees.

They stepped forward, eyes searching for him.

Riel stepped back through the forest. He shifted his skin colour first, darkening it to blend in with the night. Then changed his eyes so he could see everything clearer. But he couldn't stay this way for long. His skin tingled under the partial transition. His body fought against the unfinished shift and wanted him to revert to human or shift into a dragon.

The soldiers stepped forward, almost at the edge of the small clearing.

Riel's back muscles spasmed at the joints where his wings wanted to unfurl. He bit his lip with elongated teeth to keep from crying out. He hadn't denied his shift since he was a teen, when his father forced him to stop shifting for as long as possible just to understand what his body did.

The soldiers stepped into the forest.

He stepped back further and saw a narrow path that would take him away from the soldiers. His whole body spasmed, knocking him down on all four limbs. His face stretched forward, and he pushed himself back up to his legs. Riel stared at the path as he heard slow, methodical footsteps behind him. He had to take it. He forced his face to even out, shifting fully back to human form, and tied the sword's scabbard to his waist. It was the only way to run the path, though he would be vulnerable. His body tensed, ready to shift at any moment.

Then Riel dashed for the path.

"There!"

Riel heard a soldier crash through the trees, metal clanging with each step. Other footsteps echoed as they joined the chase. Thanks to their metal armour, they couldn't quite keep up with him.

He dodged trees and bushes until he came to a large one, with a trunk as wide as his dragon form. His body relaxed as he jumped into the tree. He reached for the lowest branch, claws out, ready to grab the bark.

Mid-jump, someone knocked him out of the air and he landed on his side. Pain shot from his elbow to his shoulder, his other side pinched by the iron armour as the soldier landed on top of him.

"Got him!" He drew his sword and aimed at Riel's neck. Metal steps on the forest floor drew closer.

Riel looked back up in the tree. He would not die at the hands of one of the *Beül's* men. He inhaled and blew the hottest air he could at the soldier. The man's armour heated around his face as he screamed and dropped the sword. Riel shoved the man off of him and jumped up.

The sounds of metal armour clanking grew louder, and Riel jumped for the tree. This time, he landed on a branch and climbed as fast as he could.

The other soldiers arrived as he was halfway up the tree. He glanced down in time to see the burned soldier below, pointing his sword up at him. One man pulled out a quiver and bow.

Once he was in the canopy, he found a branch strong enough for him to step on. An arrow raced by, missing him by an inch.

He took cover near the trunk, then took a deep breath. He untied the sword from his waist and held it in one hand. One more breath, and he ran down the length of the branch and leaped into the night. An arrow whooshed past him a split second before he shifted and beat his wings.

He flew hard, with a steady stream of arrows following in his wake. Holding the sword, he flew away. He couldn't lead the soldiers to his friends, and was thankful the soldiers couldn't keep up. Once he'd flown far enough that they couldn't see him, he circled back to his friends.

20

RORY SAT AGAINST A tree, on watch for the night. Nega was asleep beside Kuri. She'd asked Nega where Riel went, but the ogress just rolled her eyes. As a dragon shifter, he'd be fine. Luiselle slept next to her with one hand resting on Rory's thigh. She stared with unshed tears for a moment at Luiselle's fingers. Rory couldn't understand why such a tiny creature would trust her. She missed the sheep and Reinhold, and their little outdoor group.

Not a group. *Family.*

Except they weren't her family. They couldn't be. Rory longed to embrace Luiselle as a sister, create a life of meaning for the faerie, and watch her grow into a powerful woman. But joining with the faerie meant cursing her. Making a home with her would make her part of Rory's household and transfer the curse to a new location. Her own parents figured that out because they sent her to live at the chateau without them so they wouldn't suffer too.

Who curses a child, anyway? What kind of twisted person tells the family of a child that she has no life worth living? *The Seeress.* And why? No one knew. Her parents were good people, fear of the curse aside. Refugees came to her land because they were kind. They did nothing to the Seeress. Rory's heart twisted with the constraints of her life, and she rubbed her chest.

"What are you thinking about?" Kuri whispered. She hobbled over to sit beside Rory.

"Life. Fate." Rory answered.

"Do you believe in fate?" Kuri asked, her face neutral.

"I think fate is determined to control me." Rory said. Luiselle sighed in her sleep. Rory rubbed the little girl's head to settle her. "You?"

"Interesting." Kuri tilted her head, revealing her pointed ears as she studied Rory's face. "I think fate is what you make of it. Many simply use fate as an excuse to do what they want. To break or keep promises as it suits them."

Rory felt the ring pulse under her shirt and remembered her promise to the troll. "What if you have no control over your own life?"

After looking around the camp for a moment, Kuri settled her gaze on Rory. "But is it fate, or someone with more power than you?"

Rory looked at Kuri, confused. "What do you mean?"

"The King of Kehl sent an entire army into Elsass because he has power. We are on the run from him because we do not have his power." Kuri grimaced as she stretched out her legs beside Rory. "But we are not under his control, because we would not submit to his authority."

Rory mulled over her words. She was awake because she wouldn't submit to the curse of a powerful person. Because of this, she had a friend in Luiselle. And a few companions for the moment. A slight weight lifted as she thought about it. Scaling her chateau wall was a minor act of rebellion. But it was hers.

"Why do you care about that child?" Kuri asked. "She's not really your concern."

Rory looked into the elf's stone face. Her dark eyes glinted with a fierce night shine. "Because I'm human?"

Kuri nodded. "I tried to convince her she'd be better off with someone like me."

Rory's hands clenched into fists. She'd gotten back Luiselle, and the elf wanted to take her away. "Because you're a healer, or because you're an elf?"

Kuri sighed. "Either. Both." She looked down at Luiselle's sleeping form. "She has a lot of power and needs to be trained. Just imagine all her power with the emotions of a teenager. Can you help her?" Kuri narrowed her eyes at Rory. "You couldn't even kill the trochilus with her help."

Rory's heart ached. The elf was right. "No. Nega's been helping me, though. She says that I have promise."

Kuri's eyes flashed. "Still, how will you handle her? She has a broken wing that still hasn't healed from that mad King."

"Can you heal it?" Tears stung Rory's eyes.

"What if I could?" Kuri answered. "Would you leave her in my care? We could take her to the nearest town and make sure she gets to her destination."

"I..." Rory looked down at Luiselle, whose hand twitched, caressing her thigh. Rory smiled through her watery eyes. Kuri would know how to help Luiselle. Rory was not their kind. She was merely human, with skills that would put food on the table, and nothing more. And Luiselle needed more. "I would..." The ring pulsed against her, sending a sharp current of energy through her body. The flower tugged on her hair. Luiselle twitched in her sleep. Rory put her hand on her own chest, pressing the ring against her heart. "I would, but I am bound by a promise I made to her keeper."

"The troll she spoke of?" Kuri asked, surprised.

"He made me swear an oath to find her and take her home to the Rätsel caves." Rory looked up into Kuri's shimmering eyes. "And it's not fate, but I am bound to that oath. Even if I weren't, I wouldn't break my promise to her or him. I made it, I stand by it. I care about her. And I will do everything I can to get her home." Rory rubbed Luiselle's hair between her fingers. "But I don't know if I can. And when you move on to whatever your next journey is, I'm afraid I won't-"

Leaves crunching from the trees on the other side of their camp stopped Rory from continuing. She slipped Luiselle's hand from her thigh and grabbed the branch she had made into a new staff. Kuri pulled out a blade from her cloak that was ornately engraved. It was the same one used to kill the trochilus. The two quietly changed their stances. Crouched in a ready position, they waited for whatever made the noise. It came again, and they poised to strike as Riel came into view. He stopped and stood perfectly still in front of them, taking in their blades and forms.

He smirked as he held up his hands in surrender. "Nice welcome."

Kuri moved first. She sat back down and stretched her legs, but didn't wince this time. Rory followed and placed Luiselle's hand back on her thigh. The child sighed contentedly.

"Where have you been?" Kuri asked, her tone harsh in the quiet night sky.

"Hunting." He pulled out a sword from behind him. Rory recognized the dragon engraved on the wooden hilt and scabbard. He handed it to her. Kuri arched her eyebrow at him. He ignored the elf, focusing on Rory. "Now you have something to defend yourself, since Nega rarely shares hers."

Rory accepted the blade, pulled it out of the scabbard, and saw blood reflected on the hilt. She fought the bile rising from her stomach and held it up to him. "Your work?" She asked, squelching her fear of the man.

His face drooped, and he exhaled. Rory felt the hot air blast her from the other side of the camp. "Not my work. Its owner was a friend."

"Who?" Kuri asked.

"One of Louvret's pack." Riel whispered.

Kuri hobbled over and embraced Riel. "I'm so sorry."

They sat for a moment, the two mourning someone she would never know, whose death blessed Rory with the means to fight. Or at least to try. She looked away, hiding her desire to be hugged and comforted, too. But as Kuri pointed out, she didn't belong with them. Because she was human, and she carried a curse which could hurt them. She thought about what Kuri said about fate and wondered if Louvret's pack-mate believed in fate, or if he simply tried to fight back, too. It didn't always work. Rory looked down, closed her eyes, and whispered her thanks to Riel's fallen friend.

"They found me." Riel stared at the fire. "I flew off the other way, but they'll be looking for me. We'll have to leave in the morning."

Kuri nodded, then looked at Rory. "Sleep," she said, then turned to Riel. "Both of you. You need your rest, and it's my turn to keep watch."

So Rory snuggled up with Luiselle, curled her body protectively around the child, and dreamed of wolves howling in the night.

21

R ORY CAME AWAKE ALL at once to the rustling of trees and stomping of feet. She gripped the handle of her new sword, not moving to check on Luiselle, who was... gone.

She looked around, but nobody appeared. The campfire still smouldered, but the entire group was missing. Rory touched her fingers down to the spot where she had curled against Luiselle, but it wasn't even warm.

Another rustle in the trees made Rory freeze. She searched, but couldn't hear anything else. "Lu?" Rory whispered. Perhaps she shrunk herself to her faerie size. Rory stood still, making sure she didn't crush her, just in case. "Lu?"

Nothing.

There were no cloaks, canteens, packs, or weapons. Rory sat upright, the hairs on the back of her neck rising. She sensed she was being watched, but couldn't figure out from where. A predator was nearby. She thought about what Riel said and looked for any signs of soldiers. They were supposed to leave early this morning. It appeared they left and took Luiselle with them. Her heart sank as she thought about her conversation with Kuri, and she swallowed the lump in her throat. Perhaps it was for the best. She could go to Kehl and end the curse. The ring pulsed on her chest, a painful shock to her system. She would not cry. They would take care of the little faerie, Rory knew. Even so, it hurt that they'd taken her away. She rubbed the rose in her hair, and it rubbed her ear.

The leaves in the branches above and to her right moved again, so Rory crouched, preparing in case of a soldier or something else. No sounds came, but then the leaves moved again, and Rory focused on them. Another movement, this time to her right, she saw a flash of motion behind the tree trunks. It was hard to tell against the forest background. The leaves above followed the movement to her right, so she turned to keep the two sources of movement within her view.

Another crash as Rory rotated towards the sound. Footsteps beat from behind her and she turned in time to see Nega run into the camp, launch herself across the fire, and run past her.

"Nega-"

But rustling came from all three sides. Several tiny grey shapes launched themselves from the trees, landing on Nega's head. Her body jerked in multiple painful spasms. Rory stood up, about to get the creatures off Nega, when she froze. Nega shook and... laughed?

"Enough! Please!" The ogress called out to the small grey things. "That tickles!"

Rory stood at ease. Her sword dropped to her feet, clanging against the nearby stone. "Nega?" Rory asked as the swirl of motion stilled. The ogress turned to face her, squinting golden eyes.

"What?" she growled, back to her ogress self.

The small grey shapes jumped off Nega and scurried towards Rory across the ground. Rory stepped back, held her hand out to stop them until they climbed up her cloak, and sat on her arm. Three tiny squirrels blinked at her.

"Don't just stand there, give them some food!" Luiselle's tiny voice rang out. Rory held the squirrels close to her face and saw a smaller than normal faerie sitting on one of their shoulders. She looked at the other two squirrels and blinked when she found a miniaturized Riel and Kuri as well.

"What are you...?" She asked as she bent down to offer berries to the trio of furry creatures.

"Hang on!" Luiselle said. Purple light flashed in front of her, engulfing Rory and the squirrels, until she stood beside the life-sized trio. The squirrels remained on her arm. She looked up at Kuri and Riel, who both smiled with unmasked joy. Luiselle had never transformed others before, only herself. Kuri's healing and training were working.

"Luiselle found the baby squirrels a few days ago." Kuri explained, looking over at Nega, who couldn't hide her lopsided grin.

"Their momma died, and I didn't want to leave them." Luiselle cried out. "They would die!" Her eyes widened so big that tears fell from the corners. Rory nodded her agreement, still bewildered.

"So she asked me to help them learn to fend for themselves." Kuri answered.

"So you were hunting Nega?" Rory asked. "They need to learn to forage."

"Well, they already know *that!*" Luiselle said, as if it should be obvious. "But they don't know about..." she leaned in and whispered, "predators."

"So, uh, I suggested we teach them to hunt." Riel reached behind his head and scratched the base of his skull, a lopsided grin on his face. "And who better to hunt than Nega?"

Rory stood there, her mouth open, handing the squirrels more berries.

"You," Rory said to Riel, "a *dragon*, are teaching squirrel kits to hunt ogres?" She tilted her head sideways to Kuri and Nega, who each dug their toes in the dirt and looked away from her.

"Yeah!" Squealed Luiselle. "Isn't that amazing? Can we keep them?"

Rory took a deep breath. She wondered about their motley group raising a litter of squirrels, but one look in Luiselle's eyes, and there was only one answer. She knelt down to Luiselle's height, held her arm up so the squirrels could run all over the girl and make her giggle. "As long as I get to help train them next time, too!"

"Yippee!" Luiselle clapped happily before running off to feed the kits.

Rory looked up at the others. "I won't regret this, will I?" But they all just smiled back at her and motioned for her to join them at the campfire.

They sat for breakfast with some foraged food, curtesy of their hunt with the squirrels. Luiselle sat in front of Rory, closer to the fire, with the squirrels nestled in her cloak hood behind her head. Rory offered the faerie some of the carded wool to make them cozier, and Luiselle's face beamed with joy.

"Where did you learn to shrink others to your faerie size?" Rory asked her.

"Kuri taught me." She mumbled with her mouth full. "So far, it only works on other magic folk. I tried to shrink you while you were asleep by the fire, but it didn't work."

"You tried to... shrink me?" Rory looked around at the others. Nega and Riel smirked, but Kuri at least looked a little contrite.

"Well, yeah." Luiselle shrugged her shoulders. "I didn't want you to miss the fun, too." She nibbled on some white mushrooms, then turned back to look at Rory. "Kuri said you're taking me to the Rätsel caves. Why?"

Rory felt the other's gazes on her as she answered Luiselle. "Reinhold asked me to."

"Okay." The faerie faced the others. "Are you coming too?"

Rory held her breath as the three looked at each other before Kuri leaned forward and met Luiselle's gaze. "Do you want us to?" Rory looked at Riel and Nega. Nega's face was hard, and Riel's eyes held Rory's gaze while she held her breath.

"Of course." Luiselle answered. "I mean, unless you don't want to be my friends anymore. That's what happens with all my friends. Except Rory. Probably because she's not magic."

Rory's heartbeat stopped for a moment as she leaned forward and hugged the little girl. Luiselle never spoke of her family. Rory looked up at Kuri, seeking hope, but found determination.

"I'd like to stay with you for a little while longer." Kuri said. Rory let out her breath. Nega jumped up and stomped off, picking up their things.

Kuri shrugged her shoulders, then got up and walked after Nega, putting her smaller hand on Nega's back. But she shrugged it off and kept packing.

Riel inhaled the fire and put it out with one breath. Luiselle crawled around the squirrels and trailed after Kuri and Nega. Rory watched the little girl reach up to put her hand in Nega's. The ogress started and peered down at the child. Luiselle pulled Nega down until the ogress kneeled, hunched over enough for Luiselle to whisper in her ear. Nega's eyes widened. Luiselle then took the ogress' hand, put it into Kuri's before skipping away without looking back. Kuri kneeled beside her, and Rory looked away as they hugged.

"Why don't you go pick some more berries for the squirrels for the journey?" Rory suggested, as Luiselle walked over to the nearby bushes to pick some. Rory turned to find Riel at her side, watching his friends. She wondered if there was any jealousy between the three. Nega and Riel seemed very close, but not as close as she and Kuri were. It explained the ogress' determination to find her. Rory put her things in her pack, grabbing some additional mushrooms for the road. When she stood, Riel put his hand on her arm. She looked up at him, wondering about the gesture, and saw his concerned gaze.

"Are you sure about this journey?" He asked. "You don't have to make it."

"Reinhold made me swear an oath," Rory answered.

"The troll?"

Rory nodded. "He clasped my hand in his and I could feel the bond travel from my hand to my heart."

Riel sighed, then sat down to gather the rest of their supplies. "Then yes, I guess you do."

"You sound like you know what I'm talking about." Rory tried to strap the sword to her frame, but it fell out of its sheath.

"I do." Riel hid their camp by pushing leaves around and covering their footprints.

"Do you want to talk about it?" Rory tied the sword across her body. She tried to grab the hilt, but she couldn't reach it with her left hand. That wouldn't do.

"I can't. It's part of the oath I swore." He stood up.

"Fair enough." Rory tried to tie the sword to her waist, but the strap was too loose and slid down under the sword's weight.

"Just stop." Riel stood in front of her. He pushed her cloak back from her shoulders, then took the sword and scabbard. He unhooked it from the belt and undid the piece of the rope Rory used to tie her tunic close to her. Rory's cheeks reddened, startled by his close contact. Slipping the rope through the scabbard loops, he positioned it on her right side. He pulled the rope tight and checked to make sure it sat on her hip properly. He pulled the cloak forward again, took her left hand in his, his thumb brushing her palm. A new tingle spread into her fingers from his touch, and she froze. He turned her hand around in his calloused one and helped her reach down to her side to test the sword's position.

"Works?" He whispered, while Rory looked into his emerald eyes, the pupils dilated into slits. His hand still held hers in place over the sword, and she felt her blush creep up her neck.

Rory swallowed, then took a step back. She drew the sword easily. "Will my rope hold it?"

Riel smiled, his eyes back to normal. "You make excellent rope. It will hold."

Rory looked away from him, only to find Nega glaring at her.

Luiselle came running towards them, her eyes wide with fear. "You need to come!" She grabbed Rory's free hand while Nega, Riel, and Kuri all pulled their swords.

They climbed up a small hill with a clearing near the top overlooking the valley below. Except it wasn't a forest anymore. All that remained was devastation.

22

T HE CROW SAT ON a tree behind the small group as they stared at the devastation below. Where once stood a lush forest with a rapidly flowing river, now stood a desolate land. This is what the King of Kehl did to the neighbouring Elsass he invaded. And though he was now a steward by marriage, the army's destruction wasn't stewardship. The crow shuddered at the charred roots and stubs of trees, the deep grooves etched into the forest floor marking the heavy wagons that carried the trees away. What they hadn't carried away, they burned. They dammed the river with all the damaged vegetation to stop the flow of water to the southwest. All in search of the refugees.

The dragon in the group below could have stopped it. The crow cocked his head sideways. Why didn't he?

Lead them to me, the old crone's voice whispered in his mind.

He shuddered with the connection. She never left him, though he once left her.

You know she belongs with me. You promised.

He had.

How? He didn't expect an answer.

Watch them and wait. You'll see.

That was the problem. She saw. She saw everything. But her sight was incomplete because she was only one, and no longer part of the three.

The group talked, discussing something between them. He fluttered closer in the trees. The human didn't belong in the group. She neither spoke up nor hid away, but listened to them argue. She simply waited, and displayed more wisdom in that action than her entire species. The faerie child, a magic being herself,

100

belonged with the likes of the ogress and the elf. Their clans had always aligned and looked out for each other. A strange allegiance, but it was useful for their ancestors. But the child sought comfort from the human, curled up in her lap as human children do.

Foolish girl.

The dragon, he was an unknown. He shared his thoughts while the ogress and elf argued, then smirked at their banter. There were few dragon shifters anymore, ever since the young king sent hunters to the four corners to slaughter their kin. Most of them went into hiding, staying human or in the molten depths.

The crow crept closer to the group, listening carefully for anything he could use to guide them.

"We need to find out what happened," the elf said. "Then we can decide our next steps." A thoughtful plan, but it would waste time.

"No," the ogress argued. "We need to go now, east and around, away from the refugees." The crow thought her plan had the most merit. Though there were spies to the east, their smaller group would blend in among the humans. The ogress just had to cover her skin.

"But the refugees," the elf argued back.

"There isn't much we can do." The dragon's deep voice cut through. The crow smirked. He was smarter than most of their scaled breed.

"Where will we go?" Asked the ogress, a rational warrior.

"The Rätsel caves," the faerie answered as she looked directly at the crow. Did she know he listened? He hobbled over. She tilted her head before looking at the others. "That's what you promised."

"Heading to the caves takes us *into* danger, child." The ogress explained. "We should go elsewhere, at least until it's safe."

"But I'm needed there." The child answered. Her lavender eyes grew dark and unfocused for a minute, then became clear again. The four of them looked at her. The ogress shook her head.

The crow hobbled a little closer, waiting. He froze when the next words came from the human. "I don't think it's ever going to be safe again." Her soft voice drew their focus. She rubbed her chest absently, and the crow smiled to himself.

The little girl looked up at him again. She stared for a moment, then got distracted by something grey wiggling in her hood. He originally thought the furs were pelts to keep her warm, but they moved. The little girl giggled and soothed whatever it was with her fingers. He immediately recognized the look in her light purple eyes, seeing and unseeing at the same time. "It's time to go home," she said, in a voice older than her age.

The human hugged her tightly. "I agree."

The other three looked at each other. It was the dragon who spoke. "You truly want to see the Seeress?" He asked. "Nothing good comes from visiting her."

The human's eyes widened. "The Seeress lives in the caves?"

They nodded. Her body stiffened and her face grew hard. "Yes. Now more than ever." Her gaze narrowed, and she grasped her staff, her knuckles white. She was determined and brave for a human.

The crow watched the squirming grey mass poke out a small head with beaded eyes. *Ah,* he thought, *this is the way.*

The others argued below as he launched himself at the girl. She shrieked and shrunk, moving out of his way, but displaced the squirrels in her hood. The human girl looked up just as his good foot opened and snatched one of the grey squirrels. Then he returned to the tree canopy. The squirrel shrieked in his claw, fighting him with all his strength, but the crow held on. It was no match for him.

He flew up high, then looked down at them. The ogress pulled out her bow, as the rest of them stood to their feet. The child was back to normal and screamed at him to release the squirrel. He looked one last time, then flew a little ways north. The entire group followed him because of the child's love of the furry thing. *Fools.* He found a rock in a clearing. Landing so he could lean on his sore foot while pinning the squirrel in place. Then he waited.

When they came into the clearing, they stopped and stared at him. The ogress had her bow ready, drew an arrow, and took aim while the others held swords. When did the human get a sword? She was clearly out of her element with it. Her left hand trembled under its weight.

"Naughty crow, give me back my friend." The child demanded. His feathers bristled with the flow of energy around her, his skin twitched with static. She'd grown powerful. Her time with the elf was useful. The old crone would be pleased. The crow released the squirrel, who scurried back to the child. "Thank you." At least she was polite.

The others stared at him, but it was the human who approached. She knelt down, so they were at eye level.

"Rory!" the dragon called out behind her. She held up her hand to stop him. The crow tilted his head sideways. Interesting, the weak human commanded a dragon, especially this one.

The human put one hand on her chest and touched the rose at her ear. It hissed, tightened its bloom, peering at him. She soothed it with her fingers and looked the crow over. "You want to lead us?" She asked.

He bobbed his head.

"Seriously? We're talking to birds again?" The ogress grumbled. She lifted her arrow and put it back in her quiver, then slung the bow over her shoulder.

The human ignored her. For one without magic, she was uncommonly attuned to it. "To the *Rätsel* caves?" He bobbed his head. She looked at the others, and seeing their wary acceptance, she turned back to him. "Lead the way."

He flew into the canopy as the ogress threw her hands in the air. "Why do I even bother?"

We're on our way.

23

FOR THREE DAYS, RORY, Luiselle, and their eccentric companions followed the crow. For three days, Nega grumbled about following the
cursed bird, while either Kuri would tell her to stop complaining, or Riel
would smack her upside the head.

Luiselle giggled at their antics. Though annoyed by Nega's grumbling,
Rory didn't complain because they were helping her. They hadn't stopped
helping since she met them. She knew they were doing this for Luiselle. She
envied their camaraderie. The servants in her Chateau, much as she loved and
cared for them, were never really her friends. They worked in the chateau and
left her to her own devices. Rory begged Muriel to let her spin to help with
something and be around others. She watched the trio banter, teasing each
other, and her chest ached. Royalty. Human. Cursed. The titles just made
her an outsider, no matter who she was with. But amid her dark thoughts,
Luiselle would come and hug her and walk with her hand in hand.

Every morning, they rose early. Nega trained Rory, while Kuri trained
Luiselle. Riel joined in the training of both, depending on what they needed.
Sometimes he was an extra adversary for Rory to deal with, sometimes he
worked with Kuri as a magical experiment. Rory suspected he preferred the
battle to Luiselle's magic because he often fought her after being transformed
into something else. After being made into a bunny, Riel came back, his
face pale, his eyes wild. After beating Rory with his superior skill, he battled
Nega. Both relished having an equal partner to spar. Neither held back as
they fought.

With each session, Rory lasted longer, but she was out of her depth. It made her grateful for their company. It didn't help that the crow seemed to keep laughing at her. He cackled, his caw scaring away the grey jays and finches who normally kept her company.

This morning, both Rory and Luiselle were being trained in defensive tactics, Luiselle's being of the magical variety. The crow sat in the trees and watched the squirrels frolic. To Rory's relief, it never grabbed one of the squirrel kits again. Luiselle's power, when she thought the squirrels were in danger, frightened Rory more than she would admit. She hated how Kuri was right.

Today, the crow was silent. Rory looked around for him and realized too late that Nega and Riel were already attacking. She stumbled backwards before Nega sneered at her while Riel just glanced at her sideways.

"Always pay attention to your surroundings," Nega growled. "What is the point of teaching you if you won't pay attention?"

"But the crow-"

Nega lunged at her, as did Riel. She dodged to the side, then faced them. Rory kept one hand pointed at Nega, the sword focused on Riel.

Riel parried her, and she realized a moment later that he was pushing her towards Nega, who had silently come around behind her, blade drawn. Nega thrust through to Rory's side as Riel grabbed her throat, and Nega hissed in her ear, "You're dead," before shoving her to her knees in front of them. Riel held his sword up to her neck, pretending to behead her. His eyes flashed into their dragon shape, and Rory sighed.

Rory glanced at the canopy but didn't see the crow.

"You're distracted," Riel growled at her. He stabbed his own sword into the ground beside her knees. "If you allow yourself to be distracted, how will you take care of yourself? Or Luiselle?" Rory felt tears gather, but she blinked them back.

"The crow is missing," she said. Riel grabbed his blade, squinting his eyes.

"Oh, hang the bloody crow!" Nega said, punching Rory's shoulder hard enough to knock her sideways. "We're trying to teach you to be on guard. Is there any point to this training?"

But Riel stared at her, his head tilted. "Nega, I don't think-"

"Dragon, don't you dare go soft for her! She'll put us all at risk." She spun away from him, then attacked Rory. Rory dove out of the way, rolling, then getting back into a fighting stance. Nega came after her repeatedly. Rory swung her own blade defensively, but Nega sped up her attack. Her golden eyes flashed as she glared at her. Nega tripped Rory, then knocked her sword out of her grasp and held her blade to Rory's throat.

Rory froze.

"Nega?" Riel came beside them, his brow furrowed.

"We'd be better off without her. You *know* this." Nega's eyes remained fixed on Rory's, the blade scraping against skin. Rory stared back, palms up in surrender.

"Nega, stop." Riel said.

Nega's pupils dilated. The blade pulled back slightly, and Rory swallowed.

"Let her up so we can start again." Riel placed his hand on Nega's shoulder. But Nega held her strike position, her muscles taught. The blade came back to her throat.

"You're right, Nega." Rory said, and Nega's body flinched. "If it weren't for the oath the troll forced me to make, I would surrender Lu to your care. You'd be much better off without me." The ring burned at her chest. "But I can't let her go. And now I'm holding you back." A single tear escaped her eye, falling down her temple. The rose wiped it away. "What do I do?"

"Stop focusing on the birds." Nega pulled her sword back. Her body relaxed. "Learn about the creatures that want you dead." Rory nodded. Nega reached down, offered her hand until Rory took it. The ogress' gigantic frame pulled her up to her feet easily. "Again?"

Rory reached for her sword and stepped into her battle stance.

Kuri's anguished cry rang out, and all three looked around. Luiselle cried, "No!" Then there was complete silence.

Riel, Nega, and Rory gathered together so their backs faced each other, and they looked out over the forest.

A rustle came from Rory's right, and they turned together. Rory held up her sword just as something shot out from the trees. It knocked Riel over, who cried out in pain. "Run!" He yelled to them, his voice groggy. Nega and Rory ran away from him. Something brown shot out from the trees. It landed on Nega, knocking the warrior down. Nega's guttural groan sent shivers down Rory's spine, so she ran harder. She zig zagged through the forest until something knocked her over to the side. She screamed as a hand crashed into her mouth, someone straddling her.

"Easy, my dear," a man's voice said. "Stop fighting. I'm human, like you. You're safe. We're not here to hurt you." Rory stared up at him, and he loosened his hand. "We have the little child. She's safe, too. We know you're protecting her. We're here to help save you from the unnatural folk."

Rory's eyes widened as the man sat straddling her, his fingers caressing her cheek. Her whole body went rigid at his touch. His other hand held Rory's sword. The rose bud tightened and wiggled itself back into her hair, out of sight. Rory forced herself to breathe evenly, but it was difficult with the man squeezing her waist between his thighs. An angry white scar ran from his right temple, across the centre of his lips, to the left side of his chin.

"Who are you?" She asked.

The stranger didn't answer. Instead, he got off and yanked Rory up. She stumbled forward, and he grasped her hard by her wrist. He marched at a brisk pace, dragging her through the forest. She asked for Luiselle, but the man remained silent. Rory felt the bruising develop on her forearm. He held her sword hostage while his own sat on his belt.

"You don't need to worry about *them*," the stranger said. He easily overpowered her with his brute strength, directing her along a path. They walked for hours, and though she couldn't see anyone else, they didn't travel alone. Every once in a while, the man made a bird call, and someone else answered with another. Rory worried about Luiselle and the rest of her friends, their cries echoing in her ears. Tears threatened, but she forced them back, kept her eyes open to her surroundings, just as Nega taught her. Every once in a while, she'd look up and see the crow watching her before he flew away. She exhaled in relief.

Soon they found themselves at an iron gate in a massive stone wall, three stories in height. The wall itself had iron pickets sticking out from the top at least six feet into the air. The crow couldn't fit between them if he tried.

Behind them came a rider on a horse with a small bundle in front of him. A wagon with a set of iron bars followed, drawn by two other horses. Rory made out the outline of several hooded figures within it. The man beside Rory gripped her arm tightly and held her aside to let the wagon pass by. As it did, a limp green arm fell down the side and grazed the iron bars. The arm flinched, then went limp again. Rory smelled burnt flesh. She gasped, her hand covering her mouth as she fought the nausea that built up. She swallowed her bile, the burning taste stinging her throat.

Behind Nega in the wagon, she saw Riel. He sat hunched over; his green eyes narrowed to slits when they saw her. Rory stepped forward, but the man beside her yanked her back, gripping her arm so tightly she cried out. Riel jumped up and grabbed the bars. Steam rose from where his hands grasped them, but he didn't let go. They passed through the gate while he snarled at everyone, finally releasing the bars as she lost sight of him.

"Don't worry about them anymore, miss. They won't hurt you again." The man said, still gripping her arm.

"But-"

A small groan came from beside her. Rory looked at the man on the horse. The bundle moved, and a small hand dropped.

"Lu!" Rory reached for the little girl. But as the horse stepped forward through the gate, the man yanked her back yet again.

"Don't worry, we'll place the child in your room once she's tested." They followed behind, the man dragging her further into the city, still gripping her arm tightly.

"Tested? What do you mean? Where are we going?" Rory asked. Behind her, iron bars clanged as they closed off the opening to the forest beyond.

"I'm taking you to our healer to test you. To make sure you're okay." His scar reflected the sunlight, and his eyes roamed over her body. Once again, Rory swallowed back her bile.

"I'm *fine!*"

The man stopped in front of her and gripped her chin with thick, calloused fingers. Her jaw ached as he glared at her with cold, grey eyes. "We're not taking any chances. Now, get moving." He pulled her into the door of a two-storey stone building. Iron bars framed the interior of the windows.

On the table in the front room, Luiselle lay unconscious.

24

A SHORT, HOODED FIGURE hovered over Luiselle's prone body.

"Lu!" Rory tried to rush to her friend's side, but the scarred man held her back again. "Let me go!"

He shoved her roughly onto a nearby stool. "Sit," he growled. His callused hand held Rory down with a firm grip on her shoulder. "Don't move." He stepped away from the stool and moved toward the door. Rory glared at the man and wondered if he treated everyone like an animal. He blocked her only way out. She eyed her sword, but his hand gripped the hilt tight, and she knew she'd never be able to grab it fast enough.

Brown eyes framed by thick spectacles looked up at Rory and the man. She frowned at Rory. "You brought me two?" She asked, her voice raspy.

"Both girls." The man answered. "And the Blade is fetching the *Beül* to deal with the others."

The woman's mouth opened before closing again. She peered down at Lu before looking again at Rory. "The others?"

"An ogre, an elf, and a *dragon*." He spat out the words, then pointed at Rory. "Make sure she's okay and see if she has any skill that makes her useful. Otherwise we'll send her to the madam."

The woman frowned at Rory before looking at him. "And the child?"

He snorted. "You test her yet?"

The woman lifted Luiselle's hand, showing off a metal cuff that Rory had never seen. "Natural."

"If the older one has skills, the girl is her responsibility. Otherwise, we'll find her another home." He turned around to leave.

"Wait, Graus!"

He turned back to face the woman.

"The elf, if she's a healer I could-"

"King's orders, Genezra." He sneered at her. "No more unnatural help." He looked around the woman's shop. "No one wants 'em here anyway, not after they cursed the princess and left her to rot. Be thankful we're still keeping you around and don't make trouble."

The man slammed the door shut. Metal clanged, and he locked them in from the outside. Rory looked out the windows, only to find them covered in iron bars.

Genezra's home was a prison.

Icy fingers wrapped around Rory's right wrist. Rory looked in time to see a metal cuff locked around her wrist, the key on a chain around Genezra's neck. Rory grasped for it, but the woman dropped it inside her shirt. She held Rory's wrist tight and watched her face.

"What are you doing?" Rory tried to get the key's chain with her free hand. Genezra watched her for another minute, then twisted Rory's wrist until it hurt. "Ow!" She pulled Rory's sleeve back up her arm and examined it. Bruises covered her arm from Graus manhandling her. The woman dropped Rory's arm.

"You're *human?*" She asked. Her brown eyes grew round as they looked up at Rory.

"I am." Rory answered her.

"There is so much magic surrounding you!" The woman pulled Rory's head down to hers and turned it so she could see the rose. She touched it tenderly, then tried to pluck it from Rory's hair, but the rose just grabbed tighter. Rory cried out as the rose pulled on her scalp.

"Ow! Stop that!" She shoved the woman's hands away. Genezra's hood fell to her shoulders, revealing pointed ears. Each had a brass ring that created a large hole, and several brass cuffs lined her ears' helix. She was older and had deep laugh lines and wrinkles cutting into her face. "Leave the rose alone!"

"But you have no magic. Why does it cling to *you?*" The woman paced around the room. "They found you with an ogre, an elf, a *dragon,*" she stopped pacing in front of Rory and poked her hard in the stomach, "and the child! What are you, a *human,* doing with them?" The woman spat the word human, but Rory sighed, rubbing her stomach. She opened her mouth to answer, but Luiselle groaned on the table.

Rory rushed over to her side. "Lu?" She asked softly, stroking her hair. She held Luiselle's small hand in hers and rubbed her chilly fingers. "I'm here Lu."

Luiselle turned in Rory's direction, her glassy eyes unfocused. "Rory? I don't feel good."

"I know." Rory continued to rub the little girl's hand as she closed her eyes. Tears gathered in her own, and she wiped them away with her sleeve. She looked back at Genezra, who stared at Rory as if she'd never seen a human before.

"Who are you?" the woman whispered.

"I'm Rory," she said. "You're Genezra?"

The woman nodded, staring at Luiselle's hand in Rory's.

"What's wrong with her? Did the soldier hurt her?"

Genezra shook her head. "It's the iron cuff." She sat down on a stool next to Rory. "It would normally burn her skin, causing her pain, but I layered it on a wood cuff. The iron is making her sick because it's close, but this way, they don't know what she is."

"You're helping her?" Rory's eyes grew wide.

Genezra scowled at her, eyes narrowing sharply. "What's it to you?"

"Everything! Thank you." Rory's chest muscles loosened.

Luiselle called for Rory again, and Rory whispered in her ear that she was near. The faerie settled down again, and they were silent.

"I'm guessing based on the iron on the windows, doors and roof, and the iron cuff on your wrist, that you're a prisoner here?" Rory looked into Genezra's large, brown eyes.

"Aye. I was one of the many living in peace here in the village. At least until the refugees started coming through from Kehl." The woman made a tea, grabbing herbs and other items drying on the wall.

"What happened?" Rory asked.

"What do you care?" Genezra looked up and flashed her sharp incisors at Rory. "You belong with the rest of the humans."

Rory sighed and glanced at Luiselle before focusing on Genezra. "Are you an elf?" Genezra burst out laughing and Rory's cheeks heated. "What's so funny?"

"I'm a goblin, girl. We deal with the metals, not the healing arts. The iron you see everywhere? We were once the blacksmiths until they chose iron for everything." She wrinkled her nose. "That you can't tell us apart is odd. All humans can, just to know which *Beül* to call to get rid of us."

"I am learning so much." Rory sighed. All the years she'd spent in her castle, her servants spoke of the magic folk, always in a positive light. But she'd never met them until she'd joined Reinhold. Even then, he steered her away from the refugees coming through. "The ogress and the elf were teaching me about all the refugees before his men attacked us."

Genezra narrowed her eyes. "The men said they were attacking *you*. They had you pinned at their feet, a sword at your throat."

"Training me. The ogress was trying to teach me how to fight with a sword." Rory held out the palms of her hands, showing the bloody calluses that had formed. "I think I'm a pretty hopeless case." Rory glanced away from Genezra as her cheeks heated further.

"And why would you want to take up a sword?" The goblin snorted. "No other skills?"

"I promised Reinhold I would take... care of Lu."

Genezra gasped, then grabbed Rory's chin, forcing her to look directly into Genezra's eyes. "Reinhold, the shepherd?"

Rory nodded into Genezra's pinching grip. "Yes, he taught me about the sheep. That's where I met Lu."

Genezra's jaw dropped as she exhaled. She jumped up, and despite her small stature, yanked Rory up to stand as well. Genezra spun Rory around until she grabbed the rope that cinched Rory's tunic together. She pulled on it, squeezing it around Rory's waist, until it cut into her sides, and stepped over to the lamp on the other side, dragging Rory with her.

"Um... what are you -" Rory started, until Genezra held her hand up to silence her.

"You make this rope?"

"Yes..."

She spun Rory to another worktable and shoved a bunch of wool in front of her. "Show me."

Rory looked back. "But Lu..."

The goblin snapped her fingers in front of Rory's face and grabbed Rory's chin again. "She'll sleep for some time. Show me." Genezra's wrinkled face hardened. "Now."

Rory took her pack from the floor, then pulled out her carding combs and drop spindle. She combed the wool, then spun it at the table.

"How thick?" She asked, watching the spindle.

"As fine and strong as you can spin."

Genezra focused on Rory's spinning. Rory smiled to herself, and made a thin string, almost as strong as silk. When the section was done, Rory set it down in front of the Goblin, then crossed her hands over her chest. She waited while Genezra examined every single part of the length, tested its strength. She looked up at Rory, her eyes wide.

"You *are* Reinhold's! This is good," she nodded, and Rory felt her chest expand, until Genezra continued. "It's also bad. They won't want to let you go."

The soldier, Graus, came later, and once he discovered Rory's skill, had Genezra put Rory and Luiselle in a room above her shop. It was clean and had a small bed wedged into the corner. Rory placed Luiselle on the bed, and she rolled over, snuggling against a pillow at the wall. Rory thought about joining her, but sat on the edge of the bed and stared at the stone walls around her. A small window on the outside wall was big enough for Rory to climb through, but iron bars protected it, too.

Rory stood again, her legs twitching. She ran her hands along the stone walls, their rough texture opposite to the chateau walls she escaped a few months ago. They polished the stones until they gleamed, smooth. Carved embellishments told the history of Elsass, and embroidered fabrics softened the walls. She'd had a big comfortable bed with soft sheets to herself, and servants to help her with every need. They brought her everything, the wool she spun, the food she ate. But they never spent time with her. She never left the rounded walls of her tower room, ventured nowhere else after she turned twelve. They ordered her to stay put. After having freedom with Reinhold and Luiselle, and then with Nega, Kuri and Riel, Rory realized imprisonment was human nature. What they couldn't control, they locked up. Her heart raced, her hands fisted, and she fought the urge to scream at being trapped again.

Rory unclenched her fingers and traced the walls, where she found a groove notched into the stone. She traced it, a spiral spinning outwards, and a flash illuminated the room. The light spread from the centre of the spiral along the grooves through to other notches in the wall. Her eyes widened, and she gasped as the yellow glow expanded around the walls in the rooms, surrounding them, illuminating even the bars on the window.

"Runes," Luiselle sat up, hugging her knees.

"What are they for?" Rory asked.

"Protection, but you need to turn them off, or someone outside will see." At Rory's arched eyebrows, Luiselle smiled. "Trace backwards to the centre of the spiral."

Rory traced her fingers back into the spiral centre. The bar left of the window's centre was the last to stop glowing. Rory sat back down on the bed.

"Magic really likes you." Luiselle snuggled up against her side.

"I don't know why." Rory hugged her. "How do you feel?"

"Tired. Not like normal."

Rory held up Luiselle's wrist to show her the iron cuff. Luiselle nodded. "So I can't change to my other self. The goblin is smart, like her kind." Luiselle pat the bed. "This is comfy, not like sleeping on the rocks with the sheep. Or listening to Nega snore."

Rory smiled, then frowned, remembering the burning smell of Nega's arm. Her chest ached, and she grew nauseous. She rubbed the ring tucked under her shirt again. The idea of leaving the three in the iron cages made her stomach hurt, but Luiselle was her priority. She couldn't leave behind the ones who helped them. She considered them friends, even if she didn't belong. The ring on her chest pulsed with energy, and Rory sighed.

"What is it?" Luiselle asked, tucking her small hand into Rory's.

"I have to take you to Rätsel." Rory rubbed the little girl's hand with her thumb.

"But we can't leave them here." Her little hand trembled in Rory's.

Rory looked into Luiselle's large, tear-filled eyes. "No, we can't."

25

RORY WOKE UP THE next morning to see Genezra standing over her, talking to Luiselle. She bolted upright and looked around. The light filtered through the shutters on the floor, illuminating the iron bar pattern on the outside.

"Ah, the princess awakes!" Genezra said, and Rory froze. Genezra and Luiselle laughed before looking at Rory.

"I... uh..." *She knows who I am!* Rory's heartbeat faster, and she thought of several excuses she could use to dissuade the goblin from saying anything to anyone.

"Oh relax girl, I was just teasing you!" Genezra picked up Rory's hands, holding them up in the light. "No one with calluses like those is a princess! Now come on. Before Graus takes you to the spinners, you should have some bread and wine." Rory let go of the breath she held, rubbed the ring against her chest. Genezra pulled her off the bed and shooed her out the door.

"What about Luiselle?" Rory asked. Luiselle followed behind.

"I'm going to spend the day with Genezra, learning about her metalwork." Luiselle answered. "She says my hands will be useful for cleaning some of her things."

Rory narrowed her eyes at Genezra as Luiselle pushed past her to nibble on some bread. But Genezra just waved her hand as if it were nothing.

"I'll take good care of the little one, I promise."

Rory paused her motions, but Luiselle spoke. "Goblins don't lie, Rory. It's against their nature. And she's cuffed, so she's more vulnerable if she lies."

Rory looked down at Genezra's wrists, both of them cuffed with iron. "I need magic to lie, and the cuffs prevent that." She imagined a world in which she couldn't lie.

A bang from the door startled Rory out of her thoughts as the lock disengaged and Graus stepped through. He looked at the three of them, then grabbed Rory by her arm. Dragging her through the door, he pinched her arms where bruises from yesterday's march had already formed. He let go long enough to lock the door with a key from one large ring at his waist. The key was iron, like everything else. She sighed. Even if a refugee got a hold of it, they wouldn't be able to handle it without doing considerable damage to their hands.

Graus faced her, looked her up and down, and sneered. "You always dress like a boy?"

"I'm a shepherd." Rory shrugged. "I don't need to dress up for the sheep."

"They'll want to dress you finer than this," he said, motioning Rory to follow him.

"They?" She stepped behind him.

"Are you daft? The spinners. They wear proper tunics for women. Cover their hair." He touched her hair, pulling a long brown lock to his nose, but she pulled away from his fingers. "Why is it uncovered, anyway?"

"It's easier to plait and tuck under the hood of my cloak."

Graus stopped in the middle of the street and looked her over. "You're not like the other womenfolk." Then he turned and sped towards an open area. Of course not. The chateau provided more finery than Graus had ever seen in his life, but Rory preferred working outdoors with the sheep to stone walls and frippery.

Rory followed him past the old stone buildings. Iron bars crisscrossed the window shutters with plain and ornate patterns. The bigger the stone buildings, the more ornate the iron bars. They passed the most ornate building in town; the building decorated with iron roses, as beautiful as the one in Rory's hair. She peered inside and realized it was the blacksmith. She wondered at the intricacy of the workmanship, but Graus stopped up ahead, his arms crossed, waiting for her. Rory picked up her pace and entered what she assumed was the town square. It was a larger open space full of market stalls, food and other wares being bartered.

Graus shoved her through the open square as a growl came from her right. There were a set of three medium-sized cages, no bigger than something used for a lynx. Inside, her gaze found Riel's. She glanced at the other cages. Nega and Kuri each sat in one on either side of Riel. They were hunched over, their bodies curled into painful positions to avoid touching their iron prisons.

Rory took a step toward them and reached out to Riel, but Graus grabbed her wrist and dragged her off.

"Wait!" she breathed. "Please wait!" Tears stung her eyes as pain throbbed in her arm.

But Graus didn't listen. Instead, he dragged her down a side street. He shoved her into another stone building, this one with simple iron bars. She blinked her eyes, trying to adjust to the darkness after having seen the sun again.

"I'll be back to get you at supper." Graus left her in the building and locked the door.

"Well now, miss," a young girl said. She stood off to the side. "You don't look like a normal spinner."

"Hush Anna." An older woman stepped forward. She and Anna wore plain grey tunics, simple belts tied around their waists. Grey material tied their hair back, and they had fixed a red badge in the shape of a spindle on their right sleeves. "I take it you're Rory?" At Rory's nod, the older woman offered a polite smile. "Graus told us to expect you. You're to spin to earn your keep."

"My keep?" Rory asked.

"Your home," the young girl said. *Home.* Rory's mouth went dry. Her vision narrowed. She felt the tingles run up her arm until she realized the women were staring at her. The tingles dissipated. It was just a memory. As much as she didn't like Graus or the others in this village who would torture her friends, she wasn't ready to curse it.

"Well, let's see your skill." The older woman said. Rory pulled out her spindle, and the older woman laughed, lines forming at the corners of her eyes. "That's what you're using? We use these now," she said, motioning to a wheel in the corner.

"What is that?" Rory asked, leaning to touch the wheel with her fingers.

"Stop!" said the old woman. Rory jumped. "You'll hurt yourself. That spindle is sharp and spins fast. You don't want any splinters from the flax."

"Any wool?" Rory asked. "My stash is gone."

The woman nodded, then pulled some from a nearby pile. Its texture was quite coarse, not like the carded ones she made. She looked up at the woman, who crossed her arms over her chest. The young girl, Anna, tried to copy her, and Rory tried to hide her smile.

Rory dropped the spindle, fingering the wool, pulling it into a fine thread, soft and even. When she finished the wool, she handed the spindle to the older woman. The older woman just stared at Rory.

"Gran?" The young girl tugged on the older woman's sleeve. "Should we test it?"

The older woman shook her head, then set aside the thread Rory made. "You'll earn your keep." She reached into a small cabinet tucked away in the back corner of the room. "Now, show me what you can do with this!"

The young girl gasped as the older woman pulled out a yellow fleece and placed it in Rory's palm. Rory stared at it as she held it in her hand. The small amount was heavy for its size and shone in the candlelight.

"Gold fleece?"

The old woman nodded. Rory looked at it, then pulled out her combs and carded it, amazed by its softness. She had seen gold before, but nothing so delicate. Rory realized carding it too much would destroy it, so she prepared to spin as quickly as possible. She spun the wool longer and took more care, but the result was a fine golden thread she tripled to create a fine chain. When finished, she looked up to find not only Anna and her grandmother but also Graus and several other women. They looked to be about the grandmother's age. Taking in their appearance, they looked like they were all part of the same group. Three of them wore iron cuffs, the rest wore leather.

Graus whistled.

"Well, I'll be..." Anna's gran said.

Anna, who came up close, looked at the fine detail. "Where did you learn to do that?" She whispered. The chain wobbled with her breath. Anna jumped back out of the way and shoved her hands into her pockets.

"I'll take that," a large chested woman wearing deep crimson robes said from the doorway. She pulled out a coin purse and handed Rory ten gold coins. "Will that be enough?" Rory looked at Anna's grandmother, who nodded. Rory handed the chain over to the woman. Then the woman strode out of the shop, tying the chain around her waist.

Rory handed eight of the coins to Anna's grandmother, whose mouth dropped open. "What are you doing?" she asked.

"You supplied the fleece. I worked it." The other women stared at Rory as if she'd grown a second head. "What?"

"It's the rules, Rory." Anna said from beside her. "You earn your worth by making. Not supplying. They reward practice and skill here."

The other women nodded. Graus crossed his arms across his chest, his angry scar prominent in his scowl.

"That's a ridiculous rule." Rory looked at them. "I couldn't have made it without the fleece, and you supplied it. Why would I keep it all?"

Several of the women murmured to each other until Graus silenced them. He grabbed Rory's arm in that same painful spot. She flinched as several of the women backed away from him. A couple of spinners rubbed their own arms in sympathy. "She'll be back tomorrow." Graus gave her enough time to grab her things before he dragged her through the door. He locked it behind them before turning to her, dragging her down the road between the stone buildings.

"That woman's job is to supply your craft. You won't do that again."

"Why not?" Rory asked.

"Because she hasn't worked on her craft. You have." He looked at Rory as if he'd never seen her before. "You'll get paid for your work. The harder you work, the better you get paid."

Rory thought about the town blacksmith. He did good work and had the nicest home in the village. But iron bars still caged the outside, no way out or in. It was the nicest prison in the village. "Does she sheer the sheep to get the wool?"

"What?" Graus asked, stopping in the empty town square. "Yes. Of course she does. What does that have to do with anything?"

"Then she doesn't have much time to practice. Is she paid for that work?"

"She's given sustenance and a roof over her head." He pulled Rory down the street again until she yanked her arm out of his hand. Graus scowled, turning back to her. "What do you care?"

Rory gestured at her clothes. "Shepherd, remember? I know how hard it is to take care of the sheep. A shepherd checks the wool, makes sure the flock is healthy, doesn't nick the sheep. That's challenging work. You have to be gentle, firm, or risk getting a kick to the head."

A deep crease settled between Graus' brows. "What's your point?" He grabbed her wrist, forcing her to follow him.

"It's harder than spinning, and to get good wool like she did? That takes superb skill. More than spinning. She deserves more than a roof over her head."

"That's not how it's done here." He spun her around, his red face leaning down into her own. "We brought you here because you're one of us. Now, you're going to *act* like it." He shoved her against a stone wall, and Rory winced in pain. "You'll follow our rules and like them. Or I'll send that little girl who came with you to the madam. Then you'll see what other rules we like to follow." Rory gasped, and Graus took that moment to pull her forward. He yanked her arm so hard she tripped on a cobblestone and fell to her hands and knees. Sharp pain bit her knees and palms, but she stifled her cry, unwilling to let him hear. "Get up!" He yelled, then started laughing. Until it halted.

A green arm wrapped around his neck, lifting him up off his feet. Steam rose from where the arm clenched against the iron bars. The smell of burning flesh grew pungent in her nose. Rory swallowed the bile building up. Nega's gold eyes shone in the dark, her snarl clear in the gleam of her white teeth in the moonlight.

"Enough ogress!" came a voice beside Rory. A large man with a gut as wide as Luiselle was tall stood beside them. He pulled Rory against his crimson robe and Rory gagged at the stench of his sweat. "Let the soldier go." But Nega growled at him despite the pain. "I won't let him hurt the child." He said and Nega relaxed her arm. It was enough. Graus slipped out, then held her arm against the iron bars, causing her to growl again. Still, he held it there, and bile rose in Rory's throat. The smell of burning flesh was so strong she focused on the large man's sweat.

"Nega!" Rory whispered. But the wealthy man beside her just smiled.

"Enough Graus! We need them whole when we put them forward for the trials in two days." The man grabbed her jaw and held it. "So you're the one who made the belt for my Adeline? You don't look like much. But she's happy enough, and it is a beautiful piece." He shoved her into Graus, who caught her. "Make sure she's locked up tight." Then he faced Rory. "This will be your home now."

"No!" Rory shook. But the man just walked away. "No, wait, you don't understand..."

"Better get used to the idea, girl. If you want your home to be pleasant, follow the rules." Graus dragged her off to Genezra and locked her inside.

26

RORY WOKE UP THE next morning unsettled. She'd had nightmares of people burning. Riel, Nega, and Kuri's eyes glowed in the darkness before flames overtook them, their growls turning into cries of terror. She'd woken up with tears streaming down her face, mourning their loss. She'd tossed and turned, until Luiselle rubbed her back, and she stilled, calming herself for her little friend. Rory lay there, staring at the cold stone walls. She wished she were out under the night sky with her friends again, even with all the predators.

"Your hair smells gross." Luiselle said in the morning as they headed down the stairs. "I mean, Genezra has a lot of stuff that smells weird in her jars, but your hair is disgusting."

Rory swallowed and stalled on the stairs. The lingering smell of Nega's burned flesh mixed with her dreams, leaving her unsettled.

"You coming?" Luiselle asked and Rory nodded her head, before continuing and stopping cold at the bottom of the stairs. Graus had already arrived and was waiting, his arms crossed over his chest. He stared at Luiselle with one lip curled at the corner.

"He's early," Genezra said. She shoved some items into Rory's hands and stepped away from the soldier. "Here's some bread, and a small skin of water." Her eyes flashed to Luiselle, and she tilted her head to the door.

"Thank you," Rory answered her before turning to face Graus. "I'm ready."

He looked Rory over slowly, and Rory held herself still under his gaze. "Good. I was just informing Genezra that I have another person to take in the girl if she doesn't have enough work for her." Crumbs fell on the floor from Rory's day-old bread as she forced her fingers to relax.

"I have more than enough work for the child," Genezra said. Anger flashed in the goblin's eyes. She stepped in front of Luiselle, shielding the faerie with her own body.

"That may be so, but I don't know if I want you poisoning her with your ideas." He opened the door for them. "It might be best to find all three of you separate accommodations."

Rory opened her mouth to argue, but Genezra shook her head, so Rory stayed quiet. Rory followed Graus out the door, then waited as he locked it. She stepped up beside him before he could grasp her arm, and he looked down at her, surprised. She gestured to him to lead the way while she stayed behind him. Graus kept checking to see if she was there, but she kept up. As they walked through the market square, they had to dodge the townspeople gathered there.

Sneers and jeers caught her attention, and she observed some boys prodding Nega with a long stick. She watched for a moment, but Graus kept walking away and she had to run after him. As she rounded the corner, she heard a loud snap and a growl, followed by shouts and footsteps as the boys ran away. Rory smiled to herself, thankful her friends were still around, grouchy as ever.

They arrived at the spinners, and Graus unlocked the door, allowed Rory to step inside before locking her in. She found herself with Anna, and the rest of the women, so she set her spindle and pack down. The others were busy at their wheels, and Rory watched them, fascinated. Their feet pressed the pedals, and the carded wool pulled itself over the pulley, around the wheel and onto the spindle. Her eyes widened as the spindle filled up. Rory watched the woman replace the spindle with an empty one. She fed the next batch of wool through the wheel and thread it on to the spindle.

"It's so fast!"

The one woman in front of her smiled. "It is, but it takes time getting used to. And the fleece you used won't work here because it pulls too tightly."

"Where did you get them?"

The woman paused, but Anna's grandmother nodded for the woman to continue.

"Graus and the duchy who took over last year brought them with them from Kehl." The woman spoke of Kehl with venom. She took the spindle off the wheel and loaded it with the next one.

"The only good thing to come from Kehl," another woman agreed.

"Is the duchy the large man with the crimson robes? His wife, the one who bought the chain I made?" Rory asked. The woman nodded. "When did they arrive?"

"They followed the refugees about eighteen months ago." The woman sighed. "Things have changed so much since then."

"This happened before the King of Kehl became steward over Elsass?" Rory asked. She looked around at the others.

"Aye child." Anna's grandmother handed Rory some fleece, this time a silver fleece similar to yesterday's. "With the princess asleep, we're under a new rule now. And not an easy one at that."

"I didn't grow up here. What was it like before?" Rory sat down on a stool and carded the wool, careful not to break the fine strands.

The women smiled. "We had peace under the King of Elsass." Anna's grandmother smiled. "And a good trade alliance with the old King of Kehl."

"There weren't refugees, neither," another woman said. "The elves and goblins, the ogres, the shifters, the trolls, even the Seeress, lived in peace with us. They all had skills they shared with us, and we helped them, traded with them. They even helped protect the south lands from the Cave Kala."

Rory sat upright. "The Seeress?" She tempered her curiosity about the Seeress and focused back on her spinning.

"Yes, girl." Another woman said. "All the town went to the Seeress for their fortunes. At least until rumour had it, she started handing out curses instead of blessings."

"Curses?" Rory asked quietly. Her heart pounded in her ears, but she kept focused on her work so they wouldn't see how much she wanted answers.

"That was the beginning of the mistrust. Nineteen years ago, when she cursed our princess heir. Then, a few years ago, when the old King of Kehl died, more folk started running away. The new King was a tyrant to them. Then the people from Kehl followed the refugees and started taking over our town, turning people against what they call the *unnatural*." The woman snorted. "Unnatural. As if we're any better! If the Seeress hadn't lost her mind, people wouldn't have cared.

She grew distant and couldn't even protect the people from Kehl's King. No one knows why. Then people from Kehl started influencing everyone. They were malicious to everyone, but especially the *unnatural*. They'd get mean with us people too if we sided with the refugees. Most of us just wanted to keep the peaceful ways. But no one trained us to fight back."

Rory spun, focusing on the fine detail of the silver fleece in front of her. She heard the harsh tones in the way they said *Kehl*, as if they wanted to spit on the very feet of the King. They would spit on her too if they knew she was married to him.

The door opened, and the duchess stepped into the spinner's shop. She immediately focused on Rory. "What are you making today?"

Rory showed her the spindle, and she eyed it. "Silver? What good does silver rope make?" She looked away in disgust. "Let me know when you have more gold." The duchess left them, and the spinners resumed their work.

Rory looked up at Anna's grandmother, who shrugged. "How does she get in here?" Rory asked.

"As duchess, she has a key," Anna answered.

"To everything?" Rory asked.

"No, just the shops," one spinner said. "Only Graus and the duchy have keys to everything."

Rory finished the silver, twisting half of it into embroidery thread, the other half making larger and smaller chains for necklaces and bracelets. When she finished, they gave her regular wool.

"You're a hard worker, Rory," Anna said beside her. "Gran and I spoke. You're welcome to join our household."

Rory fumbled for a moment, dropped the spindle and tearing the thread she was making. Everyone looked up at her, and she struggled to speak. Rory bent down, accepting Anna's help to pick up her things. *Household.* She had to swallow twice to speak up. Anna's face remained hopeful. "I'm honoured at your request, but I'm afraid I cannot accept at the moment."

The other women glanced at each other, then back at Rory. Anna's grandmother spoke first. "We know about the child in your care. She's welcome to join our household, too."

Rory's heart beat faster. These spinners, women she'd only met yesterday, were kind enough to offer a young woman with nothing, and the child she kept, their home to stay in. If they only knew, they would curse themselves because of their kindness. But they stared at her. "Let me think about it tonight?"

Anna squeezed Rory's hand, then tilted her head sideways. "What's this?" She lifted the wooden ring up in front of Rory, still attached to her neck by the rope she'd made. Rory held out her hand, and Anna put it in her palm. It immediately heated her hand, the warmth shooting straight into her heart, tugging at it. Anna looked at her expectantly.

"My wedding ring." The room grew silent as the wheels stopped spinning. Rory's heartbeat echoed in her ears. It was odd to admit aloud she was married. She thought of her friends imprisoned in the town square. They would hate her.

"Where is your husband?" Anna asked her.

Rory took a deep breath. Their eyes held nothing but concern. "In Kehl."

The other's eyes widened, but Anna blushed. "We didn't mean to speak ill of..."

"Hush," Rory answered. "I know you didn't. My father arranged it before he passed and it's not something I wanted. But you understand why I cannot join another household?"

Anna nodded. They all continued to work for the afternoon, sharing gossip from the square, and who was trying to gain favours with Graus or the duchy. Rory took it all in as she focused on her work.

As the women gathered to leave, Anna's grandmother stopped her. "Stay a moment. Graus isn't here yet, and he'll expect to walk you home again."

Anna's grandmother offered her a small bag. Rory blinked at the weight, surprised at how heavy it felt. She tried to open the bag, but the older woman just shook her head. "Put them in your bag for later, when you'll need them." Her hand still rested on Rory's wrist, and a flash of gold glinted in her eyes. The woman winced, and the gold was gone. The woman tugged at the cuff on her wrist as Rory put the bag away.

Anna pulled a longer piece of silver rope off the spindle and pulled the rope from Rory's neck over her head. Heat spread in her chest, the ring reminding her of her oath even from the girl's fingers. She held her breath as Anna took the wool rope from the ring and threaded the silver one through it. As she did, she examined the ring itself and the engravings made into it. "A ring this special needs a handmade treasure to hold it." She placed the silver rope back around Rory's neck, and it pulsed once as it settled back to her chest. "You must go to him."

Anna said. She caught a similar flash of gold in Anna's eyes as Anna tucked the ring underneath Rory's tunic.

Graus opened the door and glared at the three of them. He studied Rory, but seeing her ready, he nodded at the door with his head. When she stepped outside, she noticed Anna and her grandmother wore iron cuffs, similar to Genezra and Luiselle's.

Graus walked her at a quick pace back to Genezra's home.

"Tomorrow is your day off." Graus sounded almost happy.

"Off?" Rory fidgeted with the unfamiliar weight in her pack.

"To watch your attackers pay their price with the *Beül*." Graus smiled at her. "You'll have a first-row seat at their trial, as their accuser. Then, the *Beül* will dole out their punishment. He will torture them as they tortured you." Graus ran his hand up Rory's arm, and she fought the urge to yank it away. "I can only imagine your relief at being rid of them."

Rory gulped. "I must get back to Luiselle." Rory answered.

Graus just grunted. His smile grew. Rory shivered as she hurried back to Genezra's home.

27

GENEZRA HAD A HEARTY stew waiting for Rory when she arrived, and she relished the food. Luiselle didn't join them over dinner, and the ring on her chest heated.

"Where's Luiselle?" Rory asked.

"Upstairs sleeping," Genezra answered.

"Asleep?"

Genezra shrugged, but her eyes glowed. "Her idea. Said something about needing her rest for tonight."

Rory relaxed a bit. "What do you know about the spinners, Anna, and her grandmother?"

Genezra's eyebrows lowered at Rory. "They're hard workers. Good people. Why?"

"They have cuffs like yours."

Genezra's eyes widened, her pupils dilating. "Not quite like mine. They have different... talents."

"Genezra..." Rory stopped. She wondered how much to trust the goblin.

Genezra placed her hand on Rory's. "Anna sent word today that you should go to bed early. You were working hard."

"Anna sent word?" Rory asked her, sitting upright.

"You didn't notice your friend out there?" Genezra asked, pointing her thumb to the window beyond. Rory glanced out the window, surprised to see a crow with a damaged foot sitting up on the stone building across the way. When it saw her, it puffed out its chest, spread its wings and flapped them twice before settling down. Rory saw something grey sitting beside it. Three small heads popped up and peered back at her. A peace offering. Lu would be pleased.

"He'll direct you," Genezra said.

"I know." Rory said. "How do I...?"

Genezra sat back down and grinned at Rory. It was her first genuine smile. "You are not magic, but it likes you. Trust it. It will open up to you."

"Thank you," she said as she climbed the stairs.

"Thank me when the child is safe. And tell her not to worry about the squirrel kits." Rory nodded and left the goblin downstairs.

She found Luiselle asleep in the bed. Rory lay down and waited for the sky to darken. When she heard the curfew called, Rory counted down another hour, her body tense. Muscles she hadn't used in a few days tensed up, and she imagined parrying with Nega again to prepare herself.

Her body's tension reminded her of the last time she counted down the hour until midnight. It felt like years, not months, since she took the chance to escape her chateau. She pulled out her pack again to check on her things. Luiselle had a pack prepared as well. She pulled out the gift from Anna's grandmother, and found some dried food, and lots of wool, the regular kind, ready for carding. Tucked in, she also found a wooden key. She looked at the cuff on Luiselle's sleeping arm and tested the key inside. It fit the cuff. Rory slipped it off, and Luiselle awoke with a start.

"Rory? What happened?" she asked, stretching. "I feel... fantastic."

Rory held up the cuff as Luiselle bounced on the bed. "I have to put it on you again." Luiselle's face dropped, and Rory put her finger under the girl's chin. "I won't lock it. If you need to transform, you can throw it off and fly away." Luiselle nodded and sighed. The little girl winced as Rory placed the cuff back on. Where her face had been bright and her eyes clear a moment ago, the cuff, loosely placed, made her ashen and tired.

Rory put the bag away but kept the key within reach at the top of her pack. "Are you ready to go?"

"What's the plan?" Luiselle asked.

"Get out of here, free the others, then get out of this town." Rory shrugged. "I don't know except to follow my gut."

"Sounds exciting." Lu rubbed her hands together. "Where do we start?"

Rory stood up, running her hands on the wall. "Here." She spun her fingers around the spiral, and stood back as the runes illuminated the walls, the beams singling out the barred windows. Rory waited. When the two bars on the right lit up, she placed her hands on them. Rory pulled the bars, but nothing happened. She pushed them, but nothing. She let go, but they stayed illuminated.

"What do I do?"

Luiselle shrugged. "I don't know."

Pulling again, Rory almost gave up when the rose in her ear pulled out a lock of her hair and twisted it around with its stem. Rory looked at the hair, then back at the bars, and twisted them. Nothing happened. She twisted them the other way, and one gave way. Twisting it with both hands, she unscrewed it from the frame. She set it down and focused on the next one. When it gave way, they could fit through the gap. Rory traced the runes backward with her finger, and everything went dark again. She shoved the iron bars in her pack.

They grabbed their things, climbed through the window, and looked down. A light rain fell, making everything slippery. A small, peaked roof overhung Genezra's entry. Rory let herself down on the ledge, then turned back to help Luiselle climb through after her. They slid to the roof edge, and Rory peered down. The stones on the building were rough to her touch, but she reached into the mortar, cut deep into the stones. Rory found her grip and lowered herself. She longed for the rope she'd used at the chateau, ages ago, but there were no rafters here to tie off to. Halfway down, she slipped and lost her grip, landing on her hip.

"Are you okay?" Luiselle asked, loud enough over the tapping of the rain.

Rory stood up, winced in pain. "Just bruised." She reached up as high as possible to catch Luiselle as she climbed down. Once within reach, Rory lifted her off the roof and set her down on her feet in front of her. Her hip groaned under Luiselle's additional weight. She pursed her fingers to her lips and pointed towards the town square. They ran, avoiding larger puddles so they wouldn't splash, and her hip loosened, the pain lessening. As they raced, a flurry of movement happened to her right. She stopped Luiselle right when the motion landed in front of her.

Rory released a breath when the crow limped in their path. It widened its wings and cawed at them.

"Shh!" Luiselle hissed at the crow. She tried to step around it, but it wouldn't let her past. "We have to get them!" Luiselle said. It still held out its wings.

"Look," Rory said, getting close to the bird. The ring pulsed at her chest. "I *know* I'm supposed to take her to the caves. Trust me, I feel it. But I can't do it alone. I need their help. The *Beül* can't kill them."

"Mrph." The crow's wings held for a moment, then retreated to its sides. It turned and hobbled to the town square. The rain continued, a little harder than before. They held back before entering the square, looking to see if anyone was around. The pouring rain meant no one ventured outside. There were no guards, no townspeople, just the three cages with Riel, Nega, and Kuri inside.

"Wait there!" Rory pointed to some barrels at a market stall. "Stay hidden." She looked at the crow. "Keep watch and keep her safe!" The rain messed with Rory's vision, because she swore she saw the crow scowl at her.

Rory raced to the first of the three cages, where Kuri sat. She pulled out the key and searched for the lock. "Kuri?" She whispered. "It's me, Rory."

"Rory? What are you doing here?" She looked around her. "Where's Lu?"

"Hiding behind the barrels." Rory fiddled with the key, placing it in the cage lock. It didn't work. "By Draconis!"

Kuri placed her hand on Rory's. "You need to leave. Now."

That's when Rory saw Kuri's cuff. She reached past the iron bars with the wooden key. Rory grabbed Kuri's wrist and shoved the key inside the cuff lock. It sprang open. She did the same with Kuri's other wrist.

"No, I'm getting you out. I just don't know how to open the cage." She placed her hand on Kuri's icy fingers, wet from the rain, then ran over to Nega's cage. Nega sat upright, having heard her at Kuri's cage. "Cuff please." Nega held out her wrists, and Rory unlocked them, then went to Riel. "Riel!" No answer. Rory called after him again, but still nothing. She walked around the side, seeing his hand in the corner. She reached in and unlocked it, only to find her own hand wrapped in his. He rubbed his thumb over her wrist. Rory looked into his questioning green eyes.

The rain stopped.

"You came back?" He asked, shaking his head. "You should have left when you had the chance."

"Yes, she should have," came Graus' loud voice from behind. Rory turned around. She gasped as Graus held Luiselle in front of him, his knife pointed at her throat.

"Leave her alone!" Kuri shouted. Nega growled, and the sound echoed in the town square.

"Now, why would I do that?" Graus asked.

"She's just a child!" Rory answered.

"She's not your child. What does it matter to you?" Graus sneered. "Or them?"

"I pledged to take care of her." Rory answered.

"What does it matter what you pledged?" Graus asked, jerking Luiselle around as he did. Rory's chest tightened. "She's in our care now."

Behind her, Riel grabbed her hand.

"Run, get out of here as soon as you have the chance," he whispered.

The rose pulled on her hair. Rory squeezed Riel's hand, keeping her eyes focused on Graus, who stood illuminated in the moonlight. "You'll help?" She whispered. The rose tugged again, and Riel squeezed her hand before letting it go.

"Step away from the cages," Graus ordered, so she did. She knew it proved that her friends were still behind bars. "Now come here, and I'll give the girl back to you."

"Rory, don't!" Riel hissed behind her. She looked over at Nega and Kuri, and they both shook their heads. She stepped out of their reach, towards Graus.

"Leave her alone!" Riel growled. "I shouldn't be in this cage. You know this." Rory scowled. She didn't want him to draw more attention to himself.

"What, because you have the king's favour?" Graus laughed. "He's hunted the rest of your kind down, and since you've done what he needs, he's done with you!"

Rory faced Riel, but his eyes were on Graus. "You're wrong. He gave me freedom."

Graus laughed again, the bitter sound echoing in the square. "Your freedom came with a purpose. And now, you completed your task, so he's given you to the *Beül.* Your brother, the king, has ordered *your* execution, just like all the others."

Rory froze, staring at Riel. His brother, the king of... *Kehl*? She glanced at Nega and Kuri, but they didn't react. It was true. His brother was the king of Kehl, which made him her-

"Move, girl," Graus called to Rory. "That's it. Come on. Hold your hands in front where I can see them."

Rory complied, walking forward to Luiselle. She held her hands together in front, fingers visible. She forced herself to focus on her friend. The little girl's face was determined, angry despite the knife at her throat. Rory raised her eyebrows and Luiselle nodded. Rory continued to step forward. Her fingers counted down.

Four. Left. Right. Left.

"Leave her alone!" Nega growled.

Three. Step. Step.

"Rory, stop!" Kuri called out.

Two. Step.

Riel growled, and it filled the square. She was close enough that she was a single lunge away from Graus.

One. Step.

None.

"Stop." Graus said. He tilted his head and stared at the side of Rory's head. The rose bloomed and spun on itself, glowing in the moonlight. "What is that?" He pointed his long knife at Rory, standing just out of arm's reach.

Rory nodded before Luiselle dropped the cuff and shrank with a pop. The cuff clanged on the stone walkway as she fluttered down to the ground, unseen by Graus. His arms widened, then he dropped the knife in favour of his sword. He saw the flicker of Luiselle's wings, and swung his sword toward her, but Rory lunged at him. She heard growls behind her as she knocked Graus over, grabbed the sword out of his hand, before jumping up. But the man grabbed her ankle, knocking her down on her knees as he kneeled over her. "Stupid girl!" he lunged at Rory with the knife in hand as she flipped over. His motion halted.

Graus's eyes widened as he looked down to see his own sword in Rory's hand thrust through his gut. Rory held it still as Graus stumbled to his knees in front of her.

"How?" He asked as his eyes glazed over, then fell sideways. Rory let go of the sword. She scrambled up, holding her trembling bloody hands out in front of her. Graus lay there, unmoving, with Rory frozen beside him.

Something light landed on her shoulder, and Luiselle whispered in her ear. "Get the keys off him, Rory."

Rory blinked, then moved. Her body shuffled forward like she was back in the river, fighting the current. She fumbled and jangled the keys; aware she made too much noise but unable to stop shaking. She got the keys free and ran back over to her friends. Kuri's cage was closest, so she fumbled through them, unable to find the right one.

Kuri placed her hand on Rory's, and Rory looked up into her eyes. "Deep breath. Use the iron one." Rory grasped the key, shoving it in the lock. It clicked, and she remembered. If any of their kind tried to grab it, they'd hurt themselves trying to escape. Rory swung open the door, offered her hand to Kuri, who stumbled, trying to get out. Luiselle flew off Rory and onto Kuri. Once on solid ground, Kuri stretched as Rory opened Nega's cage with the same key.

Nega's lock opened, and the ogress flinched as Rory helped her out. She looked down and saw Nega's open wounds from the iron yesterday.

"Sorry!" Rory whispered. Nega grunted, got out, and pointed to Riel. The ogress grabbed Graus' knife and searched for any other weapons on him. She found another sword strapped to his back.

Rory unlocked and opened Riel's cage. As she helped him out, his nostrils flared, his eyes turning to slits in front of her. "I told you to get yourself out." He growled as she helped him.

"I couldn't leave you, any of you," she said, swallowing. "You helped me when I deserved nothing from you. I consider you friends."

Riel landed on his feet, and they looked around.

The crow sat at the edge of the square. "Which way?" Rory asked.

The crow leapt into the air, flapped his wings, and headed down another laneway. Rory picked up Graus' bloody sword. All five of them followed the bird. They went down the alley and found a shack leaning against the wall. There was nowhere to go.

Rory looked up at the crow. "What, here?" The crow flew over the wall, into the trees beyond.

"The cursed bird brought us to a dead end." Nega grunted.

"Psst!" a soft voice called from the shack. The spinner who spoke of the town's old ways poked her head from behind some slats.

"Who're you?" Nega asked. Kuri elbowed her.

"Anna and her gran sent me." She stepped out of the shack, held up her wrists, shackle-free. "Through there." She pointed to a gap between some boards before disappearing behind another one. Kuri shrugged, then went in, Luiselle on her shoulder. Nega grunted and gestured to Riel.

A loud crack sounded behind them, and Rory spun around in time to see Riel lunge in front of her. A projectile meant for her hit him. Riel landed on the ground with a loud thud. An arrow stuck out of his shoulder, made Rory scream. The Beül stood with a menacing grin on his face. He notched another arrow, but Nega threw Riel over her shoulder, and shoved herself between the boards. Rory pulled her pack forward so it wouldn't get caught and followed her. The *Beül* cursed behind her, as they made it outside the town wall. She shuddered, catching her breath, holding her hand on the carved stone wall, with the sword dangling at her side.

As her friends entered the forest beyond, the *Beül* grabbed her cloak from behind and yanked her back. Rory reached out, but the sword fell out of reach. Her pack fell open, and she grabbed the first solid object she could find. She yanked out the long iron bar, twisted and pierced it through the Beül's wrist, pinning it to the wall. He let go with a yelp of pain. He tried to grab her with his other arm, but Rory spun out of the way. She found a spiral carved into the stone wall, and ran her fingers around it, from outside in, and the wall closed behind her. It severed the *Beül's* arm from the rest of him. His muffled cry came from behind the town wall.

Fighting the bile rising in her throat, she grabbed the bloody sword and her things and ran off after her friends.

28

Rory pulled up her hood to hide herself from anyone following. She searched for her friends and stepped as silent as possible in the forest. Her heart raced as she tiptoed on the forest floor, her ears on alert for anyone following them. She would rather leave her friends behind than lead the enemy to them. The ring pulsed on her chest, sending sharp currents through her body, but she wouldn't risk Luiselle and the others. Rory spotted Kuri's marks on the trees. She followed the marks until she found the crow waiting on a stump in a clearing.

"Which way?" She whispered.

The crow cawed and hopped along a small hidden path she wouldn't have found otherwise. Rory stumbled on a root and came to an abrupt stop when a blade came at her throat. She swung her sword and held it back at the last moment. Her muscles tensed and prepared to strike.

"Lower your hood," a voice growled, but Rory sighed in relief. She lifted her hands slowly and lowered her hood, revealing the red rose at her temple. "Anyone follow you?" Nega sheathed her sword.

"None that I could see, but you should probably check, anyway." Rory turned to face her, surprised by the fear in the ogress' eyes. "What's wrong? Where are they?"

Nega gestured for Rory to follow her until they found themselves on a small grassy knoll. Kuri and Luiselle leaned over Riel, who lay motionless, blood staining the grass.

Rory ran over and knelt beside Riel, his face ashen. "Oh, is he...?" She looked up at Kuri.

"Not yet, but he's close," the elf answered. Tears streamed down her face. "I can't do anything about it!"

"Why not?" Rory put her fingers on Riel's shoulder, but he flinched in pain.

"The iron arrow," Kuri whispered. "It won't let him heal."

Tears streamed down Luiselle's face. "We... we can't... pull it... out."

They stared down at Riel until Nega broke the silence. "You do it!" Nega shoved her forward.

Rory jumped back. "I can't, I'll hurt him."

Nega held up her blade to Rory's neck. "It's your fault he's hurt. You will help or I will-"

"Stop!" Kuri pushed Nega's blade to the side. She looked at Rory. "He's *dying*, Rory. You won't hurt him any more than he already is. We've tried pulling it out." Kuri held up her hands, blisters, and open wounds all throughout her palms. Luiselle revealed hers, injured the same way. "Please, you need to try. Nega already cut off the tip. We just can't get the iron shaft out."

Rory nodded, then crept close to Riel again. He wheezed, his face haggard. He was her friend, so she took a deep breath, nodded to herself, then looked at Kuri and Nega. "I need you to keep a lookout, Nega. Kuri, you hold him down. I think this will hurt." Rory reached for the shaft, sticking far enough out that she could just wrap one hand around it. Riel groaned as she did, and she stopped breathing for a moment. She pressed her other hand on his chest, then looked at Kuri, who held his shoulders.

She forced her breath out. "On three. One. Two," Rory took a deep breath. "Three." Rory yanked the shaft out as hard as possible and Riel kicked her off, crying out in pain. Tears formed in her eyes as she realized the rod was still stuck. At least more of it came out. She crawled back over to his writhing body. Nega joined Kuri, and they held him down as Rory stepped over him, one foot on either side of his ribs. She bent her knees to get as much momentum as possible. Kuri nodded to her, and Rory counted down again. This time she yanked right before three to keep Riel from tensing up. The rod came free and Rory stumbled back, falling on her rear.

Riel shifted into a large black dragon and knocked them all to the side. He came at Rory. His enormous claws pinned her down, his sharp teeth inches away from her face. She covered her face with her hands, still holding the shaft.

"Ease up Riel!" Nega yelled, punching his nose. "She pulled the shaft out!"

Riel shook his angular head, blinking slowly as if his green eyes needed to refocus. He pulled his head back slightly, and Rory held up the bloody iron rod. He sniffed at it, blinked at her again. Then he pulled his massive claws away, releasing her. He shifted and stood in front of her as she stood up.

"Rory?" He whispered, before swaying. Rory tried to catch him, but he fell on her and pinned her down again. Nega rolled him off her, then offered her a hand back up into a powerful embrace. Then Rory suddenly found herself back on her feet. Rory looked over at Luiselle and Kuri, who both smiled. She glanced at Riel, and his shoulder wound was gone.

"He'll be fine!" Kuri said. "He just needs to sleep it off." Rory nodded.

Nega punched her in the arm, knocking her off her feet again. The ogress grinned from ear to ear. She helped Rory back up, less forcefully this time.

"I knew you'd be useful."

29

R IEL AWOKE TO METAL clanging. The sharp sound of swords crashing against each other set him on edge. He rolled into a crouched position, ready for whomever was attacking.

They're hunting me now, too.

The battle sounds circled around him, starting from his left and moving to his right. Nega's growls of frustration filled the air, and Riel reached to his sides for a sword. There were no weapons nearby.

The clanging grew closer, and Riel clenched his jaw. A flash of light captured his attention from his far right, just beyond his peripheral vision. He faced the movement, and found Kuri bent over, talking to Luiselle. The disdainful crow glared at them. Kuri and Luiselle didn't even notice the flurry of activity going around as Luiselle released a flash of purple into the trees.

At least they weren't experimenting on him. Luiselle already turned him into a rabbit, making him shudder at the memory. He never wanted to be prey again.

Kuri looked up at him and smiled with her sharp Elven teeth, so he waved. Luiselle spun around and ran over and launched herself at him. She gave a solid hug for such a little child. The faerie held on for several minutes, causing him to pause before wrapping his arms around her, careful not to crush her tiny frame. He didn't deserve her kindness. She pulled back and stood at eye level with him sitting on the ground. Both her hands went to his cheeks, and she smiled, then kissed his nose. A tingling sensation spread out from the small peck, warmth spreading through him as he took in her blessing.

The tenderness caught him off guard. Tears stung his eyes, and he blinked them back. He'd done such horrible things on behalf of his brother that he didn't deserve her gift. Or her kindness,

"You are not your brother," she whispered in a deep voice far beyond her years. Her face grew serious, her lavender eyes cloudy. "You have been bound by an oath forced on you, and you will redeem yourself in the end." Then her bright smile lit him up again, and she bounded off to Kuri, who watched their exchange with a pensive smile. Riel shoved his guilt down and chose her simple acceptance instead.

The clanging sounded again, and Nega growled, followed by more clanging. It stopped, then started again. Then stopped.

"Again!" Rory's voice echoed, demanding more training.

Riel joined Kuri and Luiselle. "What's going on?" He gestured in Nega's direction.

Luiselle didn't look at him as she answered. "Kuri's teaching me how to hide messages in the trees for others to read." She looked up at him. "Then I hide them, except for only the person I want to see."

"She's brilliant." Kuri smiled.

Luiselle beamed as another flash of purple lit up the root of a nearby tree. "Can you read it?"

Riel squinted and made out marks on the tree. "I can, well done!" he told Luiselle, then gestured again to Nega and Rory. "And them?"

Kuri sighed. "Rory hasn't stopped since she woke up. I don't think Nega's ever had such a keen student, and she was the Ogre clan's trainer." More clashes sounded, and Kuri sighed again.

"How come?" Riel asked.

"She's mad," said Luiselle.

There was more clanging as Nega growled. Kuri sighed again, then looked up at the sun in the sky. "They're going to wear each other out, and then what?"

"I'll try to stop them."

Riel rolled his shoulder, happy to feel nothing left of his injury thanks to Rory. He headed towards the training, past a stream, and found them in a small clearing. He watched Rory move with light footsteps, a new fierceness focusing her. Rory advanced on Nega, more skill now than when she'd first started training, no hesitancy in her step. Nega still defended herself with little effort against Rory. The ogress had trained since she was a child, but Rory didn't hold back. Twice,

Rory advanced until she forced Nega to step back and reconvene. When Nega knocked Rory's sword out of her hands, Rory stomped after it, her brown hair blowing behind her.

"Again." Rory turned to face the ogress.

"Enough girl." Nega crossed her arms over her chest.

"No, not until I get it in my muscles. I have to get the movements right." Rory flexed her hands, fresh red welts on her palms.

"You need to rest." Nega said. She didn't budge from her stance.

"I need to practice." Rory flinched, drawing her sword.

"Nega's right Rory," Riel stepped closer. Nega's shoulders relaxed. She gave him a toothy grin as she made her way towards him.

"But..." Rory glared at them.

"You try talking some sense into that girl," Nega retorted, placing a heavy hand on Riel's shoulder. "Good to see you about." She glanced at his shoulder, concern in her eyes, but she blinked it away and walked toward camp.

Riel moved closer to Rory. She held her sword up, ready to fight, despite her trembling hands. "Put it down, Rory."

She glared at him, still holding the blade, then shook her head. "I need to train."

"You haven't trained long enough to push this hard. Your body needs rest in order to absorb what it's learned." He pressed her blade down, then took it from her hands. Clasping her elbow, he led her back to camp, towards the stream. She flinched when he crouched down and pulled her down beside him. He pulled her sleeves up and pressed her blistered hands into the water. Bruises ran up the length of Rory's arm from where Graus manhandled her. Riel fought back his growl to focus on her injuries. She had trouble unfurling her hands from the grip she used to hold the hilt of the sword. Riel massaged her hands and, one by one, stretched her fingers out. She made a sound between relief and pain as he smiled. "How will you spin if you do this to your hands?"

Rory shook her head. "Spinning doesn't matter anymore."

"Of course it does. You have a gift for it." Riel lifted her chin with one hand. "Why are you doing this to yourself?"

She flinched and looked away from him. "I need to be better."

"Better at what?" He massaged the tendons between each of her knuckles.

Rory looked over his shoulder at their friends. "I almost lost her. I couldn't defend myself against my... those people, and it nearly cost us our lives." She glanced at her hands, held by his under the water. "For two days, I missed training. You, Nega, and Kuri would have died because you were helping us."

"They would have hunted us, anyway." Riel warmed her frozen hands between his own. "You could have left us there."

"Not after everything you've done for us." She looked up at him. "You could have taken Luiselle with you and left me behind. She'd have been better off if you had. You saved me in the river. You could have let me drown. And you'd be rid of one less human." Rory looked over his shoulder again.

Riel's heart stopped for a moment while he paused his movements. "So you felt you had to help us?" He swallowed.

"No, yes... no." Rory gazed at the sky, then her hands, then back at him. A light blush crept across her freckled cheeks. "It's not repayment. You... well, you matter." Riel relaxed as he thought about her words the night before. She thought of them as friends. "I don't know why you agreed to help us. But at some point, you'll move on, hopefully after we get Lu home." Rory's shoulders dropped. "I need to be ready."

Move on? Riel shivered.

Rory didn't notice and kept on talking. "I killed Graus." She tried to pull her hands away from Riel, but he held them in his own.

"Rory, he was a horrible man..." He ground his teeth, glancing again at the bruises on her arms.

She shook her head. "I know. I feel bad that I took a life, but I don't regret saving Luiselle, and you." She shrugged her shoulders as a tear made a path down her cheek. "I didn't mean to. It was an accident. He could have killed me. He *should* have killed me. I wasn't good enough." She looked at her hands. "I failed you."

"You got us free," Riel said. "You saw Nega's arms in that cage. We couldn't get out. The iron made it impossible. Stop punishing yourself for something you have no control over." Riel reached out and wiped away another tear. His fingers skimmed the rosebud, and it bloomed before returning to its place at her temple. He brushed a lock behind her ear as his hand cradled the base of her neck. Rory's blush deepened. "You heard the Beül, he was going to come after me, anyway. Thank you for your bravery, for coming back for us. No one has ever done that for me... or for us before." Rory's eyes widened when Riel leaned into her, placing his forehead against hers. His other hand still held hers out of the water. He stilled, for the first time in the years since they forced him to take his oath. The quiet of her presence was out of place here in the forest and escaping his brother, yet it gave him peace.

He pulled back, engulfing both her hands in his, his thumb caressing the soft skin. Rory opened her mouth, then closed it as she glanced down at their hands, biting her lower lip.

Riel smiled at her nervous movements.

Her brow furrowed. She pulled her hands out of his and stood up and away from him. He let her go, his peace disappearing. "Riel?" she asked.

He knew he would not like her question. "Yes?"

"Are... are you really the bro-"

Nega's shout rose through the forest, and Riel jumped up. He grimaced in empathy when Rory grabbed the sword despite her pain, then ran quietly towards their friends.

They halted when they found Nega standing over a dead man with a sword sticking out of his armoured shoulder. The man had dark hair and a similar build to himself. They could have been cousins.

Riel approached Nega first. "From the town we left?" He asked her.

Nega nodded. "Likely a scout."

Rory came up behind them. "Which means more are on their way."

"We need to go, now." Nega said, as she and Riel started digging beside the dead man. Kuri and Luiselle started packing up camp.

"What are you doing?" Rory asked.

"Burying the body so they don't find it when we leave."

"Wait!" Rory turned to Riel. "Do you always shift into the same clothing?"

Riel frowned, unsure what to make of Rory's question. "Whatever we're wearing shifts with us. Part of our training."

Rory smiled at him, a spark in her eye, and Riel leaned towards her. "Nega has killed him with a blow to where they injured you. If you change clothes, he'll look like you. At least long enough to give us a head start."

Nega smiled. "I'm liking the way you think."

Riel did too.

30

Ilse gestured at Claude from across the courtyard. He stepped away from the sea of sycophants and walked with purpose. No one questioned his movements as he crossed over to the other side. As he arrived, Ilse bowed to him, clasped her fist over her heart, and gestured for Claude to move over to the side. Claude found her behaviour odd but kept his face neutral. A king never revealed his thoughts to anyone. His father taught him that. Turning to the side, he found a foot soldier; a runner by his manner of dress, carrying the *Beül's* symbol.

"What news?" He asked the young man.

"I have a message for you, my king." The young man bowed, and as he did, lifted a small scroll in his right hand, the blood red seal sloppily inscribed.

"Any additional words from your master?" Claude arched one eyebrow at Ilse as she shrugged.

"Only that he requests your answer as soon as you might offer it." The young man bowed again before standing at attention. Ilse had trained this runner well.

"Very well." Claude gestured for the young man to go, and Ilse took him to a guard positioned nearby. The guard escorted him to get food and rest. She returned, but stayed far enough away that he knew she couldn't eavesdrop. With the young man gone, Claude broke the seal to read the scroll while he paced along the vaulted corridor. His steps echoed off the stones, the sound disappearing into the throng of people in the courtyard. He glanced at Ilse and tried to make sense of the coded words.

The girl was *alive*? She was supposed to be dead. That's why he'd sent his soldiers to Elsass. He'd received word after her escape that she was staying near the Chateau. His men flushed her out, and she'd been on the run. Now, she had escaped the *Beül's* clutches with an elf and an ogress.

Nega! Claude's stomach turned at the thought of his cousin. If there was an uprising, Nega's warrior skills and connections with the unnatural would be instrumental. But how did the girl find such guardians? If Kuri and Nega were involved, Riel was too. The three of them had been friends since they were teenagers. *Had Riel broken his oath?* No, Claude witnessed the effects when Riel tried to break his oath before, his body writing in pain when he refused his king's demands. Riel could not deny him. Their father had made sure of that.

He reread the letter, gripped it as he studied the next lines. Riel was dead. Could it be? They'd found his body outside the village, where they escaped the *Beül* in Elsass. Even stranger was that the *Beül* was missing an arm because of a spinner. He reread the paragraph again. The spinner tested as a human but made the wall close in on itself. How *did* she escape? Was she human, or unnatural, like the rest of them? Did she develop some special tolerance to iron?

Claude looked up and closed his eyes. An iron tolerance among the unnatural would hinder his plans. Was it magical? If so, could she give it to the other unnatural folk? He'd developed weapons and armour with their weakness in mind. He gripped the letter, but forced his hands to relax before he crushed the note in front of Ilse. Though he trusted her, Ilse possessed the ability to read people far faster than anyone else he'd ever met. She'd had to, or she wouldn't be here.

"What is it, my lord?" Ilse came to stand beside him.

Claude fought the urge to pinch the bridge of his nose. He forced his voice to be calm. "The *Beül* requests I send ten of my best men to the Flachland because he's found the girl." He resumed his pacing instead. Motion while in thought gave him clarity.

"What for?" She walked beside him as he paced the length of the corridor, protecting the side that faced his guests. "If he's found the girl, he can bring her to us." At the end of the corridor, they turned and paced the other way. Ilse remained at his exposed side.

"He doesn't have her. Instead, he believes she's going to the Rätsel cave." Claude paused for a moment. Ilse did too. Allowing the girl to reach the caves was dangerous. He veered to the wall, where a torch lit the corridor.

"Shall I prepare the men to meet the Beül there?" Ilse's skirt swished as she spun around to face him. Her dress looked decadent, fitting her slight frame and position as proxy, but Claude knew she had weapons stashed in her dress. Only a fool would assume she was without power.

"No." He set the letter on fire on a nearby torch, then dropped it to the ground and ground out the embers. "Send your top one hundred."

Ilse's hands clenched at her side. "So many? After getting attacked by the Cave Kala, many of them just returned to their homes. Some of them injured."

Claude nodded. "At once. Inform the runner that the *Beül* was mistaken. The body they found was not Riel's." He turned around as Ilse bowed to his wishes. "Prepare my horse for tomorrow, and my personal guard."

Ilse paused in her bow. "Are you certain, your highness?"

Claude faced her and narrowed his gaze, but she didn't flinch. She straightened her body. While he respected her bravery and sense, he didn't appreciate how she challenged his judgement. She knew better than to question him.

"Am I to join you or to remain here?" Ilse remained calm and didn't cower under his gaze.

"You stay here." He smiled, but he knew she didn't feel any warmth in it. "I will join them on the plains, and we'll make sure Riel never poses a threat again."

"As you wish, my King," Ilse bowed to him again.

When she raised herself, he dismissed her. He resumed the party and took his place on the throne. After a few minutes, Ilse returned to his side, guarding him from any threats. He didn't expect any from within the castle. It was the threats outside of it which had him on edge. If the spinner could create an iron tolerance, had she also relieved Riel of his curse? Claude spent the rest of the night with a smile plastered on his face, wondering how his brother might betray his oath to him, when the curse should prevent it.

31

THEY WALKED FOR SEVERAL days and didn't come across any Kehl soldiers. Their routines were the same, despite Rory's exhaustion. They'd get up early. Nega would train her for a couple of hours while Kuri trained Luiselle and Riel manned the fire. The crow hopped around on his good foot, cawing at them as if he were telling them to hurry. Then they would break their fast, pack their bags and move on their way.

Kuri would leave messages for the refugees, and Rory would leave them whatever food remained uneaten. She swore the crow rolled its eyes at her when she did, but she didn't care. The refugees needed sustenance.

Luiselle's magic grew stronger thanks to Kuri's training, but her wing remained broken, and she could only flutter around in a spiral. Kuri said it was beyond her ability. Faeries required the healing of other faeries for these kinds of injuries. So they kept going. The ring on her chest pulsed, sending heat waves through her body. Enough to remind her of her oath, but it didn't hurt. She sensed if they went off course, it would change.

Rory didn't mind the reminder. Each step to take Luiselle home was another step to meet up with the Seeress. A sense of nervous energy ran through her fingers as she wondered what it would take for the Seeress to remove the curse she placed on Rory. She would inform the Seeress about the injustices the king of Kehl performed. Rory was sure the Seeress would understand and remove her curse. Then she'd break her proxy marriage and stand up to him.

They cut through the forest, stayed close to a stream, and worked their way to the Rätsel caves. As Nega reminded them, it would take a couple of weeks

146

to get there. *If only we could fly there.* After looking at Riel, Rory regretted her thought. As much as the ring weighed heavily on her chest, constantly pushing her to follow through on her promise to Reinhold, she knew they would spot Riel in the sky. As dangerous as Riel was in his dragon form, he would draw all the *Beül*'s army on her friends.

Especially, it would seem, her brother-in-law. *Your brother, the king, has ordered your execution, just like all the others.* Rory stole glances at Riel, decked in the Kehl armour. It suited him. Did he look like her husband? She could only imagine.

Riel caught her glance and smiled. She blushed, ashamed that though she admired him, she lied to him and the others. Riel didn't know her marriage made him her brother-in-law. None of them knew who she was. To them, she was simply a shepherdess who learned to spin, taking care of a faerie. They accepted her, welcomed her. Even Nega offered her... well, if not friendship, training and mentorship. So far, Nega showed her how to defend herself with a sword, and how to use her staff against one. Kuri's acceptance came with knowledge she shared about the forest and the refugees. The elf showed her what materials Nega used to make her arrows, so Rory started picking up flint and straight pieces of maple. She'd also spun some string for the tail, thin and even. Rory would leave them on Nega's blanket when she took the night shift, a small token of thanks for all her training. She was grateful they spent their time outdoors, because it kept her from thinking of their company as anything more than friends, and their motley group from succumbing to her curse.

They travelled through the forest, always in the same order. Nega up front, with Kuri close behind her, Luiselle in the middle, Rory, then Riel bringing up the end. She'd glance back to make sure Riel remained behind her. When his eyes shifted into a dragon's, Rory would focus on the forest, looking and listening for threats. When human, he'd smile and wave. She would look quickly away and keep going, focusing on Luiselle's constant chatter instead.

Today, they were heading down the side of a hill, the forest floor getting wetter as they descended.

"Shut up, you foul bird!" Nega growled. Most of the time, the crow half hopped, half flew near Luiselle. Today the crow was up near Nega, cawing at her. "For the last time, I know where I'm going." Kuri looked back at Rory. She rolled her eyes and stuck her tongue out between her jagged teeth, making Rory and Luiselle giggle. "I don't know why you're even here, but if you don't quit bugging me, I'll eat you for dinner!" It was no idle threat. They'd eaten many birds Nega had hunted over the last few days.

Distracted from trying not to laugh, Rory tripped over a branch, but Riel grabbed her by the elbow.

"She's mostly kidding." He said, grinning at Rory.

"I think he enjoys tormenting her," Rory answered, smiling back.

"Just because the girl trusts you doesn't mean I have to." Nega shooed the crow away, but he flew simply above her head, flapping his wings, just out of reach.

"Crow," Rory called out, "let her be. We don't want her distracted."

The crow landed on a branch nearby, waiting for Rory to pass by. Rory offered the crow her staff, and it landed on the hooked top, glaring at Nega. Nega looked back at Rory and the crow. The ogress pointed to her eyes, then back to the crow, before turning around and leading them into the forest.

Rory looked up to find Luiselle, Kuri and Riel staring at her. "What?" She blushed under their combined questioning glance.

"What made you offer it your staff?" Kuri asked softly, tilting her chin at the crow.

"It can't really fly through the tree canopy. It's too thick. And it has a broken leg." Rory looked down at Luiselle's glazed expression, then turned to Riel. "Why?"

"It's just, you look like the…" Riel stopped speaking and looked over Rory's shoulders at Nega and Kuri. Rory turned to see what Riel stared at. Willowy blue flames surrounded Nega and Kuri at their feet. The individual flames appeared to float just above the ground, burning nothing.

"Oooh, pretty!" Luiselle bounced on her toes before dashing forward. She reached out to touch one.

"Wait!" Rory called out, but Luiselle ignored her. Rory ran up to her, Riel close behind.

"Silly wisp. Why are you so far from the water?" She asked them, holding her palm out. The little flame leapt onto her hand and fluttered happily at her. "Where is your Navka hiding?" The rest of the blue flames hopped over to Luiselle, surrounding her, sitting on her head, embracing her with without setting her on fire.

Looking up at the others, Rory asked, "Navka?"

"Wisps are usually part of the water sprites," Kuri said, glancing sideways to Nega.

"But she called them Navka," Nega whispered, her voice deep as she watched the flames with wide eyes. Her green skin paled into a yellow colour, despite the blue light from the flames.

"What does that mean?" Rory asked.

Kuri gestured to Riel, who ran his hands through his hair. "It's hard to explain," he started. Luiselle giggled at the flames and Riel sighed. "They are eternal, able to lead the person who sees them to the desires of their heart. Or sometimes, lead men to their deaths."

"So if we desire the Rätsel caves, they'll take us?" Rory asked, smiling until she saw Riel's eyebrows furrow.

"Not necessarily," Kuri answered. "They'll take you to your desire, not to your destination, unless they're the same."

Rory looked at the blue flames, then back at her friends. "So, I may feel obligated to take Luiselle to the caves, but if it's not what I desire, then they won't take me." Rory stepped closer to Luiselle, to stand between her and the flames. She thought about her oath, and her kingdom, unsure which one held more of her desire.

"Precisely," Riel laid his hand on her arm, and stopped her from getting too close. "They aren't pure of heart, Rory. Sprites cause mischief. Especially the Navka. They enjoy vengeance."

"You're all treating them reverently, suspiciously. They're different from the usual water sprites?" Rory looked at Kuri, who nodded. "How?"

"The wisps normally come from water sprites, but there are no large bodies of water here," Nega said quietly, her wide golden eyes still staring at the flames. The ogress wrapped her arms around her waist, as if to protect herself from wisps.

"So they aren't where they should be?" Rory asked. Nega nodded without looking back. "What makes a sprite wander from what gives it power?"

"That's the thing," Kuri answered. "They might be new, searching for a place to rest or tied to something else." Several wisps approached Nega, and she stepped away from them. They paused and went back to Luiselle. The flames ignored the rest of them.

"If they are not at rest, then where are their spirits?" Rory asked.

"That's a good question," Riel whispered, staring at the blue flames. "Because Navka spirits come from very young children."

Rory's eyes widened, and she spun around and stared at the flames. "They... were children?" Her voice cracked as her hand covered her mouth.

"Yes," Luiselle looked through the flames. Her expression was soft and determined. "And we must give them peace."

"How?" Riel's voice cracked as well.

"By finding out why they remain, or burying their bodies," the faerie answered. The others nodded, an unspoken agreement to help the Navka setting their path. The ring pulsed, sending tingles through Rory's system.

Luiselle lead them now, chatting with the wisps, but the others remained silent. They glanced at each other as they slowly picked their way through the forest. Night fell, and the crow called at them incessantly. Riel took up the rear again. Kuri would reach out and brush Nega's fingers from time to time. She'd pull back when the ogress didn't wrap her larger fingers around the elf's smaller ones. The crow swooped over Nega's head several times, but she didn't even yell at it. Her golden eyes focused on the blue flames fluttering around the faerie's head. Rory had never seen the ogress look so pale. Nothing phased her except for these blue flames. Rory shivered.

Rory's ring pulsed heat repeatedly into her chest, occasionally with some sharp pains. She rubbed it and whispered for it to have patience.

The crow dived at Nega once again, but Rory hissed at it. The crow landed on a branch and stared at her. She held up her staff, so the crow could settle on it. "I get it. You want us to get to the Rätsel caves? I do too. But I can't just pick Luiselle up and take her. She'll just turn into a faerie and leave. She wants to help the Navka."

The crow rumpled its feathers, gripped her staff tighter with its good foot, and hunched its wings up over its neck.

"I don't have a say."

"*mrph.*"

"No, I don't have a say. I'm not in control here."

The crow ruffled its feathers again, then turned away from her.

"Do you talk to all the wild animals, or just the birds?" Riel stepped beside her, opposite the crow. His mouth curved up at the side, so Rory elbowed him. Riel bumped her to the side, still grinning, as she straightened and pulled away.

"I've had birds as friends for some time. Back at the-" Rory swallowed and looked ahead. "Back where I grew up, there were no others my age. So I opened up my window and left crumbs for the birds."

"Bribery?" Riel asked, his grin still in place.

"I guess so." She shrugged. "They were beautiful to watch, and I let my imagination fly away with them when they left. I... felt trapped, and they looked like freedom. They still do." She glanced at the crow, then back at Kuri and Nega, who finally held hands. "So, no, not really friends. I always wanted to fly. Must seem silly to a dragon." Rory rubbed the ring on her chest, the ache in her heart matching the heat radiating from the ring. "Any way, they're probably still back home. There are different birds here."

Riel brushed his fingers against Rory's elbow, and she looked into his thoughtful eyes. "I've seen them feed you berries and other bits of food. That's something a friend would do."

Rory smiled faintly at him, then looked at the crow. "But not him. He's on a mission."

Riel laughed, large and throaty. "That he is."

Kuri and Nega looked back at them; brows furrowed. "Grow up, Riel. This is a solemn procession." Nega growled.

"What's with her?" Rory asked Riel.

"I'm not sure," he answered her, watching the ogress. "So, where did you grow up? You weren't always a shepherd. Someone taught you to card and spin. Where's home for you?"

Rory rubbed the spot on her chest where the ring sat, thinking about how to answer. After a moment, she settled for the truth. She owed it to her friends. "I lived at the cha-"

Something sharp poked Rory in the neck. She looked up to see Riel reach out to her, as she rubbed the spot, and found something solid there. She pulled out a wooden dart with a black feather tied to it.

"Rory?" He asked. Or she thought he did. His mouth slowly made an 'O' and 'E' shape, but she didn't hear a sound. Her vision darkened around the edges, and she watched as the shadow of the crow flapping its wings expanded around her until everything turned black.

32

T HE CROW LANDED AT the old woman's entryway and dropped hard onto his injured leg. He flapped his wings to maintain his balance, but barely succeeded. Once he leaned on his good foot, he set down the feather he carried in his beak and shrieked, trying to get the Seeress' attention. When nothing happened, he did it again, hopping around. She came out, peered at him, then offered her staff as a perch. He grabbed the feather and flew up to her cane.

She looked past him, her gaze narrowed. "You failed me again?"

Before she could channel her anger, he lifted the feather in his beak, holding it in front of her eyes. She focused on it, practically crossing her eyes, trying to see it, until she looked back at him. She held out her hand, and he dropped it in.

The crone rolled it between her fingers, examining it. She sniffed the feather, then the narrow point. "Not poison." She smelled it again. "It didn't hit the girl, but the human?"

The crow bobbed his head, listening to her.

"The child is safe with the others?"

Another bob.

"Good." The crone's violet eyes darkened until they were almost black. She gazed beyond him, over the cliff edge to the forest below, but the crow understood she saw the Navka. He waited until her eyes resumed their natural colour. "The human is still alive for now, but she's in trouble." She grabbed a cluster of berries off a nearby plant, then brought the crow inside. He hopped over to the nearby perch while she boiled some water and grabbed herbs, throwing them into the pot. She selected some dried flowers hanging near the fire, and threw them in too.

When the mixture smelled foul, she pulled it from the heat, waiting for several minutes before swirling the berries in the concoction.

Once the berries dried, she held them out for the crow to take. He held his beak away. "Take it. It's your fault she didn't follow you as I asked. It will prevent her trial."

He tilted his head sideways, smelling the foul things, and stifled a gag. It came out like a garble caw.

She gripped his body until sharp pains jolted through him. "Take it, or I'll leave you in this body forever. And I'll make sure you live for a long, uncomfortable time." Another jolt of pain travelled from his beak to his good foot, making all his feathers feel like pins where they connected with his skin.

"*Mrph,*" was all the answer he gave. He gingerly picked up the berries by the stem and avoided touching anything she dipped in her pot in his mouth. She again offered him her staff as a perch and carried him outside.

"Don't return without them." She rubbed her fingers down his feathered back. A sharp tingle ran through his body, making him shudder. "Give these to the human to eat. You know I mean it. I have waited long enough for the girl to come back to me, and I will not fail."

She lifted the staff in the air, throwing the crow up, and he flew back to the human and her group, carrying the berries with him. He just hoped he wasn't too late.

33

R ORY LAY ON HER back with something pointed shoved against her shoulder. Her head throbbed; her mouth was dry. She opened her eyes, squinting at the repetitive black shapes in the sliver of light. Her body shuddered with the dampness, teeth chattering. She tried to lift herself up, but pressed her hands against her belly instead. They were bound with rope. Had she made it? She wiggled her feet and found them bound, too. She rolled over onto her side; her face rubbed against something thin, cold, and wet. It was only then she recognized the regular drum of the rainfall.

Rory blinked her eyes repeatedly as she sat up. The repetitive black shapes were metal bars, iron painted with a thick coating. She looked up to see wood slats covering her cage and below her was the same, with wet straw shoved into the corner to sleep on. The iron bars had a sheen of water. Raindrops pummelled her head. She looked at her body, her cloak was missing. She pressed her hands against her chest, sighing when she found the ring still tucked under her tunic. Her heartbeat pounded as the ring pulsed heat through her. It wasn't enough to warm her up, but it reminded her of the pain that would follow if she failed in her oath.

Rory lifted her hands and brushed her wet locks out of her eyes. The rose sat in a tight bud above her ear. Wood slats above barely kept the rain out, soaking her and the straw. The cage was small enough she couldn't stand or stretch out in it. Her heartbeat raced as she swallowed, struggling to breathe despite being in the open air of the forest. She blinked again, focusing her vision, searching for her friends. Nothing moved. But someone put her in a cage. *Where is everyone?* She

154

listened for her friends, sounds, anything. As far as she could tell, she was alone in a cage in the forest. She forced herself to breathe deeply, to focus on the things she could feel, taste, and hear. The sound of the rain. The raindrops on her face. But nothing slowed her heartbeat.

A growl came from behind her. She spun around and fell on her stomach, arms pinned underneath her. She faced a large brown bear that stalked on all fours towards her. It growled again. She shoved herself as far away from him as she could. It sniffed the air, then walked around the cage. Rory tried to circle away on the opposite side, but tripped over her own bonds. She found herself on her elbows and knees as the bear came close to her face, and sniffed her just outside the bars. She kept incredibly still, waiting for it to move again. Her breath came out in ragged wisps, heating the surrounding air. The bear growled again, its teeth bared, as she focused on the sharp yellow canines, the ends stained red from whatever it had just eaten. Rory swallowed hard. The bear roared at her, and she closed her eyes. Someone had darted her, and left her to die by a bear. When she opened them again, she stared into its eyes. They were ice blue.

"You're a shifter!" Rory gasped. She shoved herself into a kneeling position and looked the bear over. It was a normal size, its pelt clumped together from the downpour. "You're amazing!" She whispered in awe.

The bear smiled at her, then transformed into a giant heavily bearded man wearing a cloak that steadily got wet under the downpour. He stood at a ready position, his hands clenched into fists, his eyes focused on her. "Riel said you would figure it out."

"Is he…" Rory swallowed as the ring on her chest pulsed. "Are the others okay?" The man tilted his head and stared at her. Rory shifted on to her rear, then sneezed. She pulled her knees in front of her and hugged them in the cold. "What?"

"You're bound, in a cage, in the rain. Likely getting sick." He combed his fingers through his brown beard. "And you're worried about them?"

Rory nodded, the ring pulsing under her shirt sending slight shocks into her chest. "They charged me with the care of the little one. The others…" Rory sighed and looked around into the forest.

"The others?" The man crossed his arms in front of his broad chest.

"Riel, Nega and Kuri don't trust me to take care of her, so they were helping me return her home." Rory sighed and leaned back in the cage, resting her back against the iron bars. She closed her eyes, tears falling down her face, mixing with the raindrops. "I don't blame them. I would have left her in their care, but I couldn't." She looked back at the man, but he remained still, his arms crossed. "Will you please tell me what happened to them?"

"They're fine, and nearby. Among friends."

Rory nodded, sighing. "Thank you." Her friends were safe. Luiselle was safe and among friends. She'd failed, but they would take care of her. Her body relaxed.

The ring sent a jolt through her. She didn't flinch, but it was strong enough that she knew it would get worse the longer she sat in the cage. In the end, it might not matter.

Would the curse end with her death? She hoped so for Muriel's sake.

He resumed his stance, crossed clenched fists over his chest, and stared at her for a few moments. "That's it?" He asked sharply.

Rory furrowed her brows, looking at him. "Yes. Why, is there more?"

"You're in a cage, but you don't care?" The man remained still, but his body stiffened.

Rory smiled with just the corner of her mouth. "Not all cages have iron bars. At least there is fresh air in this one. My cloak would be nice to have, but since it's probably soaked, I guess it doesn't matter." He uncrossed his arms for a moment at her comment, then crossed them again with more determination. "You are not the first to control my life. I think you might be the last." Rory sneezed. "When you're ready to let me know what happens next, I'll be here," she said, gesturing with her bound hands to the surrounding cage.

The man scowled, waited for a moment, then uncrossed his arms. He shifted into a bear, then roared at her, and stalked off back into the forest nearby where he disappeared as if he'd never existed.

"Well, Jean?" Riel asked the bear as he lumbered back to them. Their group sat around a fire under a shelter with refugees. Riel clenched his fists. The bear shifted in front of him. They could see Rory from this position, but Jean's group had put up a magic shield which kept her from seeing them.

"You were right. She figured me out pretty quickly." The bear shifter crossed his arms over his enormous chest. "And she didn't care for herself, only that you four were okay." He stood there, staring down at Riel.

That's Rory. "Will you release her, then?"

Jean sighed and sat down beside him, both of them facing the cage where Rory sat. He gestured to the others seated nearby. "They're adamant that no humans pass by us or know our group. They're already rumbling that she should be dead. If it weren't for you defending her when we showed up, she would be." He shrugged his shoulders. "The only reason she isn't is because they are afraid of *you*."

Jean went silent as a few grey jays approached Rory, berries in their beaks. They slipped through the iron bars, laying them at her bound hands. She lifted her hands, one finger stuck out, so the male bird could hop on. She nuzzled its head with her forehead, checked the berries, then lowered him to his family. They slipped outside of the cage, heads tilted until she sneezed, and they flew away. Rory stared for a moment at her hand before she ate their offering. The rose in her ear stayed tight to her head.

"Never seen animals trust a human enough to feed her." Jean finally said.

"She's not like most humans, at least not with us." Riel snapped. He took a deep breath and released the heat in his breath out to the sky. Rory's face was pale, and she trembled. He wanted to blow warm air on her, to warm her up. He wanted to blow extra heat on Jean for putting her in the cage. But Jean didn't deserve his anger.

Jean looked Riel over. "You're going soft, dragon."

Riel narrowed his gaze and shrugged. "She saved our lives. She risked herself and the faerie to release us from the human town and closed the magic door on the *Beül*'s arm." Jean just stared, his face neutral. "When she thought Luiselle was in danger, she killed the man who held her."

Jean grunted, but his face remained blank. "You think she's brave?"

Riel snorted, remembering the staff she'd thrown up his nose. "It was foolish to come back when she should have kept going. She's stubborn." Riel smiled, unclenching his fists when he thought about Rory pushing Nega to train her harder. "But we're alive now because of her."

Luiselle suddenly climbed into Riel's lap. He let out an *oomph* of surprise as her elbows hit him in the gut before she settled down. "She pulled out the iron shaft from his shoulder. He tried to hurt her until Nega punched him in the nose." Riel rolled his eyes.

"Did she now?" Jean asked, smiling at Luiselle. Riel rolled his eyes. Legends of Jean de l'Ours always forgot to mention how much he adored the little ones. It didn't exactly feed his gruesome reputation. "What else did she do?" Riel hugged Luiselle tight, hoping she didn't betray her friend unwittingly under Jean's new interrogation technique.

"I see what you're doing." Luiselle said in an older voice. Her lavender eyes turned violet for a moment, making Jean shudder. Then her voice raised back to its normal childlike quality as her eyes returned to their normal shade. "Rory's always been kind. To me, to the birds, to the squirrels, to Nega, Riel, and Kuri. I don't know if she was kind to Genezra, but Genezra trusted her. Along with Hannah, and..."

"Genezra trusted her?" Jean asked.

"Yes! And Rory spun this beautiful gold and silver wool that Hannah's grandmother found." Jean opened his mouth to speak, but Luiselle kept talking. "When they paid her for the gold chain she'd made, Rory gave some of the money to Hannah's gran for the wool, but the soldiers got mad at her."

The birds came by, twittering at that moment, so Luiselle broke off pieces of the bread she was eating to give them each a sizeable piece. The three jumped off her lap and ran over to Rory,

"What are they doing?" Jean asked Luiselle.

"They want her to have enough food." Luiselle shrugged. She looked up at Kuri, who waved to her, then jumped off Riel, elbowing him again in the gut. She settled in Nega's lap, ran her hand on the ogress' cheek as Nega stared at the fire. Nega had done little else since they joined the group. A pit settled in Riel's stomach as he watched his friend relive some sort of trauma from her youth.

"Well, it's clear the faerie trusts her." Jean ran his fingers through his beard. "Does she know about everything you did to her faerie kin?"

Riel swallowed hard, shaking his head. "But what do you think of Rory?" He trusted Jean's opinion. They had often played together as children. Jean was one of the few men who could match his strength.

"She reeks of magic. It's all over her. Some of it ancient." Jean stared at Rory. "But none of it is hers. The group would allow her to live if it were."

"Jean," Riel growled, "I can't let you hurt her."

Jean faced Riel with his eyes closed, pinching the bridge of his nose. "You would destroy the remnant you created to save one human?"

Riel sighed, the pit in his stomach growing. *Please, please don't take us to the Beül!* Riel closed his eyes against the reminder of their cries for mercy. Faint aftershocks spiked his body, reminding him of the oath's pain when he fought against Claude's orders. He did everything he could to hide this group, and ended up lying low for months, shuddering underneath the pain of breaking his oath, even if it was only partially broken.

"Nega said you were now on the Beül's hit list because your brother released you. You are one of us now. The only reason they haven't tried to kill you for your crimes on behalf of your brother was they knew you were bound, forced to hunt us down. And they need you." Jean narrowed his eyes at him. "If you hadn't warned us about what was coming ahead of time, we wouldn't be here. And I wouldn't trust you at all." He crossed his arms over to his broad chest, eyes widening. "Did you swear an oath to her?" Riel shook his head. "Did she bind you to her?"

"No, I just..." Riel ran his fingers through his hair. "She calls to me." There was no pain. He simply enjoyed her presence.

Jean nodded again, then stood up, offering his hand to Riel. "It's not for me to decide, it's for them," Jean gestured to the refugees. Riel stood up after accepting the hand. "Come, the rain has let up, and they are about to show her why she must die. It would be best if you didn't get in the way."

34

R ORY NIBBLED ON THE small crumbs the birds brought her, as the bear shifter appeared in view in his human form. The rest of her group appeared with him, and Rory breathed a sigh of relief as they stepped forward, as if through an invisible curtain. Luiselle and Kuri each held one of Nega's hands. The ogress was lost in thought. Her gaze focused on something beyond Rory's cage. Rory looked behind her to see the Navka wisps gathered in a group. They glowed in the dim light, an eerie blue flame in the damp grey. Even though there were over forty of them, they swayed, synchronized. Rory shivered, then sneezed. The wisps kept dancing, not even flickering with the noise.

She turned back to her friends, watching as others came from behind the mysterious forest wall, each materializing through... nothing. Luiselle tried to run up to Rory, but Kuri held her back, and whispered to the child. Luiselle nodded and held her hand. Rory's heart stopped as the ring pulsed a sharp pain through her body, and she gasped for breath. She longed to wrap her hands around Luiselle, but at least the girl wasn't hurt.

Rory looked around at all the others. They were all different, some looking more human than others. None of them were friendly. Only one other child stood among them, studying her. This one held no fear. Riel glared at everyone, his eyes now in their dragon shape. He, Luiselle, Kuri and Nega stayed back.

The crow landed nearby the cage, hopping over on his good foot and laid some berries between the iron bars. It cawed, and Rory shook her head. It flapped its wings and cawed again, and she took them. "Thank YOU!" She sneezed the last word. She pulled out a small square of fabric from her tunic, tucked the berries in, and waited. Something was about to happen. The solemn faces made her shiver. The crow cawed again, but she focused on the bear shifter.

He walked up to Rory's cage and stood before everyone. He avoided eye contact with Riel yet looked at the others. Finally, he raised his hands so everyone could focus on him. "The dragon vouches for the human," he stated, his voice strong in the fading daylight.

Gasps rang out from the others. Some of them stared at Riel, some of them spit in disgust. Most of them growled. "She's seen us," one yelled in a deep voice. "She's human, so we can't trust her." Others yelled their agreement. But some of them sobbed. Rory watched them, women, many of them not much older than her. They held each other, a mutual understanding which bonded them together in pain. Their tears were hard to make out after the rain, but they trembled, eyes wide, watching her.

They're afraid of me?

The bear-man raised his arms until the group settled down. "They will plead her case *after* we plead ours."

"Jean," Riel broke in, stepping forward to the bear shifter. "She's on your side, I swear. She ruined the-"

"Enough, Riel." Jean yelled. Riel clenched his fists. Jean turned his ice-blue eyes on her, and she shivered. She couldn't tell if it was from them or the cold. "They will now speak for the dead."

"They?" Rory asked.

Jean gestured over her shoulder to the blue flames behind her. Rory turned and watched them glow brighter, then sway forward. One by one, they approached her cage, floating as they surrounded it. As one, they glowed as bright as day, despite the late hour. The blue light surrounded her. From one breath to the next, she stood in a blue forest, alone.

"Hello?" Rory called out, but the forest was empty. She looked around for her animal friends, but nothing moved. She peered up at the leaves. They remained still and dry, not heavy with water from the rain. Rory looked around, reached down to touch the earth. Her fingers disappeared beneath the soil, but she felt nothing. When she pulled them back up, they were clean. A screech cut through the silence. She stood up and spun to face the noise, her hand on her chest. The ring pulsed just as another screech came from behind her. Rory whirled around again. But there was nothing. Another screech echoed behind her, and she turned slower this time.

"Hello? Who's there?" The screech came again, and Rory whirled around. Her heart raced. "Please, I won't do anything to hurt you."

They all say that.

Rory startled, her body tense. She spun to face the voice but found nothing.

"Who says that?" Rory asked.

Your kind.

Again, it came from beside her ear, but Rory didn't spin this time. She took a deep breath, closed her eyes, and whispered. "My kind?"

Humans, the whispered voice hissed.

Rory sighed. "I'd like to tell you we're not all like that. I hope we aren't. But I've met some horrible people."

You don't deny it?

"I wish I could." Silence met her statement. Rory glanced around at the muted forest while she waited. The ring pulsed against her chest with its own rhythm. "Are you still there?"

We are.

"We? May I know who you are?" Her heartbeat thundered in the silence.

We *are Navka.*

"And what do you want with me?"

You are to bear witness to your crimes.

"My crimes?" She pressed her hand against the ring as it pulsed again.

Those of your kind.

The ring warmed her hand. Rory took a deep breath, then nodded. "Show me," she whispered.

Are you sure?

"You want me to bear witness? I will."

"Then come with me." A small hand placed itself in Rory's, and she discovered a small child, only five, standing beside her. The child looked up at her, blue skin pulled tight to its cheekbones. Hairless, it wore a cloak too big for its emaciated shape. The child smiled, sharp pointed teeth a mere distraction from the blue flames dancing where its eyes should be.

Rory shivered as they stepped forward.

The forest shifted before her, and Rory held the Navka's hand at the entrance to a castle. She looked for the familiar tower where she grew up. This one was more severe. It sat embedded in the mountain peak. She faced away from the castle wall and gasped as vertigo overwhelmed her. Steep steps were carved into the mountain the castle sat on, leading down below into the mist, into nothing. Rory flung herself back against the fortified walls, the large drop making her head spin..

"Silly girl. This is not real." The Navka child said, smiling with jagged teeth. Its voice was small, high pitched, but with a hiss that made the hairs on her arms stand on end.

"It looks real." Rory took a gulp of breath.

The Navka shoved Rory forward, and she flailed her arms, losing balance. She screamed, and circled forward, until she saw the Navka, upside down. She spun and floated back up, then kept spinning, no friction to slow her down.

Rory's stomach turned. "Um, how do I stop?"

The flames danced around in the Navka's eyes, mocking her. Suddenly, Rory was upright and standing beside the castle entrance again.

"Where are we?"

"The Kehl stronghold. Follow me." The Navka disappeared through the wall.

Rory's jaw dropped. "Um..." she rubbed the ring on her chest, and it pulsed once. "It's not real." She whispered to herself as she put her hand on the wall. No longer solid, she nearly fell through, coming face to face with the Navka's teeth.

I'd rather be near Riel's jaw, she thought as she stood up.

"And you would be wise. The dragon still has its heart."

"You heard my thoughts?"

The Navka smiled again. "Of course. We hear all." It turned and swiped its skeletal hand on the walls, which pushed past them in a blur, the floor moving. Rory blinked, fighting a wave of dizziness. They descended the stairs until they found themselves in a corridor full of metal bars.

"Is this... a dungeon?"

"Please, look around." It gestured towards the corridor.

Rory stepped forward. As if a bubble popped, she found herself thrust into a world of sound. The ring heated as Rory heard the wave of pain surround her. Moans, groans, sobbing, shrieking. One wail caught her attention, a small cry she would recognize anywhere. Rory glanced back at the Navka, but it gestured her to move forward. Rory stepped towards the familiar cry until she found herself outside a tiny prison cell. A hooded figure towered over a small child. Rory's heart pounded, and she clenched her fists.

"Tell me where she is!" A masculine voice demanded. Its smooth tone was familiar, but out of place.

"I don't know!" The little girl sobbed.

Rory's heart cracked. *No! It can't be.*

"It is," the Navka said from beside her.

"How..."

The little girl screamed in pain as the hooded figure reached over, then held up an iron knife and a thin piece of bloody sheer fabric. Not fabric! It was the thin gossamer material of a faerie wing. Bile rose in Rory's throat, but she swallowed it down. The hooded figured moved to the side, revealing faint lavender eyes, wide open with terror, her mouth open in pain.

Rory threw herself at the figure, but instead of tackling it to the ground, she fell through, landing on the other side. She glared at the Navka, then looked back at bloody faerie wings. One hand covered her mouth as she reached forward to her friend, her other hand disappearing through her.

A soldier appeared, stepping through the Navka into the room.

"Your highness," he bowed, ignoring the scene in front of him. "There is a letter from Elsass that arrived. It requires urgent attention."

"Very good. I'll be right there." The hooded figure crouched down near the faerie's face; his face now visible to Rory. Green eyes like Riel's stared down at her. "You're spared for now." He ran a bloody finger down the side of the faerie's cheek, as if caressing it. "You *will* tell me."

"I don't know..." she whimpered.

Rory watched the man stand up and leave with the soldier. His stride, his size, everything about him just like Riel, except for the golden hair colour, where it should be jet black. She shook her head and then looked down at the little faerie. Luiselle's tear-stained face stared back at Rory without seeing her. Small blue flames appeared one by one in the prison cell. Rory brushed her intangible fingers against Luiselle's tiny cheek. Luiselle passed out.

Rory studied the Navka, and the room shifted as they found themselves in another forest.

35

R ORY STOOD IN THE forest and faced the Navka. "Are we back?"

The Navka smiled its toothy grin. "No, somewhere else." The Navka glided across the forest floor, through the ground cover and trees without disturbing them. "Follow me."

"If you can shift us anywhere, why not bring us closer?"

The Navka twisted around and stood directly in front of Rory, sneering. "I thought you may need a moment to recover. But if you prefer..." The skeletal hand waved through the air, and the forest flew past them until they landed in the middle of an open plain full of...

Red seeped into everything in the plain, a deep rust colour, so much liquid it squished underneath Rory's feet. "Is that blood?" She looked at the Navka, whose flames dimmed in its eyes.

"We forget how much blood there was." The rasping child's voice was a quiet whisper.

Rory took the Navka's bony hand in hers, as she knelt down to face it. "Were you here when this happened?"

Startled, it peered at her, its mouth hanging open. "We were." It said, cautiously.

"You want to show me?"

It nodded. "So you will understand why you need to pay."

Rory gulped. Her palms were sweaty, but she held the Navka's hand, and hoped the Navka wouldn't notice. "Show me."

The Navka nodded. It led her to the edge of the plain, where the trunks of trees were covered in red. Rory shuddered. How many suffered to create this much of a stain on the plains? The Navka held Rory's hand and squeezed it tight. Rory squeezed it back.

Rory looked at the broad leaves that reminded her of her country's banner. She paused. "Is this Elsass?"

The Navka tilted its head sideways. "It is." It pulled on her hand, leading her to the forest. "Come."

A scream sounded from inside the forest, followed by a woman crying, "No!"

The Navka closed its eyes, and shuddered, but continued drawing Rory near. Another woman shouted, followed by more women screaming. "No, please stop!"

Rory dropped the Navka's hand and ran towards the sound.

"Why are you running?" It asked her, staying close, but exerting no effort. "It has already happened. You cannot stop it."

But Rory ran through the trees, avoiding branches as she continued. She stopped when a woman stumbled from behind a tree, crying out in pain. Not a woman, an ogress smaller than Nega. Her green hands covered her lower torso, organs spilling out. Her face twisted in agony. Rory stepped forward to help her, but the ogress collapsed.

Another cry sounded from nearby, a woman crying out. "Please, no, stop! My-"

Rory ran around the trees to get there, but stopped short when she saw a Kehl soldier cut open a pregnant troll's abdomen. The troll screamed as the soldier pulled the baby out of her womb. He threw it on the ground and crushed its head. He made a noise of disgust as the baby wriggled, then died, born too early to live. The troll stared at its dead child, a silent scream on her dirty face as the tears rolled down her cheeks.

Rory covered her mouth as her stomach groaned, then stumbled sideways and fell to all four limbs. Nothing came out, she dry heaved. A skeletal hand touched her shoulder, making her jump at the unexpected touch. The Navka's flames grew bright. "You must keep watch and see."

Rory wiped her mouth and looked at the troll, who lay watching her child, eyes glazed over, tears still flowing. Rory studied her again and remembered the face. "She's one of the group outside my cage, comforting each other?" She looked at the Navka, but it too stared at the troll.

Another soldier approached as the first cleaned its sword on nearby leaves. "Are they all disposed of?"

"Yes," the first one said. "The King of Kehl's order to eliminate the unborn is fulfilled."

"Do we bury them?" The second looked around at the carnage. Their helmets hid their faces.

"Nah," the first one said. "We're to leave them as an example to the others." He walked away, leaving the second one behind.

The second soldier waited a moment, then knelt down. He drew a rune in the sand and created a small body of water. "I'm so sorry, little ones. May you find peace." Then he followed the other soldier.

Rory watched, tears freely falling, as over forty flames emerged from the forest, floating over to the water, which spread. They circled the water, entranced, watching it grow, drawn toward it. As Rory watched, her Navka guide drew near to it, too.

"This... they, are you?" Rory whispered.

"They are."

Rory knelt beside the Navka child and took its hand in hers. The Navka squinted at her, tilting its head sideways. It reached with its free hand; a single bony finger wiped away the tears from Rory's cheek. The flames stared at her, and it pressed its lower lip up into the upper lip. "Why are you crying?"

"Because," she hiccupped. "Because this is *horrible*." She wiped her eyes with her sleeve. "You were right. I needed to see this." She squeezed the Navka's fingers. It looked at her hand. "But I have a question, if you will please answer."

"You may ask."

"How..." Rory gulped. "How long ago did this happen?"

"Two years ago." The Navka answered. "What does it matter?"

Rory sighed and looked up. "It matters to me, because they invaded this land before there was a proxy marriage between the kingdoms. It is an act of war from the King of Kehl on Elsass." She squeezed its hand again. "But either way, I understand your pain better." She looked over at the troll, lying there, still breathing, her eyes shut. "I understand their anger better."

Rory stood, still holding the Navka hands. "Is there anything else you want to show me?"

"No," came a growling voice behind them. They both turned to see Nega standing there, her axe in hand, pointed at the Navka. "You. Release her."

"She must pay." the Navka said.

"How did you-" Rory started, but Nega stepped closer to them. Her axe aimed at the Navka child.

"No," she shouted. "You leave her alone. You leave us all alone."

"Nega? What are you doing?" Rory stepped between Nega and the Navka, holding its hand to keep it away from the angry ogress.

"Rory, you fool. Don't protect them. They're going to kill you! They first torture you with their memories," she gestured around her. "Then they steal what's left of your soul before handing you over to someone who wishes you harm."

"She must pay!" The Navka flashed their teeth at Nega.

"For what?" Nega snarled back. "Did you know she feeds the wildlife?"

The Navka's hand jerked in Rory's.

"Did you know that for months she set aside food at the markers near the chateau for the refugees who passed by?"

The flames in its eyes flashed brightly before returning to normal.

"Nega," Rory argued, "I don't think you need-"

"Did you know that the faerie child trusts her? That she crushed the arm of the man who chased after them?" Nega pointed the tip of her axe, then suddenly lunged at the Navka.

The Navka cried out, and Rory caught the sight of more blood and a tiny crying ogress child, before everything went white.

36

R IEL WATCHED RORY CRY, reaching out to something he couldn't see. The Navka flames cast her in a blue glow, and she'd crawled around the cage talking to them. When she'd looked in his direction, blue flames replaced her brown eyes. He fought the urge to shift, to take out the refugee remnant and save the feisty human caged by the Navka. She stopped crying, whimpering instead "Lu!"

Riel stepped forward to help her, but Jean held him back. "She must bear witness," Jean said.

Nega twitched beside him, and he looked over at her, green hands clenched at her sides. Kuri and Luiselle stood on her other side, Kuri's face reflecting Nega's pain. He looked at their joined hands, Nega's hand squeezing the smaller so tightly, she was likely to break the elf's bones. He looked again at Kuri, who nodded at Nega's face. The ogress' gaze stared at the blue flames, as if she couldn't look away.

Riel grabbed Nega's wrist, and she turned to him. Her eyes also glowed with blue flames. "Nega?" He asked. She didn't blink. "Nega, can you see what's going on?"

"Some of them were there..." she said, her deep voice flat.

"Where?" He asked her.

"At the little faerie's torture." Nega turned back to the blue flames.

Riel focused on Luiselle, who also watched the Navka. "Lu?"

The little girl looked back at him, tears on her face. "I saw them there. I thought I was going to be one too."

169

"You see what they're showing her?" Riel asked. Luiselle shook her head. Riel looked at Kuri, her eyes closed shut in pain. "Can you?"

"No," Kuri whimpered. "Only those who have born witness to the Navka can see what they will show."

He glanced at Rory, who started dry-heaving, unable to vomit. He looked back at the ogress. "Nega? What's happening?"

"So much blood…" she whispered, her lower jaw trembling. Nega gasped. "Messa!" She dropped to her knees. Riel and Kuri looked at each other. "Messa, what have they done?"

"Who is Messa?" Luiselle asked.

"Nega's childhood friend," Riel answered.

Kuri frowned, dropping to her knees beside Nega. She ran her fingers against Nega's cheek. "Nega, my *Fürstin*, what's wrong?"

"Get her out," Nega whispered.

Jean came over to their group. "What's wrong with the warrior?"

"I'm not sure," Riel answered. "She can see what they're showing Rory."

"What? How?" Jean spun around to Rory, who kneeled, holding her hand to… nothing.

"No!" Nega yelled, standing up. Everyone from the refugee camp faced her. She dropped Kuri's hand, reached for the axe at her side.

"Nega?" Kuri asked, her voice high.

"Nega!" Riel yanked her arm.

The ogress ignored him, raising the axe toward the cage. "You. Release her."

Riel's nails grew longer, his teeth elongating as his dragon tried to shift. He turned to his old friend Jean. "What are they showing her?"

Jean watched Nega. "How they became Navka. How does the ogress know the Navka?"

"No, you leave her alone," Nega growled. "You leave us all alone."

"They approached her as a child," Kuri answered, as Riel looked back at the flames, surprised.

"Rory, you fool. They're going to kill you. They first torture you with their memories," Nega gestured around her, facing Rory. "Then they steal what's left of your soul before handing you over to someone who wishes you harm."

Riel looked at Jean, whose face went white. "Is this true?" Riel asked. "They're going to take her soul?"

"She's human. They have no soul!" One refugee cried out.

Riel's vision shifted into that of his dragon. He growled at Jean, then glared at the others. "What did you say?"

"For what?" Nega snarled. "Did you know she feeds the wildlife?" The refugees glanced at Riel, then at Jean.

"Nega!" Riel called to her, still holding her wrist. She yanked it out of his grasp, stepping forward.

"Stop her," Jean called out.

"Did you know that for months she set aside food at the markers near the chateau for the refugees who passed by?" Nega yelled, stepping forward.

Gasps came from some refugees behind them as they whispered to each other.

"Nega!" Riel stepped forward to stop her, but she approached the Navka circling Rory's cage.

"Did you know that the faerie child trusts her? That she crushed the arm of the man who chased them?"

"She hurt the *Beül?*" One woman asked.

"She did," Kuri answered. She massaged her crushed hand. "Rory saved us. Saved her." Kuri gestured to Luiselle.

Nega pointed the tip of her axe, then lunged at the flames.

"Nega no!" Riel ran after her, but it was too late. She brought the axe down in between two of the flames. A white light flashed. It spread out and knocked him down as he came behind her. He heard screams behind him. His first instinct was to shift, but he held back. Rory and Nega needed him. He sat up, the white light gone, Nega on one knee outside of Rory's cage. The blue wisps surrounded them both.

Riel looked at Rory, checking her for life. The blue flames in her eyes disappeared, and she reached out to the ogress. "Nega!" Then she dropped.

"Rory!" Riel ran, compelled to reach her. He touched her through the iron bars, burning his arm as he checked her pulse. She was still breathing, and he breathed out his fiery anger, withering the nearby branches. He turned to Nega, tears streaming down her face. The Navka surrounded her. Riel growled at them. "Stay away from her."

The Navka combined into one flame in front of Nega, shaping into a child. It reached down to touch the ogress on the shoulder. "You have nothing to fear from us, ogress. You helped the others like us as a child."

"Nega?" Rory whispered. Riel turned to see her roll over on her side, staring at the ogress. Tears flowed down her cheeks.

"I'm fine." Nega said, then fell over. Kuri rushed to Nega and cradled the ogress' large green head in her lap. She held her hands on either side of the ogress' head, sending orange light around it. The light faded, and she groaned before opening her eyes.

The Navka pulled away, looked at Nega, then back at Rory. "Why do you cry?"

"She was just a little girl." Rory sat up and hugged herself, staring at Nega. Riel wanted to pull her in his arms. "So much loss. They were her friends, and we took them all away." She sniffed. Then closed her eyes, took a deep breath, then opened them. "May I speak to them?"

The Navka watched her for a moment, then looked to Jean, and the women behind him. Riel saw some of them straighten.

"You may speak," a troll said.

"I saw you," Rory said, gesturing to the Navka. "I saw what they did. I'm so sorry. I know it doesn't bring your children back. But I see you, and I see what they did... what we allowed to happen."

"Did you really feed the refugees at the Elsass marker?" The troll asked.

Rory smiled slightly. "It doesn't matter, does it?" Riel's stomach twisted. *Don't give up!* His body shook, tense and ready to shift, to defend her.

"She did!" Luiselle ran forward, reaching into the cage, missing the bars with her little arms. She pulled out a cloth, then ran back to the troll, handing it over. "Do you recognize this?"

The troll's eyes widened as she took the cloth. She turned to the others, and they spoke among themselves. A child among them drew their attention, and they listened to him before debating amongst themselves. He kept pointing to his leg. When the troll turned back, her gaze was determined. She marched to Rory, as Riel clenched his hands, waiting for a fight.

"Why did you feed us?" She demanded.

"When I needed help, a troll and a faerie took me in." Rory smiled to herself. "When they told me you were running for your lives, I wanted to help. I know it wasn't much." The troll narrowed her eyes at her. She stared for a moment. Rory took a deep breath, then Riel stepped toward her. "I'm ready." Riel's stomach heaved.

The troll looked to the Navka and nodded.

"She lives," the flames said, then disappeared.

37

Rory sat at the fire next to her friends, bundled in her nice, warm cloak. Luiselle sat on her lap, Nega on one side, Riel on the other. Kuri sat on Nega's other side. Rory caught Riel watching her and Luiselle, and she stared into his green eyes.

Warmth spread in her cheeks. "Thank you for warming up my cloak."

Riel sighed. "You were in the rain too long." He glared at Jean, who looked back at them and shrugged.

Riel glanced at Nega. She stared into the fire, and Rory put her hand on Nega's large green one. Nega looked at Rory, startled out of her daze.

"Thank you for coming in to get me." Rory whispered.

Nega grunted as she looked back at the fire with clear eyes. "Did you see any more?"

Rory squeezed her hand. "I witnessed what happened to the children you played with as a child. We are horrible to what we fear."

"Why should they fear children?" Nega asked.

Rory sighed. "They feared you as adults. In their minds, destroying children kept you from becoming what they fear." Nega huffed as Rory's words fall free. "They were wrong and foolish. They made you into what they fear."

"You're saying they had something to do with my skill?" Nega said through clenched teeth.

"No, your skill is beyond comparison to any soldier." Rory shuddered, remembering what the Navka showed her about Nega's childhood. "And your compassion too."

Nega huffed, satisfied.

"But they gave you anger to fuel your training, didn't they?" Rory asked. "Was it their faces you saw when you swung your axe?"

Nega closed her eyes. "Still do."

Rory squeezed the ogress' hand again. "Let me know when you're ready to train me again."

Nega smiled for the first time since seeing the Navka. "So I can pretend you're a Kehl soldier?" Her eyes sparked with mischief.

Rory smiled back. "As long as I get to pretend you're one, too."

"Then eat," Nega said. "I know you aren't hungry after what you witnessed, but you're going to need your strength." Nega peered at the faerie on Rory's lap. "Did you save her some food?"

Luiselle opened her cloak and pulled out some cured meat. Rory sniffed it, her stomach clenching, unsure of whether to put anything in her stomach. She took a bite, relieved when her mouth salivated and her stomach settled. She was hungry, after all. Luiselle got off her lap to sit with Kuri, who started training her in teasing flames out from the fire.

After eating, Rory pulled open her pack, pulled her carding combs, and worked her wool. She stopped occasionally to see Luiselle's progress. Luiselle pulled up a nice sized ball of flame, holding it just above her cupped hands. Rory took her carded wool and started the drop spindle.

"Excuse me, Rory?" someone behind her asked. Rory studied the shifter, though she couldn't tell what kind.

Nega and Riel shuffled beside her, their hands reaching for their weapons. Rory breathed deeply to show she was relaxed and blinked slowly at the shifter. "How can I help you?"

The shifter's eyes widened at her question. It swallowed, looked at both Nega and Riel, before answering. "Do you have any plans for the wool you're spinning?"

Rory smiled. The two at her side relaxed their stances. Rory looked down at the belt the shifter wore, which was tattered and well used after all their travelling. "I don't have enough wool to replace the rope you have, but I can trade my belt for yours?"

"No need." The shifter turned one side of its mouth up. It reached under its cloak and pulled out some of the softest, finest wool Rory had ever seen.

Rory's eyes widened as she stared at the wool. "This is from you?" At its nod, Rory smiled. "It's beautiful." She accepted the wool, going to work on the carding and spinning it. It was a dream to work with, running through her fingers like silk, and quickly became a solid rope. The shifter accepted the rope, tied it around its waist and rejoined the others. Rory smiled.

"You're not like any human they've met." Jean said, across the fire, his eyes narrowed.

"Because I'm not like the soldiers and the *Beül*?" Rory asked him.

Jean crossed his arms in front of his broad chest. "What's your point?"

"There are wonderful humans out there." Rory closed her eyes, thinking of Muriel and the other spinners. "The King of Kehl has an agenda. He's only going to put people in certain positions that will support him." Jean combed his fingers through his beard without speaking, so Rory continued. "The others may not support him. But if he knows they will not help him purge the refugees, he'll put someone in place who will. He won't place the refugee's supporters in a place to help them."

Jean tilted his head sideways, then looked at Riel. "We need a new King of Kehl."

"I can't." Riel sighed, eating his own meal. "You know I can't."

Rory felt a tug from her side. It was the crow, pulling something out of her pocket. "There you are. Where have you been?" It held the branch from the set of berries it gave her earlier. The branch looked smaller than she remembered. "What are you doing?" She asked the crow as it took the berries and flew off. Her eyes narrowed as her gaze followed the bird away and into the forest.

"You said he released you from the oath." Jean argued with Riel. "You should take up arms against your brother. You'd be a much better leader than he ever was."

Rory agreed. Riel would be a better king than Claude. She shivered, Claude's cold eyes and blonde hair vivid in her memory. *Too bad I am married to Riel's brother.*

"No one will trust me after everything I've done because of him." Riel picked something off the ground, clenching it in his hand.

"They will, because you can change things." Jean said.

"I'm still not free from it." Riel whispered.

"But... you said... they said..." Jean argued.

"That's what that idiot Graus implied before he died." Riel answered.

"Then how do you know you aren't free?" Jean asked.

"Because I still feel its weight, its draw." Riel sighed. "It's always there. He simply has to ask me to do something, and I won't be able to resist. I know it." He gestured to the group of refugees in the background, his fist clenched. "Even now, I'm fighting the draw to finish what I started for Claude with them." Something dark oozed out of his hand, but then he opened it and popped something into his mouth.

"You're in pain?" Jean whispered.

"It never goes away when I don't do as he's asked." He shook his hand as if he had more food in it. "I've just learned to live with it."

Rory wanted to squeeze his hand in comfort and support, but let him be. It wasn't her place. It never would be.

Jean grunted as Riel put something else in his mouth. Rory watched the two tense up. Luiselle sat back on her lap, distracting her. "Ooh, a berry!" she said. Rory thought the berry looked familiar and caught the faerie's hand.

"Don't eat that!" She knocked it out of the faerie's grasp, and into the fire, where it flamed into a bright purple colour.

"What was that?" Kuri narrowed her gaze at Rory.

Rory looked for the crow. "The crow gave me berries, then took them away. It must have fallen off the stem."

"It has the colour of the Seeress' magic!" Kuri looked at Rory. Suddenly, her eyes widened, and she crawled away, backwards. Nega stood up with her axe in a ready stance. Rory turned around as Riel shifted into a dragon. A wisp of purple smoke surrounded him. His clothing tore as his body bent oddly. He snarled and growled; pain clear in his face as he collapsed before becoming his dragon self.

38

"Riel?" Rory asked, as his angular dragon head swung around. His large body took over the entire camp. The refugees scrambled away as he snapped in their direction. Rory put Luiselle behind her, slowly backing up to the shelter of the trees. His tail slammed down behind her, preventing her escape. "Lu, fly away to Kuri," she said.

"But Rory, I don't want to leave you. I am not sure I can get to her."

"I know, but see if Kuri can help you figure out what forced Riel to transform." Rory said, keeping her eyes on the dragon, her hand out. "Maybe you can help him." Rory heard a pop and felt Luiselle land in her palm. She shifted the fairy over Riel's tail, which drew her to Riel's head. She leaned back as his sharp teeth came into view and closed her eyes. He inhaled, the motion pulling her hair forward. Rory opened her eyes as Riel pushed her behind his front legs. He growled at everyone else and snapped at the refugees.

"What is wrong with you?" Nega approached, axe in hand, and he growled at her. "Knock it off, Riel!" Riel's tail knocked Nega down from behind. Rory stepped out from around him.

Kuri and Luiselle appeared behind Nega to help her up. "The berries have a lot of magic." Kuri called. "I think it was supposed to knock you out, Rory!" Riel growled at them, then pushed Rory back behind him.

Rory punched his front elbow joint. "They're not trying to hurt you!"

He snarled at her and looked at the others. His wings came down and covered her from the others, forcing her to crouch underneath their heavy leather weight.

"He's got Rory!" Luiselle yelled.

Rory crawled out of the gap between his wing and the joint from his hind leg. She looked back to see Riel snarl at her friends and the refugees. On the side, some women cowered behind a tree, faces etched with fear. Rory recognized the troll and another from her journey with the Navka. The troll was going to call out, but Rory put her finger to her lips.

"Let her go, Riel," Kuri called out. "I know you want to protect her. We're not here to hurt her, or you."

He snarled back, taking a step forward. Rory crawled over to the women.

"What's wrong with him?" One asked.

"He's doing the bidding of the King of Kehl!"

"No!" Rory whispered. "He ate a berry that was supposed to knock me out. I think he's confused."

"What do we do?" One of them asked. Her voice trembled as her hands shook.

Rory felt for them. The last time they'd seen Riel as a dragon, the king sent him to kill them. She took the troll's hand. "I will see what I can do. Stay out of his way."

Rory heard a sword drawn and discovered Nega duelling with Riel's tail. Jean, now a bear, swiped at Riel's face while jumping away from his jaws. Rory snuck around to Kuri, who worked with Luiselle on something magical. Orange mist surrounded their hands. Kuri looked up, but Rory motioned for quiet.

"We think his human side is asleep," Kuri whispered. "It's temporary. We are trying to knock his dragon side out so he can return to normal."

Rory looked at the others, some of whom were trying to approach Riel in their animal shapes. Wolves, sheep, and a deer all stood near Jean and Nega, but Riel's tail knocked them out. A familiar-looking stag stepped up. They darted back in, ready to fight, so Rory cheered them on. They parried back and forth. Despite his size, Riel held back. He was still in there.

"We're ready," Luiselle whispered.

"We need to get close to him," Kuri said.

Rory looked around and saw a tree near Jean. "Over there. I'll get over and try to distract him."

"But Rory, you could get hurt again," Luiselle said, putting her hand on Rory's arm.

"Trust me, Lu." Rory rubbed her little hand. She found a few branches on the forest floor and picked up two. Rory got on all four limbs, ready to run.

"He's in there but can't get out. We're just going to help him." She looked up as Riel knocked Nega down, and he pinned her with his claws, teeth at her face. Kuri paled. "We need to go now," Rory said. Rory ran one direction around the dragon, her friends the other.

They took position, and when Riel's teeth came near Nega's head again, Rory launched herself out of the forest. She threw the first branch at Riel's head, wedging it into his nostril. Riel reared his head back, shaking to dislodge the branch but could not remove it. He pulled his front claws off Nega to swipe at the stick, and Rory rushed forward to pull Nega back.

Rory helped Nega out, and the ogress smiled sharp teeth at her. "You threw a stick up his nose?"

"He let you go!" They ran for cover in the trees.

A wave of heat hit Rory's back. She turned as Riel finished burning the stick to ash. She held another one and turned to face him.

"Rory, get back here!" Nega grabbed her arm, but Riel roared at them.

Rory shook Nega's arm off. "We have a plan!" She said as she stepped forward toward the dragon.

"We? Who's we?" Nega asked, then gasped. Kuri and Luiselle stepped out from the Riel's other side. Jean stepped with them. *Good. They had help.* "Rory? What are you..." Nega grabbed Rory's arm again, and Riel growled.

"Enough, you big dumb dragon!" Rory yelled, pulling her arm free. Gasps came from the forest as Nega called her name again. Riel narrowed his eyes at Rory, stepping towards her, and away from Kuri and Luiselle.

That's it.

"What is wrong with you?" Rory called out. The dragon huffed, his breath hot across her face. "Tone down the heat. It could burn someone." His next breath was cooler.

I knew he's in there!

Out of the corner of her eye, she saw Riel's tail inch towards her. She held her branch in her hand. He growled at her and snapped his teeth, but Rory was ready. His tail reached to knock her down just as his teeth snapped at her, and she hit him on his nostril. He growled again, picked her up with his claws and brought her near his nose. Her arms were stuck underneath his enormous claws.

"Rory!" Nega called out, appearing with the stag.

Riel growled at them, and Rory kicked his wrist, drawing his attention back to her. "They're trying to make sure you don't hurt me, you big jerk." She watched the dragon's eyebrows furrow. "I promise they will not hurt you."

He snarled. Rory rolled her eyes.

"They won't hurt me either. Remember? The Navka spared me."

He paused, then snorted, backing away from the others. He lowered Rory, but when he saw the other shifters, he snarled at them again. Suddenly, a burst of orange hit him from the side.

Kuri!

The dragon pulled Rory out of the way of the orange magic, holding her tight to his body. His dragon hands squeezed her tight, and she struggled to breathe. The orange glow increased, and the dragon fell on his side, squeezing her against his belly. His scaled body tensed, his tail thrashed around, aimed at whomever came close. Darkness covered her as his wings wrapped themselves around her. Rory gasped for air when his body relaxed. His claws loosened. Air flooded her lungs.

Rory struggled to move, still trapped by his claws next to his body. She felt his chest rise and fall behind her, but couldn't see anything. The wing lifted as Nega peered down at her.

"You okay?" She grinned.

"I can't move," Rory said.

Jean appeared and lifted the wing up, while Nega crawled in to free Rory. Even in sleep, his claws held her tight. Riel rumbled, and they all jumped back. The wing fell back into place. They waited a moment, then lifted his wing again, the rumble in time with his breathing.

"Is he... purring?" Rory asked. Nega frowned while Jean grinned. They tried to pull his claws loose, but nothing moved. Luiselle appeared on Rory's shoulder in her faerie form and started giggling. "What's so funny?"

"You're like his little doll."

Rory rolled her eyes. "I guess I'm going to be stuck here for a while." She just hoped he didn't roll over her in his sleep.

39

Rory GRIPPED HER SWORD tighter and searched the forest for movement. The crow landed on a nearby branch. It cawed and made a fuss, but she ignored it. She had to worry about Jean. *Where was he?*

Something hit her in the head. She looked up at the crow with a light branch in its beak, ready to drop it on her. She stepped to the side, and the crow landed on the rock beside her.

"I'm not talking or listening to you." She pointed at the crow with her sword. "Those stupid berries made Riel lose his humanity, and I blame you."

The crow tilted its head sideways.

"I know you're not sorry." Rory stepped forward. The crow hopped back. "She gave you those for me. To kill me."

The crow shook its head and ruffled its feathers.

"Just be thankful Lu didn't eat them. I don't know what they would have done to her poor little body."

Rory's rose rubbed her ear, tugged her hair to her right, and she spun around, just glimpsing an enormous shadow.

The crow cawed at her.

"Be quiet."

It leapt off the rock and lunged at her, knocking the hood off her head. She spun around as it swooped back towards her, but she pulled out her staff and knocked the bird on its shoulder. It cried out and landed, then hobbled over to a nearby rock. It cawed once, then lifted its wing to inspect the damage. Rory switched back to her sword.

"Oh, grow up, you big baby." Rory said. "You should have-"

Two enormous arms encircled her from behind and pinned her arms to her body.

"You talk too much," Jean growled behind her. "Now, what are you going to do?"

Rory lifted her right foot, but Jean moved to block her kick, so she shifted and thrust her left foot on the inside of his right knee. He grunted, stumbled. Rory knocked the back of her head into his face. It was enough that he loosened his grip. Rory ignored the pain in her skull and thrust her sword pommel at Jean's wrist, forcing his arm to fold away from her. She spun around and aimed the sword at Jean, prepared to attack.

"Well, that was creative." Nega said. She leaned against a nearby tree. "You know what you did wrong?"

"I got distracted by the crow." Rory said, relaxing her stance.

"And you didn't kill me," Jean said. He pinched his nose to stop the bleeding.

"I didn't want to hurt you."

"And yet you did. A soldier doesn't care if you don't want to hurt him." Nega explained. Jean shifted into a bear, then back. His nose was fine. Rory's headache remained.

"Go for it, don't stop." Jean said. "In battle, it's kill or die."

Rory threw the sword down. "Why does *anybody* have to die? Why can't everyone just live and let everyone else live too?"

"Because your kind doesn't want that." Jean whispered. The quieter Jean got; the more Rory worried. He stepped toward her as he spoke. "They started killing us because they don't want us around. Innocents have *died* because of the murder in their hearts."

"I know." Rory said.

"Do you?" He asked. He leaned over her, bared his teeth, his face inches away from hers.

"I saw it Jean." Rory swallowed down her bile, remembering the dead ogress, the babies, Lu... "I felt their pain. I just don't want to inflict that on anyone else."

"It's them or us." Jean said. He crossed his arms in front of her, forcing Rory to step back.

Rory sighed, picking up her sword. "There are good people out there." She thought about Muriel and the others under the curse at her chateau.

"Not enough, and not since the Elsass king died."

Rory looked at him, clenching her fists. "The king of Elsass was good?"

"Jean wouldn't have been a captain of just anyone's army." Riel answered, standing behind Nega.

"You fought for... the King?" Rory asked.

Jean growled at Riel. "Good, but also a fool. Making that cursed bargain with your brother." Jean looked at Rory. "I don't know what his highness was thinking, engaging with that lunatic. He might as well have just marched us over to our graves." He looked back at Riel. "No offence."

Riel shrugged. "None taken. Maybe he knew there were no other options. Maybe if there was peace with Kehl, there wouldn't be war and more of a blood-bath."

"Perhaps. In the end, it just made it easier for Kehl to take us over." Jean clasped his hand on Riel's shoulder. "*You* should be King of Kehl."

"We've been through this." Riel said.

"I know. Come Nega, I've worked up an appetite." He let go of Riel's shoulder and walked away. "Glad you're awake."

Riel and Rory watched them disappear back to the refugee camp. "More training?"

"I feel lost, like I'm behind the others." Rory stuck her sword into the earth. "How are you feeling?"

"A doozy of a headache. Nothing I can't handle." Riel pushed his fingers against his temple, then looked back at Rory. She rubbed the back of her head in sympathy. "Kuri said I trapped you when I lost control. Did I hurt you?"

Rory smiled at him, his brow furrowed. "No, but I was relieved when you loosened your grip after you fell asleep." Rory stretched out her arms above her head. "You don't remember what happened?"

"I was eating a berry I found. The next thing I knew, I shifted and thought they were trying to hurt you. And I guess I hurt you too."

Rory put her hand on Riel's arm. "I'm fine. And I'm so sorry you went through that."

"Why are you sorry?"

"The Seeress meant those berries for me." She drooped her hand from his arm. "The crow dropped them off for me to eat, but I didn't. I kept Lu from eating one but didn't realize you found one too."

"The crow brought you those? From the Seeress?" Riel's lip curled in a sneer while his fists clenched. "For what purpose?"

"I assume they wanted me to fall asleep before the Navka got to me."

"But you're human. One of those berries could have killed you," Riel reached out and grabbed Rory's elbow.

"I know," she whispered.

"And you still want to take Luiselle to her?"

The ring pulsed again on her chest, sending a wave of heat through her. She didn't need the reminder. "I have to."

Riel nodded. "Your oath?"

"Yes." But it was more now. *She would break the curse. She could turn the tide against Kehl.*

Riel ran his fingers through his hair. "I know what that's like. I made one like it for my brother, to always protect him."

"Why?"

"My father made me." Riel sat down on a nearby rock. "At twenty-two, I am the younger brother by two years. We have half human parents. Despite a half ogress mother and a half dragon shifting father, Claude was born human. I can shift, so my father made me swear I would always follow him and protect him." He buried his head in his hand. "I was a child. I didn't know what the oath meant. Not until I was a teenager, and Claude made me do things I didn't want to do. Refusal only brings pain."

Rory sat down beside him, placed her hand on his wrist. "And now that he doesn't need you, you're to be executed?"

Riel nodded, then rotated his right hand under Rory's left and held it in place. His fingers brushed her calluses, and her hand warmed, the feeling spreading up her arm. She stared at their hands as his fingers interlaced with hers.

Riel cleared his throat. "When we get Luiselle to the Seeress, would you consider joining us?"

"Us?" Rory looked into his eyes.

Riel smiled. "Kuri, Nega, and I." He scratched the back of his head with his free hand.

"You want *me* to join *you*?" Her heartbeat thundered in her ears.

"Sure," he paused and swallowed. "We could even find a place to call home." His left hand brushed loose hair that fell in front of her eyes. His fingers caressed her temple, and she blushed. The rose bloomed.

Home. Rory closed her eyes as the single word made everything in her freeze. She exhaled a sigh. Her head throbbed where she hit Jean.

Rory let go of his hand, stood, and stepped back as Riel followed suit. She turned away and pulled out her sword from the earth. "I can't," Rory said, then faced him. "Join you, I mean."

Riel smiled with a twinkle in his eyes. "Just think about it." She enjoyed this lighter side of him. "I could light the fires. We could arrange for you to spin with the sheep shifters…"

She could see it, everything he pictured. All of them laughing around a fireplace as Rory felt at home. Then, they'd all fall asleep, never to be heard from again. Tears stung her eyes as her heart dropped. She wouldn't do that to them. "Riel stop."

He took a step towards her, reaching his hand out to touch her cheek. "Nega and Kuri respect you." He persuaded. She wondered how to make him stop. "They would have a place of their own, and-"

"I'm married." Rory said, cutting him off.

Riel's eyes widened as he froze. "Married?" He yanked his hand away from her face. She shivered in the cool air.

"Yes." Rory looked down at her feet, then took a deep breath.

"Married." Riel's lips curled at the word, looking like he was going to spit.

"Yes." Rory blinked back tears and rubbed the rose in her ear. Its stem rubbed her finger for support. She took a deep breath. "For the last year and a half. My father arranged it, and I haven't met him yet. I wanted to talk to you about that. Because I'm married to someone from…" Rory swallowed, "from Kehl."

"Kehl?" Riel stepped back. "No wonder you don't want to fight the soldiers."

"Oh, it's not that." Rory stepped forward. "Its kind of…"

"Kind of what? Funny?" Riel's eyes flashed as he clenched his fists again.

"No, the thing is… I'm married to your-"

"Riel, Rory!" Came Luiselle's voice. "I need your help!" Riel spun around and stomped off towards Luiselle.

"Riel, wait, I need to talk to you!" Rory called out.

He turned around, faced her, hands clenched, jaw pushed out. "Not now." Her heart dropped as he walked away, taking all the warmth she felt with him.

Rory followed Riel back to the group, her hand on her chest. She clutched the ring under her shirt, and wished she could get rid of it, and everything it meant. It hurt to carry the symbol of a bond with such a heartless man. The ring weighed her down more than a millstone.

As she approached, the others were arguing with each other, forcing Riel to keep the peace. Rory looked for Kuri and Nega, but couldn't see them. Luiselle stood in the centre, holding something out.

"Rory!" Luiselle called out, running to her and hiding under her cloak.

"What's wrong?" Rory pulled open the cloak to see Luiselle, the little girl's dirty face streaked with tears. Rory looked back up at the others. "What happened?"

"Tell her." Jean's voice was gruff.

"It was an accident!" Luiselle said.

"She killed them!" One of the troll women said.

"She didn't kill them, she lost them!" argued a shifter.

Sheep shifter, Rory thought. "Who?"

"Nega and Kuri," Riel said, pinching the bridge of his nose. His green eyes flashed into their dragon shape as Rory pulled Luiselle's trembling body tighter to her. Not that she could protect Luiselle from Riel as a dragon. Not anymore.

Rory took a deep breath, then spoke to Luiselle. "Lu, please tell me what happened."

"They were training me," Luiselle started, then hiccupped. "Kuri wanted to see how tiny I could make Nega. She gave me these herbs and told me to pinch them as I chanted the words. Then they shrank. It was amazing! I could do both of them fast. But then they kept getting smaller, and I lost them! Now I can't find them." Luiselle cried. "I can't find them, Rory! And what if someone stepped on them? Then Riel and Jean are going to eat me!" She pulled Rory's cloak closed around her.

Rory looked up at Jean, who rolled his eyes. Riel's eyes remained dragon-like. He took a deep breath and ran his fingers through his hair, refusing to look at her.

Rory ignored her heartache and opened up her cloak. But Luiselle tried to hide and shrink herself into her faerie form.

"Stop Lu! Stay human!" Rory said. Her voice echoed in the forest, making almost everyone jumped at her tone. Everyone except Riel, who glared at her, and Jean, who raised an eyebrow. Luiselle stayed a child but trembled.

"I'm so sorry, Rory!" Luiselle said, sobbing big heaves that shook her entire body as she stood in front of Rory.

"Lu, please calm down. Deep breaths." Rory knelt down in front of her, held her tiny chin with one finger so she could see into her eyes. She lowered her voice. "Did Kuri teach you the spell for how to make them normal again?"

Luiselle's eyes widened, and she nodded.

"Well, what was it?"

Luiselle whispered the words, her eyes darting around as if to practice. Jean and a troll yelled out in surprise as something knocked them off their feet. Kuri and Nega each grew back to their normal sizes from under them. Rory spun Luiselle around, so she was looking at her friends.

"There you go," she said.

Luiselle ran over to Kuri, then stopped in front of her. "I'm so sorry!" she said, with sobs bigger than her body. Kuri smiled at her, proud, opened her arms as Luiselle hugged her. Luiselle faced Nega, who scowled back. "Please don't eat me!"

"Just don't do that to me again." The ogress' voice was gruff. "I don't enjoy being the size of an ant."

Luiselle nodded, then looked at Riel. "Are you still mad?"

"No. It's a good thing Kuri taught you the spell to undo the changes." Luiselle nodded, he smiled, and everyone laughed. Rory smiled as well. As soon as his gaze met hers, he stopped smiling and turned away. He made the fire flash. Everyone jumped and scrambled out of the reach of the intense heat.

As Kuri and Nega looked at Riel, confusion etched on their faces, Rory felt a lump in her throat. She looked down at Luiselle. "Are you going to continue your training?" Luiselle nodded, then ran to the others. Nega tilted her head to the group, telling Rory to join them, but Rory shook her head in response. Riel stared at the fire, but she turned away. Rory returned to her earlier training spot. She swung her sword around and took out a few tree limbs until her frustration subsided. Then the weight on her chest returned. It wasn't fair. But there was nothing she could do.

"Rory?" a shifter called to her.

Rory looked up to see a female sheep shifter near her. "I thought maybe you could use this." The shifter pulled out some wool from her cloak, making Rory smiled.

"Thank you. Do you want me to make it into something?"

The sheep shifter smiled as a male shifter approached them.

"We need a swaddling cloth." He said, rubbing the female's belly. "She can knit but doesn't spin."

Rory smiled and bowed. "I am honoured." Hope bloomed, along with the rose.

40

*C**LAUDE!*

He stood under the full moon and ignored her call, then slowly turned around when he sensed her draw near. Cloaked in the traditional Seeress hood, he saw nothing of her body, but her amethyst eyes called out to him. He stared into their depths, reached for her hand, as he always did. The moment his fingers touched hers, she screamed in pain, her eyes wide with fear.

"Fayette?" He asked. He pushed the hood down from her head, revealing her silver blonde hair, and something jabbed his left hand. He examined his wrist, a small drop of blood trickling down its length. Ignoring it, he looked back into Fayette's eyes. His heart dropped seeing the anger there. She flinched when he reached for her with his hands. She'd tucked a single red rose into her silver hair, its thorns aimed at his face.

That was new.

"Where did you get the rose?" Claude asked, dropping his hands.

She planted it the night she cursed the child. Fayette looked to the side.

His gaze followed the direction of hers, to see multiple blue flames off to his right. He faced Fayette, who trembled before him.

"Why are you here?"

You don't remember?

Suddenly, they were in the courtyard outside his castle. The very spot where she'd stood before him, pregnant with another's child. They stood off to the side, watching the scene play out, a younger version of him confronting her in his anger. His heart chilled.

"It is the full moon."

And your anger hasn't ceased.

He watched his younger self clench his fists as he realized the child in her womb was not his. It sliced through his heart again. He'd seen red that day. Today, his vision grew red again.

"She forced you away from me."

I had no choice. I had to carry on the line with someone who had abilities.

"You did though. You chose her over me." Claude spoke the same words as those of his younger self.

Don't do this, the spectral Fayette beside him said as her younger self did. Her voice echoed her words back then. *She betrayed me, too. I would have been yours. I love* you!

He watched his rage take over his younger self. His body flew at her, his hands strangled her throat in anger, until she crumpled at his feet. It boiled over in him now, his fingers clenched. Claude glanced at Fayette's ghost beside him. He would do it again, except she was just a phantasm now and it wouldn't hurt her. He wished it would.

His younger self stood over her fully pregnant body, staring at his hands, amazed that he could actually hurt one of them. The revelation then still reverberated today. They weren't *immortal.* He had power over them. For the first time, he didn't have to worry that they would hurt him. He no longer needed them to protect his kingdom, or him. He had *power!*

He straightened again at the knowledge. He *still* had power.

In the vision, a deep purple blur appeared suddenly. It caught him off guard every time he witnessed the scene, even though he knew it would come. The Seeress suddenly stood over Fayette's body, staff in hand, her violet eyes pierced through the night sky. She bent down to touch Fayette's shoulder. Fayette didn't move.

With a swing of her staff, she'd blown him back to the edge of the forest. He felt the impact in his gut now, and stumbled back, watching that moment replay.

Then, in the same purple blur, she swept away. She took Fayette with her. The crone's words echoed in the night. *You will relive this every full moon until your path changes.*

His younger self laughed then, knowing the Seeress no longer had any power over him.

He faced the spectral Fayette, who looked at him with tears on her face.

Where is the man I loved?

"You destroyed him when you chose her wishes over your own." Claude turned away then. The courtyard disappeared. All that remained was the full moon. He spun around and searched for Fayette. Instead, he found a shepherdess watching him, her mouth open. She, too, had a small rose tucked into her brown hair, her dark brown eyes wide as she saw him. The blue flames flittered around beside her.

He tilted his head and wondered who she was. She pressed her hand to her heart, then disappeared, the blue flames with her. He spun around, looked for the shepherdess, but she was gone.

Claude sat up in his makeshift bed under his royal tent, gasping for breath. He could see the full moon through the open flaps. He ran his hand down his face. The dreams were stronger outside the castle walls under the full moon. Claude could still see Fayette's shocked face that night, but his heart was iron. She'd been unfaithful despite her proclamation of love. He was right in his actions.

But the girl at the end? She was new. She wore Fayette's rose. Claude knew her but couldn't see where he'd ever met with a shepherdess before. He didn't mingle with the commoners.

Who is she?

Claude grinned, then lay back down to sleep. It would come to him eventually, and he would wield his power as he always did. He would crush a human just as easily as he had crushed everyone else.

Rory sat up, wide awake, unable to breathe. She looked down at Luiselle, still asleep, curled up on her cloak. Her little chest raised and lowered in the campfire light, unaware of Rory's nightmare. The air rushed into Rory's lungs as she relaxed. She ran her fingers through her hair to the rose within, while its stem rubbed her finger back. Her hand shook as she pulled it away.

Rory gulped as she stared at the full moon above her. She couldn't get the pregnant woman with amethyst eyes out of her mind. She kept seeing the woman's panicked stare as Claude strangled the life from her. But it was no use. Their shape, their colour, their trust, reminded her of the little girl sleeping beside her.

I'm married to a monster.

Rory didn't know how she'd stepped into his memory in her dream. It was cruel. She didn't understand how there were two sets of people in her dream. It had to be the Navka. She saw their blue flames in the dream, too. They kept her from approaching the pregnant woman. Then a younger Claude killed her, while an older Claude stood next to the same woman and watched. Maybe she wasn't dead. But Rory knew Claude wouldn't let her live.

And he stared right at me.

Rory shivered under the moon, remembering the distant look in Claude's eyes. He would do the same with her. His soldiers had already tried to destroy the castle where she was supposed to be asleep. If he killed her, Elsass and all its inhabitants would be at his mercy.

And he had none.

She looked again at Luiselle, wondering what her connection to Claude was. She felt the throb of the ring on her chest and rubbed it. Sparks of pain shot into her fingers. She needed to get Luiselle to the Seeress. With the Seeress' power, Luiselle would be out of Claude's grasp. Then Rory would ask the Seeress to remove the curse, and hopefully, she could stay with her friends without putting them in danger.

Except, Riel's offer was no longer available. He didn't look or speak to her. His eyes grew cold whenever he saw her. Losing his friendship hurt more than the pain from the ring.

Rory pulled away from Luiselle, who sighed in her sleep. She leaned forward, seeing no one else up, grabbed her spindle, and sat near the fire. She wanted to make sure the wool was ready for the shifters and their little one.

"Can't sleep?" Jean's gruff voice came from her side.

"Nightmare. I didn't want to wake up Lu. She had a grueling day today."

Jean grunted his agreement as he sat across the fire from her.

"You?" Rory asked.

"My turn to watch. Riel took off, so I'm looking after everyone."

Rory looked up at Jean, whose gazed studied her.

"He left?" Rory stopped spinning.

Jean nodded. "Said he had to get some air." He pointed into the sky.

"Ah." Rory returned to spinning. "Will we be training in the morning?"

"You still want to?" Jean's voice rose in the night.

"If you're still willing to train me."

The crow landed near them and hopped around the fire towards Rory. They watched it approach her. It bobbed its head several times and flapped its wings before bowing down.

"Not one noise, crow." Rory said.

The crow bobbed its head, staring at her.

"I don't trust that bird," Jean said.

"I don't like him myself," Rory answered.

The crow huffed, ruffled its feathers, and hobbled away over to the trees.

Rory set down her spinning, the yarn neat and ready. The moon was behind the trees. It flickered in the approaching clouds. But they were travelling the wrong way from the breeze.

"Did you see that?"

"See what?" Jean yawned.

The moon remained full. Clouds passed in front of it, in line with the breeze this time. Rory shook her head, then stood up. "Never mind. I'll get more sleep now."

Jean nodded. As Rory turned around, a shadow fell out of the sky between the fire and the forest. Rory jumped back as the enormous dragon shifted into Riel. His green eyes were the same shade as the ones in her dream.

"We have a problem."

Jean straightened up, and Rory faced them both. "What's wrong?" Jean asked. Rory stepped closer to them.

"Kehl soldiers, most of them Claude's elite, have joined the *Beül* on the eastern plains."

"So close?" Jean asked.

Riel nodded. "And that's not all. Claude's personal guard joined them."

"Your brother is here?" Jean's hands clenched. "We need a plan."

Claude is here? Rory thought to herself. *I could break the curse!*

41

RORY HID BEHIND A tree near Riel, Nega, and Jean. Additional refugees were called into action against the battalion of soldiers. Kuri and Luiselle stayed behind with the other refugees. The faerie shrank them down to insect-size, and they hid in the neighbouring trees. The signal was a codeword from any of Riel's team. Something about crossing over wide water.

Rory was supposed to stay with the refugees. Riel, Nega, and Jean were confident they could handle Claude, his personal guard, and the soldiers. They didn't need Rory's help. She didn't want to help fight. She wanted to end the curse, take ownership of her life, and save her kingdom from the King of Kehl's cruelty. Luiselle nodded to Rory when she shrunk everyone. Rory couldn't shrink anyway, so she would have drawn attention to the refugees while she sat around waiting for the battle to end. She hadn't sat around waiting for the curse to take her or for a husband who wouldn't come. This was her kingdom at stake, and she would do something about it.

Rory branched off from the others, circling around the back. She used everything Nega taught her about moving softly and carried her sword in one hand, her other hand brushing against the ring on her chest. It directed her steps.

She paused behind a tree and watched the others get in position, unaware that she was near them. She couldn't blame them. It's not like they knew who she was, or why she cared. Of course, if they did, they would stop her training. Being sheltered in a castle was no way to help her kingdom. They might even use Rory's curse. But trapping her anywhere would trigger it.

"Am I doing the right thing?" Rory whispered.

The rose rubbed her ear with its stem.

"Thanks." She waited for the agreed upon signal. Jean and Nega would march into battle to surprise and take out the front guards. Then they would shoot one solitary arrow in Claude's direction. Riel would shift and take out the *Beül* and his men.

"Are we on the right path?" Rory asked. The ring pulsed once. Although the plains sloped up to the right, the ring swung that way as well. She corrected her path, yet the ring still aimed right, so she headed right. The ring bound her to her husband. The ring fell back to the centre of her chest. So she went straight. It swung left, and she followed. It pressed against her chest, so Rory slowed. She felt it pull on her neck. Rory looked around and crouched behind a large rock to her left. From there, she looked back at her friends and waited for the signal.

The sound of boots in the forest caught her attention, and she peered over the rock. Claude spoke to a man missing his right arm from the elbow down.

The Beül*!*

Rory sat back down, hand over her mouth, remembering how the wall had crushed his arm. But there he was. Rory swallowed the bile in her throat. She took a deep breath and moved closer to the two men to hear them. Their words filtered in through the forest.

The *Beül* paced back and forth and ran his left hand through his hair. "You're sure he's not dead?"

"Riel?" Claude asked, laughing. "Of course not. Aided by his dragon senses, he is quite impossible to kill."

"I shot him with an iron arrow. None of them could get it out."

"Except the human with them." Claude crossed his arms.

"She hid her powers. She controlled the runes." The *Beül* held up the stump at his elbow. "She triggered the magic in the wall to close on my arm."

"You're a fool, *Beül*. Any mortal can wield magic created by another. The oath my father made Riel take binds him to me. It doesn't matter that the Seeress created it. I wield it. I control him, with no magic myself."

"You control Riel?"

Rory caught Claude's grin from where she sat behind the rock and shivered. She clenched her hands around her ring at her chest.

"Why do you think I'm here? I will have him eliminate the refugees. We won't have to do anything." Claude put his arm on the *Beül's* shoulder. "He swore an oath to follow my lead. He can't refuse without suffering in agony. And when he's done with the massacre, you can end him. I know how he works. He'll send the others in first, and then swoop in to blow us all away with his flame. That's why I had you camp near the river. But you'll see. He'll be at my mercy."

Rory covered her mouth with her hand. The ring at her chest throbbed, and she felt its heat radiate out. The rose in her ear hissed.

She had to run back and warn them. Rory grasped her sword and crouched low, ready to race through the forest, when she heard Nega's battle cry.

She was too late.

Rory faced the *Beül* and the king of Kehl but remained crouched behind the boulder. She heard Jean's bear's roar, followed by the crash of metal, but her gaze never left the men nearby. The *Beül* spun around, yelled for his men. The King smiled, bringing tented fingers up to his nose. Rory tilted her head, watching the King, wondering what his plan would be.

One of the king's personal guard ran up. "We're under attack. Nothing major, just an ogress and a shifter."

The king nodded. "Have the men keep fighting, wear the attackers out. Claim more injury than they let on."

The soldier straightened. "Sir, there's no honour in that kind of fight."

The king laughed. "When the dragon holds you, there will be no honor in the fight. Just draw him out. I'll take care of the rest."

The *Beül* turned back to the King. "I will have my revenge."

"You shall." The king of Kehl smiled and looked towards her. She shrank back down to the ground, but the ring pulsed, and the rose tugged on her hair. She pulled up her hood down and crawled to the right, her hand coming into contact with iron clad boots. Looking up, she faced one of the king's guard, sword drawn.

He lifted it up and swung it down, but Rory rolled out of the way and kicked at his knees. She pulled up her sword just as the soldier brought his sword down again and deflected the blow. She leapt up and braced herself. The soldier lunged at Rory, and she spun out of the way, dodging blow after blow. As he lunged again, Rory spun around and thrust herself forward to deflect it, but she aimed higher and her sword plunged into the soldier's side as his sword glanced off her arm.

"Hmph!" the soldier said as he crashed to his knees. Rory cried out in pain. Blood trickled down her forearm. Three swords pointed at her neck, as the King of Kehl appeared with the *Beül* following close behind.

"She's mine!" The Beül spat at her.

"You are the one they call Rory?" The King asked her.

Rory stayed still, wondering if he recognized her, either from her trip to the castle with the Navka or from the dream. Her hood was down, and the rose hid in her hair.

"Drop your sword." One soldier stepped forward and knocked the sword from her hand. Rory didn't struggle. They would run her through if she tried. She stared back at the king. Everything about him was the same as Riel except for his hair, his eyes the exact colour of Riel's, but they narrowed in contemplation. Rory shivered, but didn't flinch. The king stepped forward until he was right before her. He reached out with his hand, and grabbed her chin, jerked it to the side. "What's this?" The king reached forward and pulled her loose hair back around her ears. "A rose? How *maiden*-like." His hand jerked away, and he put a now bloody thumb in his mouth. His eyes narrowed. "I know you."

The *Beül* pulled out his sword and sneered at Rory. "Do I get to take off her arm now, as she took off mine?"

"No." Claude said. He reached forward and grabbed Rory's hair, yanking her down until she crashed onto her knees and looked up at his face. The blades of his soldiers remained in place. He leaned down, putting his face right beside hers. "You never knelt before your king."

Rory closed her eyes. This was it. His lips were so close to hers. If Rory turned her head to the side, she could get the kiss that would break her curse, take back her life. Her stomach twisted at the very thought of kissing this monster of a man, but she tried to turn her head. The king held her hair so tight she couldn't move.

"I know you were in my dreams last night," he whispered in her ear. "Who are you?"

Looking up at him, Rory saw the single arrow land near where Claude and the *Beül* had been earlier. "You should move." Rory said.

The King let go and stepped back. He looked around as another arrow landed through a soldier. The men stumbled around, looking for their attackers. Rory grabbed her sword as she spun out of the way. Riel's dragon cry came in the distance, but Rory lunged after the King. She would kiss him and set herself free.

She ran to him and swung her sword, but he avoided her blade. He pulled out his own sword and blocked her continued attacks. Rory went for his knees, his hands, his head, anything that would cause him pain. She backed him up against the tree when she felt Riel land right beside her, breathing fire on the soldiers. Rory knocked the king's sword out of his hands and pushed her blade up to his throat. She leaned forward, her mouth almost at his.

This is it!

Riel roared as he knocked Rory down sideways, the sword no longer in her hand.

"No!"

She looked into the *Beül*'s maniacal grin as he straddled her. Riel roared again and knocked the *Beül* off her with his tail.

"Enough Riel!" the king yelled at the dragon, his lips pressed against his teeth.

Riel froze just as Nega and Jean approached their group, swords in hand. When they saw Rory on the ground, their jaws dropped as Nega glared at her.

"You will not touch the *Beül*. Back away from him." Even though she knew the king's plan, it still surprised Rory when Riel took two steps back and glared at his brother. The King smiled at his him. The *Beül* had his sword pointed at her, her own out of reach.

"Riel?" Nega called to him.

"Take them out." Claude ordered Riel as he gestured over to Jean and Nega.

Riel huffed, but knocked over Jean and Nega. Rory heard their groans as Riel's tail lingered over them, checking that they were safe. It was a minor act of rebellion, but Rory knew he was still in there, fighting the commands. Jean and Nega rolled into the shelter of the trees and disappear into the forest.

"Now. Kill her." The King pointed to Rory, but she scrambled onto her feet to face her friend. Rory's eyes widened as she realized they no longer were, not with her deceit. Riel stepped forward; his teeth bared. She was nothing to him now, and he wouldn't spare her.

"You said she was mine." The *Beül* called out.

"This is better," he said.

Riel stared at her; his eyes wide. She watched him take a deep breath, and just as she thought he would breathe fire on her, he let it out into the sky, flinching as if in pain.

The King stepped forward. "Kill the girl, Riel." He said through clenched teeth. Riel flinched again, but stepped forward. He shook his head, bared his teeth, and swung his tail out, knocking her over sideways, pinning her to the forest floor with his enormous claws. "Now."

"No," Rory whispered, while Riel tensed and shook. His dragon head fell forward, his large teeth crashed right in front of her face. He'd pinned her arms to her sides, and she closed her tear-filled eyes. "Please don't Riel."

"NOW!" The King of Kehl yelled.

Riel tensed and shook. He roared again, squeezed Rory tight in his grip, spun around, knocked Claude to the ground and launched himself into the sky. Rory watched the ground disappear below as they flew away from the battle and the refugees.

42

"PUT ME DOWN!" RIEL heard Rory yell in the loud wind. Again.

He couldn't. Not yet.

The echo of his brother's command to end Rory's life still rattled in his mind. He fought for control over his front claws, trying not to crush her. Pain shot through his body from all angles, tensing, at war with itself hearing the command to end her life, and the pitiful "please" she'd uttered when under his claws. He'd pinned her down, his fire ready to annihilate her.

His body shuddered at the thought. Somehow, hurting Rory would take a piece of him to the grave. He felt it. The pain would haunt him, much like any pain when he'd threatened Claude in his younger years or when he disobeyed him. He wanted to destroy his brother. All his cruelty would end, and the refugees would be safe. But the cursed oath he'd made to his father carried over to his brother. *I swear to protect and obey the king.* He wished the words never crossed his lips. But it was too late now.

"Put me down!" Rory called again. She pushed at his claws, trying to get him to release her. He drifted lower out of the sky before he even realized what he was doing.

He looked around, checking that Nega and Jean were back with the refugees. He saw the slight smoke signal. They were safe. For now.

"Please Riel, I need to get back to Lu!"

He flew towards a clearing. Using his wings and the updraft, he kept himself steady while he lowered himself enough so he could place Rory on the first solid branch at the top of a tall pine. He smiled as she gasped and grabbed hold for dear life. The top of the tree swayed back and forth, but he pushed himself away to a distance he knew she couldn't jump.

"Riel! What are you doing?" She hugged the tree, her feet slipping off the branches until she nearly fell. Riel frowned, put his tail out and pushed her into a sitting position, so she straddled the branch. She cradled one arm in the other. She took a deep breath, then glared at him. "What are you doing?" She repeated. He admired the fire in her eyes, her foolish bravery.

Riel flew back a few paces, then puffed smoke in her face. She coughed, nearly letting go of the tree. Riel almost felt bad for her. Almost. With every move she made, the tree swayed further to the side. But the distance from her helped clear his head. Both Claude's and Rory's commands faded from his mind. The pain dulled, too. It was still there, but no longer the extreme, sharp agony. He scowled when he remembered the *Beül* with his blade at her throat.

"Riel?" Rory asked as she gripped the tree tighter. That's when he noticed her bloody arm.

He huffed, then exhaled another breath of smoke in her face. As she coughed again, he reached over, plucked her off the tree, then flew to the safety of the ground. This time, he made sure not to pin her arms together as he carried her, then set her down.

Rory spun, looking at the different trees as Riel shifted back to human form. He ran his hands through his hair as she continued to survey the base of the trees before turning to face him.

"Nothing. No marks from Nega or Kuri. Where are they?"

Riel sighed. "They're off several miles that way." He gestured to the west.

Rory glared at him, then adjusted her cloak and started marching off in the direction he'd shown her, passing by him. He grabbed her arm as she pushed past. "Where do you think you're going?" Rory looked up at him like he'd lost his mind. Perhaps he had.

"I need to get back to Lu."

Ah, her oath.

"And put yourself at risk again? Have my brother hand you over to the *Beül* again so he could actually kill you?" Riel felt his eyes shift, his anger letting his dragon almost surface. He squeezed his eyes shut, counted to ten, but still held her arm. "What in Draconis were you thinking, going after them like that? You could have died!" Rory's eyes widened at the growl in his voice making her step back, but still he held her arm and she flinched. He took another deep breath. "*I could have killed you.*"

Rory stilled, no longer pulling away. "Why didn't you?"

Riel let go and tore a piece of fabric off his tunic. He wrapped it around the cut in her arm and pressed it with his warm hands to stop the bleeding.

"I heard them Riel. It was a trap, and I was going to warn you when I heard Nega's battle cry. Claude knew he had control over you." Rory reached up and touched his cheek. He flinched and wished he hadn't when she pulled her hand back. "He told the *Beül* that he would make sure you destroyed them all." She kept her gaze on his. "I was going to tell you it was a trap."

"You weren't supposed to be there." He placed his hands on her shoulders. "You were supposed to stay safe with the others." Rory looked away then, and as foolish as he was, he missed her gaze. She took a deep breath, pushed her small shoulders up under his hands. In his mind, he saw her again under his dragon claw, at his brother's mercy. His chest hurt, knowing he'd almost ended her life.

"I had to do *something!*" She said. "If I had told you to just sit there, while some of them hid, which I couldn't do, and your friends were off fighting, would you?" Rory crossed her arms over her chest. She released them, rubbing a hand over her chest as if it ached.

He wanted to reach out to comfort her, but he was still too angry. "You can't just run around and put yourself at risk!" His raised voice echoed off the trees as he pinched the bridge of his nose, trying to remain calm. "What would your husband say?"

Rory's eyes narrowed when she pulled away from him. As her posture changed, he regretted his words. But there was no turning back.

"My *husband* doesn't care if I live or die, so why should you?" Rory stepped back again. Riel stepped forward until she held up her hand to stop him. "*My* life doesn't matter now. What matters is my oath. Luiselle needs the safety of the Seeress, away from your brother." She stared at him, her gaze hard. "He's trying to kill her. You made an oath. You know as well as I do, I cannot walk away or do nothing to help her."

He looked away when he saw black moving in the base of the trees nearby. He crouched down low. Rory looked over, but didn't move behind him until he growled. *Foolish woman!*

The flap of wings came out through the trees, and the crow landed beside them, hopping along on his lame foot. He laid something down on the ground, and with a pop, Luiselle sprung up in her childlike form.

"Lu!" Rory rushed forward, hugged the girl, then checked her for injuries while ignoring her own.

Riel's chest ached as he watched the tenderness in Rory's embrace of the faerie. He glared at the crow before looking at Luiselle. "What happened to the others?"

"Nega and Jean came back, and they used the code words." Luiselle said. "They told me what happened. I restored the refugees and Jean, Nega and Kuri are taking them up to the Black Forest, where the Navka are joining them. Any soldiers will have to face the Navka first."

"Are they okay?" Riel asked, guilty that he'd hit them. He'd tried to make the blow look harder than it was, but he knew from experience that a hit from a dragon tail hurt badly. It was the only way to fulfill Claude's request without killing them. He hoped they'd forgive him for it. And for abandoning them to the *Beül* and his men.

"Nega was angry, so Kuri comforted her. But they're okay." At Luiselle's words, Riel sighed with relief.

"How did you find us?" Rory asked, checking Luiselle over for injuries.

"Nega pointed out where you flew, and I had the crow take me to you."

"Why?" Rory asked. "You would have been safer with them."

"After they told me how you almost died, I had to make sure you were okay." Luiselle's overly large round eyes filled with tears, and Riel felt his gut tighten.

"I'm okay," she looked over at Riel, then back at Luiselle. "Riel kept me safe."

Luiselle pulled out of Rory's arms and jumped at Riel. He wrapped his arms around the girl as she clung to him. "Thank you for keeping her safe!" Her small arms tightened around his neck, and he just held her. "I've lost everyone. I couldn't lose her too." He heard her sniff in his ear, and he smiled.

"You'd better heal her arm, then." Riel looked over at Rory, who shifted on her feet. He arched one eyebrow. The crow cawed, not one to be left out. He set the little faerie down just as Rory rolled her eyes at the bird before Luiselle's hands glowed purple over her injured arm.

Riel ran his fingers through his hair. "You can both be safe if we get you to the Seeress."

43

ORY'S BODY ACHED. FOR two days, Rory, Riel, and Luiselle picked their way through the forest, following the crow's lead. They camped at night, which allowed Rory and Riel each to keep watch every two hours so Luiselle could sleep. They took frequent breaks, ate, then continued on their way. Nobody spoke except to decide which way to go. Yesterday, Rory noticed their route was going uphill and getting steeper. Often Luiselle shifted into her faerie form, so she didn't have to scramble up the loose rocks, allowing Rory or Riel to do it for her.

Rory adjusted her pack as they waited at the base of a tree for Riel to look around. He wouldn't fly them to the *Rätsel* caves because Claude and the *Beül* could track them to where he placed Rory on the trees. They had a head start because Riel could fly faster than the army could ride or march, but they wouldn't take chances. The crow cawed, impatient as ever. Though they trusted it to take them to the Seeress, Riel didn't trust him to keep watch over them. Rory didn't bother listening to the crow's insistent noise. And the rose tugged the way to go immediately before the crow would caw, so Rory knew they were on the right track. The ring nestled on her chest sent undulating waves of heat, and the occasional shock of pain through her body, telling her to move on to complete her oath to get Luiselle to the Seeress.

She was determined to end the curse, and the pain pushed her forward.

It was just after dawn, and Luiselle still slept, her head in Rory's lap. The crow settled nearby, unwilling to be out of sight, while Riel scaled back down the tree. He looked around the area for any further threat, then sat across from them.

"Any news?" Rory asked.

"I saw their signal. They're close to the Black Forest." Riel put out the fire, avoiding Rory's gaze. She straightened her spine. His brow furrowed as he ran his hands through his hair. His body was stiff and on edge. She felt an ache in her chest, knowing their friendship was gone, but she was grateful for his company on this last leg. She would send him back to his friends as soon as they made it to the caves.

"That's good, right?" Rory asked. She did not want the refugees or the group who became her friends hurt by Claude's soldiers.

Riel nodded.

Luiselle stretched her little limbs out like a cat, causing Rory to smile at her, glad she could rest. The crow hopped over as Luiselle stood up.

Riel looked at Rory for the first time that morning, his gaze serious. "Ready?"

She grabbed a handful of the berries and mushrooms she'd saved foraging yesterday, gave some to Luiselle, and then ate the rest. "Ready!" Luiselle jumped up.

Rory nodded, her bag packed, ready to go. She tightened the rope at her waist, missing the weight of the sword she'd carried. She pressed her palm against the pulsing ring, which eased its heat for the moment.

"Let's go," Rory said.

They journeyed up the steep slope for an hour until the sun burst through a clearing encircled by a wall of rock. They glanced left to right before looking at each other. The cliff didn't seem to have an end in sight.

"Up?" Rory asked.

"Yep."

Rory looked at the steep rock face, almost smooth to the touch. She and Luiselle ran their hands over the stone. Instead of eroding the rock's face, the elements polished it instead. There was no way to climb. "Is there another way up?" Rory asked.

Riel shook his head. "Not that I know of. It appeared to be a cliff on all sides except near the top. I couldn't fly close enough because magic always pushed me away."

Rory turned to the crow. "Well? You just fly up to her?" Rory asked. The crow nodded, so she faced Luiselle. "Fly up, Lu," Rory said.

Luiselle's face turned white. "I can't! My wing only lets me fly in circles on the currents."

Rory looked up at Riel. "Can you fly her up?"

"There's nowhere for me to land, too many vines with thorns."

The crow leapt up and flapped his wings, blowing air onto the rock surface. Dust blew into their faces, and Rory sneezed.

"That doesn't help, you foul bird." Riel said. "Shouldn't you take her up?"

They both faced the crow as it shook its head and kept flapping. "I guess we wait for her to come to us?" Rory rolled her shoulders back, then stared at the rock face. A cut in the smooth surface appeared. Rory looked closer until a jagged groove aligned with the rock's granite vein and created a single step shape with two vertical grooves joined by a horizontal line in between. It reminded her of the carvings on the walls of Genezra's home.

"What is it Rory?" Luiselle asked.

Rory ran her fingers along the jagged groove, across the line, and up again. They illuminated under her fingers and spread up the cliff face. Rory's eyes widened before she stepped back and bumped into Riel, who stood behind her. As the runes lit up, pieces of rock shifted and spread out over the face of the cliff, which towered several stories above them. Rory stepped forward, put her hands on one, her foot on another. She pulled on them, and they held.

"How did you do that?" Riel whispered behind her. He moved to another set of grooves and climbed as well.

Rory looked down at Luiselle. "You coming?" Luiselle leapt, turned herself into a faerie, and landed on Rory's shoulder.

"Ready," Luiselle whispered in Rory's left ear. The rose rubbed her right ear, then they climbed.

After several minutes, Rory's body ached. She took a moment to look down, then gasped as the grooves used to get up part way retreated below her. She looked to her right, and Riel looked back at her. "I guess we just go up," he said, then kept climbing as she followed.

Riel waited on the holds near the top until Rory caught up. "What is it?" Rory asked.

"No more holds," He answered, inclining his head to the top.

While supports remained above her, there were none above Riel. She moved up another hold, and once her foot left the one below, it retreated. There were none below Riel, and none above him.

"You're stuck?" Rory asked, and he nodded, his face grim. "Can you shift into a dragon and fly off?"

He shook his head. "There's something keeping me from shifting. I felt it below too." He looked up at the cliff. "You'd better get up there."

"But Riel…" He'd put himself in danger to help them. The ring pulsed on her neck, and she could feel the grips giving way under her feet. Rory pushed herself up and over the cliff. She yanked her bag off her back and leaned back over the cliff. "Riel?" She looked down to see him staring up at her.

"Good, you're safe." He said, his body jolting as his left foot gave way.

Rory gasped and stretched down to grab his hand, but couldn't reach. Riel jerked again as his right food gave way. His eyes widened as he looked down, and his knuckles turned white as he held on, his right hand lower than his left.

"Go!" He said, as his right hand pulled back into the rock face. Rory sat back on her knees and untied the rope at her waist. She wrapped it around a nearby rock and flung it over the side of the cliff. Rory reached down, relieved to still see him holding on.

"Grab the rope!" But it was just out of reach. The rock under Riel's left hand started its retreat. He brushed the rope out of the way with his fingers. He couldn't reach, even pulling himself up with his left hand. Rory didn't think twice. She grabbed the rope, tied it under her arms, and slid down the cliff facing, reaching out for his hand.

The hold gave way as Rory felt his fingers wrap around hers. She breathed in relief until she stopped moving and Riel's weight pulled her arm out of her shoulder. Rory heard her cry of pain echo off the cliff as the rope yanked hard under her armpits.

"Rory!" Luiselle looked down at them. The crow joined her, trying to push her back from the edge.

Riel looked up at Rory in shock, then grasped the rope under her arms instead. Rory gasped in pain.

"Hold on Rory!" Riel whispered.

She nodded, her vision blurry. He reached up for the rope above her head and pulled himself up. "Keep holding on!" Riel disappeared above the cliff, and Rory hung there, one hand holding the rope at the knot settled near her neck. The other arm hung loose, sending intense pain through her shoulder.

The rope jerked above her. It jostled her limp arm, and Rory cried out in pain again.

"Rory, hang on!" Luiselle called down. Rory looked up to see her gigantic eyes watching her. "Riel is going to pull you up." Rory nodded, glad she tied the rope around her waist. Even though it hurt, she wrapped her hand around the rope and used her muscles to pull her, before her other arm gave out. The crow flapped its wings to get Luiselle to step back from the edge just as Riel's hands reached and grabbed her under her arms. He pulled her up and over the edge until she lay beside him.

Luiselle rushed to her side and moved her hands over Rory's arm. Rory cried out in pain. "Riel, hold her still." Riel held her down, but Rory was already still, shocked by Luiselle's commanding tone.

Warmth radiated from her arm through her body, and the pain disappeared. Luiselle's hands glowed purple, and when it faded, Rory sat up.

"Lu?" she asked.

Luiselle smiled up at her, pleased with herself. "Kuri taught me!"

A voice said, "Well done, Luiselle!" They looked up to see an old woman dressed in black robes standing with a staff in both hands as she watched them, her gaze in a shadow under her hood.

44

THE CROW WALKED UP and bowed to the Seeress. She held out her staff, and he flew on top of it. Rory knew the crow served her, but it was odd to witness it in person. The Seeress' face was sharp and angular. Enormous violet eyes sat deep in a wrinkled face, tight blood-red lips held in a firm line. Rory wondered if she ever smiled. Behind her was a wall of woven thorny vines.

Luiselle stood up from tending to Rory. Riel offered his hand to help Rory up. They faced the Seeress before he put himself in front of her. She glanced at him and wondered why he postured himself that way. Rory stepped around him so she could see the Seeress better.

The Seeress watched them and laughed. "My dear dragon," she sneered, "I could simply knock you both off the cliff if I wanted to."

"Grandmother!" Luiselle rushed to hold Rory's hand. "Don't do that to my friends!"

Grandmother? Riel looked at Rory, one eyebrow arched. Rory shrugged as they focused back on the Seeress.

"My dearest child, I would never hurt those who brought you home to me." She smiled at Luiselle and it transformed her face from haggard to serene, making Rory gasp. The Seeress focused on Rory as well. "You, my dear, are also a sight to behold." Rory couldn't help staring at the Seeress. "You are welcome here."

"Me?" Rory glanced at Riel.

"Of course." The Seeress smiled. "Please come in." She gestured to the wall of vines behind her. Rory peered up at Riel and found him scowling back at her. He tilted his head to the side, a gesture asking her to go as they faced the Seeress.

"Um, Seeress," he cleared his throat, bowing slightly from the shoulders. "If you would help me get back down, I..."

"No." She answered sharply. "You two will wait here. I have much to discuss with Luiselle and Rory."

"Two?" Rory asked.

She turned to the crow. "You will stay here with him." The crow cawed sadly, but she silenced him. "You didn't do as I asked. You're not being cast out only because you finally brought them to me."

She waved her hands, and the vines stretched out from behind her. They brought forward several pieces of fruit and lay them down at Riel's feet. Rory counted several apples, berries and some kind of roasted animal. How she got any animal up here... Rory shuddered. She tried to stop Riel from taking the fruit, but the Seeress interrupted her before she could say anything.

"Well? Eat." She turned to Rory and Luiselle. "Now, *ladies...*" she smirked at Rory, "please come with me."

The Seeress glided to the bramble of vines, so thick they blocked out the daylight. She wondered if she should stop her, but Luiselle skipped to her grandmother just as the vines unwound and opened themselves for her to pass through.

"Coming Rory?" Luiselle asked as she stood in the vine arbor.

Rory squared her shoulders, stepped forward, then looked back at Riel. "Will you be okay to wait here?"

He looked at the Seeress. "Not much choice." Riel shrugged. "I'll be here."

Rory faced the Seeress, who smiled with narrowed eyes. "I promise I won't hurt you." She said. The rose rubbed her ear, then tugged towards the vines.

She can lift the curse.

Rory took a deep breath, squared her shoulders, then stepped through the arbor. The vines immediately closed. She spun around in time to see Riel bite into an apple. Purple smoke wafted around him, and he collapsed as the vines closed him off from sight.

"Riel!" Rory spun around and glared at the Seeress. "What did you do to him?"

The Seeress waved Rory off as if she were nothing and walked towards a cave. Luiselle took her hand. "Grandmother didn't hurt him. He's resting. You need him, and she knows that." She pulled Rory to follow the Seeress. "Come, please."

Rory allowed Luiselle to pull her forward. The Rätsel cave had a clearing before it. Around the side was a garden, where the plants grew in groups of threes. Most of them were food or plants for healing, but Rory saw hemlock and nightshade in clusters as well. She looked back to the vines but saw nothing of Riel.

As they approached the cave, Rory's hands shook. It was dark, and almost completely black. The dappled sunlight stopped at the mouth, not even reflecting light into its depths, despite the angle. She shivered, but if she didn't enter, the curse would continue. She couldn't help her kingdom if she were asleep. Claude himself, implied in the curse, had already tried to kill her twice. Since she hadn't kissed him, she had no other choice.

The Seeress' glowing face peered out at Rory from the dark cave. Her gigantic eyes stared at her, and when the woman blinked, Rory exhaled, relieved to see the motion.

"Well? Aren't you going to come inside? Luiselle is already in, touching *every-thing*." Rory thought she heard a note of pride in the Seeress' voice.

The rose rubbed her ear, soothing her as she took a deep breath before Rory stepped inside the cave.

45

As Rory stepped into the *Rätsel* cave, she felt her ears plug, then pop. It took her eyes some time to adjust to the dark interior. Once they did, she found a very homelike setting. There was a fire near a waterfall. The opening for the water made a natural vent in the cave. The Seeress placed a bed on the other side, filled with fresh straw and topped with furs. A large worktable sat in the center, covered in bowls and jars. Varying herbs hung upside down above the table to dry. Luiselle stood on a chair to reach out and grab the herbs.

"Lu, do you even know what you're using?" Rory asked.

"Of course I do, Rory." Luiselle looked at her like she'd gone crazy. "Kuri has been teaching me. I'm going to make something so I can fix my wing with grandmother's help."

The Seeress smiled at Luiselle, then turned to Rory. "Would you like to help, Aurora?"

Rory stared at the Seeress. She hadn't heard her proper name in months. It was odd to be addressed that way. "You... you know who I am?"

"Wait, you're the *princess* Aurora?" Luiselle's outstretched hand stopped in front of her.

The Seeress laughed, the harsh tone echoing off the hard walls of the cave. It was at odds with the way she caressed Luiselle's head. "I admit, when Reinhold first found you, I was surprised. You were supposed to be asleep in the tower with everyone else."

Questions competed for attention in Rory's mind. She picked the first one. "Reinhold knew who I was? He never let on."

The Seeress' gaze narrowed. "Reinhold was the trusted guardian of my grand-daughter. He was supposed to keep her safe. To do that, we shared a connection. He was my eyes and ears on her." The Seeress' mouth tipped to one side. "And then he found you. Imagine my surprise when the curse my mother placed on you didn't work."

"Your mother? But I thought it was you!" Rory rubbed her chest. Her mind raced at the revelation that there was another Seeress. And this one hadn't placed the curse. The ring lay silent now that she'd completed her oath.

The Seeress glanced at Luiselle and then focused back on Rory. She looked Rory up and down, debating what to say next, so Rory waited. "No. My mother was powerful. She placed the curse on your family. Something to do with preventing a war." The Seeress waved her hand in the air as if it didn't matter. "You broke it, so you must be powerful yourself."

Rory laughed at the idea of having any power. She thought of the rest of her household. "It's not broken," she whispered.

The Seeress' eyes widened, and she stepped towards Rory. "What do you mean?"

Rory sighed. "The curse is on my home. I left it just as the chimes sounded. Felt it touch me when I reached in. The people in my household are all still asleep. Because I am not in my home, I am not. I..." Rory swallowed. "I was hoping you could remove the curse for me."

"Is that why you came?" The Seeress watched Rory as she nodded.

"Well, Reinhold made me swear an oath, but yes. That's why I entered your domain." Rory gestured around her.

The Seeress narrowed her gaze at Rory. "I cannot remove the curse as I did not create it. Only my mother could, and she is no longer with us."

Rory staggered back and let out the breath she'd been holding. The tension in her body disappeared, and she collapsed onto the ground as all her energy left her. The pain in her chest was worse than the sting of the curse. She looked at her lap as tears formed in the corners of her eyes, but she blinked them back. She would grieve later, in private. The rose rubbed her ear, and Luiselle ran over to hug her. Her small arms surrounded Rory's shoulders and tightened around her neck. She accepted comfort from her friend, even though there was nothing they could do.

After a moment of silence, the Seeress stepped forward until she stood at Rory's feet. "I can offer you a different solution."

Rory looked up at the Seeress, whose smile was large, but her eyes narrowed. Rory shivered.

She offered Rory her hand. "What do you know about the Seeress?"

Luiselle climbed back on the table to reach the lavender, and Rory missed her comfort. The Seeress offered her hand and helped Rory up. "Thank you."

"Not that, child, this one." The Seeress walked over to Luiselle and switched out the lavender for something else. Luiselle nodded and started mixing as the Seeress turned back to Rory. "Everyone assumes I'm the Seeress, but the *Seherin* is more. We are more. We are a trinity." She stood beside Luiselle, grabbed a second bowl, and started throwing in dashes of herbs and other powders.

"There are three *Seherin*?" Rory stepped forward; her brows furrowed. She watched the two of them work. When they both looked at her at the same moment, she saw the similarities for the first time. Purple eyes too large for most humans, though Luiselle's were lighter. They had similar postures and gestures. Rory wondered if there were wings tucked under the woman's ominous cloak.

"Not exactly. We are three. I am Violette, the eldest part of the *Seherin*. The Crone." She gestured to herself. "There are two more. The maiden," she gestured to Luiselle, "and in between, the mother. We are always three."

"The three of you make the *Seherin*?" Rory asked.

"We would," Luiselle said, her voice quiet and serious. "But he killed *maman*." She kept mixing. A memory flashed before Rory's eyes. A dream of Claude with a pregnant woman with amethyst eyes.

"You said your mother, as the Seeress, created my curse." Rory paced as the Crone watched her. "Did that make you the mother and your daughter the maiden?"

"Precisely." The Seeress nodded her approval. "My mother, Aurelie, was the Crone then, and acted as Seeress. She placed the curse. When the new maiden is born, the Crone departs, and the mother steps up to take her place."

"But everyone thinks you, as the Crone, are the Seeress, across all ages?" Rory said.

"Yes, it adds to the mystique, does it not?" The Seeress, Crone, er... *Violette*, smiled.

Rory paced. She stopped for a moment, then hesitated at Luiselle's studious face as she made her concoction. Luiselle was innocent, and Rory hated destroying that.

"Ask your question Rory. The child can handle it."

Rory looked at Violette. "I was in a dream about a week ago. In it was Claude-"

"Your husband," Violette interrupted. Luiselle scowled at Rory.

"Yes, my husband, by arrangement and by proxy *only*." Rory took a deep breath. "I never met him until a few days ago. But in this dream, he..." Rory looked at Violette, "he strangled a pregnant woman named Fayette." She looked at Luiselle then. "That was your mother?"

Luiselle frowned and nodded, then went back to her work, mixing.

Rory faced Violette. "She was your daughter, then?"

Violette turned and leaned against the table, shoulders bowed. For the first time, Rory saw her as mortal. Violette was an old woman and not the Seeress. "That was a hard day. My mother arrived to whisk Fayette away to safety, but not in time. She took Fayette to a nearby clearing, called for me to appear. She did everything she could to take care of the baby. By the time I made it, Luiselle was born. I lost both my daughter and mother." She jumped up. "I take comfort that my mother cursed him to relive that moment every full moon." She slammed her staff down on the ground, causing purple sparks to gleam around it.

"You shouldn't." Rory crossed her hands over her chest.

"Why not?" Violette scowled back at her. "You would deny me some measure of revenge?"

"The last time he dreamed, I was there." Rory stepped away from Violette, unsure of how she would take the news. But as the Crone and Seeress, she needed to know. "Every time he witnesses his own actions, he feels more right, more secure, knowing that you and the other magic folk are not immortal. It feeds his power and reaffirms to him he was right to take her life. That he is right to take the lives of everyone else who is not a human member of his, or my kingdom."

Violette's eyes widened. "You have seen this?"

"I was in his dream, where he stood with Fayette." Rory said, then sighed. "They watched his crime again. He felt no remorse. When she asked him where the man she loved went, he said she destroyed him, because she chose your mother's wishes over theirs. The dream feeds his lust for power."

Violette clutched a bunch of herbs and dried bits exploded everywhere.

46

CLAUDE THREW HIS ARMOUR at his bearer. He flung his sword on his bed, where it lodged in the headboard. His bearer ran to pull it out, but didn't have the strength.

"Leave it!" Claude yelled. He gulped down his wine while the bearer scurried out of the room with his armour.

"My king, did you at least have someone taste the wine first?" Ilse asked from the doorway. He arched an eyebrow as she curtsied before entering the room. Ilse walked up to Claude, took the goblet, drank a mouthful, then handed it back. She swallowed the wine, then walked over to the sword to pull it out of the headboard. She held it in her hand, swung it around a few times, checked for its straightness, then leaned it against Claude's bedside table. "The blade needs to be checked by the smith. It won't cut properly."

Claude gave Ilse a half smile as she leaned against the wall. "I knew I picked the right person to be my proxy." He drank the rest of contents of his goblet.

Ilse smiled back at him. "Of course." She held out her hand and Claude placed the goblet in it. She walked over and filled it up, taking a sip before handing it back to him to finish. Claude watched her swallow before taking another sip. "Why are you throwing your armour at your bearer?"

Claude clenched his fists, and gulped down the wine, then slammed the goblet down on the nearby table. "Riel disobeyed my command."

Ilse walked over to the bed, then leaned back on it. "He has always fought your command. Why should this time be any different?"

He started pacing the room. "Of course, but he cannot hold out. He always gives in to my demands."

"Then why are you worried now?" Ilse stepped into the path of his pacing.

"He *saved* her." Claude stopped, closed his eyes, and pinched the bridge of his nose. "He had her pinned down, then when she pleaded for her life, he knocked me down and flew off."

Ilse sat on the edge of his bed. "He knocked you over?"

"And saved *her*."

She tilted her head to the side. "The ogress, or the elf?"

"Neither. A human woman." One with dark brown hair that he now saw every night in his dreams, since he and the *Beül* had her. She wielded a sword and demanded retribution. Sometimes she appeared with Riel by her side, his hand on her shoulder, sometimes with Fayette, sometimes a strange hideous child with blue flames for eyes. But always her. "He had her in his grasp, then flew away with her."

"He has never failed at your bidding." Ilse stood again, then poured him another goblet of wine. She sipped it first before passing it back over. "He probably tried to spare her, but the oath would overrule him, anyway. I doubt this girl's fate was pleasant."

Claude paused. Ilse made sense, but the dreams continued. "No, she is alive. The *Beül* said she was strong, saved them from his execution."

"So he owed her a debt. Spared her life because she saved his?"

"It feels different." Claude rubbed the ring on his finger, the gift from his father, to always have a dragon protect the human king. It no longer radiated with heat, nor pulsed with power. The ring *felt* different. "I need to find that woman."

"She should be easy to locate, walking around with a dragon shifter. Especially one with a bounty on his head." Ilse stalked to the door; her mission clear. "Anything else you want to tell me about her?"

"She has dark hair, brown eyes, ruddy skin. Can fight with a sword." Claude gripped his wine goblet. "She dresses like a shepherdess, but wears a single rose in her ear."

Ilse raised an eyebrow at Claude, but he stared her down. She nodded and swept out of the room, ready to spread the word. Claude stared at his wine. He would find her. And then, when she was gone, he would end his brother.

47

R ORY FOUND A BROOM in Violette's cave and cleaned up the mess of dried herbs. Violette took a deep breath. She dumped the rest of the dried herbs into a mortal and pestle and ground them, then offered it to Luiselle.

"Here child, add this. Gently." Violette's voice came out sharp, yet she smiled to overcome it.

Luiselle did as she was told and mixed everything together, stirring carefully as Rory cleaned the floor, making a small pile near the entry.

"So," Violette started again, "Claude still lusts for power?" She sat down on one of her chairs.

Rory put the broom away, then sat with them at the table. "He has power. He is using it to destroy everyone who isn't like me."

"Like you?" Luiselle asked.

"Human. But I don't understand why. Isn't he the son of a dragon and ogress? He comes from magic."

Violette tilted her head, looked at Rory, then selected more herbs. "But that's where you're wrong, *Princess*. Claude and Riel's parents were half human as well. His father was only half dragon, his mother only half ogress." Violette mixed the dried herbs in a bowl before grinding them together. "The people of Kehl accepted their leadership because they had human parents as well. It satisfied the population that they could remain impartial."

Rory put her chin in her hand. "So while Riel inherited the dragon, Claude inherited only the human sides from both his parents?"

"I would argue he inherited his mother's ogre attitude," Violette said, "but precisely. Some children get their parents' eye colour, some their skin, some their hair. Some get their abilities."

"That would explain why he hates Riel then." Rory sat silent for a moment, watching the two work on their spell. "So, why does he hate you?"

Violette sighed, then spoke. "He was in love with Fayette. When I sent her to learn of Kehl's ways, she captivated him when they were teenagers. She loved him too." Violette checked Luiselle's mix, then nodded at her. The little girl disrobed and let her full-size wings open. Violette whispered something over the mix, then spread it over Luiselle's broken wing. A purple haze wrapped around the little girl.

"But we must stay as the three. The eldest daughter is to take on the mantel of Seherin power. She was supposed to learn the ways of the world and rejoin us. And she was to procreate with someone with power. My mother had already selected the man for the ritual, an Elsass bear shifter."

Rory's faced almost crashed on the table at the news. "Jean de l'Ours? Does he know he's her father?"

Violette shook her head. They were silent as they watched Luiselle's broken wing stitch itself back together, weaving a web of layers and fine skin over it. Rory's eyes widened when the spell finished. Luiselle's wing matched the other three. She jumped and clapped. Suddenly, she shrank with a pop, and flew around the room. Rory smiled, listening to her tiny laughter. She zipped by Rory, landed on her shoulder, and touched the rose. It bloomed, and they both giggled as she flew away.

Finally Luiselle went back to the table, transformed back into her human form and hugged her grandmother. "Thank you!"

Violette beamed, then focused back on Rory. She continued her mix. "But you are wrong about something else, *Princess*. You are not entirely human either."

Rory laughed, picking up the dried lavender. The harsh tones echoed in the cave. "Of course not. I'm cursed."

"That's not what I meant, Aurora." Violette paused. "Your mother, rest her soul, was my younger sister. Half human, half Faerie."

Rory dropped the lavender. Sprigs fell across the table. "What? I have no magic."

Violette nodded to Luiselle, who spoke. "Not of your making. But it finds you. And you use it. Don't you wonder why the rose accepts you, my great grandmother Aurelie's rose? Why you saw the runes?"

"But the iron? It doesn't hurt me." Rory stood up and started pacing. "Everyone who knows me knows I'm not at all magic. Lu couldn't even shrink me like the others." The rose rubbed her ear until she rubbed its soft petals back.

Violette stood and faced her. "But I assure you, you are like us, in your way. And we'll prove it." The Crone lifted her hand, palm out, then blew the powder she'd made into Rory's face. A purple haze started at the corner of her eyes, making Rory blink twice before everything went black.

She stood by a fire in the middle of a moonlit clearing with Violette and Luiselle. Except, they looked different from in the cave. Here they wore deep purple robes with intricate black embroidery, lining them from hood to base. Rory found herself dressed the same way.

"Come Aurora," Violette beckoned. Her face glowed from within, and Rory realized she was no longer Violette, but the Crone.

Rory stood between the two. "What's going on?" She asked, crossing her arms over her chest.

"You're going to become one of us," Violette said.

"What?" Luiselle asked. "How?" The young girl's face looked older than her years, and Rory understood that in this magic plane, Luiselle was the Maiden here. But Rory only thought of her as Lu.

"Aurora is cursed." Violette shrugged as if it meant nothing. "The only way to remove the curse is for Aurora to cease existing." Rory tensed at the Crone's words. She didn't want to be cursed, but she wanted to live. The Crone waved her hands around her and an iridescent purple glow shined above purple flames. The glow turned into a face, and Rory gasped when she recognized the shape.

"Mother, why do you call me from the spirits?" Fayette asked. The tone was neither angry nor pleasant, just a voice.

"So you can rejoin us and complete the *Seherin* triad once more."

Fayette looked around, her gaze landing on Luiselle. Her smile broke free, but didn't reach her eyes. "Daughter! How I've missed you!"

"Maman?"

Fayette materialized and stood with her spectral body next to Luiselle. She knelt down, so they faced each other, and ran her purple illuminated hand down the child's face. Luiselle leaned into the touch, but didn't fall through as Rory expected her to.

Rory's hand touched her throat, the tender touch of a mother and daughter, something she'd never experienced. Muriel was the closest she'd had to a mother, but kept her distance because of Rory's status. Rory felt tears run down her cheeks. She'd left the only mother figure she'd known asleep with the curse. *But maybe,* Rory thought, *Muriel could wake up if she followed the Crone's instructions.*

"You made it back?" Fayette asked.

Luiselle nodded. "Thanks to Rory." She pointed to Rory, and Fayette faced her. Fayette glanced around and she scowled.

"*You* brought her back *here*?" Fayette asked. Her brow furrowed, and her eyes flashed before Rory stepped back. "Why?" Fayette stepped towards Rory, her hands clenched. If Fayette weren't an apparition, Rory would swear she had white knuckles.

"We..." Rory swallowed. "We were under attack. There was a dragon. We thought he was burning down the rosebush and we had to stop him." She rubbed the flower at her ear. "Then they captured Lu with a net and Reinhold made me swear an oath to find her and bring her here." Rory rubbed the ring on her chest. "And I did."

"You!" Fayette spun around, facing her mother. "You had her brought here when I told you she shouldn't come. That it was safer for her with Reinhold."

The Crone lifted her chin. "I did what was best for my grandchild. If it weren't for this one, I would have let her be." The Crone gestured to Rory. "She would have been fine tending the sheep with Reinhold had this one not escaped the curse."

Fayette faced Rory again. "You are Aurora of Elsass?" Rory nodded. Fayette bowed to her. "I saw you in his dream. You are connected to Claude."

"I am married by proxy."

Fayette turned towards the Crone. "Why is she here?"

The Crone smiled. "She is your cousin. She will be your vessel. All your power, all of you, can inhabit in her."

Rory stumbled backwards. "What do you mean?"

"You cannot live with the curse. You will always be in hiding. This way, you can live. And we can have our power again." The Crone turned to Luiselle. "Take her hand, child." Luiselle did as she was told and took Rory's right hand. The simple grasp caused power to flow through her, a tingle that ran from her hand, through her heart, down to her toes. It was nothing like the curse that grew sharper over time. Instead, her limbs lost the feeling of weight, as if she had Nega's strength times ten. "Take mine." Luiselle took the Crone's hand in hers, and the Crone seized Rory's left hand. The tingling stopped, but she felt the energy flow through her, from one hand to the next.

Luiselle gasped.

Rory frowned.

The Crone smiled and nodded her head.

Fayette flew into Rory's chest. Rory blinked until her vision became purple. She stumbled, but the others held her in place. She gasped, her hands in the others' hold.

What do you see? Fayette whispered. Her words were like a thought that wasn't her own.

"We are in a castle," Rory said.

It was a grand hall, full of banners, the colours of her kingdom. A celebration. They stood off to the side. A trumpet rang out and hundreds of people faced the elevated dais at the corner. A man and woman stood up, the woman holding a baby. Rory saw her own face reflected in her mother's. She looked at the infant. "Is that me?"

Yes. Your naming ceremony.

Rory watched the kingdom toast to her long life. Her parents, faint memories in her mind until now, looked happy, smitten with the child in her mother's arms. Rory longed to reach out and touch their faces, hug them as Fayette had hugged Luiselle. But this was a memory, nothing more.

"Were you there?" She asked Fayette.

Over there under the banner.

Rory saw a child who looked so similar to Luiselle, she looked a second time. It was only their hair colour that distinguished them.

A hooded figure appeared amid the crowd.

"Welcome Seeress!" The King proclaimed to the old woman, who pulled back her hood. She had violet eyes, similar to the Crone holding her hand, but her gaze was sharper, her wrinkles more pronounced. The people parted for her when she walked up to the dais. The Seeress held a staff with a hooked end on it, and a crow came to rest upon it. She bowed before the King and Queen without lowering her gaze. The Queen held her baby to be seen by the Seeress.

"Mother, we have named her Aurora," the Queen said, smiling. "We wanted a name that reflected you a little."

"She is beautiful, daughter," the Seeress said. Her eyes glazed over, and she put her hand on the child. As she stood, her eyes became completely violet, with no white or black in them. She blinked and gasped, yanking her hand away.

"What is it, mother?" The Queen asked.

The Seeress jerked her body and retreated. The crow flew off. Murmuring grew from the crowd until someone shouted out for a blessing. The Seeress stumbled back, afraid of the crowd, afraid of her parents.

Afraid of... me?

"Aurelie?" Her father asked. "What's happening? Are you ill?"

The Seeress narrowed her gaze and put her hand back on Aurora. She nodded once to herself. Purple smoke expanded around the three of them as she spoke.

"As Aurora's nineteenth year rings at midnight,

"So the curse begins.

"Asleep, the household, one and all."

The Queen tried to pull Aurora away from the Seeress' grasp, but the Seeress' other arm grasped the Queen and held both her and the child in her grip. Baby Aurora cried.

"Where she calls home, there she'll lie,

"To sleep until kissed by the King of Kehl,

"Whose love must overcome hate,

"To unify their lands."

Her Father tried to pull them apart, but he couldn't before she pronounced the curse.

Without an heir, their lands will fall to waste.

"What did you do?" Her mother broke free of the Seeress' grasp and held Aurora tight to her chest. Her father stood between them, his arm on the sword by his side.

The room, once loud from the celebratory chants of the crowd, fell silent except for baby Aurora's cries. The Seeress looked around at everyone. They pulled away from her, flinched and looked away as her gaze travelled over them. She squared her shoulders and stared at the King and Queen of Elsass. "I have saved your kingdom from tyranny."

"How could you?" Her mother, tears in her eyes, stared at Aurora.

Her father, red with anger, drew his sword and pointed it at the Seeress. The Queen placed her hand on her husband's and held him back. She pleaded with him with her eyes. Other soldiers drew their arms and pointed them at the Seeress, too. Among them stood a teen boy with ice-blue eyes that reminded Rory of Jean.

The King blew out a harsh breath. "You are being met with more mercy than you deserve. You are not welcome here. Leave now, or I will spill your blood."

The Seeress nodded once, no hint of sadness on her face, harsh compared to the Queen's. Purple smoke enveloped the Seeress so deep that light couldn't penetrate. When it dissipated, she was gone, along with the little girl in the corner.

Everything went black.

"Wait," Rory felt herself grip the Crone's and Luiselle's hands. "What did she see?" She loosened her grip on the child's hand.

The scene shifted, and Rory witnessed a battle. Humans against the shifters, faeries, elves, ogres, and others; a bloodbath. A dragon swooped above them all, blowing fire on the magical, and Rory's heart stopped. She tried to rub the ring on her chest, but Luiselle and the Crone still held her in their tight grasp. In the distance, she saw Claude, directing Riel to kill them all. At Claude's side, Rory saw herself, older, yelling and wringing her hands. She watched as she try to stop Claude, to tell Riel to stop, but it was no use. Claude laughed, then pushed her off the platform into the battle below where she perished under the iron hooves of the soldier's horses. A child stood next to him, a scar from his right temple to his chin, cheering their soldiers on.

My son? Rory wondered as she saw his dark hair, so similar to hers.

Your son with Claude, Fayette answered.

It flashed to another gruesome battle, with a man leading them. Rory recognized the scar on his face. Her son lead a group of soldiers into a town and butchered everyone in it. Men, women, children, animals, all slaughtered. They did not distinguish human from faerie or elf or anyone else. He didn't just command his men to attack; he joined in, slaughtering the innocent. And he laughed. The laughter echoed in Rory's mind as tears streamed down her face.

"My mother tried to spare you, and this from happening." The Crone whispered.

They thrust Rory back to where they met Fayette. Fayette's emotions mixed with her own.

"So your mother took away my choice?" Rory lifted her hands to wipe away her tears, but Luiselle and the Crone still held them tight in their grasp. Her whole body tensed up as she tugged. "She took away my life!"

"My mother spared you from being with that monster." The Crone answered. "And this way, your heir would not be subject to his brutality. Look at what he did to Luiselle."

"Because of your and grandmother's meddling!" Fayette hissed at her mother through Rory.

"She could have told my parents and asked them to reconsider," Rory said. "She could have warned me!"

The Crone gripped her hand. "And what would they have done? They pledged you to him as a baby." The Crone shook her head. "They would have risked war with Kehl then."

"Maybe, maybe not. I have my own power. You said it yourself. I could have done things to stop him. She could have sent the right people to train me to be stronger, more capable. I could have done *something! Anything!* But now you'll never know." Rory glared at the Crone. She felt Fayette rise in her, take over. Rory fought it, but Fayette won, and her body jerked. She felt Fayette's anger overflow. "And if you hadn't interfered, he would have been with me. He *loved* me." She said through Rory, her voice echoing. "I could have prevented this, too. Until you arranged for me to be with Jean, thinking it was Claude!"

Fayette let go of Rory, and she fell to her knees. She looked up to see Fayette hovering in front of them.

"Claude would have turned your child into a monster, Fayette. He hurt your child, cut the wing right from her back. He would not have listened to you." The Crone argued. Fayette crossed her arms.

"So your mother foresaw that I would be meek under the hand of Claude." Rory waited for the Crone's nod. "Did she foresee Claude would kill Fayette in his anger, or that I would climb out of the tower and not be asleep? Did she see that two years before my curse took place, he would invade and start the war, anyway?" Rory clenched her hands into fists, making the Crone grimace. She shook as she faced the Crone, loosening her hands.

"No," the Crone faced her, but tilted her head in defiance.

"Then none of us will ever know if her vision would come to pass. Or if my family could have separated themselves from him because of her vision. Your mother took their choices away."

Rory yanked her hand out of the Crone's, and rubbed Luiselle's hand with her own, soothing her from the grip she'd held before. Luiselle squeezed her hand back.

"Join us," the Crone said to Rory. "When you join us, you are no longer Aurora, and your curse will cease. Your servants freed. Isn't that what you want?" She offered her hand to Rory.

Rory swallowed as she saw Muriel's face again, in pain from the curse. She almost placed her hand in the Crone's, when she remembered Nega and her friend's faces, the refugees asking her to spin yarn.

She pulled her hand back. "But what of my kingdom? No heir means it's cursed. The refugees will be decimated, and Claude will ravage them."

"We will destroy him," the Crone said, smiling. It was jagged and menacing, every bit the Seeress now. "We will have our revenge on him. You will fight for your kingdom. We will have our complete power."

Rory shook her head. Revenge sounded good, but no heir still meant her kingdom's demise. "I can't." She whispered. The Seeress would once again control Rory's life on her terms. This time, she wouldn't stand for it. She stood straight. "I won't."

"It doesn't matter. Fayette can merge with you, anyway." She signalled to Fayette and tried to grasp Rory's hand, but Fayette and Luiselle stepped back.

"I will not merge with her, mother." Fayette crossed her arms over her chest. "You have no right to ask that of us. You will not force us into any more machinations that you do not comprehend." Fayette turned to Luiselle. "As much as I long to be with you, be your mother, I cannot. Do you understand?" She knelt so Luiselle could run into her arms, embracing her.

"Don't you see Fayette?" The Crone faced her daughter's apparition. "You could have your relationship with Luiselle again, be with her properly. Take the chance."

"No, mother."

"It's okay, maman," Luiselle hugged her. "Though I will always miss you, I love Rory as she is."

Rory brushed away a tear, then knelt beside them. "I cannot stay with you, Lu." Rory rubbed Luiselle's arm. "We will all fall under the curse if I make your home mine."

"I know. You need to stop him." Luiselle said. They both knew Claude's evil. "And Riel will help you."

A purple light flashed before they returned to the cave. Violette collapsed on the floor, her energy gone as Luiselle helped her into a chair. Where she'd been a strong, menacing Seeress, now an old woman with little energy, remained.

"I cannot force you without Fayette and Luiselle's help." Violette wiped her brow, then drew her gaze to Rory. "There is one thing you need to know before you leave."

Rory crossed her arms and waited.

Violette's breath grew haggard. "The ring you wear, that bound you to your oath," she gestured to Rory's chest.

"My wedding ring." Rory pulled it out and held it up.

"In a way," Violette said, then sighed. "It is also more. That ring is also what Riel swore his oath to Claude on. Specifically to his father, to protect its bearer and obey them at all costs. Claude wore it to command Riel."

Rory's jaw dropped, and she stared at the ring.

"Its magic lies in binding. One to another by oath, either forced, or in one such as marriage. Mother created it for that purpose. It's why Reinhold could bind you to your oath for Luiselle. So because you bear it, he is bound to you, and you are now his to protect." Violette smiled, her eyes glinted. "And he is yours to command. Use him to destroy his brother, as his brother used him to destroy everyone else."

48

Rory stepped out of the mouth of the cave into the sunshine and felt it warm her body. She still shivered from the revelations of what her future could have held, but the sun helped. She drifted to the vines barricading the path as they untangled themselves.

"Rory, wait!" Luiselle ran after her, and hugged Rory's legs so tight they gave way and she fell. "You can still stay with us. Grandmother won't force you to do anything."

She sat up and ran her fingers over Luiselle's cheek, brushing a lock of her hair away from her face. "I can't Lu. I can't put you in danger like that."

"Why not?" The girl pouted.

"You know why. If I stay, this will be my home and then we'll all fall asleep. Your great grandmother meant for it to be the castle at Elsass, but it is wherever I call home." Rory took a deep breath. "You and your grandmother would forever sleep because of me. Because Claude will never break the curse." She pulled out the ring and held it up for Luiselle. "I vowed to protect you. To bring you here to safety. You won't be safe with me here."

"I don't want you to go. Everybody goes and leaves me behind." Tears fell down her cheek.

Rory wrapped her arms around the little girl, her own tears gathering. She felt a tug at her ear, and as she brushed her fingers over the rose, it came to her hand. She lifted the rose to Luiselle's cheek. The rose snagged a lock of Luiselle's hair, and tucked itself behind her ear, as it had done with Rory. She brushed the spot above her own ear and missed its presence.

"Rory, your flower!" Luiselle touched the rose, and its stem rubbed her ear.

"So you have each other, okay?" Rory hugged Luiselle one last time and stood. The vines parted to create an opening, and she saw Riel sit up, rub his head. Rory walked backwards towards the vine's opening.

"Rory, don't go!" Luiselle cried. Violette came out of the cave, kneeling beside Lusielle, and hugged her tight as she sobbed. Twice Luiselle tried to change into a faerie, but Violette rubbed her back and the shifting stopped. Rory's heart ripped in two. She wiped her eyes, but it did nothing against the flood of tears breaking free.

Violette waved her hands as she stepped back, pulling Lusielle with her. The vines closed Rory off again, criss-crossing in layers until the solid mass hid Luiselle away from her.

She placed her tear-soaked hand on the vines, and they angled their thorns away from her. "Please take care of them," she whispered. The vines shuddered, rippling from her hand, then heading towards the rest of the vines. When Rory pulled her hands away, the entire vine aimed its thorns out. A vine tendril with no thorns came out and wiped away her tears, then offered her one large thorn.

She took it in her hand and stared. It was too big to fit inside her palm. A single reminder they would protect Luiselle.

"Thank you," she whispered. She tucked it into her tunic pocket before she turned away.

Riel watched Rory stare at the vines as they closed. He wanted to wrap his arms around her, comfort her and dry her tears, but the vines did it for him.

He'd woken recently, with a headache from the blasted crow's incessant cawing. He wondered if Rory would ever come out. The Seeress had welcomed her, and he was relieved to see she wasn't staying. Perhaps she'd changed her mind and would come with him to Kuri and Nega. They could be friends. It didn't feel right, but it was better than not having her in his life. He puffed out his chest, and that's when he realized he no longer needed to worry about getting down. He could shift again. The Seeress had lifted her spell.

"Rory, are you ready to go?"

Eyes red from crying, she turned to face him. He stepped toward her and brushed his hand over her ear just as Rory pulled away from him, and he noticed what was missing. "Where's your rose?"

"With Lu." Her voice was quiet, withdrawn, as she looked back at the vines.

"Are you alright?" He asked, turning her chin to him.

She nodded, but her eyes were flat. No spark remained, and he felt it in his chest.

"I can fly now. Do you want to ride back to Kuri and Nega?" He asked, seeing if he could delight her in flight. She'd never been afraid of it, but he'd only carried her in his claws, or that one time dangling from Nega's arm. He shuddered when he remembered almost losing her then.

But Rory stepped back away from him. "I have to go to Kehl."

Riel stepped towards her, and she held up her hands to stop him. "I think I mentioned you could come with us. We'd be glad to have you." He swallowed. "I would like you to join us."

Rory shook her head. "You don't know what you're asking." She rubbed her chest and Riel saw a chain hanging down.

"Of course I do. We like you Rory."

Rory smiled, but there was pain in her eyes. "Riel, you'll have to go without me. I'm going to Kehl."

Riel growled. He placed both hands on her shoulders and fought the urge to pick her up and fly off. She pushed his arms up and spun away, a defiant move which made him admire her training with Nega. But he saw the ring on the chain around her neck as she swung away. Something about it called to him.

"Is that..." He swallowed. *It couldn't be.* "Is that your wedding ring?"

Rory's shoulders dropped. "Yes."

"To the man of Kehl." He wanted to spit out the name of his own kingdom in disgust, but he held back. He wished Rory was not married and if the man hadn't claimed her as his bride, it meant she could still come with them. He could protect her. Still be friends. It was enough. It had to be.

Rory straightened and turned to face him. It wasn't defiance he found in her eyes, but resignation. She held up the ring in front of him. Intricate patterns covered it, too big for her to wear. It reminded him of...

No.

"You recognize it." Rory said.

"It can't be." Riel shook his head. He stepped closer to it, drawn by the ring as he always would be. "How did you get this?"

"It is my wedding ring, given to me on the day of my proxy marriage."

Riel looked at her... *no*... she wasn't, she couldn't be.

"I understand you are bound by the oaths you made on this ring to your father to protect its bearer." She smiled sadly. "The Seeress explained it to me."

"That means you're..." Riel paced.

"Aurora of Elsass." She stood straight, her bearing at one with her title. He saw it then. She wasn't just a shepherdess.

Riel staggered sideways as though Nega punched him in the shoulder. "You're married to my brother." He stepped out of her proximity but just as quickly, walked back to her.

"Yes," she whispered.

"You're supposed to be asleep." A jolt went through him as he remembered meeting her, her request to look in on the chateau's inhabitants.

Rory simply held out her hands, presenting herself as she was. Riel stopped his pacing and looked back at Rory and the ring.

"I saw your castle. Everyone's asleep. So you can't be..."

Rory looked away. "Everyone in my home is asleep. I thought if I could leave, not have a home, it would stop the curse." She stared over the edge of the cliff to the forest below, toward Kehl.

Riel paced, running his hands through his hair, then looked at her. "You can rally the refugees. If they know you're alive, they'll have hope! They'll have someone to lead them, and..." He stepped back and began his shift, ready to fly and take her with him.

"Stop!" Rory's command echoed back from the vines, and he fell silent. The urge to speak was strong, but his tongue was stuck to the roof of his mouth. His body, which had partially shifted, retreated painfully to its human form, his bones cracking and resetting quickly.

If he had any doubt that she had Claude's ring, Riel lost it now. All the times he'd protected her, felt the need to take her to safety, asked her to come with him, were because of the ring. He glared at her, and she sighed.

"I see. It really forces you to obey me, doesn't it?" She looked up at him, her eyes watery. He thought for a moment he wanted to hug her. But as she squared her shoulders again, her gaze resolved.

Riel crossed his arms over his chest, his only act of defiance. She stood with authority, and it terrified him.

"Come here Riel."

No. But he stepped forward, his body obeying the weight of her words. Once again, he loathed the ring.

"Give me your hand," she said, holding the ring flat in her palm.

No! He shook his head, looked into her eyes, and pleaded with her not to do it. *Don't command me!* But his hand covered hers.

Rory placed her other hand on his cheek, a gentle gesture at odds with what he knew was coming. The Seeress knew Rory could use him against his brother. He remembered the aftershocks of their dual commands in the forest. He couldn't fight them both.

"You are a good man, Riel. If only you had been..." Rory shook her head and placed her hand on top of his with the ring underneath. "I know what it's like to be bound to this ring."

He braced himself, readied his mind to be bent to her will, and wondered if anyone could resist its corrupting power. He closed his eyes, ready for the power to settle over him as it always did with his brother's every command. As it did now with her current command. He made himself ready to be used as a weapon. Again. And for the pain that would come.

"As bearer of this ring, I command..." Rory hiccupped. Riel opened his eyes to see tears streaming down her face. His heartbeat thundered in his ears. He wanted to wipe away her tears, but that was foolish. He scowled at her instead. "I command..." She searched his gaze, then took a deep breath. "I command you to be released from any oath you ever made on this ring, and not beholden to it henceforth."

Riel's tongue loosened to release a roar. Rory flinched at the sound. He shifted into his dragon self and launched himself into the air, feeling lighter than he ever had before. There was no pain. No commands echoed in his mind, nothing but his own thoughts, and they were for his friends. He stretched his whole body, feeling release. He looked down to see Rory, knocked on the ground, wiping a tear as she watched him fly. For a moment he thought he ought to go down to her, comfort her, take her with him. But he realized now, any draw to her had not been because of her, but the ring she bore.

He was free, so he flew off into the night to his loyal friends.

49

Rory took one last look around her. She stared at the outline of the Kehl Castle which sat South, from the *Rätsel* cave plateau. She could walk to it in a few days if she aligned her path to the stars and the sun.

Rory peered down the edge of the cliff, near where she and Riel climbed. She refastened the rope that was wrapped around the rock back to her waist. She found the same rune at the top, and rubbed it, then peered down. The grooves appeared again, making her sigh in resignation. Going down would be difficult. She would have to guess at the holds for her feet. Too bad she freed Riel before he could fly her down.

But he *left*.

Tears formed in the corner of her eyes. She needed to know if the seeress was correct. Riel hadn't even known she had the ring, and she'd never intentionally used it against him. But no longer bound, he'd flown away, not once looking back. She envied his freedom, wished she could soar alongside of him. She was free from her oath to help Luiselle, but she was still bound to protect the girl.

Rory couldn't stay, or Luiselle would be at risk.

She hoped Riel went to Kuri and Nega. As much as she wanted to join them, their group was stronger without her. With Jean, they could hold their own against the *Beül* and Claude's army. She would only hold them back, and if they became part of her home...

She hoped they would distract the soldiers so she could get to Kehl.

As Rory mused, the rune faded, and so did the grooves in the wall. It wasn't the time to plan or hide; now was the time for action. She was unsure how much she could do alone. She felt the weight of the ring on her chest and tucked in under her tunic. But she also felt its silence. Rory grabbed her things, rubbed the rune, and peered down, taking a deep breath. She turned backwards and started the climb back down the cliff face.

Rory stepped her feet down on the ground faster than she expected, surprised at how uneventful it felt on the way down. But it had come with a price. Her body ached more than on the climb up. But not having to support a heavy shifter made her way easier. The light faded in the afternoon sun as she stepped into the forest.

She picked up a piece of wood to use as a staff and thought again about learning to shepherd from Reinhold. Tears formed again, but Rory blinked them away. She was on her own. She could leave it all behind, live off the land. Except, it felt wrong with so many people suffering. She needed to think like the Princess, no Queen, that she was. And when she thought about it, Riel was better serving her kingdom on the front lines, saving her people, than being her personal escort. Queens shouldn't put their desires above their people's needs. They needed to think of their people.

Rory paused and clenched her fists.

Just once. Just once, she wanted *something* for herself, her own happiness. First, her own grandmother cursed her. She lost her mother. Her own father sent her away out of fear. Then, she'd been married to a monster of a king. Without her consent. The Seeress named him in the curse, but he didn't care. He'd attacked her kingdom, hurt its citizens, and tried to kill her more than once. The one thing she'd done for herself was escape from the tower.

Muriel's face as she succumbed to the curse flashed in her memory.

She escaped as much for her household as she did for herself. And she'd found a place, even if it wasn't home. Until Reinhold forced the oath out of her to take care of Lu. The worst part was he hadn't needed the oath. She would have helped Lu, anyway.

Rory wiped a tear away as she thought about her farewell to Lu. The Seeress, her aunt, tried to force her to lose herself and allow Fayette to take over. Her hands clenched again around her staff.

She swung it around, lunged, and struck a tree. The branch made its mark, and she struck again, pretending it was the old Seeress. *For cursing me!* It shattered, and she found another branch.

Rory lunged and struck at another tree, saw Claude's sneering face as he hurt Luiselle.

She thought about the refugees and the babies, pictured the Kehl soldiers and the *Beül*. Rory stabbed at the tree repeatedly and didn't stop until the branch shattered in her hands.

She picked up another branch, swung around and struck another tree, and saw the current Seeress, Violette. *You tried to use me!*

She swung the branch; thought about Riel and backed away.

A tear spilled down her cheek. It wasn't his fault. His own oath, courtesy of the old Seeress, trapped him too. She bore the ring, and it was why he'd helped her, why they'd connected. He hadn't chosen her; the ring forced him to protect her. His invitation to join Kuri, Nega, and him was nothing more than a means to keep her close, protect her because she bore the very thing he'd sworn an oath to. The one thing he loathed.

He just hadn't realized it.

Tears cascaded down her cheeks, and her body lost its strength. She gripped the wood tight in one hand, wiped her eyes with the other. She missed him. But he wouldn't miss her.

She was alone. Everyone stayed with her to help Luiselle. Because the child had power. They all left when they realized Rory had no power of her own.

No one chose her.

The branch fell, and she collapsed to the ground. Silent sobs shook her body.

Who wanted a cursed princess? No one. How could she blame them?

The lengthening shadows from the trees hid the warmth of the sun, making her shiver. A caw sounded beside her, and she faced the limping crow.

"You're not staying with Violette and Lu?" She brushed away the lingering moisture on her face. Noticing the sting in her hands, which were red and swollen from wielding the fragmented branches, Rory pulled out the splinters as the crow hopped over to her. She found a smooth branch that worked as a staff. It had a hooked end and was the only weapon she had left.

Rory held it out, and the crow perched on it. "I'm going to Kehl. If you don't want to come with me, leave me now."

The crow looked at her, then tilted its head South.

"Thank you for the company."

A few hours later, Rory found a place to hide in a cluster of trees. She was tired from both the climb and the walk, but more so from the constant lookout. Finding a decent rock that would cut the north wind, she wrapped her cloak around herself and laid the staff down next to her. The crow flew up to a branch above to rest for the night. Rory pulled her hood over her head, hiding her face from the outside. She could pretend it was just another night with the sheep.

But she barely slept. She woke up to forest noises and dreaming of Riel. The forest made her nervous, but the dreams left her trembling. She was relieved to see Riel coming back, along with Nega and Kuri, when suddenly Riel's hair changed. He grabbed her throat, lifted her off her feet, and when she cried out for him to stop, Claude's voice would come out, laughing.

You let him go, and you've lost!

Rory woke up, her icy fingers rubbing her throat. It was tender to the touch, and she gasped for air. She sat up and rubbed her arms under her cloak, trying to warm herself up. She stared up at the sky, searched for Draconis to the North. When she saw it, she closed her eyes and wished...

She opened them again. Wishes wouldn't do her any good. She could wish they never placed her in this position. But all she really had to do was find a room, call it home, and she'd be asleep. And those who served her would be free. She could wish for friends, but she would curse them if she stayed too long, and they felt like home. And she would leave those who needed her to take a stand with Claude as their king. He would eliminate them, and the curse would spread to everyone.

The sound of moving leaves brought her back to the moment, and she peered from behind her cloak. A medium-sized shadow blocked the light momentarily, and Rory reached for her staff, careful not to make a noise. The rustle of leaves was uneven in front of her, and she tried to listen to the intruder's footsteps. As the noise grew closer, Rory counted to three and flung her hood up at the same time as she lunged with her staff... aimed at the crow who hobbled along in the leaves. It leapt backwards, flapping its wings, cawing at her, defensive against her attack.

"What are you doing?" She whispered.

The crow picked up something in its beak and hopped over. Rory settled back against her rock and held out her hand.

"Mrh!" It laid down some berries and mushrooms in her hand.

"Are they poisoned this time?"

"Caw!" The crow lifted his chin as if she was being ridiculous.

"You know I have to ask." She said and smiled. She popped a few berries in her mouth, enjoying the burst of flavour. "Thank you."

The crow hopped over again and pulled on her cloak.

"What are you doing?"

It hopped inside her cloak, setting its warm body against her chest.

"You're cold too?"

"Mrh." It leaned against her, and she felt it reverberate in her body. The subtle movement of the crow's breath and vibrations brought tears to her eyes. The simple connection to a bird made her feel like she wasn't so alone.

"You should know that I'm cursed," Rory said. "I'll never have a home because of it. It's why I enjoyed being a shepherd. No home." She looked back up at Draconis. "So if you're hoping for a home from me, you won't get one." The crow didn't answer.

Who are you talking to?

Rory jumped up and knocked the crow out of her cloak. She grabbed the staff and spun around to face the Navka child.

Rory gasped. "What are you doing here?" Her voice echoed in the forest, and she looked around to see if anything noticed her presence. She focused back on the Navka, its childlike body and blue flamed eyes. "I thought you were protecting the refugees." She whispered.

"We are."

"But you're here."

"We are many."

"Are you connected to each other?" She asked as she sat back down, nestled against the rock, and opened her cloak. The crow harrumphed, then hopped back inside.

"In a way. We are aware of each other." The Navka stared at Rory.

Rory sighed. "I appreciate your company, but is there something else you want?"

"You cannot stop him, you know." The Navka child stared at her, unblinking.

"I can try."

"You cannot change him." The child tilted its head, blue flames dancing where its eyes should be. *"He has let his hatred cloud his judgment for too long. You will not convince him."*

Rory crossed her arms over her chest. "Are you certain?"

"He hates all who are not human or animal, all that he cannot control. And he will stop at nothing to destroy us all. He is ruthless in his mission. And once he has you, he will destroy you, too." The Navka paused. *"You know this. "*

Rory took a deep breath, then sighed. "Yes, I know."

"Then why not join the others? Why are you trying to convince him to change? His heart is hard. His soul is black. He believes he is right in our persecution. You will fail."

"Because there has to be another way." Rory answered. "The Seeress who cursed me spoke of his heart. That once his heart changed, and we kissed, the curse would break."

"And you will live happily ever after?" Rory heard the sneer. *"It's foolish to think he would love you and that's the end. He must pay for his crimes."*

"If the Seeress missed me being awake, maybe she missed something else." Rory mused and shrugged; her chest tight. "I have to try."

"Then you are a fool, and you will lose everything."

Rory nodded. "I am a fool, with nothing to lose." She thought about her kingdom again. "And everything to gain."

The Navka stared at her a moment, then sat down beside her.

"You're staying?"

"Sleep. We will keep watch while you rest. You will need it."

When Rory woke, she found the Navka smiling at her. When she smiled back, the air popped, and they disappeared. She found the crow sitting nearby. It pointed to the ground with its beak, where there were more berries and mushrooms gathered.

"Many thanks," she said. They watched a squirrel scurry by, and the crow flapped its wings once, then angled its head towards the squirrel. "Much as I'd like some meat, I don't want to draw attention to myself with a fire."

With the morning sun to her left, Rory finished her breakfast and continued on her journey, staff in hand. She stopped by the nearby pond, took a sip, and thanked the local Navka for their help.

They walked for a day and a half. The trees became less dense, allowing her to see the clear sky. The shadows were short, and she took rest from the heat in a small crop of trees next to a clearing. Rory peered out to see a road marked with signs similar to the post where she used to leave food for the refugees. One arm pointed to Elsass, another to Kehl, and two more to locations she hadn't yet been to.

She wondered if she should take the marked trail to get there sooner, or follow alongside of it, under the cover of the trees. The latter made more sense, because anyone coming upon her from Kehl would assume as a sole woman travelling with a crow for a companion, that she was ripe for attack. Or worse, the Seeress.

That thought gave her pause, and she stared at the crow, who had once again found food for her. "Is it guilt that makes you feed me?"

The crow bowed down low, then bobbed its head.

"I forgive you, friend."

Rory thought she saw a tear escape its eye, but it turned away.

As she ate, the forest grew quiet. The crow flapped its wings silently. She nodded and pressed her fingers to her lips. She looked around for any predators, but nothing moved. Remembering the lynx, Rory looked into the trees but saw nothing.

In the distance, she heard a rumble, so she closed her eyes to discern where the sound came from. It was down a road she hadn't travelled. Rory ran into the woods, pulled her hood up over her head, peered around the trees, and waited. The rumbling grew louder and more distinct, the sound of horse hooves on the ground. Many of them. She lay in wait as the first soldiers approached the signs, then carefully looked around before heading towards Kehl. More hooves thundered, counting at least twenty soldiers. The *Beül's* team, if she wasn't mistaken.

Behind them, followed another two-dozen soldiers. Finally, the *Beül* himself appeared, holding onto the horse with his left arm. For a moment Rory felt guilty about crushing the man's arm, but when she remembered his hatred and how he tried to kill them, she set it aside. She noticed behind the parade came a small cage on a cart.

The soldiers stopped at the signpost.

"Are you sure you want to return to Kehl?" One soldier asked the *Beül*.

"I must." The *Beül* said. "The king needs to know what happened."

"He won't be happy with you." The soldier said. "Or any of us."

The *Beül* grunted. "I know. But I brought him a gift to curb his disappointment."

Disappointment? Rory focused on the soldiers, realizing they limped and stumbled, with various parts of their bodies in makeshift slings. Their armour was dented and broken, some of it burned. Rory knew they came from Riel and his friends! She smiled at the damage inflicted by him, glad he was no longer bound to serve them.

"Let's go get this over with," the soldier said. He spun his horse back on the path to Kehl, and Rory noticed his one leg dangling awkwardly. This was not a victory march, but a retreat. The King would be furious!

Rory smiled as their horses ambled by, noting all their injuries. But her joy was short-lived. As the cart passed by, iron bars held a small red-haired captive.

Rory's heart sank when she saw Kuri, bruised, beaten, and burned inside the cage.

50

*T*WO DAYS EARLIER.

Riel flew over the forest towards his friends and saw the large swath of land cut by the *Beül's* soldiers. He avoided their trail and flew around to the other side, low over the trees so their scouts wouldn't spot him.

Riel wanted to do aerial acrobatics because he didn't work for them anymore. He thought about taking them all out now, but wanted his friends safe first.

Then they would burn.

Riel's own anger startled him. He never felt bloodlust before. After all the things Claude forced him to do, all those he'd slain in his brother's name, he wanted revenge and freedom. They'd used him, and he wanted to show them just how wrong it was.

Riel shook his head. Vengeance would cloud his mind, and if he wanted to stop them altogether, he couldn't afford to be blinded by it.

There. A small waft of smoke, Kuri's making from the smell of it, drew him to the refugees.

No, he couldn't lose his temper, not with the remnant at the *Beül's* mercy. Riel would be strong for them. He found a small clearing near their camp and landed, then shifted so he wouldn't surprise them. He walked towards the camp, using his dragon vision, saw Nega move before she drew her sword across his neck.

It took her a moment to recognize him before she pulled back and smiled with her pointed teeth.

"Good to see you!" She slapped him on the shoulder, then looked back around him. "Alone?"

"Yes," he said, his voice raw. He rubbed his hand over his chest. "Alone." Then he pushed past her towards their group. The ache in his chest was the only pain he now carried.

Nega grabbed his arm, her strength holding him back. "Where are they?"

Riel growled at Nega until he saw her worried expression. "With the Seeress." He turned towards the camp. "We need to hurry. The *Beül* is on his way with his army."

Nega nodded, then followed him. "I knew Luiselle would stay with the Seeress. But I thought Rory might come back with you now that she no longer has to worry about her oath." They entered the camp together, and Riel's footprints drew everyone's attention. He didn't bother to be quiet, not with the army so close.

"Riel!" Kuri jumped up, ran over to throw her arms around him. When she pulled back, she looked at him and Nega, then scowled back at Riel. "Where's Rory?"

Riel clenched his hands at his sides and swallowed hard. "Rory is heading to Kehl."

"Whatever for?" Kuri stepped back and looked him over.

"She's going to betray us?" Jean growled from behind Riel. A few refugees turned to face him.

Riel took a deep breath before answering, Rory's tear-stained face the last thing he remembered. "No, she won't betray us."

"How can you be sure?" Jean said, stepping forward, his hands clenched. The shifter's body shook with the effort to hold back his anger.

"I believe she's going after Claude."

"Alone?" Kuri asked. She glanced at Nega, then back at Riel, her brow furrowed. "Why would she do that? It's suicide."

"Because Claude can't ignore her." The group stared at him like he'd lost his mind. Maybe he had. He hadn't been himself since Rory broke his curse. Maybe he was even more himself now. He took a deep breath. "Rory is Aurora of Elsass, Queen of Kehl." And then he told them about the ring, the curse and her refusal to join them. Once he finished, they stared at him. "Now, we have to deal with the *Beül*. I, for one, am looking forward to fighting him today." He rubbed his hands together.

"You're truly free?" Kuri asked.

"I am," Riel grinned. He felt feral, his cheeks high on his face in a smile. "But if you doubt, let's go test it out."

They set up their plan. The refugees would hide again, this time in their normal size. Riel would pretend to fight for Kehl at the *Beül's* command until Jean and Nega attacked, then he would breathe fire on the *Beül's* soldiers.

Later, Riel and Nega waited for the soldiers near the edge of their camp, further away, to protect the refugees while Jean waited in another set of trees.

"Are you okay?" Nega asked him.

"For the first time in years." He scanned the trees for movement.

Nega put her large green hand on his forearm. Her touch was so gentle, he wondered if she was well. "Did she know?"

Riel sighed. "No, I don't think she did." He looked down at the brushes.

"Do you remember when I asked you why she drew you to her?" She paused until his eyes found hers. "You said it wasn't the same. It felt different."

Riel grunted. "I was wrong." There was no motion as he looked into the trees. He felt the coming attack but couldn't see it.

"So she was controlling you this whole time?" When he didn't answer, Nega growled.

"What?" He spat.

"You're mad at her because she was controlling you." Nega punched him.

"Wouldn't you be mad at her?" He faced the trees. Something wasn't right. The forest was too silent.

Nega nodded. "Yes, if I thought it was intentional."

"You don't think it was?" Riel glared at Nega. "You didn't trust her from the beginning."

"True," Nega answered as she watched the trees. "She had the softest hands I've ever seen. Never seen someone that soft want to stay and fight or live outdoors before. And her skill at spinning. It all makes sense."

A tree snapped as they waited, but a rabbit scurried by and they both exhaled.

"Exactly." The hairs on Riel's neck raised. But none of the soldiers were near.

"So why, when she could have used you to bring your brother down, did she let you go?" Riel grew silent and Nega peered at him before facing ahead of the impending attack. "She was told to use you and your oath, but didn't. You could have been her weapon. She could have released you from Claude's oath only. Rory set you free from everyone. It's who she is, how she treats everyone."

Riel stayed silent. He focused on the forest, yet saw Rory's tear-filled face. He blinked the image away and kept surveying the area, ignoring the pain in his chest.

"Is her curse broken?" Nega asked.

"What?" Riel stared at her.

"I assume that's why she wanted to go to the Seeress, to break her curse." Nega scanned the forest for movement.

Her *curse*. "I didn't ask," Riel whispered. He thought about how her household was still asleep. The times she said she couldn't be with them, with him. He thought it was just her marriage... but he'd mentioned a home. "She was protecting us from her curse." Then he thought about how she went after Claude. "She wasn't trying to kill him. She tried to kiss him."

"Exactly. That girl has no bloodlust at all." Nega nodded. "Are you still angry at her?"

Riel thought for a moment. "No. Are you?" His chest tightened, as he worried about her facing her curse, and Claude, alone.

"Nope, not since she pulled the arrow out of your shoulder." Nega grew quiet. "So are we going to-"

Kuri's cry of pain rang out in the woods behind them. Without a second thought, they ran to her. Breaking through to the camp, they found the refugees and Kuri fighting off soldiers, Kuri's blade drawn. It clashed against the soldier's steel, ringing out in the forest. Nega roared and leapt into the fray, joining the elf, taking on the larger soldiers.

Riel didn't have space to shift, or a clear aim at the soldiers. But when he heard the *Beül* laugh behind them, he could no longer control his rage. He leapt and shifted, and knocked the Beül off his horse.

"Stop Riel!" The *Beül* shouted. "Your brother forbid you to hurt me or his men!"

Riel smiled; his lip curled over jagged teeth. The *Beül's* eyes widened as Riel picked him up in his claws and threw him over the horse. The loyal beast didn't flinch. Riel's tail lashed out and knocked many of the soldiers over, breathing fire over others, burning them through their armour.

One soldier jumped on his back, his blade sliced the leather-like skin of his wing. Riel cried out in pain, using his tail to knock the man down, then pinned him with his claws. The soldier sneered at him before he glanced to his right. Riel gathered heat into his lungs, then exhaled flames in the direction the soldier glanced. He immolated another soldier, poised to strike his other wing. Then he forced him and under his claws, who snapped at the soldier's face, his teeth inches away. The man whimpered, but Riel picked him up and threw him against a group advancing on the refugees. He and the rest of the soldiers collapsed and didn't move.

Riel hoped his friends found a place out of his way. With his rage, he was no longer safe to be around. He felt blades trying to pierce through his armoured scales, but his tail knocked them down. Men cried out in pain, many collapsed on the ground in the carnage. But they kept coming, wave after wave. Riel kept his flames aimed at them, and he welcomed the smell of burning Kehl flesh.

He herded a small group of soldiers away from his friends and approached them. He stalked his prey, eyes narrowed. Suddenly, a whistle sounded, followed by a call for retreat. The soldiers who could move, ran away. Riel gave chase, but his large body couldn't fit through the forest. He stalled, and turned back, relieved to see the refugees coming out of their hiding places.

Nega's cry of pain caught his attention. "They have Kuri!" she yelled, clutching her sword in one hand. Her other arm dangled at her side and swayed with her motions before she collapsed into Jean's arms.

51

R ORY FOLLOWED THE *BEÜL's* men towards Kehl from the shelter of the forest beside the path. She stayed near Kuri, who cried out when the cage jostled and threw her against the iron bars. Though Rory hated to hear her friend in pain, she was relieved Kuri was alive. Every time Kuri groaned, her eyes were closed. The rain that poured off and on during their trip didn't help things and kept everyone's pace slow.

As they approached Kehl, the rain stopped. The soldiers set up camp for the night in a forest clearing off the main path. Their bruised and battered bodies made slow progress. Rory stayed far enough away so the soldiers wouldn't find her during their watch. Not that they were looking for her.

Kuri's cage sat away from the fire, the soldiers ignoring her. Rory wanted to check on her friend, but never learned perfect stealth from Nega. She didn't want to reveal herself until she had a plan.

Rory looked at the crow, who sat beside her with some berries and mushrooms. "You can check on her." It shook its head. "And take her some berries. She'll be hungry, if she can eat."

"*Mrph!*"

"Please. They won't suspect you, and I don't want to lose her." Rory pressed her hands together. "I need to know if I can help her." Rory handed the crow a small cloth with some flax seed that she'd collected as they followed. "Take this to her. It will help with her swelling."

"Mrph!" the crow answered, then picked up the berries. She folded them into the cloth with the flaxseed. She tied it with a piece of the rope from her belt, then held the pouch with the small string hanging out. "Can you carry it?"

The crow tugged on the string, then hopped to the side. He flew into the trees as Rory crawled closer. The bird flew down quietly to the side of Kuri's cage and hopped over. The crow let out a quiet caw, and Rory watched the shadow curled up on the floor rise slightly. Kuri must have seen the crow because she sat all the way up. She cradled one arm in her other, then placed it in her lap. She reached her good hand between the bars to take the crow's offering.

Rory saw Kuri hold the pouch up in the moonlight. She placed it in her injured hand and struggled to open the pouch up one-handed. Rory felt bad about Kuri's limited mobility when the elf gasped. She looked at the crow, then held up the piece of rope. She searched the forest but couldn't see where Rory was. Kuri tied the piece of rope back around the fabric, gave it back to the crow, and it flew over to where Rory hid. The elf watched the crow, and when it landed in front of her, it dropped the cloth and rope. Kuri held up her good hand and waved.

She ate the food and then curled up on the cage floor. Rory packed away the cloth and rope and backed away from her current hiding spot.

"She looks bad," she said to the crow.

It bobbed its head.

"We have to get her out, but how?" Rory sat for a moment. Her mind drifted back to the town with the iron bars. "I have to be the one to release her." She sat for a while. "What do I do?" She asked. She looked up at the stars as Draconis winked at her. Rory closed her eyes, listening around her. The leaves rustled in the breeze, crickets chirped, and drops fell off the leaves into small puddles.

Water!

Rory's eyes jerked open. She crawled over to a stream and prayed it fed into a pond or river nearby.

"Navka?" Rory asked. Nothing moved. "How do I call them?" She asked the crow, who hopped along beside her. The crow came up to the stream, pointed to it with its beak, and made a circular motion. Rory dipped her fingers in and made the same motion. "Navka?" She whispered again. Rory looked around. Nothing. She sat back down on her heels, shoulders dropped, feeling the ache in her chest. A small tear fell off her cheek. She brushed it with her fingers, then tried one last time. "Navka?" She whispered as she swirled the water with her fingers.

What is it you want, Aurora of Elsass?

Rory looked up to see tiny blue flames illuminating the forest, one by one. She smiled, relieved.

"I would like your help, please."

The flames danced for a moment. *You cannot just call us on a whim.* They flickered out until only one remained. She felt it in her gut, the disappointment that they wouldn't help her.

Why the tears? The last one asked. *We felt them in the water.*

"The soldiers over there," Rory pointed to them with her thumb. "They have my friend, an elf named Kuri. A healer. I need help to save her."

Soldiers? The whisper grew harsh. Two flames reappeared.

"Yes," Rory said. "Kehl's soldiers, the *Beül's* men."

More flames reappeared before her.

"I was hoping you could distract them while I help her get free."

Distract? How? They asked, more flames appearing with every moment.

"I don't know." Her hair fell into her vision without the rose. She pushed the locks behind her ear. "Is there something you can do?"

Silence answered her. However, more flames appeared, too many for her to count. *We have no plan.* The blue flames brightened the forest until she saw shadows dancing around the flames. The blue light was surreal and terrifying.

"Just appear," Rory said. "Like you are now."

How would this help? We want revenge.

"You are terrifying in number, especially if you move around, surrounding them, getting them to panic."

When?

"Give me time to get in position near my friend in the cage. It would help if you could avoid illuminating the cage."

Done. The flames extinguished out, and she quickly scrambled to the area where she'd seen Kuri before.

"Can you make sure she's awake?" Rory asked the crow.

It bobbed its head and flew over to the cage, and made a muffled sound. Kuri sat up, carefully cradling her arm. The crow hopped to where the latch was. Kuri tilted her head, so the crow hopped back to her, flapped its wings, and hopped again to the cage gate. Kuri manoeuvred herself in place.

"*Beül!*" a soldier yelled. A few others cried out in surprise. Horses whinnied, but otherwise they showed no fear. The Navka were not after them. The *Beül* himself stumbled up frozen as dozens of flames appeared around them. Soldiers stepped back from the flames. The horses pawed the ground, sensing the surrounding soldiers' fear. One soldier glanced back, found more Navka, and bumped into the other soldiers. Sweat ran down their temples.

Rory crept to the end of the cage, the cloak over her head, shielding her face. She glanced at the soldiers, then up at Kuri's bruised face. "Rory?" Kuri whispered.

"Hi Kuri," Rory said. "Can you walk?"

Kuri nodded.

"Leave us be, Navka!" The *Beül* yelled at them. "We are not afraid of you."

Rory slid the iron bar that secured the cage over.

You should be! They hissed. The soldiers jerked upright, then many of them fell to the forest floor. Some of their eyes held blue flames before they went vacant and stopped breathing.

The *Beül's* eyes widened, but he stood up taller. "I will not cower to you." He said.

Rory opened the end of the cage, but the resounding screech echoed through the trees. Rory and the *Beül* stared at each other, before he yelled, "The elf, she's escaping!"

The soldiers remained immobilized, their faces white with fear as the blue flames touched the top of their heads. Shouts and groans came from a few. The others had their mouths open in silent screams. Many of the men turned blue, their chests no longer moving.

Rory shoved the cage door open, grabbed Kuri's arm, and dragged her out. Kuri groaned with pain. "Sorry Kuri, we have to go."

Together, they stumbled into the trees. The forest floor dulled the sound of footsteps behind them, but the leaves rustled with movement.

You will not escape, Beül*! We will have our revenge!*

Rory turned back as the *Beül* chased them with a sword. Rory set Kuri down, grabbed her staff, and prepared to defend them with what she had. "Stay out of sight!" She said to her friend as her hood fell off her head.

She stood her ground as the *Beül* approached. He held his sword in his good arm, ready to fight. "You!" He said through clenched teeth. "I will take pleasure in killing you!"

Rory pulled herself to her full height, pulled out the ring, and held it up in front of her. "You would hurt your Queen?" Her heart pounded, her body shook, but she held herself strong.

"You are not my Queen!"

"I am Aurora of Elsass, your queen by marriage."

The *Beül* stopped moving for a moment, his eyes narrowed. "You lie."

"I have the king's ring." She held it up.

"You consort with *them!* You are no queen of mine!" He lunged after her. His sword came down in a full arc. Rory deflected it with her staff. It splintered as it broke in half. He came at her again, but she dove out of the way. She kicked her feet at his knee as he swung the sword toward her, the blade missing her shoulder. He advanced again, though she jumped out of the way. Again, and she kicked, but missed him. He swung close enough that she moved to the side and swung what she had left of her staff. She jabbed the broken end into his injured arm.

The *Beül's* face reddened, his eyes bulged before he lunged at her again. Rory dove out of the way, but tripped on a root, dropped the fragments of her staff. He took advantage and swung his sword again. At the last moment, Rory crossed her arms in self defense and closed her eyes. But the swing never made contact.

Instead, she heard wings flap, making her open her eyes to see the crow claw at the *Beül's* face. He stepped back out of the way as blood poured out of his eyes, before he dropped to his knees. The crow pecked and pulled the man's eye out of the sockets. It clawed his neck, and blood spurted out of it just as the Beül brought the sword down.

Rory gasped as the crow took the blow to its shoulder, partially severing the wing from its body.

"No!" Rory scrambled to get up. Her voice echoed in the forest. She spun around, but nothing moved. No soldiers, no blue flames.

"Rory?" Kuri asked, her voice weak. "The crow!" She pointed to a purple glow that shrouded the crow, who lay gasping on the *Beül's* chest. It rose and fell slightly in the eery light.

Rory ran over to the *Beül*. "You... *evil*... cursed... woman!" He spat out each word. "You've... ruined... everything..." He rasped before taking his last breath.

Rory reached down and cradled the crow. She lifted it carefully off the *Beül* and brought it over to Kuri. "Can you heal it?" She asked as she laid the crow down beside her. Rory stroked the crow's feathers near its head, careful to avoid its injury.

Kuri shook her head. The crow shuddered as her tears gathered. The purple glow grew brighter. Its radiance forced her to look away. When she looked back, both Kuri and she gasped.

A small, cloaked figure lay where the crow had, blood spilling out of the deep cut through its collarbone. It breathed raggedly, so Rory reached down, gently turning the figure over to its side. As she did, the hood fell away and Rory stared into Reinhold's eyes.

"What? Reinhold! I don't understand!" She ran her fingers along his temple and held his good hand.

He lifted his good arm and brushed his hand against Rory's cheek. His thumb wiped away her tears. "It's good to speak to you again, child."

"Kuri?" She looked at her friend, whose eyes were wide in surprise.

Kuri's skin colour was grey in the moonlight. She shook her head sadly, still cradling her arm. "There's nothing I can do."

"No! Kuri, there must be something-"

"Listen Rory," the troll coughed out. "I'm sorry I bound you, but I worked for her."

Rory put one hand on his on her cheek and squeezed his other. "Why a crow? Why not just lead us yourself?"

"Her doing." He coughed, blood still poured from his shoulder. "You need to stop the king. Find a way." He coughed again.

"I don't know how." She answered in tears. "I can't do it without you."

"You must. You're stronger than you know, than they ever gave you credit for." He coughed again. "I knew it the moment I saw you awake outside your chateau."

"But-"

"Trust yourself, your instincts." He coughed, his arm grew limp. Rory held it to her cheek, tears streaming over their hands. His chest stopped moving, and Rory carefully lowered his hand to his heart. Rory brushed her tears away as her body shook with sobs. After several moments, she noticed Kuri trying to hug her with her good arm. Rory wiped her face on her sleeves.

Kuri stood up.

"What are you doing?" Rory asked as Kuri limped back towards the camp. Rory stood up to follow as Kuri checked the soldiers for things. Kuri found a satchel in one soldier's things, the bag she normally wore. Kuri sat down and mixed a concoction, then drank it.

"So what now?" Kuri asked.

Rory faced the carnage, then stepped around two soldiers. The early morning light filtered through the trees. She found a soldier close to her in size and stripped him of his weapons. She found another closer to Kuri's size and stripped him of his weapons and armour, and a set of clothes to bring to Kuri. It was slow work, but she got it done before noon.

Much of Kuri's swelling had gone down, and she no longer looked grey. She flexed her injured arm.

"Now," Rory unfastened two of the horses from where they'd been tied. "Now, you take me to the king."

52

CLAUDE AND ILSE STOOD in the watchtower, off to the side, watching the soldier clutch the Seeress' arm as he dragged her to the gate. She put up a good fight, but staggered when he knocked her with his pommel. While he cheered at making the old hag weak, he narrowed his eyes on the pair. The soldier was on the small side. How could this soldier subdue the Seeress when the *Beül* couldn't?

The soldier hit the Seeress, and she fell to the ground. Her hood fell off, and his eyes widened. The Seeress he brought was... "Fayette?" The whispered name escaped his lips. Ilse faced him for a moment as he continued to watch. The soldier punched Fayette to make sure she moved as blood trickled down her bruised cheek.

"She's wearing iron cuffs," Ilse said.

Claude nodded as Fayette fell to all four limbs. The rusted iron peeked out of the long cloak, her wrists red and blistered underneath.

"The *Beül* sent me with a gift for the King." The soldier yelled to the gatekeeper.

"Interesting," Ilse said. "*He* didn't apprehend her."

"The *Beül* would want to bring me this prize himself." Claude answered. "He has failed too much to miss witnessing my joy at seeing her brought in."

"Perhaps your brother distracts him?" Ilse asked.

Claude nodded at the possibility.

"Will you let us in?" The soldier yelled. He took his sword, yanked on Fayette's hair, and pulled it back sharply, her neck exposed to his blade. She cried out in pain. "Or do you want me to execute her here?"

Claude swallowed. His hands twitched. "Order them in."

"Do you want to meet with them?" Ilse asked. "Or shall I?"

Claude ran his fingers through his beard. He wanted to run his fingers on Fayette's neck, see if she truly lived, feel her pulse slowly disappear. His fingers twitched again. The faerie *lied*.

"Find out what game they're playing at," he said, stretching his fingers out to steady them. "Then kill them."

Ilse didn't rush out the door. Her fingers twitched, then went still.

"You have something to ask?"

"You don't want to handle this?" she asked.

Claude stared at her, but she held his gaze without flinching. He always respected that about her. She never showed fear, even when she should.

"This is a trap, nothing more." He waved his hands to dismiss her. "Putting me in the same room would give them time to spring it."

Ilse bowed and righted herself. "Of course. Forgive my question, my king."

He waved to the door as Ilse marched off to talk to the men at the gate.

"Laniel," Claude commanded.

"Yes, my king?" The soldier behind the door entered.

"Watch Ilse's interrogation," Claude ordered. "If there is a problem, alert me immediately. Especially if the problem is with Ilse."

Laniel bowed before him and left. Claude heard the gate rise and the bridge lower to the other side. He clenched his hands, wondering what Riel was playing at, and where he found this imposter.

53

R ORY CAUGHT KURI'S GAZE as the elf shoved her into the castle. Other soldiers escorted her away. Kuri's illusion of Rory as the Seeress would fail without her presence to keep it going. But Rory knew they had to part now. Kuri saluted the Kehl soldiers, then returned to their horses. Kuri said she had to return to the *Beül* to hunt Riel. Rory agreed. Kuri had to join their friends and protect the refugees.

The gate closed behind her; the sound echoed in her mind. She fought the desire to run back outside into freedom and faced the armed guards. She ignored her racing heart and sweaty palms, and clasped the staff she still held, loosening her grip to appear relaxed. The soldiers stared at her with mixed reactions. Some with outright hatred, but others with curiosity. Some even displayed a reverence which surprised her. She was glad not everyone feared the Seeress. Rory purposely leaned on her staff, showing the iron shackles that revealed her restrained powers.

Nobody moved until a woman strode through, and they allowed her to pass. She didn't dress as one of the court. She wore armour over her dress and carried a sword with her. Her blond hair was short, like a soldier. Rory envied her, both for her presence and her freedom.

"Seeress," she said, walking back through the soldiers. "Follow me."

Rory adopted a hobble with her staff and followed the woman. A pair of soldiers followed closely behind. Rory wondered how long it would take for the illusion to fall. Sweat poured down her back, but she kept her face neutral.

They passed narrow corridors, then went underground. They passed several prisoners held behind iron doors. She'd seen this before, shuddering as she remembered Luiselle's time here. When the woman turned to the right, Rory expected another prison chamber. Instead, she found a room with a single chair in the back, and the only open window to the outdoors.

"Sit," the woman commanded. Efficient in all her movements, she reminded Rory of Nega, but human and tiny. Rory sat down in the open chair, facing with her back to the soldiers. The woman stood in the entry, then dismissed the soldiers behind her with a wave of her hand. She made a show of displaying the pommel of her sword and the additional smaller blades in her belt.

She stood staring at Rory, studying her intently, head to toe. Rory remained calm, but didn't flinch, yet she recognized the moment the illusion faded. The woman's eyes widened, then she nodded.

"You're not Fayette." Her voice held no malice or anger. She didn't move.

"I am not." Rory confirmed. She didn't know this woman. Evidently, Claude didn't want to be in the same room. This threw off Rory's plans. She couldn't convince Claude to kiss her and break the curse if he wouldn't show. Especially if she didn't look like Fayette.

"The resemblance was impressive. Your skill or that of the person posing as the soldier with you?"

"What do you think?" Rory leaned forward on her staff, revealing the iron cuffs again.

The woman placed her hands on her hips. "I think the iron cuffs directly on your wrist mean you couldn't place the spell. The welts disappeared, which means it was part of the illusion." She placed her hand on the hilt of her sword. "So, that makes you a human." The woman licked her teeth under her lips and made a sucking noise before her grin spread across her face. "That's too bad. Makes you easy to dispatch. I'm almost disappointed."

Rory swallowed. "And that's what you'll do, dispatch me?"

The woman lunged and Rory jumped up, tripping backwards and rolling out of the way of the blade aimed at her throat. Rory's cloak spun around as she pivoted to face the woman and lunged forward. She twisted out of the way, but the woman's sword pierced through Rory's cloak, sliced it down the side as it struck the stone wall joint while Rory pulled away.

The woman smiled at her. "You're more than I expected." She yanked the blade from the stone, but it snapped. They both looked at the partially wedged blade in the stone, then back at each other. The woman examined the broken blade and frowned. "Pity, that was my favourite sword." She tossed the handle over to the side of the room. Her eyes narrowed, but twinkled in delight as she focused on Rory. She smiled as she reached both arms to her sides and pulled two smaller blades. "But combat up close is much more fun."

Again, the woman reminded Rory of Nega. Their fighting styles were similar, but Nega simply fought. She didn't relish her victories. This woman attacked with a focused look. Rory grabbed her staff and deflected the woman's blows multiple times. She lunged at Rory, but Rory deflected again, slamming her staff into the woman's side to put space between them. Rory's breath grew ragged, but the woman in front of her looked calm.

"You surprise me." The woman rubbed her side. "I don't normally like surprises, but this is excellent." She spun the small blades in her hands between her fingers and stepped forward. "But the king, he despises surprises." She stepped forward again until Rory backed away. "Who trained you to defend yourself?"

"I'm a shepherd," Rory answered. She shrugged as if it made no difference, but she kept her eyes on the woman. She wouldn't give Nega's name, or they'd realize who she was. The woman moved forward one slight movement at a time. "You're not much different from a lynx I once fought against."

The woman smiled, pleased. "I am honoured you compare me to such a noble predator." She took another step forward. "What happened to the lynx?"

"It no longer stole my sheep." Rory stepped to the side.

"What's your name?" The woman asked as she mirrored Rory's movements.

"What does it matter when you're trying to kill me?" Rory retorted. She stepped forward, and around the blade wedged in the wall. Its sharp edges could still do some damage.

"So I may honour you in your death." The woman spun her blades around in her hand. "Most do not last this long with me. I am glad to have the challenge." The woman bowed to Rory without looking away. "I am Ilse, the King's proxy and personal guard."

Rory paused a moment, swallowed before answering. This was the woman who stood in her place at the throne with Claude? "I am Rory," she said to Ilse.

"Rory, shepherd, trained to fight lynx and other predators, I honour you in your death." The woman lunged at Rory again, her body within striking distance. Rory deflected the blades with her staff, getting in another blow to the woman's side, then moving away. Ilse didn't back away, but lunged with more strength.

The two women fought and took turns attacking and deflecting, until Ilse swung her leg out as she struck and tripped Rory, knocking her down on her back. Ilse's blade came to Rory's throat, and she held still, stared into Ilse's eyes. *This is it. This is all there is. At least Muriel and my home will awaken.*

"Shepherd Rory, you have been an honour to fight." Ilse flipped her blade in her hand and moved to slash Rory's throat. Rory closed her eyes, waiting for the feel of warm blood, but she heard a gasp.

Rory opened her eyes to see Ilse staring at her neck.

"Where did you get this?" Ilse whispered, holding something up. Rory saw the ring, held in the blade's tip.

"Are you finished, Ilse?" A man's voice came from the corridor.

"Groan!" Ilse whispered to Rory. Rory stared blankly at Ilse. Ilse rolled her eyes, then punched Rory in the gut, and Rory let out a noise between a wheeze and a gasp. "I'm fine Laniel." Ilse called out. She reached into her belt and pulled out a skin and cut into it. The bright red liquid sprayed everywhere, and Ilse flung it around and painted it across Rory's neck. "I have to do this." Ilse whispered as she cut Rory's neck. It stung, but Ilse had only scraped the skin. "Pretend you're dead, or soon you will be," she whispered to Rory. Then she stood up as a man walked into the room.

Rory stopped moving and closed her eyes, facing away from them. She fought the urge to breathe.

"You're just in time to clean up after me," Ilse said. Rory heard the swoosh as Ilse spun her blades around. Rory felt her face redden.

"By Draconis! Ilse, why do you always leave such a bloodbath behind you?" Rory heard the man run his fingers through his beard.

"She didn't cooperate." There was a pause in the conversation. Rory's lungs burned.

"Was she Fayette?" the man asked.

"No, just a sick joke played by some shepherd. Likely trying to inspire the population into an uprising."

Rory heard the metal rub against itself as he moved. He was covered in armour. "Very well, I'll go inform the king that you eliminated her. Apparently, in quite the massacre." There was the sound of steps heading out, then he yelled, "Clean up your own mess this time!" Finally, footsteps disappeared down the corridor.

Rory felt a boot tap her on the shoulder. "You can stop pretending. He's gone now." Rory gasped for breath. She turned to look into Ilse's face, her smile replaced with pressed lips and a scowl. "Now, tell me who you really are, and where you got this ring." Ilse held a blade to Rory's throat, the tip pointing into the skin without piercing it.

She took a calming breath, despite Ilse's blade. "It is my wedding ring." Rory answered.

"That can't be. They delivered it to the cursed Princess of Elsass." Ilse's eyes narrowed and the blade pierced Rory's skin. "Speak. Now."

"I am Aurora of Elsass," she said.

"You lie." Ilse's face reddened, and her eyes bulged. "The chateau is still asleep under the curse."

"You're right," Rory said. "It is. But I left as the curse fell. I have no other home, so the chateau and those who live in it remain asleep." She remembered Muriel's prone body.

"You lie."

Rory sighed. Closed her eyes and breathed out. "Muriel, my servant, gave me the ring on the eve of my eighteenth birthday. The ring bound Riel to me, until I released him."

The blade dropped away from Rory's neck. "You released him?"

Rory nodded.

Ilse sat back hard as she searched Rory's eyes. Panic replaced her confidence. "Now, how will we defeat him?"

54

THE LIGHT FADED AND darkness fell as Riel, Jean and Nega made their way to Kehl.

"We need to find shelter for the night," Jean said. Riel nodded.

"No." Nega stood in front of him, drawing her sword, placing it at Jean's neck before either of them blinked. "We keep going."

Jean growled at her as his eyes shimmered. Riel knew Jean was near his transformation. Their tempers were all on the surface.

"Nega," Riel's voice was low. "You need to rest."

She arched her eyebrow up at him. "You'd rest if they kidnapped Rory?"

Jean laughed, but Riel scowled at him, then crossed his arms over his chest. "I know Kuri. She would want you to heal."

Nega's lip curled up in a snarl. "She also knows I would not allow them to torture *her*." She huffed, spinning around to stick her sword into the ground before clutching her limp arm.

Jean glanced at Riel and shrugged.

Riel went to Nega and braced himself for her reaction when he placed his hand on her shoulder. Instead, her solid shoulders sank under his touch. He was used to her ogress frame towering over him, but she looked small.

"Nega?" he asked.

"I failed her."

Riel turned her around to face him, surprised by a single tear travelling down her cheek.

"I will help you find Rory, save the kingdom." Nega had a moment of light in her eyes before it faded. "But then you must promise to end my life for not protecting hers."

Riel's heart hammered. "Nega..."

She placed her good arm on his shoulder. "I am her bodyguard, her sworn protector, and I failed her. The honour of my kind deserves it."

Riel shook his head. "I can't-"

"You must."

Riel swallowed. He would not fight her now, nor end her life later. "I-"

"Riel, Nega, come over here!" Jean's voice came from a nearby clearing.

Nega grabbed her sword before they picked their way through the forest to where Jean stood.

Riel smelled the death and decay before he saw it. It mixed into the earthy scent of the forest floor, but it was there. The stench did not prepare him for the scene in front of him. The forest's silence was remarkable. Even the trees were still.

A small battalion of soldiers, all strewn about, lifeless except for the blue flames that danced around their heads.

"Navka!" Nega's sharp whisper broke, deafening compared to the silence.

The three of them stood staring at the bodies and the Navka.

"Riel." Jean pointed to the bodies. "Their armour is burned."

Riel saw the blackened armour. "They're the ones who attacked us?" He whispered, then studied the carnage. He recognized some of them from battle. Except, one of them was missing armour altogether, and another his armour and his clothes. Iron bars caught his attention in the fading light.

"There!" He pointed to the cage, then hurried over, picking their path through the deceased. When they got to the cage, the gate hung open.

"She's not here!" Nega cried. With relief or desperation, Riel couldn't be sure. The empty cage was a positive sign.

"Let's fan out and see if we can find her." Jean suggested. He and Nega each took a different path through the carnage while Riel walked around the perimeter. Two blue flames danced over something in a clearing.

"Over here!" Riel called until the others hurried over. They made their way to the blue flames, each one hovering over a body. Riel bent over the first one as the others watched. Nega wouldn't approach them, but Jean would protect him from anything else. He looked at the body under one blue flame. "Troll." They both looked at him with questioning glances, but neither said anything.

Riel left the dead troll and walked over to the other body with a disfigured face. He was missing one arm, but the signet for the *Beül* was on the one that remained.

Riel straightened and yelled, breathing fire up into the sky. He felt lighter, the threat of the *Beül* gone, but frustration boiled in his gut. He wouldn't get his revenge against the man who destroyed so many in Kehl.

"Riel?" Jean asked.

Riel stared at the Beül. He had a gash across his neck, and something pulled his eyes from their sockets. Riel clenched his fists, then turned back to his friends. "The *Beül* is dead."

Both of his friends clenched their fists.

"Where is Kuri?" Nega whispered.

"Right here," came Kuri's voice. They whirled around to find her dressed as a soldier.

Nega's eyes widened. She dropped her sword and rushed over to her, ran her good hand over the elf's face. "You're okay?" She asked. Kuri nodded and Nega pulled the elf in a one-armed embrace, ignoring the burn of her arm against the armour. Nega dropped to her knees in front of Kuri, who ran her fingers through the ogress' cropped hair.

Riel and Jean made their way over to them. They each gave her a slap on the back before she reached down and tilted Nega's face up.

"Let's do something about that arm." They made their way to a rock outside the carnage, where two horses waited for them. Kuri started making something to go on Nega's limp arm.

"How did you escape?" Nega asked. She placed her good hand on Kuri's arm, halting her movements.

Kuri smiled, put her hand on Nega's cheek, then continued mixing. "Rory saved me. Along with the Navka, and the troll."

Riel's heart pounded as he faced Kuri. "Rory? How? Where? I left her at the *Rätsel* caves."

"She was heading to the castle at Kehl when she saw me in that cage." Kuri spread her mixture on Nega's limp arm, whispered a few words and an orange glow appeared. Then she continued to tell them what Rory did.

Riel found it hard to swallow. His fists got tighter as he listened to the story, and he felt the flames burn within him. When she got to Reinhold, his jaw dropped. "The Seeress forced the troll to be a crow?" He blew a hot breath into the air above them. A few leaves on the trees withered in the heat.

Kuri nodded.

Riel looked around. "Where is she?"

"In the castle at Kehl, to confront Claude." Kuri patted Nega's arm, then stood to face Riel.

"She's trying to break the curse? Alone?" Riel ran his fingers through his hair. "Does she think he'll listen to her once she's queen?"

"No, she hoped he'd listen to Fayette." Kuri said. "She thought maybe being Fayette would change his mind, but they wouldn't let me accompany her."

"The illusion is likely gone by now," Jean said.

"She's a fool!" Nega ground her teeth, jumping up. She stretched both her arms above her head. "What was she thinking?"

Kuri held Nega's uninjured hand in hers and stared at Riel. "She said it was time to be the queen her kingdom needed."

Riel closed his eyes. "Claude will see right through her. She'll die, or worse, he'll torture her, get an heir, and then eliminate her. He will know she has no recourse, nowhere to turn. She isn't strong enough to kill him."

"She believes she can convince him to end the curse." Kuri said.

"She won't." He glared at his friend. "You know she won't. He won't bend to anyone. Why didn't you convince her not to?" Riel felt his temperature rise and looked at the sky, dissipating more heat. Then he faced his friends again. "He'll destroy her," he said. He closed his eyes and saw her tear-stained face as he flew away. "If I hadn't left her..."

"If you hadn't left her, we wouldn't be here," Jean said, putting his hand on Riel's shoulder.

Nega carried the same guilt in her eyes, but Kuri's eyes were soft as she looked back at him. "You can't make Rory do anything she doesn't want to do."

"I should have taken her with me. At least she would be safe." He felt the hot air build in his lungs.

"It was her choice, Riel. You would never force her. You're not Claude." Kuri said. "And that's a good thing."

Riel spun around and blew fire on a nearby log. Flames erupted high into the forest canopy, and he relished the blazing heat before he inhaled the flames and blew the heat back into the sky.

A small hand clasped his elbow. "I'm sorry Riel." Kuri offered, and he hugged his friend tight, grateful Rory helped save her.

He faced her, his shoulders sagged as his anger left him. "What do we do now?"

Kuri smiled at him. "I'm glad you asked." She rubbed her hands together, her nose wrinkling as she grinned, eyes filled with mischief. "Because I have an idea." The three gawked at her. Kuri was a healer, not a strategist.

"And that is?" Jean asked.

Kuri smirked at Riel. He stepped away from her focus, his heartbeat thundering in his ears. "It's time to make you king," she said.

55

"WE NEED TO GO to another room." Ilse said, standing. She offered a hand to Rory, ready to move.

"Wait, how did I get the king's ring?"

Ilse smiled at Rory. "It's a long story, but it involves a magical duplicate that sits on Claude's hand and sending the real one to my aunt Muriel."

Rory didn't move. "My servant is your aunt?"

Ilse nodded. "No time for that now. We need to get going."

Ilse moved down the corridor first, then signalled for Rory to follow. After they made it to the end, Ilse pushed Rory behind a banner. Two soldiers walked by. From the shadows, Rory saw the two nod to Ilse before going on their way. Once they passed, Ilse peered around the corner, then motioned for Rory to follow her again. They travelled this way for several corridors.

Ilse gasped, then shoved Rory into a room behind a door. Ilse straightened as the door closed, left ajar. Rory glanced around the room and discovered she was in the throne room. One larger and one smaller throne at the end, flanked on either side by dragons and ogres. The room itself was stone, imposing and regal, while the king's banners hung above. Torches lit both sides, suspended on large columns. Small windows sat between the columns, allowing the sunlight to illuminate the dust in the air. It was large enough to have a squad of soldiers or a small group of guests, or perhaps a few dragons. In the middle sat a dining table, set for two. Rory was the only person inside.

"Ilse."

Rory swallowed, her mouth dry as she recognized Claude's voice.

"Laniel told me you left a mess of that imposter pretending to be Fayette."

The swoosh of skirts told Rory that Ilse bowed. "I was questioning her when her spell faded." Rory stood between an enormous banner and the back of the door.

"Did she offer anything useful?"

"She was skilled in defence." Rory heard the smile in Ilse's voice and thought Nega would be proud of her.

"But not skilled enough." Claude's voice sent a shiver down Rory's spine.

"Never, my lord." Another swoosh of skirts.

"What did she look like when the spell faded?" Claude spoke as if he didn't care, but Rory understood his calculating mind.

"Dark brown hair, pleated, fair skin, brown eyes. Your regular beauty."

Ilse gasped, and Rory covered her mouth with her hand. Rory had no weapons on her, nothing to save her new ally.

"Did she have a rose at her temple?" Claude's voice seethed. Rory fought her desire to step out of the shadows and confront the man, but held her breath.

"No, my lord." Ilse's voice squeaked. Rory eyed the torch under the enormous banner. Would the flames work? She was no dragon, but the king's robes could catch fire. If he didn't call the guard first. Rory heard the slap of something against the stone, then Ilse spoke. Her voice rasped. "I beg your pardon, my Lord, but what does the rose have to do with her?"

"Your description matched the woman Riel sided with, but she had a rose in her ear." Claude's voice grew quiet with each word. "You are my proxy, Ilse. Chosen, because you are skilled and I would have you by my side. Have I made a grave mistake?"

"No, my lord." Ilse's damaged voice made Rory wince. "You said you did not wish to attend."

The door opened, and Rory pressed herself behind the banner against the wall. Ilse came into sight, walking backwards on the tips of her toes with the King's large hands around her throat. He towered over her. Ilse's face turned red as she stared up at the king, her gaze unflinching.

Two soldiers appeared behind him, passed the threshold into the room. "Leave us alone. Stay outside the chamber. I will take care of this myself." Ilse's vision glazed over as Claude dropped her. She crumpled to the floor, gasping for breath. The soldiers paused for a moment. "I said leave!" Claude let Ilse gasp for breath twice more before lunging at her and picking her up by her throat again. Her feet dangled off the floor as his hands choked the life out of her. The soldiers disappeared but left the door open.

Claude dropped her again just as Ilse started losing consciousness. His smile was the same as when he called Riel to kill Rory in the forest. He had the upper hand, and Rory watched his cruelty again.

"Ilse," he sucked in with his teeth. She opened her eyes. "You should have had Laniel fetch me. I had such high hopes for you. When this mess was over, you would have given me powerful sons. Warriors." Claude grabbed her hair from behind and forced her to look up at him. "And we had such fun practicing."

Ilse whispered something to Claude, but Rory couldn't hear it. His face turned red with anger as he punched her in the jaw. She lay immobilized on the floor, and Rory put her fist in her mouth to muffle her scream. She checked if Ilse was breathing, but the little warrior's chest no longer rose and fell. A single tear fell down Rory's face as she watched Claude straighten himself before calling his guard in.

"Dispose of her." Claude ordered as they stepped in. There was only a brief hesitation as one soldier stepped forward and picked up Ilse's lifeless body. "Go find the woman she brought in." Rory saw Ilse's face as they walked by. For a moment, Ilse appeared to wink at her, but Rory blinked and saw Ilse's lifeless body.

Once the soldiers left, Rory struggled to breathe. She was alone with Claude. They left the door ajar. Rory would have to be quick or catch him off guard. The king swept one of the place settings aside and the dishes crashed on the floor. He stomped up the steps to the dais and threw himself down on his throne. He grumbled something about never pretending and ran his hand through his hair. The gesture reminded her of Riel, except his hair was the wrong colour.

Rory pulled out her ring. She took a deep breath and closed her eyes. Putting her hands in her pockets, she ran her fingers over the large single thorn given to her from the vine. She thought of how Luiselle was now safe, and Riel was free. If nothing else, when she was gone, she had helped. They would have to lead her people without her.

When Rory opened her eyes again, a grey jay sat in the window. A bird sat in each window, hopping around. Rory listened for movement around the corner, but there were none.

Taking one more deep breath, she tucked the ring back in her tunic, then stepped forward and stalked towards the throne.

"Claude, I believe you were looking for me." She stared at his stunned face. "Well, here I am."

56

"WHAT DO YOU MEAN, prepare me to be King?" Riel ran his hands through his hair, staring at the woodland creatures scurrying up the trees. "Rory broke my curse, but Claude is still alive. If she can convince him, she'll be queen with him."

Nega smacked Riel upside the head. He blinked back stars before he focused on the ogress again. "No one here wants Claude to be king. And no one wants Rory stuck with that selfish clod." She put her hand on his shoulder. "Do you?"

"My parents didn't want me to rule." Riel answered. "I wouldn't know how."

"You love your kingdom," said Jean. "It's more than your brother can offer. The residents would rally behind you, human and all other because you are both."

"The people in the village didn't exactly welcome us." Riel said.

"Because their leaders didn't welcome us," Kuri said. "With violence threatening them, if they didn't follow the *Beül's* men, would you stand up to them? Think of the humans who helped us escape."

They stood silent for a moment. As they did, the birds chirped, and the squirrels ran across the branches overhead. Riel smiled, remembering how the little animals fed Rory. *Too bad they can't help now,* Riel thought to himself.

Unless they could.

"What's your plan?" Riel asked Kuri.

"We need a large group to present you as king to the castle, so Rory can get close to Claude." Kuri responded. They all waited for her to continue. "That's all I have." She shrugged as they looked at each other. "I'm a healer, not a war strategist."

"And I am glad for that," Nega said, taking Kuri's hand in hers. The ogress looked at the others. "We need enough residents to support Riel's claim to the kingdom. Or at least the appearance of that."

"My illusion skills aren't that strong," Kuri gestured wildly. "I can't conjure up an entire army."

"I can rally the refugees," offered Jean. "They would support us in trying to get rid of Claude."

"Rory doesn't have much time," Riel said. "Not if they know who she is."

A gray jay landed next to them. "Perhaps we could help," a small voice came from the jay. Half a dozen more birds landed beside them, along with more squirrels.

Riel looked down at the grey jay. "You birds and squirrels *want* to help?"

"Silly!" The closest jay put an insect on the rock before it morphed into Luiselle. The one beside her did something similar, and up popped the Seeress.

"What are *you* doing here?" Jean growled at them but glared at the Seeress. His eyes narrowed, and he crossed his arms over his broad chest.

"I know you're angry with me, Jean, for using you and Fayette, but it was my mother's iron will." She looked around at the others. "I am merely trying to help you succeed now."

Luiselle reached over and took Riel's hand in hers, the slight gesture comforting. Riel gently squeezed her little hand, more thankful for her support than he would have thought. He knelt down beside her, looked her in the eye. "So what's your plan, little one?"

Luiselle smiled. Her lavender eyes brightened, then sought her grandmother. "She will conjure up the army while I sneak you inside."

"Why?" Riel faced the Seeress. "Why now?"

"His cruelty needs to stop, and you need to take his place." Luiselle answered, leaning into him, her face at his ear. "And you love her," she whispered.

Riel peered at the little girl. He opened his mouth to argue, but his tongue stuck to the roof, which was now dry. He swallowed and shook his head. "She's not mine to love." His stomach flipped as he said the words.

"No," Luiselle said. "She belongs to her kingdom. And that's in jeopardy, thanks to your brother." She stepped back and addressed the others, too. "If we don't act now, there won't be another chance."

"You've seen this?" Jean asked the Seeress. He changed his stance, ready to fight.

The Seeress shook her head before answering. "I don't need to see the future to know Elsass and Kehl are running out of time. If she succeeds in her plan, you will need to become a leader to help with your kingdom. If not, then the kingdom needs to see you stand up to your brother, so they have hope."

Hope is a dangerous thing, Riel thought, running his hands through his hair. Yet it warmed his heart, fighting with the acidic terror that they could lose everything. In Luiselle's hair, Rory's rose bloomed. Riel nodded.

The rest of their small group set off to the castle at Kehl.

57

"A ND WHO, EXACTLY, ARE *you?*" Claude asked, rubbing his fingers through his beard. Rory shivered. The motion reminded her of Riel.

"I am Aurora of Elsass, your queen."

Claude smiled, but his eyes narrowed. "I don't believe you."

Rory stepped forward and walked with purpose towards the throne, then stopped when Claude's hands twitched near a strange protrusion in the throne. "Why not?"

He gestured to her body. "You don't look or act like a queen."

"What should a queen look like?"

Claude laughed. "Not like a pitiful shepherd girl. You don't look royal at all, no finery."

"Finery doesn't matter without the support of your people. It's merely a display of wealth." Rory pointed to the painting of the ogress queen to Claude's left. "Your mother was a queen. A good one at that. She's not dressed much differently than any of your warriors."

Claude sneered at her; his lips curled in disgust. "She was a warrior. You want to take her place as queen?" He asked and gestured to the smaller throne at his side. "You want to stand alongside me as I rule my land?"

"*Our* land." Rory crossed her arms in front of her. "You are only the consort in *my* kingdom."

Claude laughed. Harsh and unyielding, the sound echoed off the stone walls and small glass windows. He shook his head, but his eyes never left hers. "You are brave or foolish. I'm not sure which."

"The greater opinion is that I'm a fool." Rory said, smiling. "I met your brother when you were trying to burn down my chateau and threw my staff at his nose."

Claude grew silent. He narrowed his eyes as he stood at his throne. Raised on the dais, he towered over Rory. "You control my brother. He wouldn't kill you when I commanded him." Claude placed his hands together behind his back. He attempted to put her at ease, but she knew enough of Claude to keep her guard up. "Tell me, Aurora of Elsass, where is my brother now?"

Rory pictured Riel above her, flying away after his release. *Free.* She fought back tears and focused on Claude. Sentiment would not help in the King's presence. She shrugged to make herself seem at ease. "I don't know."

"I don't believe you." Claude stepped down from the dais, and Rory forced herself to hold her ground. "He was ready to crush you, yet didn't. You know more than you're letting on." He stepped down to the floor and stood several feet away from her.

Rory shrugged again. "I don't know where he is." She relaxed her fingers.

"Liar." His quiet voice through clenched teeth made Rory's skin crawl. It was worse than when he yelled. "I don't believe you're Aurora of Elsass. Your chateau is still asleep. Everyone who tries to get inside succumbs to the curse with the sharp pain of limbs going still. Right before their eyes close and they don't wake up. My soldiers have been trying to get in for months. They can't even get past the forest's edge now." He stepped toward her. "You're *not* my queen."

Rory reached into her tunic and pulled out the fine chain she'd spun to hold up the ring on its side, the distinctive markings visible to Claude. "And yet, I have your betrothal ring."

He paused mid-step, several feet away. His gaze went to the ring, then back to Rory. "That's not the betrothal ring I had made."

"No," Rory said. "It's your ring, the one that bound Riel to follow your command." She walked towards the left, around Claude in a slow circle, still displaying her ring. Her gaze never left his. He followed her with his eyes, but didn't move, his hands clenched at his side. "Your proxy switched it from your very palm and sent it to me."

"Your plea and command." His eyes widened. "You bear the ring, you command the dragon." He faced her, his cheeks reddening, eyes bulging. "Do you have him awaiting a signal to attack me? You will force me to allow you at my side because you control my brother?"

Rory continued in a circle around Claude, closer to the dais. She thought of Claude's words and smiled. Perhaps she could convince him this way. "He is gathering an army as we speak." She hoped he couldn't tell she was lying.

"What is it you want, Aurora of Elsass?" They faced each other, Rory at the dais steps, Claude far enough away that she could sidestep if he attacked.

Rory stepped backwards up the stairs. Claude's nose flared, his eyes widened as she stepped her way backwards. She didn't falter until stood at the throne, towering over Claude.

"What I want, Claude of Kehl, is peace for our kingdoms. I will take my rightful place..." Rory stepped backwards, then sat in the King's throne, not the consort's. "Here."

"You will *not* be queen here." Claude put his foot on the first step.

Rory placed her hand on the protrusion of the throne, and Claude halted. Rory grinned and pulled the sword out of its secret location. Claude's eyes widened.

"You are a prepared king." Rory held the sword in front of her, turning it so she could see Claude on both sides of the sharp blade. "But I imagine a king who declared war by entering Elsass and killed its inhabitants before the promised betrothal alliance has to be."

Rory watched Claude's eyes narrow briefly before he smirked. "I can assure you; I would never attack a country I built an alliance with. You are misinformed." He said and rose another step.

Rory stood and held the blade to his throat, making him pause. "The Navka do *not* misinform." Claude flinched, so Rory continued. "Did you know the Navka are born from the deaths of children? I bore witness to the murders of those helpless babies and their mothers when we were not yet married. I believe you said you couldn't be with me because of other issues. Those issues were the slaughter of my kingdom's residents." Rory paused. Claude's throat bobbed as he swallowed. "Instead of marrying me, you attacked my kingdom and, therefore, declared war. What other countries are you invading? Who else do I have to broker peace with?"

"You think you can stop me?" Claude whispered, his jaw hard, his eyes narrowed. "What is it you want?" He stood on the third last step of the raised dais, eye level with her. She held the sword at his neck, firm in her grasp. "Are you here to kill me? You crushed my *Beül's* arm. My brother is under your control. You already attacked me. Are you trying to retaliate? Declare war?"

Rory paused, choosing her words.

"Here's what I think, *Aurora*." Claude pushed his throat into the blade of the sword, cutting his skin so blood dripped out. "You would have killed me already if that was your goal. But it isn't. You still need me. The question is why?"

Rory kept her blade firm, but her stomach flipped as Claude's eyes widened. His smile broke through, his eyes glinted.

"You need *me* to break the curse."

58

RIEL HATED BEING SMALL. The castle walls, corridors and rooms were generous, to both accommodate his dragon shifter father and his ogress mother. Both of them were half human, but that hadn't affected their size or their abilities. Riel could run through the castle as his grown dragon self without bumping into anything. Except for brief periods during his adolescent growth spurts.

Now, he rode a rat scurrying through gaps in the walls and led his friends to find Rory. And Claude.

His chest tightened, and he growled under his breath. Luiselle looked at him as she sat in front, on the rat. She put her hands on his where they held the rat's fur on either side of her, making sure she wouldn't fall off.

"Remember, she's strong," her tiny voice said.

Riel thought of all the times Rory didn't give up on her training with Nega. "I know. But I don't trust Claude. He's always been able to read people and takes what they value most. It will be no different for Rory."

Riel directed the rat to the left.

"Where do you think they are?"

"The throne room." Riel's nose wrinkled, his lip lifted in a snarl. "As a child, he was obsessed with sitting on the throne. Father used to let him pretend to dictate the people on his knee. He'll be there now."

"And Rory?"

"If she's confronting him, she'll be in there with him. But if she failed in her mission, she'll be in the dungeons." Or at the gallows.

Riel directed the rat to the right. The rat slowed down, and they peered through the opening of the kitchen, directly below the throne room of the grand hall. It was more active than Riel remembered, with many servants preparing a large roast and several portions of fish.

"They should have been here yesterday!" One servant complained. "It will be such a waste of food if they don't show up."

"Doesn't matter to his *majesty*." The other said. "Best to be prepared either way."

Ah, they were cooking for the Beül and his team, he thought. They would wait a long time.

From their small corner, Riel glanced around. Nega and Kuri approached behind him on another rat. Kuri sat in front of the ogress, who looked more yellow than her usual green.

"Not enjoying the ride?" He asked and smirked.

She glared back, fist at her mouth, hand on her stomach. After a moment, she pulled her fist away. "I am *never* doing this again."

Riel smiled. Kuri was safe in Nega's arms. Nega would do anything for Rory. Even ride on a rat again. As Riel searched the room, he realized how much the ogress and elf respected and admired Rory. She would make a good queen, except for her horrible king. They had to remove Claude as king and break her curse.

There.

The hole above the copper pot hanger should take them to the throne room. But they would need a diversion, or the servants would spot the rats.

"Stay here," he said. "When I distract the servants, head for that opening." He pointed to the corner, getting off the rat and shifting into an insect sized dragon. Nega switched onto Luiselle's rat, sheltering the faerie as Riel had. He hoped Nega wouldn't vomit.

He climbed up the wall, high enough that he could fly quickly over to the hearth. When the space was clear, he launched himself to glide over. As he flew, one servant stepped in his way, and he bumped into the woman's elbow. Large fingers tried to stop him, but he took off again. Riel sighed with relief until he realized he flew in the wrong direction. He swung back, glided down, and landed near the hearth.

He took a deep breath when the servants stepped away. Just before he fuelled the flames, a bright orange blur knocked him over. Riel looked up to stare into the crouched form of a calico cat. Its orange paw swiped at him, and he dove out of the way towards the fire. A second white paw blocked his path just as large sharp teeth crashed down. Riel crouched as tight as he could, but the bite never came.

"Get out, you mangy thing." A servant drove the cat away with a broom. She shook her head. "It's here for the rats, but that cat just trips us up."

Riel waited for the servant to step away from the fire. When she did, the cat stalked back in quick movements. Riel took a deep breath and fuelled the flames. They flared high, burning the meat. The servants yelled from the heat flash in the room. As they ran over with pots of water, he climbed up onto the hearth and launched himself into flight. The orange cat swiped at him, claws extended, but missed. The rats scurried through the opening as Riel met them. He felt bad for the servants. He breathed some of the fire back into his lungs, lowering the flames, then disappeared into the hole above.

He met them at the next opening and stared into the room. It was not as he remembered.

"This isn't the throne room." Kuri said from the rat.

Riel shifted to his human form and stepped outside the opening to look around. The arched colonnade ran lengthwise in both directions. "It's the corridor outside the throne room."

"Which way?" Luiselle asked. She slid off the rat as Kuri did the same. Nega fell off, landing on all four limbs. For a moment, she appeared to kiss the floor. Luiselle touched the nose of the rats, who scurried back into the hole.

"We head along the wall behind the banners there to those doors." Riel pointed them out.

They nodded before Riel led the way. Nega took up the rear. They walked under the banners, then sprinted at the gaps. Nega carried Luiselle on her shoulders to keep the faerie from falling behind.

As they approached the door, thunderous footsteps approached from two large soldiers. They flung the doors open.

"Duck!" Riel threw himself down to avoid the door as it swung over head. Once it cleared, he looked back at the others. Luiselle rubbed her elbow, and they all peered at him from the floor.

As their group stood, the soldiers stood in place, swords drawn. Kuri and Luiselle stood beside him, as Nega gasped.

Rory sat on the throne, its hidden defensive broadsword drawn, the tip pointed at Claude's throat. She was regal and poised with the sword in her hand. She looked every bit a queen. Glancing at the soldiers, he wondered what they would do if they were faithful to Claude.

"I wouldn't move if I were you." Rory's calm voice echoed from the throne.

The soldiers gasped. "My king?" One soldier addressed Claude.

"Remain where you are." Claude said, facing Rory. She was the threat to him.

"But sir..."

"I would do as he says," Rory said.

"She got the upper hand on Claude?" Nega asked, surprised. She smiled and wiggled her fingers. Riel chuckled at the ogress's pride.

Riel watched the scene, everyone still, then focused his gaze on Rory. Her sword hand was steady as she held the blade. But her other hand, on the throne, gripped it tightly. White knuckles gave away her tension. She hadn't defeated Claude. Not yet.

"My King, I hate to interrupt," one soldier gestured to them with his sword. "But we are under attack."

"By whom?" Claude asked, still staring at Rory.

"By your brother in his dragon form. He secured the help of the ogres and the *Skrzak*. There are several hundred encamped in the forest."

Rory's eyes widened. She had not expected this. Riel's chest ached when he realized she truly expected to be alone to confront his brother. If Riel saw her surprise from the floor, Claude wouldn't miss it.

"Not at your command?" Claude asked.

"Does it matter?" Rory retorted.

"Not really." Claude said.

"When did she become so shrewd?" Kuri whispered to Riel, holding Luiselle's hand in her own.

"That was my influence." Nega stood on his other side, fist thudding her chest.

Riel watched Claude, who focused so much on Rory that the soldiers didn't matter. Claude's fingers stretched wide at his sides, bent at the fingertips. He grinned at Claude's frustration.

"Send a few warning shots out into the encampment," he ordered. "Use the incendiaries."

Riel felt the soldiers tense above him. "But sir, the forest will burn."

"It is of no consequence. Go. NOW!"

One soldier left, the other stood in the doorway, at attention. "And her, my king?"

"Stay there Laniel. She's no threat." Claude's hands clenched into fists, then relaxed. "In fact, bow to your *queen*, Aurora of Elsass. She is here to take her rightful place at my side."

Riel's heart raced.

"But, sir, your neck," Laniel argued.

"The queen *needs* me." Claude said, holding his hands at his side. He held three fingers pointed down just on the back of his leg, out of Rory's view.

Riel scowled at his brother. Nega gasped beside him.

"We need to shift back to normal," Riel said to Luiselle. She dropped her bag and started the spell.

"Sir?" The doubt in Laniel's voice rang out. Claude retracted a finger, leaving two behind.

"Hurry, Lu," Riel said.

"She's working on it!" Kuri said.

"Now, my *queen*, we have much to discuss." Claude left only his index finger pointed.

"Now, Lu!" Nega joined.

"Discuss what?" Rory asked.

A purple glow gathered around them. Claude closed his fist and lunged at Rory just as Laniel rushed into the room.

59

Rory held her breath. Blood bloomed on Claude's neck as he cut himself on the throne's blade. Her eyes widened and her jaw dropped as he knocked the sword from her hands. She struggled to hold on to it as Claude pushed forward. He reached to the Consort's chair, grabbed a small acinaces blade and spun around. He yanked Rory forward, throwing her down the steps. She kept up until the last step, where she tripped and fell, landed on her hands and knees. Claude leapt down beside her, grabbed her hair, yanked her up on her knees with a cry of pain, her head back, neck exposed. The small blade held across it, and she felt his breath at her ear.

"Stand up, my queen. Slowly."

Rory carefully placed one foot down, then the other, trying not to cut herself on the blade. She closed her eyes for a moment, reaching into her own pockets, to find... nothing but the large thorn from the Crone's vine. She gripped it, comforted by its presence. Claude yanked back on her hair, forcing her chin up.

With her head held at a sharp angle, she just made out a purple glow. The soldier at the door yelped before metal crashed against the stone walls.

"Oh, Aurora. You *lied* to your king." He released her hair enough that she could see the door. There Riel stood, sword drawn, along with Kuri, and... *Luiselle?* Nega bent over the soldier. "How will we ever get on if you won't. Tell. Me. The. Truth?" A yank on her hair punctuated each word.

"Let the queen go." Riel stepped forward, but Claude yanked Rory's hair, continuing to stretch her neck. She breathed in through her teeth in order not to cry out. Claude didn't deserve her pain. Riel paused inside the doorway.

"You see why I should be king?" Claude asked. "You are not willing to sacrifice to get your desires."

"He won't kill me," Rory said to Riel, staring at him. "Not yet."

Claude laughed behind Rory. His chest shook, but the blade held still at her throat. "You are foolish."

"If you do not break the curse and produce an heir with me, you give up my kingdom."

"Ah, but I already have your kingdom." He pushed her forward and stepped with her, closer to Riel. "I did before your curse even fell upon you."

"Perhaps," Rory said. "The Seeress cursed our kingdoms if you rule it without me and anyone from my line on the throne."

"That old bat knew nothing of the future." Claude said, laughing. "I'll bet she didn't even see you'd escape its effects."

Riel stepped sideways and Claude scraped the edge of the blade up and down her neck. Her skin felt raw until Riel stopped moving.

"Maybe," Rory gulped as the blade held still. "But she said our child would rule both kingdoms with incredible power." She ignored the vision Fayette had given her and made up one of her own. "His rule would expand the kingdoms with his might."

The blade pulled back a little. Claude's grip on her hair loosened. "And how do you know this?"

"I saw him, in a vision." A single tear poured down her cheek. She told him the truth. "He was just like you."

They stood like that for a moment. Rory and Claude faced her friends, his enemies, in silence. No one moved until several soldiers ran down the hall. Nega tossed Laniel into the throne room, and he grunted in pain as she faced the onslaught. Rory saw the glint in Nega's eye as soldiers surrounded her friends. Riel didn't face away from Claude and Rory. Kuri and Luiselle started weaving the orange elvish and the purple faerie magic together.

Rory heard the cries of soldiers as the magic hit them, or Nega's sword and axe took them out. The sound was constant as all the soldiers ran through the magic barricade. Claude cursed when he realized some of his soldiers took Riel's side. They fought against themselves, trying to convince the other soldiers to stop. Hope bubbled in Rory, as the soldiers stood up to Claude for the first time, alongside Riel.

He would make a wonderful king, she thought as pain travelled up her taught neck muscles. *If only the Seeress named him instead...*

In the throne room, Laniel stood and drew his blade as Riel faced him from the doorway. More soldiers approached and forced Kuri and Nega back against Riel on the threshold. Rory searched for Luiselle, but saw nothing until a purple cloud wove above the soldiers.

"Take out the faerie!" Claude's voice echoed in the hall.

A small net flew above them, and the purple cloud stopped. Soldiers who advanced on everyone.

Rory's heart broke. "No!"

The grip on her hair tightened. "You will watch your friends die now, Aurora of Elsass." Claude whispered in her ear. "Then Laniel will bind you in the royal rooms. There, you will be my queen in every way, until the Seeress' prophecy comes true. You will bear my son. I will make those rooms your household. You will sleep forever. I will be king and raise our son to rule with an iron fist."

Rory saw it all, just as Claude described. After everything she had seen him do to the babies, the women, to Fayette and Luiselle, the refugees... he would not hesitate. Not when everything was in his grasp.

He would never change his heart.

She looked up at Riel. He entered the fight alongside his friends but kept glancing back at Claude. Nega fought with a warrior cry, while Kuri was sweating with the power she unleashed on the soldiers. Rory knew it went against her elvish healer ways, but she fought anyway. Rory couldn't find Luiselle in the group. The soldiers pushed ahead. Rory's tears fell, and Claude laughed.

There was only one thing she could do to save her kingdom, her friends. Remove the current king.

"This is a beautiful room." Rory said. "Laniel, please leave."

Claude tightened his grip. "Laniel, you will stay!"

The soldier looked between them; sword ready.

"We can spend eternity in this beautiful room." Rory said. She sighed. Peace settled within, and her body relaxed.

"What?" Claude asked, yanking her hair again. It wasn't enough to make her tense. Not anymore.

"Because this throne room," Rory cleared her throat, "and only this throne room, I make my household, with everyone in it."

As soon as the words finished, Rory felt the sharp tingles of the curse hit her feet. Claude threw her down as he cried out in pain, and she landed on her hands and knees, the stabbing pain in all her limbs. She crawled to the doorway; her grip frozen on the thorn. She tried to let it go, but couldn't, and leaned on her knuckles.

"Stay back! The Curse!" Laniel said as he fell, too.

"No!" Riel flinched while Nega yanked him back over the threshold. The soldiers stopped fighting, distracted by the cries of pain in the throne room. Rory heard the clang of metal disappear down the hallway. *Cowards.*

"Shoot her with an arrow!" Claude's speech slurred. He crawled beside her, the small blade still in his hand.

Rory's right arm gave out, and she fell to her side, staring back at everyone.

"Give me your hand!" Nega called out from the door, her long arm outstretched, her face grimaced, and brow sweaty. Rory reached up with her left hand, but everything from the elbow down hung limp. She couldn't feel the floor as her fingertips grazed its surface. Rory's body gave up from the sharp pain until she slumped over on her side. She tilted her head to the door, pulled her arm over her chest, and fought for breath as she fell on her back. A shadow covered her, her vision blackened at the corners.

"Rory!" Riel called from the door, panic in his voice as it deepened.

"Go!" Rory said, then faced the shadow. Claude pulled himself on top of her, holding the knife up to her throat. She made one last attempt to throw her arms in a defensive move, but felt nothing happen. His hand twitched, ready to strike when everything went black.

60

S ILENCE DESCENDED AS RIEL reached for Rory. Pain laced up his arm as far as it went into the throne room. He yanked it back, flexed his fingers to dissipate the tingling, then ran his fingers through his hair. Despite the violent pain of the curse, they looked peaceful. Rory slept, her eyes closed, her mouth slightly open, her jaw relaxed. Claude collapsed on top of her, with the tip of the acinaces blade pressed into her neck. There was no blood, not yet. They were frozen, their chests didn't even rise and fall. Claude's normally shrewd look and penetrating gaze relaxed in slumber. Riel had never seen him at peace.

"Well, Rory's wording was effective." Kuri stood beside him, placing her hand into the throne room, flinched, then removed it. "I thought it would expand."

"Eventually it will. Great grandmother was very specific in her wording," Luiselle said from beside Kuri. She was at her normal height, her wings spread wide.

Riel frowned at the cut in her chin. "Are you okay?"

Before she could answer, a shout rang out from behind the subdued soldiers. "The king! This is mutiny!" A soldier pushed through, advanced on Nega and triggered a wave of onslaught.

The soldiers allegiant to Claude pushed against the small band who defended Riel and his friends. Luiselle conjured more purple smoke, but it wasn't as effective as before. Riel worried that her little body was unused to the power needed in battle. He deflected swords aimed at them and stepped in front to protect her. They forced him sideways until the side of his leg entered the room. The sharp pain of the curse shot from his little toe up to his knee. Riel deflected another blow and spun out of the way of a soldier. He pulled his leg out of the room and watched the soldier fall inside. He collapsed, shock mixed with pain in his wide, terrified eyes. Riel reached in quickly, clasped the man's hand tightly before it fell asleep, and pulled him so his head was inside the door. He lay there, unable to do anything but watch the action from their feet.

Another soldier lunged his sword at Riel's stomach, but he sidestepped at the last moment. There was precious little room to fight. Kuri and Luiselle's magic faded, and Kuri's growing weakness distracted Nega.

As his friends suffered, his anger grew. He'd lost Rory, he wouldn't lose them too. He took a deep breath, stepped into a gap, and leapt as high as he could, then transformed into his dragon shape. When he landed, he blew hot air all over his brother's soldiers. They screamed in pain, drawing the attention of the soldiers who still attacked Nega. They paused mid strike, distracted by the shadow looming over them all. Nega took advantage by shoving three of them into the throne room. They tripped over the immobilized soldier on the floor, screamed and within seconds fell asleep too. Nega growled at the remaining soldiers while they stepped back, swords dropped, hands up in surrender. She tied them up using the banner, while others burned by the armour on their body collapsed and groaned in pain. Only the soldiers who had fought alongside them remained.

Nega frowned at the soldier, still lying across the threshold. He struggled to breathe. "If I pull you out, will you be any more trouble?"

"No!" He rasped. Nega reached down and yanked him up, hand at his throat, his legs dangling. The soldier gasped as life returned to his body, his eyes wide. He stared at Riel. "You... You saved me!" His hoarse voice echoed out in the corridor. The rest of the soldiers silently stared at Riel. "My prince, I... I thank you."

"You mean your king." The Seeress stood at the end of the corridor, surrounded by several small blue flames, and accompanied by Jean. Many of the soldiers gasped. Riel shifted back into his human shape.

The soldiers grumbled to each other. "You want Claude as your king? Be my guest." Riel gestured back to the throne room and stood aside. "Let me know how that goes." He crossed his arms over his chest and stared them all down, looking at each man in the eye one by one.

"Only the king can break the curse once his heart changes and kisses the princess." Kuri said. "How many of you think Claude's heart will change?"

"It doesn't matter anyway," said the soldier they saved. "Even if his heart changed, he's asleep too. He can't kiss her."

"Captain?" A soldier who fought beside Nega in battle called.

He swallowed. "Our king is asleep, possibly never to awaken." He looked each soldier in the eyes. "We have been loyal to King Claude's every whim." The captain gestured to Riel as he faced his men. "I have never enjoyed doing Claude's work. I have fought beside Riel, and he would make an excellent king."

Several men nodded in agreement. Then a clang as one man pushed forward. "Riel was the King's mercenary, as loyal to Claude as we were. What changed?" The man stared at Riel.

Nega growled at him and swung her blade back and forth. The man ignored Nega and focused on Riel.

"Claude misused an oath made to our father on a very special ring." Riel put a hand on Nega's arm to stop her posturing. "I would have rebelled against Claude's tyranny long ago, if not for that."

"Then you are not free!" The man thumped his chest for emphasis.

"I am." Riel said softly.

"How?" asked the captain. "Claude would never let you go."

Riel nodded. "He even sent the *Beül* after me." He looked back at Rory. Her necklace spilled onto the floor, the ring visible. Then faced everyone. "The queen's betrothal ring was that same ring. She set me free." The soldiers looked around to stare at Rory as Riel rubbed his chest, trying to ease the ache which grew in it. If she hadn't released him, then maybe she wouldn't have fallen asleep.

"She also eliminated the *Beül*," Kuri said, "with the help of the Navka." She gestured to the Seeress and the blue flames.

The soldiers looked at each other. "What now?" The captain asked them. "We have a king, but no queen. With no heir, the kingdom remains cursed."

"And if it's broken, Claude returns," said Kuri. Many of the soldiers stopped talking.

"So we leave Rory cursed?" Luiselle asked in a small voice.

"Child," the Seeress came to her, rubbed the top of her head. "Rory sacrificed herself to stop him. She wouldn't want us to dishonour that."

Riel stared at Rory, his heartbeat racing as her loss made him numb. Everyone remained silent. When he finally looked at them, they were staring at him. "What?"

"It's your call, my king." Kuri said, as she knelt before him. Nega bowed. The Seeress did as well. Many of the soldiers took a knee.

Luiselle stomped over to stand in front of him instead of bowing like the others.

"You are now the king." She said, her eyes narrowed, a purple glow at her hands.

"I know," Riel whispered. "I have to think of everyone now."

"No, you don't." Tears gathered in the corner of her eyes. "Everyone has left me. Please don't take Rory away from me, too!"

"Luiselle!" the Seeress said.

"You are king, and your heart changed." Luiselle's lavender eyes glowed with her tears. "Claude forced you to kidnap me, but you fought to save everyone. You wouldn't have taken the mantle before. I saw it. They trapped you, but she freed you. You *love* her. Even though she was married to another, you would have chosen her." Riel closed his eyes at her words. Until Luiselle took his hand in hers. "And she loves you. *You* are the king who is to break her curse." Riel shook his head, but Luiselle fluttered until she was at eye level. "She set you free. Free to do anything. Everything. Free to stand up to Claude, free to save your kingdom's inhabitants."

"Claude no longer has his *weapons*," the captain offered. "He neither has you, nor the *Beül*, to do his bidding."

"And you love her," said Kuri. She held Nega's hand. "Could you honestly live as king without her?"

Riel sighed and studied Rory. "How do we get her out?"

61

E will help.

Riel watched the Navka flames glide forward. They passed through the threshold, spirits uninhibited by the curse. They merged to create the child with blue eyes for flames. The soldiers behind him gasped. The child pointed to the captain.

"You, the one who gave us water, stand at the door." While Riel pondered their words, the captain did as the Navka asked him.

The Navka child reached under Claude and pulled out a rope. Riel realized it was the one Rory tied to her waist, the same one she'd willingly tied to herself as she'd jumped off the cliff to save him. They tied its end to the ring and removed the silver chain from around her neck. It still looped through the ring, tied to one end, holding the other in their hand. The child glided over to the captain and stopped near the door frame.

The rope didn't reach him.

"Now what?" Nega ran her hand down her face. "We can't just leave her like that. She deserves better."

"Here, use this." The Seeress took Jean's arm as she approached, holding her staff out to the captain. The captain held the end with the hook aimed out towards the Navka. They looped the silver rope onto the hooked end, then glided back to join the captain.

The child placed its hand on his arm. The captain shuddered under the child's touch. *"You have nothing to fear from us, captain. We know what happened. You redeem yourself by saving the queen."* Riel didn't understand what the Navka meant, but the captain relaxed under their touch, and he pulled the staff. The rope and necklace grew taught.

"Will it hold?" Riel asked, staring at the ring.

"We'll find out," Jean said.

The captain pulled, but Rory's body didn't move. Claude's weight added to the resistance. He pulled harder. When Rory's body inched towards them, everyone sighed. Riel watched the blade in Claude's hand get perilously closer to her neck as the Captain pulled on the rope. As the tip pierced her skin, he yelled for them to stop.

Everyone turned and faced him. He looked around.

"My King?" The captain asked.

"The blade," he pointed to it. "Come around to this side."

The captain dragged the rope to the other side of the doorway. It disappeared under Claude's elbow, then slid up his forearm and under his wrist, lifting the blade up and away from Rory's neck. There was a cut but no blood.

"She's going to bleed when she's pulled through the threshold." Kuri started rifling through her pack. Luiselle did the same.

The captain pulled the staff until the chain made it through the threshold. Another soldier jumped in to grab the chain, and with Claude's acinaces blade slowly moving away from Rory's throat, it sped up. Until she got closer to the threshold. When she was within reach, they stopped.

"Captain?" Riel stared at him.

"My king," he said. "We can't pull her through without Claude waking up first."

Riel ran his fingers through his hair as he studied them. Claude's body leaned over Rory's, almost tumbling through the threshold. One powerful tug and he would fall through. Riel wasn't sure what to do with Claude if they broke the curse, but for Rory's sake, he had to try. Either way, he didn't want his brother to wake up first. Rory's lifeless body made Riel unfocused. He felt out of control, and he fought the urge to shift. His eyes widened.

"Stand back."

"Your highness?" Kuri put her hand on his arm.

Nega dragged her away, and he shifted into his dragon form. He turned sideways in the door frame and braced himself as he swung his tail into the room.

Sharp pain immediately traveled up his tail to the edge of the doorway. Riel wedged the tip between Claude and Rory, lifting Claude slightly until his tail grew numb. He shifted Claude, but the numbing made his tail give way and Claude dropped onto Rory's legs. Riel yanked his tail out of the space.

"Riel?" Nega asked. Riel glared at her and waited for the sharp pain lacing back down to the tip to dissipate. When it subsided, he took a deep breath and tried again. He quickly wedged his tail under Claude, further in this time, as the sharp pain sped up his tail, quicker than before. Riel growled, and as he felt the numbness hit, he lifted his tail up with a large force, and threw Claude off Rory toward the throne. He didn't have time to hear Claude's thump with satisfaction. He yanked his tail out again, groaned as the pain washed over him again. When it subsided, he shifted back into his human form. Claude lay limp at the bottom stairs of the throne room. The Captain pulled Rory through the opening, her head on the other side of the threshold.

"She should be awake," the soldier who'd been in her position said.

Kuri and Luiselle considered each other, then focused on Rory. "She's not bleeding yet," Kuri said. "Maybe because the rest of her organs are still asleep?"

Riel stared at Rory's peaceful face. Her eyes remained closed, and her mouth was open.

"Well?" Nega punched him in the shoulder. Soldiers gasped at her treatment of Riel. She peeked at them. "Um... Well, my king?"

"Kiss her to break the curse," Luiselle said.

"I know." He stared at Rory.

The little faerie took his hand. "So, what are you waiting for?"

"It feels wrong to kiss her when she's asleep." He looked down at her. "No permission."

Luiselle smiled back at him. "You'll make an excellent king, Riel." She unfurled her wings and fluttered up to meet him face to face. She leaned forward and kissed him on the nose. "But I want Rory back."

Riel smiled as Luiselle lowered herself back down. He looked down at Rory and reviewed the curse wording in his mind. He smiled when he realized the one thing the Seeress never specified. Riel knelt down beside her, her head turned slightly sideways. He ran his fingers gently over her cheek, then took a deep breath as he reached into the doorway. Beads of sweat trickled down his temples. Pain ran up his arm as he reached for her hand and pulled it through the threshold.

The numbness didn't take hold before the pain subsided. He waited until it was thoroughly gone before doing anything.

Riel brushed his other fingers over her cheek, then looked up at his friends, still holding Rory's hand in his. Everyone watched him. Kuri and Nega held hands so tightly their knuckles were white. The Seeress and Jean stood beside them, his arms at his sides, hands in fists.

"It's time, King Riel," the Seeress gestured to him.

Riel's heart thundered in his chest. He caressed her cheek and kissed the first knuckle of her hand. "Rory," he whispered, then kissed the next one. "It's time to wake up." He kissed the third. "Please Rory, my queen." His heartbeat was all he could hear. A tear escaped. "Please, my love." He kissed the fourth knuckle.

Nothing happened, and Riel turned Rory's hand in his so that her palm faced him. He kissed her palm. "Please, Rory?" Then her wrist. "I need you here. I love you."

He held her palm to his tear-stained cheek and waited.

62

R ORY GASPED FOR AIR. There was pain, nothing but pain. It shot through her body; the jolt reaching all her extremities at the same time. She opened her eyes, or thought she did, but all she saw was white and black jagged lines criss-crossing her vision with every pulse of pain. Each one hit with each beat of her heart, which thundered in her ears. She tried to scream in pain, but her tongue was stuck to the roof of her mouth, seized in the same pain as her body. Rory tried to move, but everything was in agony. Her body didn't respond, and her back hurt.

Rory stilled in the pain, focusing on the hurt. It was different. Pressure built up against the pain shooting through her body with every frenetic heartbeat. But it bounced off her back and into her body. And the back of her legs.

She lay down on something hard.

I am awake?

She ignored the jolts, focusing on other sensations in her body. Something wet slid down her neck, and something warm pressed against it.

Something squeezed her right hand, and her palm felt something rough. She wished she could see.

Sounds filtered past her heartbeat. It was slower, making the pulses of pain less frequent, too. Rory focused on the sounds. Some of them were higher, some lower. And one seemed to vibrate right from her fingertips.

Her vision greyed, the lightning bolts faded. The room darkened. A hand moved her head to the side, a deep voice murmuring reassuring words to her as something pressed against her neck.

"Ow!" This was an unfamiliar pain, centered in one location.

"Hold still, love." A gentle hand stroked her cheek. "Kuri and Luiselle need to heal that cut."

Riel? He's here? Rory tried to sit up, but couldn't move. Then she froze. *What did he say?*

She tried to move again. Hands held her on either side of her head, while another hand pressed into her neck. She felt a soothing warmth radiate from both places and she closed her eyes to the now orange and purple light which radiated from her peripheral vision. Her pain disappeared.

"Rory?" Luiselle's voice came from beside her. "Rory, open your eyes." Rory opened them to see large, light purple eyes staring at hers, upside down. "You're awake!" She squealed and hugged Rory's head. She lifted one hand to Luiselle's head. Her other still wouldn't move.

"I'm awake?" Rory's throat hurt and her voice came out with a rasp.

I am awake!

Luiselle disappeared and Kuri's face appeared upside down above her. She held out a finger and Rory looked at it as she moved it across her vision. "Glad you're back with us." she said, then disappeared too.

She looked over at her hand, found it trapped between Riel's hand and his cheek.

"You're okay?" Rory asked. She rubbed his cheekbone with her thumb.

He nodded. "Are you?" He reached forward and stroked her cheek with his other hand.

Rory smiled. "I'm awake. You broke the curse."

Riel smiled back. "Can you sit up?" He pulled his hand away from her cheek and held her other hand. Rory nodded, so he helped her sit up for a moment. When she motioned to stand, he helped her up, one hand on her back, the other holding her hand. Fully upright, she swayed, her legs wobbled, and he pulled her into his arms, hugging her tight.

"Rory," he whispered, his breath in her ear.

She hugged him, then leaned back. His gaze was on hers and she opened her mouth as he leaned in. Rory caught the glint of light behind Riel just as Nega yelled at him. Rory shoved Riel sideways. He let go of her in surprise, and she fell just as the throne's blade stabbed where Riel had been.

Claude quickly pivoted and lunged back at Riel. "I will end you, brother. The kingdom is not yours." His face was purple with rage, and he flinched as he stepped forward. Rory understood Claude's pain. If not for Kuri and Luiselle's healing, she'd still feel the curse's effects, too.

Riel drew his sword and glanced at Rory before engaging Claude. Rory watched Claude's stilted movements. One hand on the sword, the other held against his chest.

"You will not have Kehl, Riel." He lunged at him with the blade.

"Maybe not, but you cannot have it." He defended himself from Claude and fought back.

"What do you want?" Claude used his anger to fuel his aggression, and attacked Riel quickly, forcing him to defend himself.

"Freedom from you." Riel spat.

"I'll make sure you're never free."

Nega growled and approached the men fighting, but Laniel, the soldier who also suffered from the curse, stopped her with his blade. "You know how this works, ogress. The stronger brother wins the crown. This is the way of dragons and your kind."

Rory looked around at the crowd. All had their blades drawn to watch the fight between the brothers. They eyed each other. Rory wondered who would remain unscathed as the two men fought for power for the kingdoms of Kehl and Elsass.

My kingdoms.

Rory stepped forward, but Kuri held her elbow. "Don't do it, Rory." she said.

Claude lunged again and lost his balance. Riel quickly counter attacked, knocked Claude's sword out of his hand, and tripped him. Claude landed on his back with Riel's sword aimed at his throat. Riel stared at his brother and exhaled.

"You can't do it." Claude sneered at his brother. "That's why you'd never make a good king Riel. You can't do what's needed to make sure everyone stays in line."

"I don't like your way of leading." Riel said, his blade still in place.

Rory approached Riel, who scowled. Claude smiled at him. The glint in his eyes made Rory shiver. He looked at her chest, then back at Riel. "Kill Aurora, Riel."

Rory looked up at Riel and found him smiling at Claude. He leaned over, face to face with his brother. "No."

Claude's face grew red again. "She doesn't bear the ring. It doesn't protect her." Then he smiled and narrowed his eyes. "Which means she no longer controls you, either." Claude jumped up suddenly, the sword cutting across Riel's left shoulder. As he reached for the blade with his other hand, Rory saw Claude flinch with the effort, before he spun around, grabbed Luiselle, and held the blade to her throat.

Everyone yelled, some for Claude, some for Luiselle, some for Riel. The hazy glow of purple surrounded the Seeress, but Claude slammed the pommel onto the joint of Luiselle's wing. The faerie cried out in pain, kicked him in the knee, and Claude flinched. Blood darkened the tunic near his rib.

"Stop, Seeress, or I will end your line now." The purple cloud dissipated in his words.

Rory searched for a blade, or any other weapon, but nothing was within reach. Even her pockets were empty. She eyed the growing red stain at Claude's ribs, and her eyes widened.

Rory stepped forward. "Let her go, and I'll come with you."

"Rory, no!" Riel said.

Luiselle cried out in pain as Claude smiled. "Your heart is too big, Aurora. But I accept your trade. Come here."

"Rory, don't!" Luiselle said.

Rory stepped forward in between them. "Let her go, I will come. They won't make it in time." Claude loosened his grip and Luiselle popped into her smaller form. Rory stepped forward to distract Claude from where she fell.

Claude ignored Luiselle, and when Rory was close enough, he grabbed her by the throat and lifted her off her feet.

"What now, *my queen?*" Claude said, smirking at her. "I win." He glanced down and stomped on Luiselle's compact form below.

No! Rory centred her gaze on Claude, looked deep into his eyes, then kicked out at the bloodstain on his rib. Something sharp hurt her heal, but she struck true. Claude's eyes widened, and he dropped Rory, who fell backwards. Claude stumbled back and pulled his shirt away from his body. Blood gushed out of the wound on his side. Claude wheezed, and every breath he took led to bubbles of air coming out from the injury. He dropped to his knees as Rory stood up over him. She knocked the blade out of his hands, yanked the thorn out of his ribs, and Claude collapsed on the floor in front of her.

Everyone stopped, and the only sound was Claude's faded breaths. Then nothing.

"Rory?" Luiselle's tiny voice came from the floor.

"Lu!" Rory picked up Luiselle's small body off the floor, cradled her into her hand, and brought her over to Kuri and the Seeress. Rory didn't breathe as they murmured to her. "Can you shift back, Lu?" Rory sat down in front of the Seeress, tears on her face.

"I'll... try." After a purple glow surrounded her, Luiselle transformed into a child. She had bruises all over her body, and a cut in her neck. Kuri and the Seeress immediately worked together to heal her. Rory watched, able to breathe again as Luiselle's wing mended and the bruises faded from her skin. Rory sighed, crying as the little girl hugged her tightly. It didn't matter that her little arms strangled her neck. Her strength made Rory smile through her tears.

When she let go, Rory looked around. She saw the acinaces sword laying at Claude's side. Rory picked it up and turned to face everyone staring at her. She walked over to Riel, whose eyes were on her throat. She stopped two paces in front of him and swallowed.

"King Riel of Kehl, I believe this belongs to you." She offered the sword to him.

Armour clanged as everyone knelt down, joining Kuri, Luiselle and the Seeress on the floor. They called out "My King!"

Rory watched them in awe, and knelt, but Riel took the sword from her hand and kept her standing. "Only if you're my queen, love." He took one hand and brushed her cheek.

"Love?" Rory asked.

"I broke the curse..." he said, grinning, and Rory smiled. "You're a widow now, so..."

Rory frowned. "But you want your freedom."

"And you gave it to me," he said.

Rory sighed. "And I have to lead... here. In these walls."

"Yes, I know. But it turns out, I also want *you*, if you'll have me. Here. Outside. Anywhere."

Rory smiled. Her heart felt light. "I love you too."

Rory closed her eyes, but just before his lips found hers, she stopped. She pulled back, making Riel look at her, his brow furrowed. Rory brushed a lock of hair behind her ear as she looked around at the others.

"Any objections?" Everyone looked down and away. Rory focused on Laniel and the Captain. "If there are, take them up with her." Rory pointed to Nega, who had a feral grin on her face.

"That's right! You'll have to go through me!" Nega said, as Rory focused on Riel.

"Can I kiss you now?" He whispered, smiling.

"By all means."

His lips pressed gently against hers, and Rory finally found home.

Epilogue

LUISELLE CLIMBED ONTO THE chair behind Rory, determined to fix the queen's hair. Muriel was busy pulling out the right gown for the naming ceremony later, so the task fell to her. As Luiselle did her best to restore Rory's locks to their former glory, Rory stared out the window and sighed.

"Do you want to talk about it?" Luiselle asked.

"I just miss being outdoors." Rory tilted up her head to look at Luiselle and smiled, but it didn't reach her eyes. "These days, I'm always inside the castle walls. I'm too busy to do anything outside."

Luiselle bent down and kissed Rory on her forehead, then tilted Rory's head forward so she could gaze out the window at her kingdom.

Are you near? She asked her grandmother through the mental link they had established. It was difficult without her mother to complete the triad, but they had succeeded.

Laniel is escorting me up, her grandmother responded.

A few minutes later, the Seeress entered the Queen's private greeting rooms. She spotted Rory and Luiselle at the window. Luiselle didn't have to look at the Seeress. She felt her surprise at seeing Rory so haggard.

"Hello Seeress," Rory said through the reflection in the window.

"My Queen," she bowed before her.

"Grandmother!" Luiselle ran over and threw her arms around her grandmother in an enormous hug. She knew her grandmother relished them, and though she was nearing nine, she was just as happy to give her hugs. Her grandmother pulled back and patted Luiselle's cheek warmly.

"Is everything ready for the ceremony?" The Seeress asked Rory.

"Everything is ready." Rory answered. She sighed as the Seeress glanced at Luiselle.

She has bags under her eyes, her grandmother noted.

The Seeress approached Rory, bowed her head, then touched Rory's chin. She lifted it to see the dark circles around the Queen's eyes, contrasted with her pale skin and limp, charred hair. "Are you unwell, my Queen? I have foreseen no illness."

"Bah! She just needs some sleep!" Muriel said from the corner of the room.

Luiselle nodded, then focused back on Rory's hair. The magic out of her fingers glowed purple, and restored some of the lustre of Rory's hair, and brought colour back into her cheeks.

Rory smiled. "That's true Muriel. Right now, my responsibilities are quite high."

"Where is the king? Is Riel not helping?" The Seeress frowned. Luiselle knew her gran cast out to see where Riel was. If he wasn't careful, he'd get an earful from her grandmother.

Rory's smile brightened. "Riel has gone flying." Her smile shrank. "I envy him that ability."

The Seeress spun around. Her eyes flashed. "And the babes aren't with you?"

Luiselle giggled. "Relax grandmother. He takes them flying so Rory can rest."

The Seeress' jaw dropped. "*Flying?*" Luiselle almost giggled at her look of astonishment. "Not even one hundred days old and without the naming ceremony and he's taking them *flying?*"

Rory laughed for the first time today. She put her hand on the Seeress' shoulder. "It's the way of the dragon." Rory shrugged. "The twins are fine in Riel's care. Sometimes no rocking motion will comfort them, and Riel takes one in each hand, er... claw, and flies with them. Something about the wind. They go right to sleep. He gives me a moment to myself to rest without their cries to be fed or held."

"*That* is why you're supposed to have a nursemaid," Muriel stated. She held a dress in each arm. Rory stood and pointed to the dress on Muriel's left. She handed the dress over. "But no one wants to nurse them. It gets too hot."

Luiselle jumped down from the chair again. "Rory, I'm not done fixing your hair." She reached out and pulled one particularly black lock of hair and cast a restoration spell on it.

Rory stared at Muriel and pointed to the changing lock of hair. "Would you want to nurse my twins when this is the result?"

"No milady," Muriel answered, trying to hide her grin. "Here, let me help you into this one, and then Lu can continue her work with your hair."

As Rory stepped behind the privacy screen, her grandmother crooked her finger at Luiselle. "Are you using enough lavender?"

"Of course gran!" Luiselle rolled her eyes even though it made her grandmother's gaze narrow on her. Luiselle tried to be serious. "Very few leaders have a kingdom to run and try to raise dragon twins. Everyone is very helpful, Riel especially. But they had to divide tasks to accomplish them, so they rarely get to work together anymore."

Her grandmother rubbed her chin. Her violet eyes looked up to the ceiling, clouding over for a moment. "Perhaps we should arrange for some time for them together."

"That's a wonderful idea." Riel answered from the door. He entered with Kuri and Nega following, each carrying a sleeping twin in their arms. Kuri carried the little girl, firstborn, and Nega, the little boy.

Dragon hearing! Luiselle rolled her eyes. Even though she'd been living at the castle to train with her friends, she never got used to it.

"Where is Ilse?" Riel asked.

"She's out looking into our defences for the ceremony." Luiselle stated. "She'll be along soon."

Rory stepped out from behind the screen. A smile lit up her tired eyes when she saw the babies and Riel. He held out his hand to her for her, and she stepped into his arms.

"What's a wonderful idea?" Rory asked. She and Riel stared at their children and Luiselle winked at her grandmother. They both whispered a restoration spell as they held hands, and a faint purple glow illuminated Rory's hair until it was back to normal.

Riel looked everyone in the eye one by one, and they all nodded. "They had some time with papa, now it's your turn."

"My turn?" She looked up at him, confused.

"To get some freedom in the skies."

Rory's eyes brightened, but then she shook her head. "But the ceremony-"

"Isn't for three hours," Riel said. "The babes will need their rest, and we have Muriel, Luiselle, a healing elf, our own personal warrior ogress, Ilse and the guard, and the Seeress." He tilted Rory's chin up to him and kissed her gently. "They'll be fine, love, and you need a break. We can even go visit the sheep grazing at the chateau."

Rory blushed. "But..."

"Let us give you a moment of peace," Kuri said. "As you've worked hard to do it for everyone else in the kingdom."

And she had, Luiselle thought. As king and queen, they set about a new order, restoring the refugees to their lands, uniting Kehl and Elsass, and squashing the rebellions who tried to keep Claude's way of entitled thinking. It had taken time, but in the end, it was Rory's mercy that won everyone over to her side. A mercy which tempered the lethal justice of a dragon king.

"Go on Rory," Luiselle pushed her. "You want to be outdoors again."

Rory looked at all her friends and nodded. Riel walked her out the door when she stopped and pulled back. "Wait!" She glared at the Seeress for a moment, then marched over to her, determination now filling her formerly tired eyes.

"No predictions!" She said, poking her finger at the Seeress. Luiselle struggled not to laugh.

"My queen?" The Seeress asked. Luiselle giggled at the look of confusion on her grandmother's face.

"I mean it. No looking into their futures. No insights, no curses, no warnings." The Queen studied the Seeress. Riel had his arms crossed over his chest.

"But the Seeress always bless-"

"Yes, bless them, of course. Wish them well. But no visions, no thoughts, no curses, no... implied future. No meddling." She stared at the Seeress. "I won't have them live under the shadow of a mysterious curse or be perceived as a threat simply because they live. They will have enough threats in their lifetime as it is. We will raise them, and we will face things as they come. I don't want *anyone* to know what you see. Even you. No more machinations. There are enough of those without your powers helping or hindering." Rory took the Seeress' hand in hers. "Swear it."

The Seeress looked at Luiselle. "I've already sworn." Silently, she whispered her thoughts to her grandmother. *She needs this.*

The Seeress looked Rory in the eyes. "I swear it."

Rory transformed in front of them. As if they had lifted a weight off her shoulders, she stood taller, calmer, less worn than a moment ago. The single oath did more for Rory than any restoration spell could.

"I never meant to worry you with my presence," the Seeress said, bowing before her.

"I know, aunt," she said, caressing the Seeress' cheek. "You are always welcome here, as family."

Then Rory took Riel's hand and left the room.

"May I see them?" The Seeress asked. Nega and Kuri glanced at each other, then offered views of the babies. Nega narrowed her eyes and Luiselle knew the ogress would run with the babes if she thought anything would go amiss. The Seeress smiled, and Luiselle stood beside her.

Rosy cheeks greeted them. The boy's pink lips sucked on his thumb, and the girl yawned in her sleep. They were beautiful, and Luiselle never tired of seeing their faces.

Luiselle ran her fingers on their foreheads and smiled, then looked back at her grandmother.

Rory had nothing to worry about with her babies. She and her grandmother had seen it long before today. Luiselle wanted to relieve Rory of her worry, but the Queen was right. Trials would come for their kingdom and friends, but they would be okay. But that kind of knowledge would be a curse itself. So she wouldn't tell a soul.

REVIEWS

Enjoy this Book? You can make a big difference.

As a newly published author, honest reviews are the best way that I can get my books into the hands of new readers.

If you enjoyed this book, I would be grateful if you could spend just a view minutes leaving a review on your favourite platform or on Goodreads.

Thank you very much!

NEWSLETTER

D EAR READERS,

If you enjoyed this book, please sign up for my newsletter, Fitzpatrick's Fables. It's the best way that I can stay connected with you. I occasionally send newsletters with details on new releases, special offers, and other bits of news that relate to the Rose World Tales.

If you sign up for the mailing list, I'll send you a free copy of my Rose World Tale short story prequel, Escape (coming soon).

You can sign up for Fitzpatrick's Fables at https://mailchi.mp/72277261381 f/fitzpatricks-fables

Acknowledgments

Thank you!

There are numerous people to thank who have helped me on this journey. First, I'd like to thank my *Alpha Readers* from the *Writing in Community* program who commented on every segment and witnessed the rebirth of <u>Awake</u> in 2021. Without your generous support, and comments asking for more of Rory and her adventures, this wouldn't be here. JF, PK, PS, MK, and the rest, thank you for all your comments and reading.

I would also like to thank my *Beta Readers* for your generous time and feedback, and for not just patting me on the back, but pushing me to make Rory's story better. You are amazing.

Thanks to my development editor Allison Fairfax and my line editor Sandreannie.

Finally, thanks to my husband and son for your support. The fact that you gave me time and space to just create has given me more than I could ever say.

Inspiration

There are a number of different references to European middle age and older creatures. I tried not to get my information from Wikipedia, but took inspiration from a variety of sources. Here are a few of them:

Sleeping Beauty References:

Charles Perrault's The Sleeping Beauty in the Wood: https://www.pitt.edu/~dash/perrault01.html

Sleeping Beauty Myths: https://essexmyth.wordpress.com/2017/05/29/sleeping-beauty-and-the-fates-of-mythology/

Sultan's Son: https://folklorethursday.com/folktales/unravelling-sexual-mystique-sleeping-beauty/

Other:

For commentary on some other obscure fairy tales see http://www.sarahbeth-durst.com/fairytales.htm

For information on spinning: https://spinoffmagazine.com/spinning-silk-is-not-scary/

For information on sheep: http://livestocktrail.illinois.edu/sheepnet/paperDisplay.cfm?ContentID=1 and

http://www.sheep101.info/201/behavior.html

Medieval Creatures: https://vocal.media/horror/the-15-most-bizarre-monsters-from-medieval-folklore

Skrzak: https://en.wikipedia.org/wiki/Skrzak

Boginka (Navka): https://en.wikipedia.org/wiki/Slavic_water_spirits

Blemmyes (Headless Men): https://en.wikipedia.org/wiki/Headless_men

Jean de l'Ours: https://en.wikipedia.org/wiki/Jean_de_l%27Ours

Trolls: https://en.wikipedia.org/wiki/Troll

About H. C. Fitzpatrick

Architect by day, author by night, H. C. Fitzpatrick is an author out of Toronto, Ontario, Canada. You can find her book reviews, news about latest works, and a sign up for her newsletter at:

http://hcfitzpatrick.com

ALSO BY H. C. FITZPATRICK

Coming Soon:

Escape:
A Rose World Tale prequel featuring your favourite faerie and the wolf-shifter who helped her escape.

Cloaked:
The second Rose World Tale.